FAILSTATE
LEGENDS

JOHN W. OTTE

MARCHER
LORD
PRESS

FAILSTATE: LEGENDS by John W. Otte
Published by Marcher Lord Press
8345 Pepperridge Drive
Colorado Springs, CO 80920
www.marcherlordpress.com

MARCHER LORD PRESS and the MARCHER LORD PRESS logo are trademarks of Marcher Lord Press. Absence of ^{TM} in connection with marks of Marcher Lord Press or other parties does not indicate an absence of trademark protection of those marks.

This is a work of fiction. Names, characters, places, and incidents are products of the author's imagination or are used fictitiously. Any similarity to actual people, organizations, and/or events is purely coincidental.

Scriptures quoted are from THE HOLY BIBLE, NEW INTERNATIONAL VERSION®, NIV® Copyright © 1973, 1978, 1984, 2011 by Biblica, Inc.™ Used by permission. All rights reserved worldwide.

The author is represented by MacGregor Literary Inc. of Hillsboro, OR.

Cover Illustrator: Carlo Garde
Colorist: Katja Louhio
Cover Designer, Typesetter, Editor: Jeff Gerke

Library of Congress Cataloging-in-Publication Data
An application to register this book for cataloging has been filed with the Library of Congress.
International Standard Book Number: 978-1-935929-94-9

Printed in the United States of America

For Micah
Already one of God's great heroes
May you have a lifetime of adventures

PROLOGUE

LEGENDS STARED DOWN at me from the walls. I squirmed under their scrutiny. I could almost hear them whispering to each other, *Who does this kid think he is? Does he really think he deserves to be here?*

Of course I didn't.

No, that wasn't entirely true. I had earned a vigilante license four months earlier. I had even gone on a fifteen city victory tour over the summer to celebrate the fact. But now that the initial rush had worn off, now that I had returned to New Chayton, now that I was sitting in the Vigilante Oversight Commission's office waiting to meet my liaison officer, I felt woefully inadequate.

Especially given the office's decor. I felt like I was sitting in a doctor's waiting room, what with the plain white walls, the dull blue chairs, and the flimsy-looking end table with an obviously fake potted plant. A small hole had been cut into one wall where a young lady sat behind a pane of very thick glass. Next to that window was a steel door with a narrow window cut into it.

But what really caught my attention were the pictures. I recognized about half of the heroes whose portraits dotted the walls: Etzal'el, Meridian, Gal Strife, Howling Vibe. Some were vibrant color photos, others had faded black and white. The one thing I couldn't help but notice was how well-dressed they all were. Each one wore pristine spandex or battle armor of some kind.

I resisted the urge to straighten my costume. Next to them, I probably looked like a thug, in my well-worn camo pants, dark sweatshirt, long gloves, and full hood of a material that hid my face but still allowed me to see through.

I got up to look at one large picture, a grainy photo bleached brown by age. A broad-chested man with arms the width of car tires grinned at me. His costume was simple: an army uniform, three stripes on his sleeve. A small golden plate at the bottom of the frame labeled the man as Sarge.

So this was Sarge. He had been a pillar in the superhero community decades earlier, a veteran of both World Wars and a man who helped found the modern VOC. In spite of that, I still winced at his name. Someone like him deserved a truly epic name. But then, I wasn't really one to judge. After all, I called myself "Failstate."

"Failsafe?"

A pity not everyone did. I faced the receptionist. She was a perky young woman with blond hair, which was pulled back in a tight ponytail. Even still, I got the feeling she could kick my rear end.

I took in a deep breath. *God, here goes everything. Please don't let me make a fool of myself.* "Actually, it's Failstate."

Her smile didn't falter. "Oh. Terribly sorry. Are you ready to go in, Failstate?"

She ushered me from the waiting room into the inner office.

Somehow I'd expected more. I had imagined the VOC New Chayton office to be a high-tech command center. I was expecting commandos to be conferring around maps of the city, or a gigantic digital display with the status of known criminals. Instead, it looked more like an office park. A dozen cubicles made of chest-high dividers filled the center of a room, half of them containing men and women in sharp suits. Muted conversations drifted through the room along with the clicking of computer keyboards. Somewhere from within the maze of cubicles came the smell of cheap coffee and popcorn.

The receptionist led me to a back office, one with a large glass wall that overlooked the central workspace. She rapped on the door and then opened it, motioning for me to go through.

Sitting behind a plain metal desk was a barrel-chested man with a tightly trimmed goatee on a chiseled jaw. He glanced up at me with his steely eyes, and his lip twitched into a snarl.

"Failstate." His voice sounded like rocks being ground into gravel.

"Agent Sexton."

He glared at me for a few moments. Then he waved a hand at a chair opposite his desk. He turned back to his computer and kept working.

I suppose I shouldn't have been surprised at his welcome. Agent Edward Sexton and I had encountered each other shortly before I'd received my license. I couldn't say I'd been happy when I'd learned he would be my government liaison officer, but since the Vigilante Oversight Commission granted all licenses, I didn't say anything. Heroes never argued with the VOC, not if they wanted to keep their status.

I looked around the office. Sexton sat at a metal desk that looked like it belonged in a school. A stack of file folders balanced in a tray on one corner. A large phone was set in the other corner. The wall behind Sexton's desk was dotted with pictures of him shaking hands with different heroes. Some of the heroes' smiles actually looked genuine. I easily spotted Meridian in his full costume. And next to that one was Raze, a hero from L.A. The only picture that didn't have Sexton in it was a large picture of Sarge standing next to an unfurled American flag.

Sexton finally glanced in my direction. "So here we are. I'll be honest: When I was at VOC headquarters in D.C. back in July, I tried to talk Director Bentley out of this, but he insisted that we proceed. I can't say I'm too happy about it."

I winced. "Look, I know that the way I received my license—on a reality TV show—was unorthodox—"

"That's one way of putting it," Sexton grumbled.

My jaw clenched. "But I'm here, and I'm licensed, and I'm willing to do the hard work."

"I don't doubt any of that, rookie. But we need more than some C-list teenage celebrity right now. The world's a dangerous place, becoming more so every day. There could be dozens of superpowered criminals out there right now plotting death and destruction against the people of this city.

"Now normally, New Chayton is protected by five licensed heroes, plus whatever amateurs don't get in our way. But let's see here." He ticked off the names on each finger. "The Living Quark is still on medical leave after tangling with Asylum. Shadowfall and Nightsilver were captured by the Order of the Fourth Eye six months ago, and we have no idea if they're even alive anymore. And as for the Hoplite, my superiors sent her on a top secret mission two months ago, and I have no idea when she'll be back. So who does that leave us on the front line? You. In a state of failure."

I bristled and sat up straighter in my chair. "That's not what my name—"

Sexton blew out a long sigh. "But we play the hand we're dealt, huh?" He picked up a paper from his desk and glanced at it. "Since you have accepted a government vigilante license, you will be expected to comport yourself in an acceptable manner. You represent the United States government and will be expected to conduct yourself as such. Understood?"

"Uh . . ."

Sexton sighed. "It means you can't kill anyone, kid. Okay?"

Oh. Why didn't he just say so? I nodded.

He looked at the paper again. "You will be expected to go on regular patrols through New Chayton and report your activities to the VOC in a timely manner. From time to time, we will expect your assistance with certain matters. The government will provide you a monthly stipend of $3,000 for your services."

Up until now, to finance my heroic exploits I had been creating sculptures in my garage and selling them. Three thousand dollars? Had I ever made that much in a month before?

Sexton looked at me skeptically. "Is that going to be your uniform?"

"For now." I tugged at my pants, suddenly self-conscious about the fraying patches. "My powers . . . well, they eat through anything I wear. I tend to go through costumes quickly."

Sexton blew out a long breath. "That is unfortunate. At the very least, you should design a logo identifying yourself. Right now, you look like a common thief, not a licensed hero."

My cheeks burned beneath the hood.

"Speaking of your powers, have you developed any new talents? Or do you still just break stuff?"

"Well . . ." I ground my teeth together. "Over the summer I figured out how to use my power to open a car lock."

Sexton stared at me. "Car locks?"

I nodded.

He sighed and mopped a hand over his face. "Maybe we'll get you in contact with Dr. Olympus. If anyone can help someone as . . . someone like you, it's her. Moving on. Do you have a unique catchphrase?"

I thought about it for a moment. "'Try not to break anything'?"

Sexton didn't blink for a long time. Then he sighed and set the paper to one side of the desk. "We'll leave that one blank for now."

For the next hour, he droned on about procedures and paperwork.

I tried to pay attention, I really did, but Sexton's words blended into a buzzing that I barely followed. I was about to ask for a break when one word snapped me back to reality.

". . . mentor should be here any minute now." Sexton leaned back in his chair.

Wait, mentor? "What are you talking about?"

Sexton glowered at me. "As I was saying, since you are under the age of twenty-one, the VOC has assigned you a mentor to help acclimate you to your new role as a licensed hero."

Someone knocked at the door, and it popped open. A large man stepped in, wearing black slacks and turtleneck. A full cowl covered his face from his nose up and over his hair. A radiant golden starburst was set between his eyes.

"M-Meridian?" I stumbled to my feet to face him.

The older superhero nodded and shook my hand. He squeezed hard, a definite warning. "Hello, Failstate. Good to meet you *for the first time*."

My jaw clicked shut. The first time. Of course. Six months earlier, I had accidentally uncovered Meridian's secret identity. It was still hard for me to believe that Meridian, a hero I had idolized since childhood, was really Alexander Magnus, the multibillionaire who produced *America's Next Superhero*. It was a complicated relationship.

"Meridian has agreed to come out of retirement only to the extent that he will serve as your mentor," Sexton said. "I suggest you listen to his advice, Failstate. That'll save all of us a lot of headaches."

Meridian snorted. "Oh, come on, Sexton. I'm sure Failstate will do just fine."

"Uh huh." Sexton stalked around his desk and stood next to me, his arms crossed over his chest. "From what I've seen of him, Failstate hasn't been getting by on skill. If he wants to hang with the big boys, he's going to need a lot more than just dumb luck."

My cheeks burned. I wished I could carve a hole in the floor and hide.

Meridian squeezed my shoulder. "He'll do fine."

Something crashed in the outer office, and a burst of light illuminated Sexton's office.

The VOC agent glanced through the large window and laughed. "Well, then let's see if that's true. I'd say we have a situation on our hands."

I turned and looked out the window. A small fire blazed among the cubicles. I dashed through the door.

The inferno was centered around a thin man in an orange prison jumpsuit. Flames radiated out from his body but did not consume him or his clothing. He snarled at the agents surrounding him and flashed teeth that were pointed.

Pyrotrack. He was a lieutenant for the Blue Eclipse Boys street gang. Six months earlier, a superpowered friend of mine named Veritas and I had defeated Pyrotrack and he was arrested. While I had been away from New Chayton over the summer, I had tried to keep track of his trial, but I hadn't learned much. Why he was in the VOC office and not in prison baffled me.

Meridian nudged me toward the door. "You're up, kid."

"Me?" My voice squeaked, and I winced.

Sexton crossed his arms. "Sure. Pyrotrack claimed he was ready to name names in the Blue Eclipse Boys hierarchy and insisted the talk happen here. Apparently this is an escape attempt. You're a licensed hero—and what a happy coincidence that you happen to be right here. Go."

I took a deep breath and slipped out of the office.

While I was still three yards away, Pyrotrack tossed a fireball at the receptionist, who ducked behind a cubicle wall. Then he whirled on me.

"Failstate!" A gob of flame burst from his mouth, its heat bleeding through my mask. "I've dreamed of this for a long time."

He clapped his hands together and a long tongue of flame ripped through the air. I dove to my left, rolling as best as I could and coming up in a crouch behind a desk. The room quickly cleared of agents. A cubicle in the corner caught on fire. Pyrotrack roared and threw another fireball, which spattered against the metal desk and melted it.

I had to end the fight and fast. There was no telling what kind of damage Pyrotrack could cause. I glanced at the ceiling. Why weren't the fire sprinklers going off?

"I will roast your guts and turn you to ashes, Failure-state!" Pyrotrack unleashed another blast of flames that knocked the agents surrounding him off their feet.

"How long did it take you to think of that one?" I concentrated on my power. I channeled the energy into a quick burst that sliced through a sprinkler head above Pyrotrack. Water gushed out of the pipe, dousing the flames on the villain's body.

Pyrotrack sputtered for a moment, steam gushing from his body. "Did you really think that would be enough to stop me?" A new blast of flames erupted from his arms and quickly spread up to his back and chest.

Actually, I had thought it might, but I couldn't admit as much in front of Sexton or Meridian. Instead, I dropped into a ready stance. Hopefully I appeared confident.

With an inarticulate roar, Pyrotrack charged. Flames exploded from his arms. For a split second, I froze. What could I do? What could I—?

In that moment, my power flared out of control, ripping a small hole in the floor between Pyrotrack and me.

Just enough to trip Pyrotrack.

He smacked his forehead against the floor. The flames dancing across his body guttered and winked out. Water continued to douse the cubicles, and the steam made the place look like a sauna.

Pyrotrack pushed himself to his knees. Blood trickled from the corner of his left eye. "I'll gut you for that!"

I figured he might. So, before he could reignite, I charged forward. Two could play that game. I channeled my power around my fist and punched him as hard as I could. He thrashed on the floor for a moment, then went limp and lay still.

For a heartbeat, the only sounds in the office were the crackling of the fire still consuming the cubicles and the spray of water spewing from the broken pipe.

Then Sexton stomped over to Pyrotrack. He stared at the fallen villain for a few moments and then whirled on me.

"What did you do?" His tone was almost accusatory.

Meridian laughed. "He solved your problem, Sexton. Our new hero packs quite the punch."

I felt as though I were glowing under his praise. I smiled and relaxed.

But in that momentary pause, my control lapsed, and my power flared. The lights overhead flickered and one by one, the bulbs burst, showering sparks throughout the office. We were plunged into an eerie darkness.

"Maybe we should go with 'Try not to break anything' after all." Sexton's voice had turned to ice.

White light flared in front of me. Meridian's hands glowed, casting bright light into the darkened office. He offered me a thin smile. "Don't worry, kid. We'll work on it."

I sighed. Great first day on the job.

CHAPTER 1

MY STOMACH FLIPPED as the bus ground to a halt. I wished for a trumpet fanfare or a burst of fireworks, something to announce my return to the streets of New Chayton. Tonight I would patrol the city as a licensed hero.

It was a pity I had to rely on public transportation to get there. I really had to get a car. But if I had three grand a month coming in, that would soon be no problem. Maybe I'd even be able to find something with my first stipend check, whenever that would arrive.

Choosing the neighborhood to patrol was tricky. I spent hours poring over maps of the city before I finally decided on downtown. Plenty of banks and corporate headquarters. Best of all, I'd heard *he* had been seen there recently. That was all I needed to convince me.

At the next stop, I made sure I was the only one to slip from the bus. As soon as it had rumbled down the street, I ducked behind a dumpster and dropped my knapsack.

I had been practicing my quick-change over the summer. Off went the civvies, and on went the costume. Boots, gloves, hood. Finally, I tugged off the necklace I constantly wore around my neck while in my alter-ego of Robin Laughlin. The red crystal tied into the hemp-rope braid kept my powers in check. I took it off when I meant business.

The moment the crystal broke contact with my skin, a wave of needles swept through me, pricking me from the inside out until it balled into a dull throb behind my eyes. I snared my power, reining it in, but I still braced myself just in case. Every now and then, it got away from me.

Thankfully, nothing happened. With a grim nod, I set out. The skyscrapers of downtown New Chayton soared over me, glass walls that warped and twisted the reflected street lights. A lone street sweeper growled down one of the roads, sucking in the trash that had collected in the gutter. I tried to stick to the shadows. That wasn't easy, thanks to the bright street lights. Downtown appeared dead. I didn't see or hear anyone for the first forty-five minutes.

Then an explosion boomed from the upper levels of a parking garage. It sounded like two cars smashing into each other. I looked up, in time to see a tire sail out of the garage and bounce off a building all the way across the street. Definitely worth checking out, even if it was only an accident.

I charged for the nearest door and took the stairs two at a time. I was almost out of breath by the time I reached the fourth floor. Another loud bang sounded, and a momentary burst of light flashed over the walls through a narrow window.

I hesitated. What kind of an accident tossed a tire that hard? This had to be a villain. So charging into combat wouldn't be wise. Better to maintain an element of surprise if I could. I eased the door open and slipped through.

The deck was mostly empty, just a few high end cars parked in a row to my right. An expensive sports car had been flipped onto its side and was missing one of its rear tires. The overhead lights swayed and cast dancing shadows along the walls.

A man in golden tights cackled, his muscles rippling beneath the shining material. His wild grey hair defied gravity, forming a mane around his head. "Did you really think you could defeat the Golden Slinker?

He'd spotted me already? I sank behind a parked car. So much for surprise!

"I, who once battled Dr. Olympus to a standstill? I, who cause all mere mortals to tremble in fear?"

I readied myself for battle, but then the Slinker whirled away from me and kept laughing. Why would he turn his back to me, unless . . .

I poked my head above my hiding place. Sure enough, the Slinker stood over a hero, one tied up with thick chains. I recognized him immediately. How could I not? I had seen his blue uniform with the white rising star logo often enough. In spite of the fact that he was tied up, his green-gold eyes still glinted with quiet confidence.

Gauntlet smirked but didn't answer.

"You have nothing to say? No insult? No pleading for your life? I would have thought that one with your vaunted strength would have put up more of a fight. Alas, I suppose it's not to be." The Slinker stood over Gauntlet and cocked his fist back. "If you believe in a god, now's the time to—"

No way was I going to let this happen! I readied myself to leap out, but then the hood of nearby car rattled. I frowned at it. What was shaking it?

"Shhhhhhh." Gauntlet smirked at the villain, but I could see a hint of tension in his eyes.

"I beg your pardon?"

Gauntlet shushed him. "You wanna hear a secret?"

The car hood rattled again, the metal actually vibrating. I glanced at Gauntlet. His gaze flicked toward the car. His face pinched into a look of concentration, but then he turned his attention back to the villain.

"I suppose. What's your secret?"

The car hood clattered. I knew what I had to do. I sliced through the hinges that held the hood in place. In a screech of tearing metal, the hood ripped free and smashed the Slinker across the back of his head. The villain collapsed in a heap.

"I don't have super strength. I'm really telekinetic." Gauntlet shook his head sadly, then glanced around the darkened garage. "You know, I had that under control." He flexed his arms and the chains snapped apart.

"I could tell." I stepped out of my hiding place.

Gauntlet shrugged off the links and stepped over the Slinker's fallen form to envelop me in a crushing hug. "Good to see you, little brother."

I hugged him back. Strangely, I'd missed Gauntlet over the summer. No way I would have predicted that.

I took a step back and nodded to the supervillain. "So, the Golden Slinker, huh? Didn't know he was back in town."

"You've been busy." Gauntlet rolled the villain onto the car hood and twisted the metal around the Slinker's arms. "Besides, there's not much to tell. Dude's just been stealing cars. Kind of sad, really."

Frustration bled through my brother's words. I gritted my teeth.

"Look," I said, "I know this sort of work isn't what you want. If there's any way I can help you—"

He shook his head. "We've been over this. If I'm going to get a license, I'm going to do it solo." He offered me a toothy smile. "So, first night back on the job, huh? Where are you heading?"

I shrugged. "Nowhere in particular. Now that I see you're working here, I'll head over to Club Row."

"Don't let me stop you. I was thinking of swinging by Hogtown in a little bit."

There was an eagerness in his voice. "What's up? Anything I should know about?"

Gauntlet smirked. "Nothing big enough for a high-and-mighty licensed hero. There's this gang called the HazMats. They've been making inroads into the neighborhood the last few months. Nasty bunch. They're mostly into dealing this new drug called 'Blade' and some other stuff too. But I do have something . . . big in the works."

"Oh, yeah? What's that?"

His smirk grew wider. "Sorry. Trade secret." He grabbed the edge of the hood wrapped around the Slinker. The metal groaned as Gauntlet picked up the unconscious villain and flipped him up onto his shoulder. The Slinker's head lolled to one side. "On second thought, tell you what: I'll take this wiggler to the nearest precinct and then we can get caught up. You know Garibaldi's down on Club Row?"

I nodded. It was a bar and grill down near New Chayton University.

"Meet me there in thirty, okay?"

He charged for the half-wall and leapt into the open air. I rushed to the concrete barrier and peeked over the edge. Gauntlet floated to the ground below and then walked off into the shadows.

I sighed. Looked like I was going to have to get my civvies and catch another bus.

CHAPTER 2

I SHIFTED IN MY SEAT and glanced at my watch. Nearly eleven. Sure, it had taken me a little while to get back into my civvies, but I had been waiting for Ben in the restaurant for close to an hour. I was sure that he'd probably had to answer a lot of questions at the police station when he'd showed up with the Slinker, but this was getting ridiculous.

I looked around the restaurant. The room was cozy, only a dozen tables and booths, with brick walls punctuated by rustic wooden beams. The lights were turned down low, so much so that I wondered how anyone could see their food. Pictures of rambling fields and forests hung on the walls and low strains of violin music drifted through the air. It seemed like a nice place to take a date. Why would Ben want to come here?

The door banged open. I craned my neck around to see if it was Ben. It wasn't.

It was a zombie.

At least, it looked like one. His skin was a putrid shade of green, and it looked like his cheeks were puckered and falling apart. He wore a tattered New Chayton University sweatshirt. But even from halfway across the restaurant, I could tell he was wearing makeup. The pseudo-zombie shambled to the hostess's podium and practically fell on top of it.

"C'mon, Jessica." The zombie had a surprisingly high-pitched voice. "The zombie crawl's just no fun without you!"

Before the hostess could reply, the manager stormed over to the door. "Get out! I told you guys already, I don't want any of you in here tonight!"

The zombie tried to protest, but the manager steered him out the door. The manager turned around and chewed out the rapidly blushing hostess and then headed back for the kitchen.

I sighed and resumed my inspection of the restaurant. Most of the patrons were college students, although there were a few older couples as well. There was even a booth full of high school girls, at least six of them.

I risked a peek in their direction and froze. One of them was absolutely gorgeous. Long, wavy, red hair, warm brown eyes that sparkled even from the shadows. She was dressed in a sweater and jeans. For a moment, our eyes met. She smiled, a brilliant flash of teeth.

My heart stuttered. Should I go over and speak to her? She wasn't looking away. I could maybe introduce myself, get her number. I'd never done anything like that before, but then, I'd never been a licensed hero before either. Of course, I couldn't reveal that to her, but maybe it would translate into some confidence. Given the swarm of bees rocketing through me, it hadn't kicked in yet, but that could change before I made it to her booth.

But then the redhead dipped her head toward one of her friends and whispered something. The two of them peeked over at me and started giggling.

I turned away, my cheeks burning. I took a big sip of my water, wishing I had my hood over my face. I tried to hide behind the menu, hoping they would forget about me soon. After a few minutes, I risked another glance. The redhead had disappeared.

I sighed. This was ridiculous. Ben obviously wasn't coming. Maybe he had been held up at the precinct. Or I suppose he could have found more trouble on his way. But it'd be silly for me to stick around any longer. I left.

The street outside the restaurant was mostly deserted. A row of darkened one story office buildings stretched down the block. Across the street, neon signs from different bars and nightclubs painted the night with their garish colors. Cars cruised by, and the drivers honked and shouted at the folks gathered at the club entrances. The sounds of crowds at nearby clubs drifted past me. I headed across the street toward the alley where I had stashed my costume. I could go back out on patrol again, maybe keep an eye on Club Row. Things would probably pick up once the bars closed.

I heard a shriek.

My head snapped around. It had come from the restaurant's parking lot.

"Get away from me!" A woman's voice.

I sprinted into the parking lot and looked around. Half a dozen cars were crammed as close to Garibaldi's as possible, and the pavement was broken and uneven. No sign of any trouble. My gaze landed on an alley that ran along the back of the buildings. Maybe the problem was back there.

Sure enough, three men had backed a young lady up against a chain link fence. My pulse quickened when I saw her. It was the redhead from the restaurant! She looked ready to clamber up the fence if she could. Her face twisted with fear, and she sobbed.

Her attackers continued to advance without saying a word. They wore dull grey scrubs, like what my mom wore to work. One of them had long, stringy hair. They didn't walk so much as shuffle. Obviously they were part of that zombie crawl the other guy had mentioned. But why mess with this girl? Were all three of them drunk or high?

Didn't matter. I had to help, costumed or not. I charged down the alley and threw myself at the center man's knees. He crumpled and fell on top of me. I shoved him away and swept the legs out from beneath the next attacker. Then I launched myself into the knees of the third guy. He toppled over backward.

I whirled on the girl. Our gazes locked. Her lips trembled, and her chest heaved. In that moment, I wanted nothing more than to stand up and hug her. She looked like she could use one.

But then the first zombie I tackled got back to his feet and lunged at her. I launched myself onto his back and wrapped an arm around his neck. The other two were shambling to their feet as well.

"Run!" I shouted.

She shot past me and disappeared down the alley.

I shoved the zombie away from me and turned to his partners. Something about them didn't look right. One of them appeared to be missing a few vertebrae from his neck—his head lolled to one side so far it almost tipped over sideways.

Another's skin was a putrid shade of grey. The third had a dark void where his right eye should be.

I sighed. "Okay, guys. I don't know what you've been up to tonight, and while I love the cosplay, enough is enough."

It was their silence that creeped me out the most. The one with the wobbly neck lurched for me.

I knocked his hands away. "Great makeup job, by the way, and you're really selling it, but knock it off before I call the cops."

Wobbly Neck lunged for me again. I slapped his arm away again. His face contorted into a snarl, and he charged. This time I didn't hold back. I snared his arm and punched for his elbow.

My fist broke clean through him.

With a dry sigh, his arm fell off in my hand.

I stared at the severed limb and quickly tossed it away. "Ew!"

Wobbly Neck inspected his stump but didn't seem all that concerned. Neither did his companions. Instead, they hissed and clacked their jaws at me and charged.

I bumped up against the chainlink fence. This wasn't good. When I had gone out on patrol tonight, I had expected to find some trouble. I just never thought it'd take the form of three honest-to-goodness zombies.

CHAPTER 3

THE ZOMBIES LUNGED for me again. They slapped the chainlink. I ducked underneath their outstretched arms. The zombies slowly turned to face me. As they did, they moaned and clacked their teeth. Were they capable of communication?

I held up my hands in what I hoped would seem like a non-threatening manner. "All right, guys. Let's calm down here. Nobody else has to get hurt."

The one-eyed zombie snarled and stumbled forward with his fingers outstretched and curled into claws. I backpedaled and fingered my necklace. It would be nice to have my powers for this fight, but there was no way I wanted anyone who stumbled upon this confrontation to see my true, disfigured face. But I probably couldn't count on these three staying put while I went to go change into my costume. Still, they weren't moving very fast.

The wobbly-necked zombie groaned at me.

I held up a finger. "Hold that thought, okay?"

I sprinted down the alley and rounded a corner, nearly tripping over a garbage can. Thankfully, the streets had emptied. I skidded to a halt next to a closed bar and found my duffel bag tucked underneath a parked car covered in tickets with a parking boot on its back tire. I ducked into a nearby alley and slipped into my costume. Then it was another mad dash back to the alley behind the restaurant.

The zombies hadn't made it far. They had shuffled their way up the alley and were into the parking lot, weaving between the parked cars.

I leapt in front of them and held up my hands. "That's far enough!"

Maybe they recognized me even with the costume on. The wobbly-necked zombie I partially disarmed snarled at me and charged. Or maybe they were just being zombies.

I channeled my power around my fist and struck him in the chest as hard as I could. I could feel the bone crack beneath my fist, and the zombie's head snapped around, flopping down to the other side. But it didn't show any outward pain. It grabbed my sweatshirt and pulled at my arms. His friends latched on as well and tried to drag parts of my body toward their mouths.

"Get off!" I shouted and unleashed a burst of my power.

Nothing happened. Not to them, anyway.

I couldn't move. Somehow my clothing had turned as rigid as stone. I was trapped within my shirt and pants, stuck in an uncomfortable pose. The zombies scratched at the material. It sounded like they were clawing at metal. One of them tried biting my arm at the wrist but I couldn't feel it at all. What was happening? Had I done this to myself?

Something shifted inside me, and my clothing returned to normal. I stumbled and fell. The zombies fell on top of me in a pile. They thrashed their legs and limbs. One of them bit my arm. I hissed. It didn't feel like he broke the skin, but I probably wouldn't be so lucky next time.

I rammed an elbow into one of their faces and twisted free of another's hands. They kept snaring me in their claws. Then my power surged and tore through the pavement underneath me. A nearby car alarm went off, blaring in the night. The zombies stared at the new sound.

I clearly wasn't strong enough to take them on in a head-to-head fight, especially not when I was outnumbered. What I needed was a plan. Or a weapon.

There. One of the signs near the parking lot entrance was bent over, as if a car had hit it. I ran to the sign and used my power to saw through the bottom of the sign. It clattered to the sidewalk. I hefted up the sign, which was too unwieldy to use as I wanted. I sent a burst of power into the post to sheer it off into a three foot long club.

But that's not what actually happened.

Instead, the metal post turned soft like taffy in my hands and oozed through my fingers.

What was going on? I shook my hands, trying to free myself from the metallic goop. The post twisted and sagged. It became rigid once again. The now-warped signpost hit the ground with a loud clatter, which I could barely hear over the droning car alarm. I looked around the parking lot. Why wasn't anyone coming to see what was going on?

Apparently the zombies were done with the noisy car. The wobbly-necked zombie groaned and started for me in a stumbling lope. I lashed out with my power and carved a deep rut into the sidewalk. He stepped right into the hole and tripped.

His jaw cracked as he hit, then he thrashed for a moment and went still.

The other two didn't seem to notice what happened to their friend. They charged. I ducked the one-eyed zombie's outstretched hands and kicked him solidly in the knee. The joint snapped, and he went down. I jogged back out of his flailing grasp. He wasn't out of the fight yet, though. He dragged himself across the sidewalk. So long as I kept moving, I figured I could keep away from him.

That left the long-haired zombie. He twisted his head to one side, then the other, as if studying me for a weakness. Then he clacked his teeth and charged—

Only to vanish in a blast of smoke.

A wave of decay swept over me. I gagged on the rancid smell and waved my hands to clear the air. Once the smoke cleared, I realized I was alone. The other two zombies had vanished as well.

"What did you do to my car?"

I whipped around at the angry voice. A young man, maybe in his mid-thirties, stood at the edge of the parking lot. He glared at me, and I turned around to see why. The droning car alarm was coming from a sports car, one with a large gash carved into its side.

I turned back to the angry man, but he was already on his cellphone. "Hello, 911?"

My shoulders slumped. This was definitely not what I was hoping for on my first night back.

CHAPTER 4

THE POLICE DETECTIVE, who had identified himself as Emil Wong, glared at me over his glasses and clicked his pen a few times. "You really expect me to buy this?"

I sighed and sat down on the hood of the wrecked car. Police cars blocked the parking lot entrance, and officers milled through the lot. One of them was taking pictures of the area.

Apparently the cops had attracted the attention of the zombie crawl participants. Half the crowd pressed up against the police line were zombies. These were obviously fake zombies, their putrid skin nothing more than make-up. But it was an uncomfortable reminder of what had happened. And now I would have to tell the story for a third time. Wong had grilled me every time, probably trying to see if I'd slip up.

"Look, I'm sure someone saw me fighting the zombies." I gestured at the crowd of on-lookers. They pressed up against the yellow-tape border the police had erected around the parking lot.

Wong shook his head. "Yeah, you'd think so. But nobody's coming forward."

"Are you calling me a liar?" I drew myself up to full height so I could look him eye-to-throat.

He smirked at me. "Look, kid, I watched your little show. I know what a screw-up you are. Here's what I think happened: I think that you had one of your 'accidents,' wrecked that car, and now you're making up a zombie fight to cover for yourself."

My gaze darted to the twisted parking sign. Thankfully, the police detective couldn't see my eyes or he might have gotten nastier.

"You can talk to the girl. She saw the zombies—"

"Right, the girl you allegedly saved. Any idea what her name is? Phone number? See her in the crowd right now?"

"No."

"So . . . no witnesses and damage to an extremely expensive sports car. Great start to your career, huh?"

I bit back a sharp response. Tonight had gone badly enough. I doubted that getting into an argument with the police would help matters any.

Then my night got worse. Agent Sexton ducked under the police line, a scowl etched onto his face. A police officer tried to stop him. Sexton flashed his ID and then marched toward us. Just what I needed.

Wong turned to the VOC agent and rubbed the back of his neck. "Just what I need."

My head snapped around. Was the police detective telepathic?

"Evening, Detective Wong," Sexton said. "I hear we had an incident. It's a shame I heard about it on the news and not from you." Sexton smiled, but he clearly wasn't happy.

"I was just about to call you." Wong still wouldn't meet Sexton's glare.

"I'm sure." Sexton turned his gaze to me. "So what happened?"

I launched into the tale once again. Sexton's expression didn't change, remaining stone-faced throughout. When I wrapped it up, Sexton turned to Wong.

"So does any of the evidence support what Failstate says?" Sexton asked.

"Well, there's the car." Wong waved a hand at the parking lot. "But aside from that, there are no eyewitnesses to the fight. Besides, there was a zombie pub crawl tonight. Costumed zombies everywhere. Bunch of kids from the U put it on." Wong pointed to the zombies watching from behind the yellow tape. "I think Failstate here stumbled over one of those 'zombies' and freaked out."

My cheeks burned underneath my mask. Even from this distance, I could tell that those "zombies" weren't real. What I'd fought had been something altogether different.

"Now wait just a minute here!" Sexton said. "May I remind you that Failstate has a government vigilante license? As such, you will show him the appropriate respect, Detective. Do I make myself clear?" Sexton thumped Wong in the chest with his finger to punctuate each point. "Now why don't you go double-check and make sure that there were no eyewitnesses? Somebody must have seen something."

Wong stomped away, rubbing his chest and grumbling.

I looked at Sexton, surprise radiating through me. Given how much hostility he'd shown me earlier in the week, I never would have expected him to defend me. "Thank you, sir."

He glared at me. "Get something straight, Rookie: I didn't do that for you. Wong's always had a problem with the VOC. He's mixed it up with Nightsilver on so many occasions I've lost track. If I didn't keep him in his place, we'd pay for it down the line. But I don't buy your story for a minute."

"I'm telling you: The zombies were real!"

"I highly doubt that. You know how many crackpot super-villains have tried to reanimate the dead? Dozens. Maybe hundreds over the last century or so. And not a single one of them succeeded." Now he jabbed me in the chest. "You'd better hope we find something that points us in the right direction, or there's a good chance your career as a licensed hero will be the shortest ever."

With that parting shot, Sexton marched off.

Well, if Wong and Sexton didn't believe me, that didn't let me off the hook. I could do some investigating. I crossed my arms and studied the scene. Ten feet away, the crowd still pressed up against the police tape. At least a quarter of them were dressed as zombies. Wong's theory that I had mistaken them for the zombies I'd fought seemed ludicrous. None of them wore those odd grey scrubs. Most of these people looked to be college-aged, maybe a little older. That made sense, given what Detective Wong had said.

My gaze landed on one person who stood out of the crowd. Not because he wasn't dressed like a zombie, since there were plenty of club-goers who weren't. No, this man stood out because he looked far too old to be out clubbing on a Monday night. He looked to be in his mid-fifties, mostly bald save for a horseshoe of grey-and-brown hair. Stubble lined his jaw. He stood at the edge of the crowd, craning to see above everyone else.

"Excuse me!" I shouted toward him. I jogged toward the police line.

The man shifted on his feet, glancing around as if he were looking for an escape route.

"Hey, Dr. Ayers!" One of the zombies, a college-aged woman in a ratty cheerleading costume and half her face painted green, shouted. "What are you doing here?"

The man winced and waved at the young woman.

"A doctor?" I asked.

He wouldn't look at my face. "Ah, yes. Yes. I work at the university."

"Oh." I frowned. "The cheer-zombie had a good question, then. What are you doing here? You're not exactly dressed for the clubs."

His cheeks reddened. "I was going for a walk."

"Through Club Row, Dr. Ayers?"

He nodded once, his eyes darting toward my mask. "It helps clear my mind. Can I . . . can I go now?"

I nodded. Dr. Ayers scurried away, ducking his head. Huh. Weird.

I turned around to see what else was happening. The police were dispersing the on-lookers. Wong had vanished. So had Sexton. I set my jaw. They may have dismissed me, but I wasn't done yet. Not by a long shot.

CHAPTER 5

I SQUINTED AGAINST the rising sun and shoved my hands deeper into my pockets. I walked up the driveway toward my home, a modest two-story house nestled in South Bend, an inner-ring suburb of New Chayton. Rather than go inside, I circled around to the back, slipping into the detached garage.

Thankfully, Mom's minivan didn't fit in the garage, leaving most of it empty. A row of boxes lined the wall to my left, each one labeled with thick black letters. To the right was a well-worn couch, a plaid monstrosity I had found sitting on a curb. I stashed the duffel bag holding my costume near the door and paused to breathe deeply, letting the odd mix of gasoline and an unidentifiable tang soothe me for a moment. I loved coming out here. Before my dad died, he and I used to spend hours out here, testing out my powers, seeing what I was capable of. The smell always reminded me of him.

Toward the back of the garage was his workbench, which I had adopted as my own. I wasn't handy like Dad. I had no idea what most of the tools that hung on the pegboard actually did. But I had made this my inner sanctum, the place I could go to escape it all.

I flopped down onto the couch and pulled out a large laptop from its hiding place underneath the couch. It was thick and sturdy and bordered with solid rubber. It was the first thing I'd bought after winning my license, something I could use for research and to compile a crime-fighting database. As soon as the computer switched on, I fired up a web browser but then paused. What should I search for? Zombie sightings?

The door to the garage creaked open. I slapped the laptop shut. Who might be creeping in this early in the morning?

My mom poked her head in the door and smiled sheepishly. "I was wondering if you were out here. Did you have a good night?"

I smiled, all too aware that it felt thin and forced. "Not really, no."

"Oh. I'm sorry to hear that." She stepped inside the garage, wrapping her right arm around herself in a half-hug. "Did you see Ben at all?"

Stop that! I winced at my own pettiness. Ben had always been Mom's favorite. We all knew it. Things had gotten better between Mom and me in the past few months, but some of the old resentment lingered. *Sorry, God. Keep working on me.*

"Yeah," I said. "I was planning on going over to his place in the next day or two."

She brightened. "Great."

"So what's going on, Mom? Are you off to work or something?"

She shook her head. "You have a visitor."

I did? I glanced at my watch. Who would come to see me at six-thirty in the morning?

Mom stepped out of the way, and Alexander Magnus walked into the garage. Even without his costume as Meridian, Magnus was an imposing presence. His greying hair was pulled back and slicked down into a severe widow's peak. His black suit, impeccably tailored, looked completely out of place in my dingy garage. But somehow, the way Magnus carried himself made it seem like it was the garage's fault.

He leaned heavily on a cane topped with a snarling gargoyle.

"Good to see you, Robin." His voice was low, a bare growl.

I winced at the mention of my full name. I wished he would call me "Rob," like everyone else.

"Well, I'll get out of the way," Mom said. "I'm sure you two have . . ." Her voice trailed off. She gave a quick half-curtsey to Magnus—which looked odd, since she was wearing jeans— and scurried out the door.

"I understand you had a busy night last night." Magnus strolled through the garage, his gaze roaming over the boxes and other items stacked along the walls. "I almost expected you to be asleep when I got here."

"I don't sleep, sir." It was true, I didn't. Something about my powers made sleep unnecessary.

"Good. Crime doesn't either."

I laughed. He skewered me with a sharp glare. Oh. He wasn't kidding.

I coughed. "What can I do for you, Mr. Magnus?"

He looked around the garage again. "This your secret lair?"

"It's a start," I said.

"Barely. I suppose we'll have to make do with what you have for now, but the VOC can help here. They have grant money available to help heroes set up their headquarters. But that's a discussion for another time. Come on, get the garage door open. I have a present for you."

I frowned but did as I was told, hitting the button so the garage door could rattle to the top. I blinked at what waited for me outside.

A beat-up car sat in our driveway, a blue Toyota Camry. The paint across the hood was splotchy, dotted with a wide white pattern as if someone had spilled something on it. Rust nibbled at the doors' edges.

I turned to Magnus. "What is that thing?"

"The Failmobile."

I blinked and turned back to it again. "The who?"

Magnus shrugged. "The name's a work in progress."

Good, because I didn't like it. If we called this the "Failmobile," people would probably expect me to make a mess of things. That wasn't all that encouraging. "Does it have a different name?"

"Not really. Well, it has a serial number: DK-207."

"DK?" I asked.

"Short for 'Darius Kahahane,' the man who designed it. He creates vehicles for licensed heroes all the time. He designed the third . . . no, fourth version of the Photon Cycle for me."

"Oh." I liked the sound of "DK." It sounded like "decay," which was a good way to describe what my powers did. "So why'd you bring this here?" I asked.

Magnus smiled. "It's yours, Robin. I suggest you get it inside the garage so I can show you all the bells and whistles."

He tossed a set of keys to me.

I was so numb from surprise that my arm didn't even twitch. The keys ricocheted off my chest and fell to the ground.

Seriously, someone was giving me a superhero car? With bells and whistles even? Who cared if it looked like it should be crushed into a tiny cube—this was completely awesome!

I retrieved the keys and darted forward, dropping into the driver's seat. The interior didn't look much better than the exterior. The driver's side armrest had cracked and was falling to pieces. The back seat was covered in stains that I couldn't identify and probably didn't want to. I turned the key. The engine sputtered and sounded ready to die at any moment, but the car rolled into the garage easily enough.

Before I could get out of the car, Magnus pulled the garage door shut behind us and then slid into the passenger seat. "Don't let her outward appearance fool you. This baby is tough. Remind you of anyone you know?" He winked. "It's got an experimental engine that can outpace most race cars. The doors and windows are bulletproof. And the front end is a reinforced ram that can go through most obstacles like they're made of paper. Best of all, it has a state-of-the-art camouflage system. Right now, it's in 'civilian mode,' so you can drive it to school or wherever."

Wait. It was in a *mode*? That meant there were other modes . . .

Magnus opened the center compartment between the seats and pulled down part of the fabric wall, revealing three buttons. The left-most button was lit by a green glow. "But let's say you're going out on patrol. You don't want Failstate to be seen in the same car as Robin Laughlin, so . . ." Magnus stabbed the middle one with his finger, and it lit up green.

A shimmering wave of energy rippled over the car's exterior. I poked my head out of the window and gasped. The paint color had changed to red. And unless my eyes were fooling me, it appeared as though the front end had reshaped itself ever so slightly.

"The onboard computer will randomly pick an appearance so you can remain incognito. But let's say that you want people to know you're in the neighborhood. Then you use suppression mode."

He hit the right-most button. A low rumbling swept through the car, and it felt as though the Camry grew. The red hood vanished, replaced with gleaming steel. The car seemed to rise from the ground by six inches. I hopped out and gawked. Gone was the nondescript Camry. In its place sat a miniature tank. No way would I want to see that rolling down my street.

And then it shrunk, the exterior resuming its faded and mottled blue. Magnus slipped out again and offered me an expectant look.

I fumbled with finding the right words. "But . . . why?"

Magnus ran his hand along the roof. "I know the VOC gives you peanuts for a stipend. They mean well, but three grand a month will barely keep you in spandex once things really get hopping. You need a leg up, and I'm more than happy to help." He rolled his shoulders, his face turning sour. "Besides, it's not like I have anyone else to give it to."

I froze, thinking immediately of my friend, Mike. Not only was he the superhero Veritas, but he was also Magnus's son. Had something happened between Magnus and his son that I didn't know about?

Before I could ask, Magnus stalked around the car. "One other item: Are you doing anything this Thursday?"

From his tone, it was clear I shouldn't be. "No, sir. School doesn't start for another week and a half."

"Good. I've made an appointment for you to see Dr. Olympus at her lab. We'll take my private plane."

My head felt as though it were spinning. Dr. Olympus was a living legend in the superhero community. She had fought crime in St. Louis for close to three decades. She was a genius by any definition of the word. "Why?"

"Oh, no reason." But from the way he looked away from me, fiddling with the top of his cane, told me that there was a reason.

"What did Agent Sexton tell you?" I asked.

Magnus grimaced. "He said something about you seeing a couple of zombies and that your powers malfunctioned."

I groaned and sat on the couch.

Magnus settled in next to me. "Why don't you tell me what happened?"

I launched into the story. Magnus didn't react as I described the battle.

When I wrapped up, he sighed. "Look, kid, Sexton may be a jerk, but he's right on one thing. No one has ever reanimated the dead. It's impossible. You can ask Dr. Olympus when we see her."

I made a sour face. "Do I really have to?"

Magnus nodded. "Now that you're an official fixture of the community, it's good to get out there and meet other licensed heroes, start establishing your reputation. And the Doc is a sweetheart . . . most of the time."

I mopped a hand over my face, ignoring the itch of my suppressed powers as they swept over my body. "Okay."

"Excellent. I'll send a car for you at 7:00 Thursday morning." Magnus started for the door. "Take good care of the car, Robin, and it'll serve you well." He hesitated in the doorway. "You wouldn't happen to be going to that church of yours, would you?"

I nodded. "Tonight's the big school year kick-off. Wouldn't miss it for the world."

Magnus grunted and nodded. "If you see my son there, tell him . . ." He looked down at his feet, frowning. "Never mind."

He stepped through the door. A black limo waited for him at the end of the driveway. I watched as he slipped into the back the sleek car pulled away. It was still early morning, but now I couldn't wait to get to church that night and find Mike. Apparently we had quite a bit to talk about.

CHAPTER

6

I SPENT MOST OF THE DAY fiddling with DK, trying to figure out every bell and whistle. There was a police transmission interceptor, an array of surveillance devices, and a remote control that hid in the top of the glove compartment. I wanted nothing more than to take DK out and put it through its paces. But knowing my luck, I'd wind up crashing the thing just pulling out of the driveway. Besides, even if I did go out for a joyride, all I'd be doing would be trying to escape the mystery of the zombies.

When 6:00 p.m. finally rolled around, I figured it would be best to take a break and go to youth group. That's what I usually did on Tuesday nights. I slid behind the wheel of the car and took a deep breath to calm my slam-dancing nerves. I double-checked that DK's civilian mode was activated, and then, with one final quick prayer for empty streets and understanding drivers, I slipped the car into reverse and backed out of my driveway.

Something about driving my own car through the streets of South Bend made me sit up a little taller. Who cared if it looked like a wreck? It was mine! I cranked up the stereo, enjoying the way the sound system thudded the song into my chest. It was too bad that we didn't live farther from church: It would have been a good night for a longer drive.

At least four dozen vehicles of all shapes and sizes were jammed into Mount Calvary Christian Church's parking lot when I arrived and a long line of cars snaked out to the street as parents dropped off their kids. I whistled. What was going on? I had never seen Mount Calvary this busy for youth group.

I walked up to the church building, a rebuilt school, and walked through the hallways to the gym. What I saw in the gym caused me to stop right where I stood. Granted, it had been a few weeks since I'd been able to go to youth group, but the gym had been transformed.

Before, it had looked like a gym, with scuffed hardwood floors and bare cinderblock walls painted a garish mix of white and red stripes. Now, though, the floor was covered with carpeted mats, and while the walls were still white and red, most of them had been covered with long banners of different colors. A purple one had a glittering crown surrounded by the words, "Royal Priesthood." A green banner had an image of a basin of water and a towel and sported the phrase, "Foot Washers." There were half a dozen others, each bearing a different symbol with accompanying words.

At the other end of the gym was a stage filled with amps and a large steel scaffolding. The praise band conferred quietly with each other, the lead guitarist noodling on his instrument as they spoke. Two folding tables piled high with electronic equipment stood to my left, facing the band.

At least a hundred teenagers wandered through the gym, forming little clots in the flow of bodies. Some of the attendees I recognized, many I didn't. But I really wanted to find only one person in the sea of bodies.

I wound through the chattering mass, straining to see over everyone else. I nodded greetings at some of the other attendees. Where was Mike?

I had made it barely a quarter of the way through the crowd when I ran into Pastor Grant, one of the only adults in the room. P.G., as he insisted we call him, was in his mid-thirties, a little on the pudgy side, with brown hair that I think he kept untamed to hide the fact that he was balding. He wore baggy cargo pants and a button-down shirt he had left open to reveal a vintage t-shirt for a video game.

When P.G. saw me, his eyes widened with surprise. Remembering what he knew about me, probably. But then he got over his shock and stepped forward, slapping my arm with a little too much enthusiasm.

"Rob! Good to see you again. How . . . uh, how was your summer?" Pastor Grant practically vibrated with nervous energy.

Ever since I'd had to reveal my superhero identity to P.G., he'd never really acted normal around me.

I forced a big smile to my face. "It was great, P.G. Thanks for asking. Have you seen Mike?"

P.G. brightened immediately. "I think he's back at the sound booth working on my laptop. Stupid thing crashed when I hooked it up to the projector."

"Thanks."

I headed back through the sea of bodies until I made it to the sound board at the back of the gym. Two guys my age were fiddling with the knobs and dials, arguing over volume settings.

Michael Rickman hunched over a scuffed laptop, his face pinched in concentration. He ran a hand through his red hair. He frowned for a moment and then looked up. He smiled. He came around the table and slapped me on the back. "Rob, it's so good to see you! I was hoping you'd be here tonight! So how was the tour?"

I grimaced.

Mike laughed at my expression. "Say no more. I heard about most of it already. Dad seemed to take particular pleasure in reminding me that I didn't win and you did. But I am glad you're back."

"So am I." I looked around the gym again. The band had started to warm up, and their riffs nearly drowned out our words. The attendees drifted toward the chairs. "So what have I missed here? Looks like you guys have really renovated."

Mike shook his head. "Not really. Just the carpet and banners. Let's see, over the summer, P.G. did an eight-week series on what Christians are supposed to be. Most of it is leftovers from that. And we've been trying to get everyone to bring their friends on Tuesdays."

"Looks like it worked."

Mike dismissed my words with a wave of his hand, but I couldn't miss the proud glow in his eyes. "It's nothing, really. Just doing our best with what God's given us."

For some reason, his words pricked my conscience about the zombies. I hesitated and cast an uncertain look at the guys working on the sound board. "Speaking of which, I may need your help unraveling something. You game?"

"Uh, yeah. I guess so." Mike checked his watch. "Listen, I'd better fix this laptop or P.G. will have a meltdown. We'll talk later, okay?" His smile broadened. "I really am glad you're here, Rob. I think you're going to enjoy yourself tonight."

I frowned. There was something in his tone of voice, a hint that he wasn't telling me everything. But before I could ask for an explanation, he shooed me away from the sound board.

I found a seat toward the back just as the band started the first real song. The lead singer directed us through a rousing series of songs, thanking God for His presence and the time we had with Him. They were just ordinary praise songs, normally the sort of thing I wouldn't enjoy. But I couldn't help but smile. It felt right to be there. I had missed it more than I knew.

Once the band wound down, P.G. launched into his lesson. I tried to concentrate, I really did. But my mind kept drifting back to the zombies. Could there be more of them out there? Sure, no one had been hurt the previous night, but that was luck. Maybe I should leave, get out on patrol, or . . .

I shook my head, trying to clear it. I risked another peek at my watch. It was only 7:00 p.m. Even this late in the summer, it wouldn't be quite dark enough yet. The chances of a zombie attack happening during daylight seemed unlikely. I tried to calm my mind but found it wasn't so easy. I forced myself to focus on what P.G. was saying.

"And now, I want to bring someone up to talk to all of you about a new program at Mount Calvary. Charlene?"

P.G. stepped aside, extending a hand, and an angel walked up on stage and joined him.

No, not an angel, although it was easy to understand why I might have been mistaken. A beautiful young lady smiled sheepishly as P.G. handed her a wireless mic. Then recognition slammed into me. It was the redhead from the restaurant, the one I'd saved from the zombies! I could hardly believe it.

She tucked a long lock of red hair behind her ear and dipped her gaze from the audience. She wore a simple jean skirt and a green t-shirt, loose enough that she wasn't flaunting her body, but I couldn't help but notice how incredibly attractive she was.

"Thanks, P.G.. Uh, hi, everyone. My name is Charlene Gardner." Her voice was like auditory honey. It was so sweet I could listen to her all night. "P.G. and I have been working out some ideas for us to give back to the community. After all, Christ does call on us to be servants, and we want to see that start to happen.

"We're going to be starting some servant event programs here at the church. We're lining up opportunities to volunteer in a local soup kitchen, the food shelf, and a women's shelter. Plus we're going to start donation campaigns for winter coats and stuff like that." Her eyes had positively lit up, brown beacons that sucked me in. "I think it's great for us to do this. Like P.G. was saying earlier tonight, we're called on to be the hands of Christ in this world. It's so important that we live out that calling every day, you know?"

"Is this chick for real?" someone whispered behind me.

I turned in my chair and shot the guy what I hoped was a menacing look. "Shut up."

The whisperer raised his hands in mock surrender, but I could tell from his expression he wasn't sorry in the least.

"I just know that, with all of your help, we'll make a tremendous difference in this world." Charlene blushed furiously for a moment. "Thank you."

She scurried off stage. I craned my neck to see where she had gone.

Someone dropped into the chair next to me. Mike. He smirked at me.

"So do you want to meet her?"

"Uh . . . I actually have already," I said.

Mike's mouth twitched into a smile. "What?"

"Yeah. Last night."

"You mean, as . . . you know?" Mike mimed pulling a mask over his face.

"Not exactly."

Mike stared at me and then laughed. "Okay, now this, I have to hear. Stick around, okay?"

No problem. Going out on patrol was suddenly the furthest thing from my mind.

CHAPTER 7

I BOUNCED ON MY HEELS while everyone else filed out of the gym. My mind flipped with every passing moment. What if Charlene had left already? Given the swarm of bodies flowing through the doors, she could have escaped, and I would have no way of knowing. Just my luck! Maybe if I took a quick walk around the gym, look for Mike or . . . her. No, I couldn't approach her by myself. I'd probably swallow my own tongue.

"Hey!"

I whirled around at Mike's shouted greeting. He had Charlene in tow. My breath slammed to a halt in the back of my mouth, and I suddenly felt way too hot.

"Robin Laughlin, meet Charlene Gardner. Charlene, this is my friend Rob I was telling you about."

Her eyes lit up again, which was almost enough to squash my rising panic. What had Mike told her? For a moment, I could almost imagine the conversation: *Yeah, my friend, Rob? He's a superhero who got my sister killed. And when he's not*

*wearing his mask or that necklace, he's incredibly repulsive. Oh,
and he stole the license that should have belonged to me.* No, Mike
wouldn't do that, would he?

Then her lips pulled into a wide grin. "You were the guy in
the restaurant last night. And then . . . in the alley."

I nodded. "I'm really glad to see you made it out safely."

"Same here. Whatever happened with those guys?"

I froze. Should I tell her the truth? The last thing I wanted to
do was freak her out. "It was just some college kids, I think."

She frowned. "Really? They seemed so realistic. Huh."

Time to change the subject. "I-I really enjoyed your speech
tonight." My head started bobbing. "Those servant events
sound great."

"I know, right? I mean, just think of how many lives we'll
be able to touch."

My head kept bouncing, as if my neck were a spring. I
couldn't help myself! "It sounds great!"

Her head tipped to one side for a moment. "Are you going
to join us?"

Spend time with her? Absolutely! But before I could say
a word, an image of Agent Sexton popped into my head.
Knowing him, he'd want my priority to be patrolling the city,
not hanging out with a girl.

"If I can, I will. But I'm usually pretty . . . well . . ."

Her face fell.

"That's not because Rob doesn't care," Mike added quickly.
"The thing is . . . he's already engaged in a lot of . . . charity
work."

I shot a questioning look at him. He shrugged.

"Oh, yeah. My schedule is just packed with . . . charity
work."

"Really?" she asked. Her eyes lit up again. "Where? I'm always looking for a new place to volunteer."

Ice sluiced through my veins. "Well, it's not so much a place as it is a . . . state of mind."

What did that even mean? Charlene gave Mike a puzzled look.

"So how long have you been coming to Mount Calvary?" I asked.

"Since July. Some friends told me about it, and I had to check it out."

"That's why I started coming here too." Mike put his arm around me. "I was in a pretty dark place, and this guy helped me through it. He suggested I start coming here and, well . . . here I am."

"That's wonderful!" Charlene glanced at her watch. "Well, I hate to do this, but I have to get going. It was good to see you again, Mike, and it was nice to officially meet you, Rob." She ducked her head. "And thank you for saving me last night."

Mike elbowed me in the gut and whispered, "Phone number."

"Phone number!" I blurted.

Charlene's eyes widened.

"I mean . . . could I get your phone number? Maybe we could hang out sometime?" I probably looked like a lost puppy.

Her lips pursed into a thin line, but then she smiled. "Absolutely. But, you know, I live in New Kidron. It's not like our paths are going to cross that much besides here." She fished out a scrap of paper from her purse and scribbled a number on it. "See you around."

She disappeared into the crowd.

Mike turned to me. "'State of mind'?"

"'Charity work'?"

"Oh, do you have a better way of describing what you do?" he asked.

He had me there. "Okay, fine." I looked in vain for Charlene in the crowd, then I sighed. "Can we talk? I've got a problem I need your help with."

He nodded. "Let me just take a look around, see if there's anything else I can help with, and I'll be right with you, okay?"

Half an hour later, Mike walked with me out to DK. The night air was just beginning to cool, enough to raise goose-bumps across my arm. The parking lot had pretty much emptied out. The only cars left were mine, Mike's, and P.G.'s, which meant it was probably safe for us to talk. We leaned against Mike's car, and I told him about what happened the night before. He listened to the story quietly, his brow knitting into a deeper and deeper frown.

When I finished, I opened my hands. "Any ideas?"

Mike began pacing a tight circle. "Nothing's leaping immediately to mind. Zombies, huh? Well, whatever it is, I'm sure you'll figure it out."

"I was hoping that *we* could figure it out. Could you come on patrol with me?"

Mike hesitated, a split second of awkward silence. "I suppose. I don't know if I'll be able to get away for a few days. Have you considered asking Ben?"

"I did ask him. He didn't seem all that interested."

"Huh. Well, call me in a day or two, and we'll see what we can make happen, okay?"

I clapped him on the back and climbed into DK. I fished my costume out of the back and quickly changed, then started up the engine and activated the patrol mode. Hopefully I'd find some leads out on the streets.

CHAPTER 8

MAGNUS'S CORPORATE JET was plush. The seats were comfortable, and there was a private TV available for each one. A steward offered to get me something to drink. I asked for an orange juice. Magnus settled into a chair and opened a paper. His body language made it clear he wasn't interested in conversation. I fished a novel out of my bag and started reading.

I had barely made it through two chapters when the plane shifted. I frowned and looked out the window. Were we descending already? I glanced at my watch. Barely half an hour had passed.

"How fast are we traveling?" I asked. "Have we reached St. Louis already?"

Magnus laughed. "St. Louis? The doc doesn't live there anymore. No, we flew to Fargo."

North Dakota? I pressed up against the window. Sure enough, nothing but flat farmland. "Why does she live here?"

Magnus gritted his teeth. "Some cold calculus. The doc needs certain resources from the local colleges, but this is out of the way enough that if one of the doc's experiments goes haywire . . . Well, you get the idea."

My eyes widened at the thought. That wasn't very reassuring.

After we left the airport, Magnus hailed a taxi and we climbed into the backseat. Magnus barked directions to the driver to take us to the center of town.

As we drove, I pulled my cell phone out of my pocket and fiddled with it for a moment. Maybe I should give Charlene a quick call while we were on our way. Calling her only two days after meeting her wouldn't be too soon, would it? Maybe just a text?

"Know someone in town?" Magnus asked.

I stammered for a moment. "I met . . . well . . ."

Magnus nodded, a knowing glint in his eye. "Gotcha. Can I give you a piece of advice?"

"That's supposed to be your job, right?"

Magnus grimaced. "I suppose so. Be careful who you give your heart to. That's good advice in general, but especially so given what we do." He glanced at the back of the cab driver's head. "There are a lot of ways a person can get hurt. Remember that."

Cold sluiced down my back. I knew all too well that Magnus was speaking from personal experience. I had learned just a few months ago how messed up his love life had truly been. I slid the phone back in my pocket, suddenly not all that eager to speak to Charlene. At least, I wouldn't until I knew more about her and her intentions.

The cab didn't deposit us near one of the colleges. Instead, it left us at the edge of what looked like a bean field. I turned a slow circle. In the middle of the city? Weird. The nearest buildings were at least six blocks away. A freeway overpass peeked over the top of some of the buildings. The sound of distant cars wove together into a constant thrum. Wind whipped across the field, setting the plants swaying in a gentle undulating motion.

"C'mon, we don't want to keep the doc waiting." Magnus strode out into the middle of the field. Once we reached the middle, he pulled out his cell phone and dialed a number. "We're here."

A low groan sounded, barely audible over the roar of the cars on the nearby freeway. A section of the dirt peeled back, revealing a staircase that led underneath the field. I started for the entrance, but Magnus held out an arm to block my path. He pulled something out of his pocket and handed it to me. It was a hood, similar to the one I wore as part of my costume. I glanced at Magnus and saw that he had pulled on a half mask, the same one he had worn at the VOC headquarters. He nodded for me to put on my hood.

I did so, but I left my necklace on. There was no telling what kind of equipment Dr. Olympus would have in her lab. Given what had been happening with my powers, I figured it best not to run the risk of me frying something important.

Magnus led me down the set of stairs, and the door ground shut behind us, sealing with an audible hiss. Overhead lights flickered on, illuminating dull green brick walls with a scuffed cement floor. A large security camera toward the top of the wall on my right swiveled to glare at us. A faint smell that reminded me of my high school chemistry lab tickled my nose. Magnus set out down the hall, and his footsteps echoed as he walked.

I paused as we walked past a scorch mark that had ripped a gouge in the wall at waist height.

"What do you know about Dr. Olympus, kid?" Magnus asked.

"Just what they say on the news. She's brilliant but also a crafty warrior. Not someone you want to mess with."

Magnus snorted. "Oh, is that all? Well, I suppose all of that is true, but it doesn't do her justice. The doc has three distinct personalities. The one I hope we can talk to today is Athena. An absolute genius and usually calm. But if we were going into battle, we'd want Artemis with us. I've fought alongside her plenty of times." His voice drifted off.

I frowned. "What about the third personality?"

He grimaced. "Let's just say that if she starts coming on to you, flirting, get out of there quick."

What did that mean? We reached a set of metal doors, which ground open, revealing an airy and well-lit laboratory. No, it was much too big to be a typical lab. More like a science factory warehouse.

It was at least half the size of a football field. The room was filled with black-topped tables. Each one was piled with papers, three open laptops, and a bubbling collection of beakers and test tubes. One row was covered with a disassembled machine, with circuits and wires scattered over the tables. A complex molecular model made of wooden sticks and multicolored balls sat on the table nearest to me. A large white board, filled with scribbles and equations, dominated one wall, easily thirty feet long and four feet high.

Along another wall was at least a dozen machines, one of which was a large metal loop covered with balls. On the third wall were a series of unmarked doors with ten feet of space between them. Lurking in the far corner was what appeared to be a ten-foot tall robot with thick arms that ended in claws.

I took a cautious step inside, but I accidentally jostled the molecular model.

"Don't touch that!"

A woman appeared next to me, her blond hair pulled up into some sort of twist. She wore black goggles that covered her eyes and a white lab coat over a black tactical suit. She was frighteningly gorgeous, so much so that I looked away from her immediately.

"That's my cure for cancer," she said. "Or a new recipe for a buffalo wing sauce. I can't remember which. Either way, be careful."

"Doc." Magnus nodded.

"Meridian. So this is Failstate? Let's get started."

Dr. Olympus took me by the arm and dragged me deeper into the lab. She planted me onto a tall stool and turned to one of the tables. She yanked open a drawer and rummaged through it, pulling out a blood-pressure device, a stethoscope, and a big box with a large needle poking out of it.

I leaned away from her, casting a worried look at Magnus.

"So the VOC 'helpfully' provided me with your dossier," she said. "A little thin on the details, but you're new, so I guess that's forgivable." She produced a manila folder and flipped it open, rifling through the contents. "Says here that your power is to . . . 'break things?'" She gave me a questioning look.

My cheeks burned under her intense scrutiny. "Yeah, I guess. I met with a scientist once who thought that I created 'potential failstates within molecular bonds.'" I hesitated. Should I tell her about what happened the other night? Well, she was a doctor . . . "But lately I've been having trouble." I recounted the story of my costume turning rigid and the signpost becoming like taffy.

Dr. Olympus listened with a frown, then grabbed my hand and yanked me off the stool. "We'll get to the bottom of this."

She led me a few steps and then shoved me into another chair, one that was surrounded by the large metal loop I noticed earlier.

Olympus picked up a stapler and tossed it to me. "When I tell you, destroy that."

"You want me to destroy your stapler?"

"It's not that big of a deal. I've got half a dozen others . . . somewhere. I think. Hang on a sec." She stepped over to a console and entered something on a keyboard. A low whine filled the air, and the loop began to rotate around me. A strange prickling sensation washed over me. Olympus turned and nodded. "Okay, go ahead."

"Sure, I just gotta . . ." I reached under my hood and untied my necklace. The normal itching sensation I felt while wearing it swept through my body and coalesced into a dull throb between my eyes. I felt my face draw up into its monstrous form beneath the mask.

"Hold on. What's that?" Olympus slapped a button on the console the loop froze. She snatched the necklace out of my hand.

"That red crystal mutes my powers," I said. "I have to wear it or else . . ."

She looked at me expectantly, but I didn't want to say anything else. The last thing I wanted to do was reveal my true face to her or Magnus.

"Or else what?" Olympus prompted.

I grabbed the edges of my seat and dug in my fingers. No way. Not going to happen.

Magnus knelt down next to me. "Look, kid, it's okay. We're all friends here. And the Doc won't be able to help you unless you're honest with her."

"Okay. Just remember: You asked for this. If I don't wear that necklace, I look . . ." I pulled off the hood . . . "like this."

Olympus jumped backward, the color draining from her face. Magnus slapped a hand over his mouth.

I sighed. I understood their reactions all too well. Without the necklace, my face was completely disfigured. My eyes bled onto my cheeks, making them little more than inky pools. In this state, I really didn't have a nose, just a nub that appeared to have been twisted off. My skin became parchment thin, cracked in places and looked ready to disintegrate.

Olympus pursed her lips and cocked her head to one side. Her eyebrows twitched up her forehead. "Well, that's interesting." She turned back to the controls. "Please put the hood back on and destroy the stapler."

I dropped the hood back in place and focused my attention on the stapler. I willed it to dissolve. Layer by layer, the stapler withered and blew away. Within a few moments, it had disappeared, completely destroyed.

Dr. Olympus adjusted her goggles, then straightened up and blew out a long breath. "Well, whoever you consulted with before is an idiot."

"Excuse me?" I asked.

"You don't create any sort of 'failstate' in molecular bonds. Based on what you've just shown me, that explanation is ludicrous for a variety of reasons."

"Like what, Doc?" Magnus asked.

"The law of the conservation of mass, for starters. If all your protégé did was destroy molecular bonds, then yes, the stapler would have fallen apart. But its mass would have remained as individual atoms. That's not the case, as my readings clearly show. Instead, Failstate—maybe you should consider a name change?—converted most of the stapler into energy and sent it . . . away."

I looked around. "Where?"

"Good question. Could be you absorbed it. Or redirected it to another dimension or somewhere else in the space/time continuum. Without further testing, I'd have no way of knowing for certain."

"But what about that business with his clothes going rigid and the signpost turning to goo?" Magnus asked.

"Ah. I have a theory about that. I think your powers can do more than just 'break things.' I think you can also temporarily alter an object's physical state."

I stared at her, unsure I heard her correctly. That didn't make any sense. "I've never been able to do anything like that before."

"I suspect you have, only on a subconscious level. According to your dossier, you've brought four buildings down on yourself in the past year."

"It was only two," I said, feeling defensive.

"Four, two, doesn't matter. The principle is the same. That much debris raining down on you should have pulverized you. The fact that you're still alive tells me you've been using your transmuting power without even knowing it. Maybe you convert your clothing into temporary armor each time. One way to know for certain. Hold a second."

She walked down the row of machines and then ducked between two of them. When she returned, she was holding a sledgehammer. "Hold still." With a petite grunt, she swung as hard as she could and hit me in the chest.

I was blasted off my chair and thrown twenty feet through the air until I slammed into the whiteboard. I slid down the wall. I clambered up to my feet. Much to my surprise, my chest ached only lightly. "Are you out of your mind?" I demanded.

She sauntered toward me with the hammer held across the back of her neck. "The fact that you can talk still tells me I didn't break any ribs."

"What if you were wrong?"

"I have sixteen doctorates, Failstate. Pretty sure an MD is one of them. Or maybe two." She tossed the sledgehammer off to one side. "But this confirms my hypothesis. And given the readings I collected, this opens up new possibilities. One moment."

She disappeared again, this time stepping through a door on one side of the lab.

"You okay, kid?" Magnus asked.

"Why did we come here again?"

"Look, the Doc is unorthodox, but she gets . . ." His voice trailed off and he took a step away from me.

Dr. Olympus returned with two swords.

I threw up my hands in surrender. "Hey, wait a minute! The sledgehammer worked, but I'm not comfortable with you trying to slice and dice me!"

She laughed. "I'm not going to attack you with these. They're for you."

I looked from her to the swords. Even though they were still in their sheaths, they looked like katanas with slightly curved blades. "What?"

She nodded. "I designed these for Raze a few years ago, but I believe they'll work for you also. A device in the hilt will channel your destructive energy along the blades, making them capable of slicing through just about anything. Or should, anyway."

She tossed me one of the swords. I tentatively pulled the sword from its scabbard. The moment the blade slid free, it felt as though the breath had been sucked out of me. The blade hummed and sparked. Huh. That was interesting. I swung the sword around in an arc. For a moment, I pictured myself wielding these blades like some sort of ninja, slicing through anything that got in my way.

I blanched at the thought. I wasn't trained for swordplay. I'd probably slice my own arm off.

"I appreciate the thought, Dr. Olympus, but I'm afraid that I just wouldn't know what to do with these."

"No worries." She reached into her lab coat and pulled out what appeared to be a ray gun, which she leveled at my head.

With a cry, I ducked just as she fired. Heat flashed over my head. "What is your problem?"

"This?" She showed me the gun. "This is a cognitive imprinting beam. It will download the requisite skills into your cerebral cortex in seconds. Although there is a ten percent chance it will give you a partial lobotomy. Only one way to know for sure. Hold still . . ."

"Wait!" I held up my hands to protect my face. "Swords aren't really my thing!"

She shrugged. "Just trying to help." She took back the swords and cradled one for a moment.

A physical change came over her. She seemed to grow larger, stand taller.

"Uh-oh," Magnus said.

With a snarl, Dr. Olympus tore the goggles from her face, revealing wild green eyes. "You are a fool not to accept these weapons, Failstate. They are the finest ever forged and would make you a force to be reckoned with! Only a coward would refuse this gift."

Given the way her fingers curled around the hilt, I suspected that Dr. Olympus was about to give me a first-hand demonstration on how to use them.

Magnus quickly stepped between us. "Let's just settle down, Doc, okay?"

"Of course you would defend his bloodless actions, Meridian. You were never one for head-to-head combat. Are you at least teaching him the code?"

"Code?" My voice came out as a squeak.

Magnus sighed. "It's not a 'code' per se. Nothing formal. But there are certain ways that heroes like us are supposed to interact."

"Yes." Olympus took a deep breath and seemed to soften. Her features became even more stunning and her eyes smoldered. She traced Magnus's jawline with her finger. "Interaction is always good, right, Meridian?"

Magnus cleared his throat. "Not now, Doc. For example, Failstate, any time you enter another licensed hero's territory, you should always check in with that hero as soon as possible. Common courtesy."

Now Dr. Olympus turned her hungry gaze on me. "If you don't, it could lead to unfortunate misunderstandings." She ran a hand along my shoulder, her fingers lingering a bit too long on my back.

Heat flashed over me. I seemed to remember Magnus saying something about this sort of situation, but my thoughts were so jumbled I couldn't remember exactly.

Magnus caught her hand and maneuvered himself between Dr. Olympus and me.

"So for example," she said, "if you had to go to Los Angeles, you'd want to contact the local VOC office so they could get you in touch with Raze. It's possible he might be able to help you. At the very least, if you've registered your presence there, he won't get upset if he stumbles on you at some point."

"Okay." I nodded. "So if I went to New Orleans, I'd check in with Elemental. Or if I'm in Seattle, I contact Downtime." My eyes widened and I smiled. "Or if I went to New York, I'd get to meet Etzal'el, right?"

Both Magnus and Dr. Olympus froze. They exchanged worried looks.

"Don't ever go to New York," Magnus said. "You do not want to mess with Etzal'el."

"The man is a force of nature, completely uncontrollable," Dr. Olympus said.

I frowned. "But he's a licensed hero."

Magnus sighed. "The only reason the VOC gave Etzal'el his license is because they couldn't stop him. No one can. You'd better hope you never cross paths with him."

That warning sucked the air out of the lab. Dr. Olympus settled down, seeming to shrink again. She retrieved her goggles and we got back to work. She conducted a series of tests that took the rest of the afternoon, collecting readings and blood samples and cheek swabs. After three hours, she dismissed us tersely.

On our way out, I glanced back at the lab doors. "She's not entirely all there, is she?"

Magnus shook his head. "Not really, no."

"What happened?"

Magnus rubbed the back of his neck. "The Doc used to be able to control her personality shifts. If she needed brains, she'd be Athena. If she was going to fight, she'd be Artemis. And then there was Aphrodite. But then she tangled with Mind Master. He somehow disrupted her higher brain functions, and she hasn't been able to control the shifts since."

What felt like a great weight settled on me. I suddenly remembered what Sexton had said about the Living Quark being on medical leave. And now Dr. Olympus. Was that what I had to look forward to as a licensed hero? Constant battles, and always with the threat of being broken or worse?

As if he had read my mind, Magnus clapped his hand on my shoulder. "Don't worry about it, kid. We walk a tough road, but it's worth it. And you're going to be just fine."

I hoped he was right.

CHAPTER 9

"THIS IS JUST GREAT. I'm so glad I took the time to come with you."

I glanced over at Veritas, unsure if he was being sarcastic or not. My friend, dressed in his red-and-blue tights, was hard to read in costume. A mask covered his entire face, revealing only his eyes and his hair. He drummed his fingers on DK's armrest.

"What are you complaining about? I'm the one who flew to Fargo and back today."

He turned and met my gaze. Although I couldn't be sure, it looked like he smiled. "Sorry. This is just . . . hard. A lot more difficult than I thought it would be."

I grimaced. "You're thinking about her, aren't you?"

Veritas shifted in his seat. "Kind of."

Oh, shoot. I should have known. Just a few months earlier, Lux, Veritas's partner—his half-sister—had been killed while waiting to go on patrol with me. While Veritas and I had worked together after that, it had been to uncover the identity of her murderers. But after solving that case, our unofficial partnership had gone inactive. We didn't go out on patrol together. Come to think of it, I hadn't heard any news about Veritas since then.

"What's going on with you?" I asked.

His eyes carried his smirk all too well. "I thought I was the one who saw the truth."

"It's contagious. Start talking."

Veritas sighed. "It's nothing, really. Don't worry about me."

"Mike . . ."

He glared at me. "It's. Nothing." He coughed into his hand. "So what's on the schedule for tonight?"

I put DK into gear. "Let's go see what we can find."

Three hours later, we were cruising through New Chayton's warehouse district, the buzz of the police scanner playing quietly in the background. The empty bag from a burger joint rolled in the back seat, filling the air with its greasy smell. Veritas was stuffing the last few fries into his mouth when a muffled explosion sounded in the distance.

I twisted in my seat and tried to get a bearing on where the explosion had come from. "Any idea?"

Veritas shook his head.

The police scanner squawked at us. "All units, respond to a Code Omega in the Warehouse District. Coordinate with rescue efforts and maintain perimeter. Please respond."

Veritas yanked his mask in place. "Let's go!"

"What's going on?"

He glanced at me. "Code Omega? Superpowered emergency. Didn't Sexton tell you anything?"

Another thing the good agent had failed to mention. I hit the "suppression mode" button, and the vehicle growled and grew larger. I floored it, and the engine roared. I made a U-turn in the middle of the street and headed out, looking for the lights from the police cars.

I saw them soon enough. Police cars blocked the street. I pulled up by the impromptu barricade and got out. One of the patrol officers rushed to my side. "What's going on?" I asked.

"Some sort of disturbance two blocks down." The cop pointed down the street. A large cloud of dust billowed through the streets.

"All right." Then I realized that he was looking to me for instructions. To *me*. "Well, uh . . . maintain the perimeter, contact the VOC, and keep any civilians in the area safe."

The cop nodded and rushed off to his colleagues.

That would take some getting used to. I turned to Veritas. "You ready?"

"Would it matter if I said no?"

"Not really."

"Then I'm almost ready. Hold on a sec."

Veritas bowed his head and closed his eyes. I winced. How stupid was I? Before I went into battle, it'd be best to entrust it to God. I mimicked Veritas's posture. *God, the only way this will turn out okay is if You're with me. Guide my actions, keep me safe, and help me do what You need me to do.*

We charged down the street, rushing into the dust cloud.

Loud smacks and cracks echoed between the buildings. Then a body came tumbling through the air and slammed onto the street. The pavement cracked, but whoever it was staggered to his feet. He glanced at us, his blue costume dirty but his usual cocky half-grin in place.

"Good to see you, little brother," Gauntlet said. "Here to help?"

CHAPTER 10

"WHAT ARE YOU DOING HERE?" I asked.

Gauntlet dusted himself off. "Selling Girl Scout cookies. Want some Thin Mints?"

I stifled the sharp retort clawing up my throat. "So what are we facing?"

"Not really sure." Gauntlet hesitated. For a split second, uncertainty darted across his face. Then just as quickly it was replaced by the usual bravado. "Well, at least you two can witness my heroics. Be sure to get the details right for the press, okay?"

"We'll do our best," Veritas said.

Gauntlet looked down the street and took a deep breath. Then he turned to me and motioned with a quick bow. "Licensed heroes first."

That wasn't good. If Gauntlet wasn't charging into battle head-first, it meant he was a lot more nervous than he let on. I set out down the street, my hands clenched into tight fists.

Large warehouses towered over me on both sides of the street. Most looked like they had seen better days—they all had dull paint and cracked windows. I passed by a bus stop enclosure that had been partially covered with graffiti.

Sweat poured down my forehead and stung my eyes. Each step set off a jangle of raw nerves. My power, instead of thrumming in the background as it usually did, spiked and flared. At any moment, I just knew I would break something—or transform it into molasses.

"So how'd you wind up in this fight?" Veritas asked Gauntlet.

"Well, I was out on patrol. Hadn't found anything special yet. Then I heard this big 'boom.' Sounded like someone blew a hole in the side of a building. So I started off in the direction of the noise. Found this big guy. When he saw me, he attacked. I thought I was holding my own but then he got in a lucky punch and bam! I'm rolling to a stop next to you two."

"Any idea who he was?" Veritas asked.

Gauntlet hesitated again. "No clue. He wasn't wearing a costume. It was weird, actually. It looked like he was wearing scrubs."

My head snapped around. "Grey scrubs?"

Gauntlet frowned. "How'd you know?"

"Lucky guess." I didn't like coincidences. Not now, not ever. "Was it a zombie?"

Veritas almost said something, but I held up my hand for him to keep quiet. Off in the distance, someone was stomping around on the pavement. The tremors wormed through my boots and into my feet. I turned to the others and signaled: two fingers to my eyes, then a sharp jab around the corner. Palm up, a stopping motion.

"What?" Gauntlet asked.

I sighed. "I'm going to take a look. Stay here."

"Why didn't he just say that?" Veritas asked.

"Give a guy a license, and he goes all special forces on you." Gauntlet flashed a crooked grin at me.

I grumbled under my breath but crept forward, inching along the building wall. Once I reached the corner, I carefully poked my head around to see what was happening.

A large man in torn grey scrubs stood in the middle of the street. He was almost as big as the minivan he stood next to. Thick arms hung down almost to his knees. His hair, a mottled mix of black, red, and orange, hung in ragged clumps down around his shoulders and onto his chest. He glared around the street then stomped toward another vehicle. Well, not really stomped. More like staggered. One of his knees didn't seem to work correctly. His left leg flopped and bent as he moved. And I could hear his moaning and clacking from where I hid.

"Oh, great. Another one."

The man turned until his eyes were locked on me. His lips twitched into a snarl, and he tried to bellow. I think. At least, it looked like it was supposed to be a bellow. Instead, the creature released a dry hiss in my direction.

The zombie slammed his fists into the road, the pavement exploding in a spiderweb of cracks. The zombie picked up a chunk of asphalt the size of a car engine and hurled it at me.

I ducked back behind the corner just as the chunk slammed into the building.

A shower of debris rained down onto my head and shoulders. I winced. "Yeah, we've got another zombie."

"Another one?" Gauntlet asked. "You've tangled with one of these before?"

"Three, actually." I ground my teeth together. "We can play catch-up later. Right now, let's go!"

"Hold it!" Veritas held up a hand, his eyes pinched by a frown. He cocked his head to one side. "Listen."

I did as I was told, holding my breath. Off in the distance, I heard more sirens. There were some loud voices from a few blocks away as well, if I had to guess. But that was it.

Wait. Where were the noises from the zombie?

I risked a peek around the corner, ready to duck if the zombie hurled another chunk of pavement at me. The street appeared empty, as if the zombie man had disappeared completely. I counted to thirty and then slipped around the building, stepping carefully over the crushed pavement. I frowned. Had the zombie vanished?

"He's not here." I motioned behind me for Veritas and Gauntlet to join me.

Veritas looked around the empty street. Gauntlet did so as well. For the first time, I noticed the wrecked cars. Apparently the zombie had been beating on them at some point, shattering the windows and crushing the hoods. Some poor road crew would have a difficult job fixing these potholes.

"Do you think he turned invisible?" Gauntlet asked.

"An invisible zombie? C'mon," Veritas said.

I frowned. Like that would be any more ridiculous than a zombie at all. I started to shush him, when something slammed into the pavement next to me. The impact threw me off my feet and I hit the ground hard.

The zombie towered over me, hissing and clacking his jaw. He raised his fists over his head. I rolled a split second before he shattered the ground where I had just been. The zombie cocked his fist back, clearly ready to pulverize me.

Gauntlet darted forward, snaring the zombie's fist and dragging it backward. The zombie thrashed and twisted, yanking Guantlet off his feet. The zombie caught Gauntlet by his shoulders and legs and tossed him at a brick wall.

Gauntlet tumbled end over end through the air. I frowned. It looked like he was slowing down in midair. He tumbled one more time into a standing position and dropped to the ground, looking no more the worse for wear than if he'd stepped off a bus.

Veritas dashed passed me. The zombie swung a fist at him, but Veritas easily ducked. He darted in, peppering the nightmare creature with a series of jabs and punches. The zombie didn't appear affected, but Veritas didn't stop. The few times the zombie tried to fight back, Veritas easily ducked.

"Veritas, down!"

At Gauntlet's shout, Veritas ducked and rolled to his right.

Gauntlet hurled a car at the zombie.

But before the car could hit, the zombie plucked it out of the air. He turned a tight circle and threw it back at Gauntlet, who only barely managed to dive out of the way. The car slammed into a nearby building, punching a hole through its wall.

"You gonna do something, Failstate, or are you just supervising?" Gauntlet shouted.

My cheeks burned. I dashed forward, marshaling my power around my fists. The zombie swung at me, but I ducked, and his fist sliced the air over my head. I darted in and hit his stomach with a focused punch of my power.

Pain lanced up my arm, exploding through my fingers. It felt as though I hit a solid metal plate. Worse, the zombie didn't show any sign that he had felt my punch.

I darted around the massive creature and jabbed at his kidneys. The blow once again hurt me more than the zombie. He whirled and backhanded me. Stars exploded through my vision, and I slammed into a parked car.

My power flared.

Oh, no.

The car door I was leaning against melted, oozing down over my shoulders and dripping to the pavement. The strange thing was that the metal wasn't hot. It had simply liquefied, but only for an instant. In a split second, the metal hardened, trapping me in its embrace. I pulled and thrashed against it, trying to get free, but it was no use. The warped metal shackled me to the ground.

Veritas glanced in my direction, his eyes wide. He waved to Gauntlet. "Help him! I'll distract!"

Gauntlet charged to my side and knelt down next to me. He tried to wrap his fingers around my restraints, but the metal had molded to my shoulders, creating an impossibly tight seal. Gauntlet grumbled and smacked a fist against part of the metal, sending a sharp spike of pain through me.

"Ow! Don't do that again!" I said.

"You have any bright ideas?"

"Yeah. Back off a sec."

I closed my eyes and focused. I couldn't lose control, not again. Not like this. Instead, I pictured a ball of destructive energy radiating from my body, chewing through the metal and freeing me.

Almost instantly, I felt the metal holding me down dissolve. I leapt to my feet, steadied by Gauntlet.

"Let's end this," I said.

Gauntlet nodded, then disappeared.

I whirled around in time to see him sliding across the ground, a large car engine smashed against his chest. The zombie had ripped the engine out of one of the cars!

I whirled on my opponent. Veritas was on the zombie's back and was trying to subdue him with a choke hold. Maybe not the best idea for a creature that didn't breathe anymore, but I didn't have any better ideas.

The zombie pawed at him, trying to catch him, but Veritas managed to dodge most of his attempts. So the zombie lunged backward, and slammed into the pavement. The creature got up, but Veritas didn't. He lay on the street, groaning.

Enough. This was my responsibility. I was the licensed hero. I had to end this.

"Hey! Gruesome! You and me!"

The zombie's lips twisted back in a snarl, revealing surprisingly gleaming teeth. He clacked and hissed at me, pawing at the ground with his hands in a way that reminded me of the apes at the new Chayton Zoo. Then he charged, arms cocked back to destroy me.

I braced myself. I wouldn't run. I wouldn't retreat. I lashed out, slicing through a nearby streetlight and another on the opposite side of the street. The poles tottered and fell toward the zombie.

The first of the poles clubbed the zombie over the back of the head, and he dropped to the street. His head hit the pavement hard enough that his chin shattered. Then the second pole smashed the creature over the back of his head. I charged in and kicked him in the face. Then, surrounding my fists with my power, I lashed out and punched him as hard as I could in the back of the neck.

The zombie exploded in a burst of dust.

I coughed and hacked as the foul-smelling debris swirled around me. I waved it away as much as I could, but I had a feeling that I would be using a handy-vac on my costume when I got home to get rid of it all.

When the dust settled, I found that the zombie had vanished completely. Weird.

I ran to Veritas's side and knelt down next to him. His eyes fluttered open and he nodded to me. I checked on my brother.

Gauntlet shoved the engine block off of him with a groan. "Well, that was fun. Let's not do that again. Ever. Okay?"

I grinned. "Sure thing."

Then I looked around me at the wreckage. At least four buildings had taken severe damage. A dozen cars had been completely totaled. And that didn't include the cracks and craters in the street's pavement. I swallowed a groan. I might have defeated the zombie, but this still felt like a loss. A big one. I realized I'd better brace myself for another tongue-lashing from Agent Sexton.

CHAPTER 11

"OH, COME ON, KID. You really expect me to believe that one?" Sexton looked ready to spit fireballs.

Veritas ducked slightly and refused to meet his gaze. Gauntlet, however, still wore his usual half-smirk. That probably wasn't helping. I knew how infuriating it was when he grinned at me. I could only imagine how a government official would react.

The three of us stood near the police car barricade, which had grown considerably during our fight. Now fire trucks and ambulances added their lights to those of the police cars, and the emergency personnel milled around. Most of them were giving us a wide berth, although a few shot dirty looks in my direction. They weren't helping the situation either.

"Everything I've told you is true, Agent Sexton." I pointed to my friends. "They can back me up on what happened."

"Like I'm going to take the word of two amateurs." Sexton crossed his arms over his chest. "Unless you're making these two your sidekicks?"

I could do that? Maybe Sexton had told me I could have sidekicks, maybe he hadn't. That would make things a whole lot simpler. I could always use a partner, and either Gauntlet or Veritas—or, preferably, both—would be a colossal help to me going forward. Maybe I could have a whole team of them!

Except Gauntlet and Veritas were both shaking their heads. Gauntlet actually laughed.

"Sir," Veritas said, "with all due respect, does it really matter if we are or aren't? Do you really think all three of us are lying?"

Sexton sighed. "Look, do you understand how stupid all of this sounds? You guys fought a super-strong zombie that, despite its strength, was so flimsy that it exploded into dust when Failstate punched him. Well, isn't that convenient? Now there's no forensic evidence!"

I glanced in the direction of where we had fought the zombie. A few crime scene techs were heading down the street with vacuums. Maybe they'd get lucky and find some samples, but I had my doubts.

"So imagine what would happen if I went back to my superiors and told them that Failstate and his two amateur friends insist that they fought the undead—even though no one has ever successfully reanimated the dead, remember? They'd bust me and reassign you to a new liaison officer."

That actually didn't seem too bad, but I didn't think pointing that out would be such a good idea. "Look, I know this sounds really weird. If I hadn't fought zombies twice now, I wouldn't believe it either."

Sexton glared at me. "My suggestion, Failstate, is you start taking your license seriously. You wouldn't be the first hero to lose his status, and believe me, I'd be more than happy to boot you myself. Now, are you busy tomorrow?"

From the tone of his voice, I knew that I had better clear my schedule. I shook my head.

"Good. Meet me at City Hall at one. The mayor wants to see you."

The VOC agent signaled for one of his underlings to come over to him. We had clearly been dismissed. Gauntlet snorted and stomped away. Veritas and I followed him.

Once we were out of earshot, Gauntlet whirled on us. "Who does that moron think he is?"

I sighed. "Right or wrong, he's my VOC liaison officer. And I suppose it's his job to be skeptical."

"Well, he's certainly got that part down." Gauntlet clapped a hand on my shoulder. "Are you doing okay? What happened with you and the car door?"

I gritted my teeth. How would Gauntlet react if I told him my powers were fluctuating again? Would he still support me?

"I don't know. I've been having some . . . problems. I can't really talk about it right now."

"You sure?" Gauntlet asked.

I nodded.

"Well, okay. If you change your mind, swing by the apartment, okay? I've got this idea I want to try with you, should be kind of fun."

It was still odd to think of Ben in his own apartment instead of with us at home.

Gauntlet knelt and tensed his legs. Then, with a great leap, he burst from the pavement and shot up to the top of the highest building, disappearing onto the roof. Figures that he would have learned how to fly.

Veritas stepped closer to me. "Seriously, what's going on?"

I sighed. "I don't know. I saw Dr. Olympus this morning, but she only had theories."

Veritas blew out a long breath and motioned for me to follow him. We left the area and headed back for DK.

"I know it's a little frustrating, but this sort of thing happens. At least, that's what I understand. Dad went through something similar when he was younger. For a while, his powers intensified to the point where all he could do was shoot lasers at people. A year later, all he could muster were light shows and holograms. It took him a while to get things back to normal again."

I gaped at Veritas. "Why didn't he say anything to me about that?"

Veritas laughed bitterly, a short bark. "What, the great Meridian admit that he was anything less than perfect? You don't know my father very well."

My stomach soured. How could I trust Magnus if he wasn't going to level with me about these sorts of things? Was he really going to be that much of a help for me? Of course, he had given me DK. I fished the keys out of my pocket and keyed the locks. I opened the door but didn't get in.

"What's going on?" Veritas asked.

"These zombies . . ." I looked back over my shoulder at Agent Sexton. "If what he says is true, then this shouldn't be possible. So what could be causing this?"

Veritas shifted on his feet. "I don't know."

"I mean, the dead are supposed to rise when Jesus comes back, right? Do you think that's what's going on?"

"Somehow I don't think He meant a zombie apocalypse."

I chuckled. "Well, yeah, I guess. But what if these guys have souls? What if they can be rescued? Or cured and made whole again? Did we just murder someone back there?"

Veritas shook his head. "Absolutely not. Have any of the zombies you've seen seemed capable of reasoning, Failstate? We didn't have any choice here."

"I guess."

Veritas glanced at his watch. "Look, I hate to say this, but I have to get home. Some of us still need to sleep at night. I'll see you at Mount Calvary on Sunday?"

I nodded.

"Sounds great." Veritas hesitated for a moment. "You sure you're okay?"

"Yes. I am."

I hated lying to my friend, but hopefully, what I said would be true eventually.

CHAPTER 12

CITY HALL WAS A GLEAMING SKYSCRAPER in the heart of downtown New Chayton. I found a parking spot two blocks away. I held my breath as I attempted to parallel park DK. With DK in suppression mode, I was pretty sure I didn't want to hit the cars near me. I'd probably wind up destroying them.

I attracted more than a few curious looks as I fished out change for the parking meter. That was understandable. I probably looked ridiculous, a superhero digging through his pockets for enough quarters to buy two hours' time. Maybe I would have been exempt, but I didn't want to take any chances. Once the meter was fed, I set out for the building.

I hauled open the glass door and stepped into the lobby. I paused in the door to soak it all in. City Hall's lobby was a circular room that towered twenty feet over my head. Set in the center of the room was a large fountain that shot jets of water in an intricate dance. A marble rosette surrounded the fountain and was bordered by a number of planters with large green bushes and small trees. A coffeehouse was to my right, a security station to my left. The guard manning the station sat up, his hand darting toward his gun.

I held up my hands. Then I slowly pulled out my superhero license, a small purple card made of plastic. I handed it to the guard.

The guard's eyes narrowed. He didn't take his gaze off of me. Instead, he ran the license through a card reader in his station. His eyes flicked to the readout for just a second. He must have been placated by what he saw. He sat down again and motioned for me to keep going.

I retrieved my license and walked around the fountain.

An information desk had been set up on the far side of the room. The receptionist gave me an equally chilly welcome. She looked me up and down before she asked, "Can I help you?"

"My name is Failstate. I have a 1:00 meeting with the mayor."

"Uh huh." She looked down at the computer on her desk. "Well, I'll be. Head on over to the elevators and take them to the top floor." She pointed past her desk.

I nodded my thanks and walked to where she had pointed. The elevator arrived after only a short wait, and soon, I was riding to the top.

My fellow passengers shied away from me. Though the elevator was almost full, I still had a good foot and a half between the others and me. Eventually, the elevator emptied, and I rode to the top of the building by myself.

The elevator opened to a small office that reminded me of VOC headquarters. Instead of cubicles, though, clusters of desks dotted the open area with men and women hunched over their computers or talking into their phones. A few shot a glance in my direction, but that was about it.

A young man in his mid-twenties stood next to a large set of wooden doors. He appeared to be an inch or two taller than me and was a little on the skinny side. He smiled and waved when he saw me. "Failstate? Over here?"

I crossed to him.

He took my hand and pumped it vigorously. "I'm Agent Kensignton with the VOC. Well, I'm only a probationary agent, actually. But I have to tell you, I was thrilled when Agent Sexton asked me to come to this meeting. I am such a big fan."

A fan? Really? "You are?"

Kensington nodded. "Of course! You were my favorite on *America's Next Superhero*. I must have worn out three cell phones voting for you. I was so glad when I heard you got the license!"

I smiled, then realized that Kensington couldn't see my expression through the hood. "Is Agent Sexton here?"

"Oh, yes, they're all waiting for you."

Wait, all? "Who else is here?"

"Well, Mayor Reilly, obviously. And Agent Sexton. And Police Chief Blackthorn. Oh, and Fire Chief Thompson said she wanted to talk to you about what happened last night."

A weight settled into my stomach. I was pretty sure I was going to vomit before I even stepped into the meeting. I felt like I had been summoned to the principal's office.

"So, come on, let's get in there!" Kensington dragged me to the doors and pulled one of them open. Without waiting to see if I was ready, he shoved me through.

I stumbled to a halt in a plush office. A bank of windows looked out over the New Chayton skyline. A large wooden desk sat to my right with a high-backed leather chair behind it. A cluster of blue couches were to my left, forming a half circle. On the wall was a seal for the City of New Chayton, a large hawk in flight carrying two olive branches.

Mayor Reilly rose from her seat underneath the seal and walked toward me, her hand out and a smile on her face. I had met her only once before, shortly after I'd received my license. She was a nice woman, a little on the plump side, with streaks of grey through her otherwise auburn hair. She was dressed smartly in a dark skirt and coat. "Failstate, so good of you to join us. I'd like to introduce you to Chief Blackthorn . . ."

Blackthorn was an older gentlemen, maybe in his early sixties. His hair had thinned out, revealing a pockmarked scalp. His face was lined with wrinkles, mostly around his eyes, and I couldn't tell if most of them had come from laughing or scowling. His uniform was covered with ribbons. He didn't rise from his seat, but he did nod curtly in my direction.

". . . Fire Chief Thompson . . ."

Ms. Thompson was in her forties, with a large halo of black hair that seemed to defy gravity. She was taller than me, and she looked tough. She smiled at me, but it was obviously forced.

". . . and of course, you know Agent Sexton."

All too well. Sexton didn't even bother to glance in my direction.

Mayor Reilly ushered me to a seat on the couch nearest to Sexton. Kensington flitted past me and took up a position behind Sexton. "How was the traffic on the way down?" Mayor Reilly asked.

"It was fine, ma'am," I said.

The mayor laughed. "Failstate, now that you're a licensed hero, we're going to be seeing a lot of each other. You don't have to call me 'ma'am.'"

"I'm sorry . . . uh, Mayor Reilly."

"Very good." She sat down in her chair and clapped her hands on her knees. "Well, now that the introductions are out of the way, let's get started." She turned to Sexton. "How is the Living Quark doing?"

Sexton shifted on his chair. "A little better. The doctors inform me that he managed to walk from his bed to the bathroom today. Unfortunately, his cognitive abilities haven't improved."

Mayor Reilly nodded. "And Shadowfall and Nightsilver?"

"We're still holding out hope that the Order of the Fourth Eye will release them unharmed, but that possibility is looking more and more unlikely."

"And you still can't tell me where the Hoplite is?"

Sexton shrugged. "I don't even know myself."

"I see." The mayor's gaze shifted to me. "So that leaves us with Failstate."

Everyone in the room turned to face me. I squirmed in my chair. This was just like my recurring nightmare of being up in the front of class for a presentation I hadn't prepared. At least I was fully clothed.

"That's just wonderful," Thompson said. "Did you see what he did to the warehouse district?"

"That wasn't my fault," I said.

"That doesn't enter into it." Thompson turned to the mayor. "Do you realize why Jenkins isn't here right now? He's down surveying Failstate and his cronies' damage."

"Who's Jenkins?" I whispered to Kensington.

"Head of public works for the city," he replied.

"He's already estimating that the cost to fix the road will run into hundreds of thousands of dollars!" Thompson said.

"That may be," Mayor Reilly said, "but do you remember what happened the last time Krazney Potok released his minions on the city? He nearly leveled an entire neighborhood before Meridian stopped him . . ."

"Exactly my point! If someone like Potok were to unleash a giant robot or some genetically modified creature, how likely is it that Failstate would be able to stop them?" Thompson turned to Sexton. "Can't the VOC bring in someone else, at least until the Hoplite is back?"

Sexton almost answered, but Agent Kensington interrupted him. "Ma'am, the VOC has every confidence in Failstate. Otherwise we wouldn't have given him a license."

Sexton glared at his subordinate, but then shrugged. "He has a point."

"Well, I still don't like this," Thompson said. "This is just a disaster waiting to happen."

"Hey!"

All eyes were on me once again. It took me a moment to realize that yes, I had actually spoken. Best to just press on.

"I'm sorry about the Living Quark and . . . and the others, but I'm here, and I have the license. I may not be as great as Meridian in his prime, but I promise you I'll do my best. If you'll trust me, that is."

Thompson glanced at Mayor Reilly, her skepticism painted across her face. Worse, I saw its echo on the mayor's face as well. And based on the smirk that tugged on Sexton's lips, he was enjoying himself.

Then Chief Blackthorn cleared his throat. I stifled a groan. From the sour look on his face, I had a feeling he was going to shovel the final clod of dirt onto my grave.

"I think I've heard enough. I've been doing police work for thirty-five years now, and I've seen guys like this come and go. Some have been good, lots have been just okay, and a few have turned out to be disasters. And based on what I've seen, I think I've got a good bead on Failstate."

Here it came.

"I say we let the kid do his thing."

I sat back in my chair. Wow. Thompson scowled and shook her head. Sexton looked like he had been chewing on glass. The only one who seemed pleased with Blackthorn's pronouncement was Kensington. He beamed at me.

Blackthorn turned to Mayor Reilly. "But that's just my opinion, Your Honor. Take it or leave it."

Reilly pursed her lips, then turned to Sexton. "You brought the phone, I trust?"

Sexton stammered for a moment. "Uh . . . yes, Your Honor, we did. Just give us a moment to set it up." He got out of his chair and slapped Kensington on the arm. The two of them walked over to the mayor's desk and opened a briefcase on it.

I leaned over to Blackthorn. "Thank you, sir. But if you don't mind me asking, why stick up for me?"

Blackthorn rubbed his knees before meeting my gaze. "I remember a number of years ago, back when I was just a beat cop, I had a run-in with a clown in a costume. He was just a kid, a little younger than you, but he thought he was the best thing to ever hit New Chayton. I was sure he was going to be dead within a week. And sure, he screwed up every now and then, but he learned each time. The kid turned out okay. Better than that, actually. Maybe you know him. Went by the name 'Meridian.'"

"You're kidding!"

He shook his head. "I don't know how you're going to turn out, son. But I do know this: New Chayton needs a hero right about now. And we've got one in you. The best thing we can do is let you do your thing."

Kensington returned to the group and handed me a cell phone. I nearly choked when I saw it: a sleek smartphone, bordered with black rubber in a stainless steel case.

"Do you have a cell of your own?" Kensington asked.

I fished my phone out of my pocket and handed it to him. The VOC agent looked it over, then pulled a cord out of his pocket. He used it to hook the two phones together, then pressed a button on the smartphone's side. "I'm transferring your data," he explained. "You'll be able to use this as your personal phone, with the same number, but you'll also be able to use it to contact the VOC at any time. This also has a direct line to Mayor Reilly, Chief Blackthorn, and Chief Thompson, and vice versa."

"In case we run into a situation that requires your expertise," Blackthorn said.

Kensington handed me the phone. It was extremely light, but it felt as though he'd handed me a brick. My situation suddenly seemed even more real, as if I had been playing make-believe up until then. I was it. The group in the mayor's office—no, the entire city—was counting on me to do big things for them, to protect them and keep them safe. I just hoped I was up to the task.

Chief Blackthorn rose from his chair and stuck out his hand. "Good luck, Failstate. Make us proud."

I rose and shook his hand. "Anything in particular I can help you with?"

He frowned, and the lines in his forehead deepened. "Maybe keep an eye out on Hogtown. I'm not saying spend all your time there. New Chayton's a big place, after all. But after you and Veritas took out Pyrotrack, the Blue Eclipse Boys have been losing ground to the HazMats. It hasn't escalated into a full turf war yet, but maybe, if they know you're watching, it won't."

I nodded. "Anything else?"

He shook his head. "But if anything else comes up, I'll call you. Mayor Reilly, good day."

Chief Thompson left shortly thereafter as well. I spent another half hour with the mayor, mostly making small talk. She tried to press me into making an appearance with her at the soon-to-be-reopened Hawkeye Mall that weekend. I declined, claiming to be too busy, but in reality, I didn't want to make public appearances. While I may have been New Chayton's only hero, I knew I wasn't ready for playing the celebrity just yet.

Finally, Sexton and Kensington walked with me out of the mayor's office. She offered me one more friendly wave before sitting down behind her desk. I strode back to the elevator with the two VOC agents flanking me.

"That went well," Kensington said.

Sexton glared at him, then turned to me. "Look here, kid, I don't know how you snowed Blackthorn. I suppose he is practically senile. Don't think for a second that this somehow means you're in the clear. You reek of disaster, and I'm the one who will have to clean up after you. Got it?" He stomped off.

I wondered for a moment if he was planning to take the stairs. Maybe going down fifty stories would help him cool off.

"Don't worry about it," Kensington said. "He'll warm up to you eventually."

I appreciated Kensington's optimism, but I suspected the only way Sexton would warm up to me was if I used a blowtorch on him.

CHAPTER 13

WHEN I RETURNED home from patrol early Sunday morning, I found that Mom was already dressed for church and headed for her car.

"You coming this morning?" she asked as she adjusted one of her earrings. "Need a ride?"

I perked up immediately. There was a good chance that Charlene would be there, and I hadn't worked up the courage to actually call her, especially after Magnus's "pep talk" in Fargo. I dashed into the house and ran through the shower, put on clothes and my necklace, then leapt down the stairs and into Mom's van. I practically vibrated in the passenger seat as she drove.

She glanced at me when we were about halfway there. "What's with you? I don't think I've seen you this excited since your big trip."

I grimaced. "I'm just excited to see someone at church. That's all."

A smile tugged at the corners of Mom's mouth. "'Someone?' As in, 'someone you should introduce to your loving mother?'"

"Nothing like that." I couldn't help but smirk as well. "Maybe someday, though."

Mom snorted. "When we get home, you're telling me everything, got it?"

I laughed. Even though it felt good to kid with Mom, I still felt a bit uncomfortable. It was moments like this one that made me hopeful that our relationship had turned the corner.

We pulled up to Mount Calvary, and I bolted out of the car. Up the stairs into the building, down the hall, and to the left into the gym. I skidded to a halt and found . . . no one there.

I frowned and glanced at my watch. The service was supposed to start in an hour, and yet none of the chairs were set up. The stage was mostly empty. Where was everyone?

P.G. strolled into the gym carrying a steaming cup of coffee. He froze when he saw me. "Rob? You okay?"

"Sure, P.G. Why do you ask?"

"You're not in trouble again, are you?"

His question stung. Agent Sexton would probably answer differently than I would, but I didn't want to bother P.G. "I hope not."

He relaxed. "Well, then, you're the first to arrive to help set up. Go grab a stack of chairs and start schlepping." He pointed to a collection of towers made of chairs that filled one corner of the gym.

I groaned. If I would have known arriving at church this early would mean physical labor, I would have driven myself over. With a sigh, I went over to the chairs and got to work. I carried a stack from the pile and started arranging them around the end of the stage. I had set up ten chairs when two female volunteers, two giggly soon-to-be freshmen, joined us. A few moments later, three guys, brothers whose names I couldn't remember, began working on the other side. With each new arrival, I craned my neck around to see if Charlene was one of them. She would be one to help out like this, right?

A half hour before the service started, Mike strolled into the gym. He greeted some of the crew, but his face froze when he saw me. He waved me over, a sly smile spreading across his lips.

"I'm not the person you were hoping to see, huh?" he asked.

"Stay out of my mind," I shot back with a smile of my own.

"I don't need telepathy to read you right now." Mike clapped me on the shoulder. "Hey, P.G., I'm going to borrow Rob to get the sound equipment ready, okay?"

P.G. didn't turn from his work on stage but gave us a thumbs up.

Mike led me back to the sound booth and started removing the hard covers from the devices.

"You realize I don't know anything about this stuff, right?" I asked.

A smile blossomed on Mike's face. He leaned over the sound board and fiddled with a set of sliders. I frowned. What was he doing?

"Hey."

I turned. Charlene smiled at me. My mouth went dry instantly.

She had pinned her hair up in a braid that wrapped around her head, almost like a crown. While most everyone who attended wore jeans and t-shirts to worship, she wore a dark green dress that reached to just below her knees, and she had cinched a wide black belt around her waist. She looked like she was ready for some sort of semi-formal dance. For a moment, I panicked. Had P.G. announced something like that for today? No, of course not. Mike wasn't dressed up. So what was going on?

"I was hoping that one of you could help me set up my display?" She didn't look at Mike. But then, why would she? She probably knew he had to finish work on the sound board.

I smiled and nodded. She led me out of the gym and toward the main sanctuary.

Mount Calvary had started its life as an elementary school. It was easy to tell when we crossed out of the original building. The scuffed linoleum on the floor gave way to newer tiles. We entered a large atrium at least thirty feet wide. A vaulted ceiling soared overhead, supported by dark wooden pillars. The carpet was a rich blue, flecked with darker dots. A large mural dominated one wall, depicting Jesus preaching to a crowd. The other walls were dotted with portraits of the staff, a painting of a small country church in winter, along with a number of Bible verses painted directly on the wall.

Adult members of the church milled around in the open space, gathering in small knots. Singing drifted from the open doors to the sanctuary—probably the choir warming up. I spotted Mom chatting with two of her friends. All three of them held cups of coffee. When Mom saw me, her gaze darted to Charlene. Her eyes widened, and a small smile flashed across her face. I blushed. I was going to hear about this afterward.

Charlene led me to a closet off the atrium. Inside were piles of fold-away tables and an assortment of music stands, easels, and posters scattered in the corners. She grabbed one end of a table and started sliding it toward the door. That was all the prompting I needed. I grabbed the other end. Charlene led the way across the atrium to a spot near the sanctuary's entrance. A folded piece of cardboard and a stack of brochures were already waiting for us.

"Thanks for helping me." Charlene locked the table legs into place. "P.G. and I are hoping to raise awareness with the adults about the mission projects."

That explained the dress! If Charlene were going to man the table during the service to talk to the adults, she would naturally want to look her best.

Charlene spread red fabric over the table. I picked up the display and opened it. Dozens of pictures dotted the inside, with the message "Well done, good and faithful servant" written over them in six-inch letters. Some of the pictures depicted teenagers working with smiling African children in what appeared to be a crumbling school building. A few showed other teenagers working with spades and rakes inside a weed-infested vacant lot.

I spotted Charlene in a few of the Africa photos. Though she was wearing sweat-stained clothing and her face was smudged, she was gorgeous. My eyes were drawn right to her. Heat shot through my cheeks. I set the display on the table.

Charlene came around and started setting out the brochures.

"What do you think you kids are doing?"

I turned at the sharp voice. An elderly man dressed in a rumpled blue suit glared at us.

"I'm sorry?" Charlene asked.

"Why are you cluttering up the narthex with that garbage?" The man brushed past me and snatched a brochure out of Charlene's hand.

"We're trying to raise awareness about the youth group's mission trips next summer, and—"

The old man snorted. "Which I suppose you'll expect us to pay for. You kids think you own this place, don't you?"

Charlene blushed furiously, and her head dipped. "I don't think that at all, sir. If you're upset, maybe you could talk to Pastor Grant and—"

"Why would I talk to him? He's not the real pastor here." The man crumpled up the brochure and tossed it onto the table. "He's part of the problem anyway, coming in here and making all that racket while we're trying to really worship God."

Charlene mumbled more apologies.

I wanted to pop the old crow. Seemed like I was loving the idea of coming to this girl's rescue. I looked around for someone to help, but none of the adults in earshot seemed all that interested in what was happening. Actually, most of them seemed to be doing their best to avoid eye contact with me.

"It'd be better if Pastor Redder would bring you people in line, focus on what really matters!"

"You mean following Jesus' example in serving others doesn't count?" The words slipped out of my mouth before I could think about what I was doing.

The old man whirled on me, his eyes wide and his nostrils flaring. "What was that?"

My heart imploded. What was I doing? The last thing I needed this morning was a fight with some old guy in church. What if he had a heart attack? But I couldn't exactly back down now. "I'm sorry if you're upset, sir, I really am. But I'm not sure this is the best way to deal with it. You're attacking fellow Christians in church. You see that, right? We haven't done anything wrong."

"You are cluttering up our worship area with this . . . nonsense!"

"Isn't it our worship area too? I mean, we may worship down in the gym, but Charlene and I are part of the Church, aren't we? Or has Pastor Grant been teaching us the wrong stuff?"

Purple crept up the man's neck and bled into his face. "How dare you talk to me like that! Do you know who I am? You need to remember your place."

I couldn't help myself. "'Don't let anyone look down on you because you are young, but set an example for the believers in speech, in conduct, in love, in faith and in purity.'"

"I suppose that 'pastor' of yours taught you that?"

I nodded. "But only because the Apostle Paul taught it to him first. That's from First Timothy, sir. I'm sorry you're upset, but look at yourself. What kind of example in speech, conduct, and love are you setting for us right now?"

The old man seethed. For a moment, I thought his head would literally explode. He jabbed a quaking finger in my face. "I'm going to speak to Pastor Redder about this!" He stormed away.

I blew out a long, shaky breath. I had a feeling that I had made a serious mistake, but I couldn't help myself. I couldn't let him talk to Charlene like that. I turned to her.

Tears pooled in her eyes.

Oops. Had that been her grandfather or something? I touched her shoulder. "Are you okay?"

She nodded and offered me a weak smile. "Thanks." She grabbed the crumpled up brochure. "Let's get out of here."

"Don't you have to be at the table or something?"

She laughed and shook her head. "No. Why?"

Then why was she so dressed up? "I just thought . . ."

"Let's just go find a place down in the gym." She smiled and dipped her head for a moment. "Would you . . . would you sit with me?"

Like she had to ask? "Absolutely."

We started back for the gym, but Charlene's cell phone jangled. She pulled it out and glanced at the screen. Her face paled.

I tried to peek over her shoulder. "What's wrong?"

"I . . . uh . . ." She winced. "I have to go. I'm . . . I'm sorry." She rushed out of the church.

I stared after her. What had just happened? I had come here, hoping to find peace, but I suspected that I'd leave with only more questions.

CHAPTER
14

THE WORSHIP SERVICE in the gym turned out to be fine. P.G. was apparently wrapping up a sermon series on being in the world but not of the world and made a lot of references to things he had said in previous weeks. While I got some new thoughts out of it, my mind kept drifting. I was worried that the old guy from the main sanctuary would come rushing into the gym with Pastor Redder and chew me out. But mostly, I thought about Charlene. I wished she could have stayed. It would have been nice to just sit next to her for a little while.

It also would have helped on the ride home. Mom quizzed me about this "special someone" the whole way. I couldn't tell her much. My only escape was when she started lunch. As we ate, we talked about her work. She wound up telling me little stories about the nurses at the hospital, which was a welcome distraction.

Halfway through lunch, the front door to our house banged open. A moment later, Ben breezed into the kitchen. He whisked over to Mom and kissed her cheek.

A sparkle zinged through Mom's eyes. "What are you doing here, sweetie?"

"What, a son can't come home to see his favorite girl?" Ben asked.

Mom smiled. "You ran out of change to do your laundry again, didn't you?"

Ben chuckled and walked over to the stove. He picked up a plate and helped himself to some food. "Well, there is that too." He smirked at me. "You're in my spot, Rob."

I returned his smirk. "I've upgraded."

Ben laughed and dropped into my old seat. "Fair enough." He turned to Mom, and the two of them fell into a conversation, with Ben prompting Mom to tell him story after story. I didn't mind. After all, I had heard most of them already.

After lunch, I slipped out to the garage and headed for the couch and my laptop.

"Hey."

I jumped. Ben stood in the open doorway. I braced myself for some sort of joke or quip. Instead, Ben strolled into the garage. He ran a hand along DK's hood. "Nice wheels." Tension bled through his voice. "Been saving up your allowance?"

"Meridian bought it for me."

"Ah." A frown twitched across Ben's forehead, but then disappeared into a smile. "Well, then, get in your fancy car, and let's go for a drive. I've got an idea I want to try."

CHAPTER 15

FIRST WE STOPPED at Ben's apartment, a small building near New Chayton University. He came out with three large boxes stacked on top of each other. Even though it looked like he was about to drop them all, I knew he had the whole thing stabilized with his telekinetic powers. Showing off yet again.

Once the boxes were stacked in DK's trunk, Ben slid into passenger seat and rapped on the dashboard. "Drive."

"Are we going anywhere in particular?" I asked.

"Head south, out of town. I'll tell you when we get there."

Ben leaned back in the seat and stared out the window. He spoke only to give me directions. Finally, we pulled off onto a gravel road that wound through a stand of trees. I squinted into the afternoon sun. Ben directed me to park next to a rundown garage that titled precariously to one side.

I glanced at Ben. "So where are we?"

"An abandoned farm. No onlookers for at least two miles." He smiled. "Perfect place to practice."

Practice what?

Ben just got out of DK and retrieved the boxes. He led me a hundred yards past a burned out house and a partially destroyed barn into an empty field and set the boxes down in front of him. He ripped one of them open and pulled out a dinner plate.

"What are you doing?" I asked.

Ben smiled. "I've been refining my telekinesis. Of course, I can still make myself look like I'm super strong and blast things around. But I need to work on my finer control. Moving small things, stuff like that."

"Like flying?"

Ben actually blushed. "I haven't figured that out yet. It's more like big hops right now. Hence why I need to practice. And no offense, Rob, but you can always work on your control as well." He balanced the plate on the tip of his finger and gave it a small twirl. The plate wobbled at first, but without Ben touching it, it picked up speed until it was whirring in a tight circle, balanced perfectly. "Consider this poor man's skeet shooting."

He flicked his finger, and the plate jetted off into the air. I flinched at the speed. Good thing Ben hadn't been aiming it at me. It looked like that would have hurt.

"Are you serious?" I asked.

Ben got another plate and started it spinning on his finger. "Completely. Break this one. Oh, and lose the necklace. Let's see what Failstate's range is."

I hesitated, looking around. The field we were standing in was bordered by tall trees. I couldn't see any houses, but that didn't mean that there weren't any onlookers.

Ben must have sensed my hesitation. He caught the plate in his hand. "Relax, Rob. I've been coming out here for the past six weeks. I've checked the area thoroughly. Your secret will be safe." He gave me a lopsided grin. "Unless you're worried I'm going to blab or something."

That didn't reassure me. But I knew Ben. He had a way of bending reality to his will. Even though I drove, he wouldn't let us leave until I at least gave this a try. I sighed and untied the necklace. The transformation rushed over me, the dull throb of my powers thudding between my eyes. I gasped.

Tension flashed over Ben's face, and he looked down at the ground.

"Do you want me to go back to the car and get my mask?" I asked.

Ben shook his head. "No, it's fine. Sorry." He started the plate spinning again. "So let's give this a shot, shall we?"

"So you're going to throw the plate, and I'm supposed to destroy it?"

"That's the gist of it."

I gritted my teeth and looked down the field where Ben's first plate had landed. "I don't know if I can do that. I mean, my range is pretty limited."

"That's kind of the point, isn't it?" Ben carefully passed the plate from one hand to the other. "You won't know what you're capable of until you push yourself. Ready?"

Not really, but I wasn't about to admit that to Ben. I set myself, fists clenched and knees bent. Maybe that would help.

The plate screamed past my face, so close I could've sworn I felt it take a hunk of skin with it. I jumped and flailed. The plate shot through the air. Then it crashed into the ground a hundred yards away.

Ben clucked his tongue at me. "That wasn't good."

"You nearly took my ear off!"

"You think the people you're fighting aren't going to be shooting things at you?" He pulled out another plate. "Let's try it again." He started the plate spinning.

I blew out a shaky breath and set myself again. Focus. Maintain control. Be ready for when—

Once again, the plate zinged past me close enough that I could feel it split the air. I lashed out, trying to direct a bolt of destructive energy straight through it.

I missed. The plate sailed off to the other end of the field.

"Did you at least try that time?" Ben asked.

I glared at him.

He held up his hands in surrender and got another plate.

"So how have you been? I mean besides the rampaging zombies business."

"Okay, I guess. I mean, school hasn't started yet, so there's no drama there. Check back with me on Tuesday."

"But there is drama somewhere else?" He gave me a knowing smile. He set the plate on its edge and spun it on its side in the middle of his palm. "What's her name?"

My mouth went dry. "How did you—"

He chuckled. "Lucky guess. Spill."

Once again, I hesitated. Granted, things between Ben and me were good, better than they had been for a long time, but some of our past problems were related to girls. One in particular.

Ben must have read my mind somehow. He caught the plate in his other hand and scowled at me. "Give me a little credit, Rob. There's no way I'd want to go through that again."

"How is Elizabeth?" I asked. "Have you heard anything from her?"

Ben shook his head. "No, but that's the point of witness protection, isn't it?"

Elizabeth Booth, a girl both of us had liked, had been moved from New Chayton by the VOC last spring. I wasn't happy about that. She and I had become good friends. But I knew Ben was taking it particularly badly. They had dated for months, gone to prom together. I had expected that, even with Ben leaving for college, they would have stayed together.

"For what it's worth, I'm sorry."

Ben smiled, an obviously forced grin, and started the plate spinning again. "No worries. Besides, we were talking about your pathetic love life, not mine. So who is she?"

"Charlene Gardner, new girl at church."

"Is she hot?"

I snorted. "Yes, she is. But she's also very nice. At least, that's what Mike tells me."

Ben frowned. "You don't know for yourself? You've talked to this girl, right?"

I thumped a fist against my thigh. "Well, yeah . . . technically."

"'Technically?' Rob, please tell me that you've called her."

"I . . . that is, I've been meaning to—"

Ben sighed and shook his head. He flicked a hand in my direction, and my cell phone jumped in my pocket. It slid free and danced in front of my face.

"No time like the present," Ben said. "Nice phone, by the way."

I snatched the phone out of the air. I turned it over in my hands a few times but then stuffed it back in my pocket. "Maybe later. But I will call her, okay? You happy now?"

"Ecstatic." Ben chuckled. "You ever need any help in romancing her, you let me know, okay?"

I gave him a sidelong glance.

"You know, advice and whatever. I'm here to help."

Just the opening I needed. "That's good. I still haven't chosen a deputy."

Ben laughed. "I'm nobody's sidekick."

"But—"

"No. Besides, I'm still working on cracking open the HazMats in Hogtown."

"How's that going?" I asked.

"Good. I've got some solid leads. I should have it wrapped up in a week or two." He tossed the plate up in the air. Before it could fall back down, it caught in the air and spun faster and faster. "Now, let's do this."

He cocked his hand back.

I lashed out and destroyed the plate before he could throw it.

Ben glanced over his head where the plate had been. "That's cheating, you know."

"Says who? There a rule book I should know about?"

Ben's smile broadened. "Oh, that's how you want it, huh?" He stomped his foot and five plates burst from the box, taking up orbit around him. As one, they began to spin until I could hear them whirring. "Let's see how you do against more than one."

He threw his arms forward as if hugging the air, and the plates rocketed toward me.

I snapped my hands up and created a barrier of destructive energy that shredded the plates before they could touch me. I peeked at Ben, only to see him lob another five plates at me. Once again, I destroyed them with my shield.

"C'mon, Rob, you can do better than that! Stop hiding behind your power and take them out one by one!"

"Why should I?" I asked. "Where did you get all of these anyway?"

"Garage sale." He kicked over the second box and launched five more into the air.

He wasn't going to stop, not until I did as he asked. I back-pedaled, trying to increase the distance between us. Maybe that would give me a little more time to work.

Ben laughed at me. "You think that's going to help?"

Probably not, but I nodded anyway. I danced back and forth, trying to stay loose and ready.

Ben waved his arms in a large pattern, as if directing the plates that spun through the air around him. Then, in a succession of quick blows, he sent the plates rocketing across the field.

I braced myself and flicked my hand at the first one. A blast of destructive energy disintegrated it in midair. I lashed out, catching the second and then the third. While I didn't completely destroy them, I demolished most of them. I missed the fourth. And the fifth. And that last plate was arcing right for my chest with enough force behind it I was pretty sure that it'd hurt if it hit. I fired again and missed.

My heart hammered in my chest, and my power flared. I didn't destroy the plate. It slammed into my chest and splashed over the front of my shirt like liquid. I tripped over my own feet and fell to the ground. The liquefied plate evaporated.

Ben ran up to me. "Are you okay?" He looked me over. "What was that?"

"Yeah, that's the other thing. I've been having trouble with my powers."

"I noticed when we were fighting that brute." Ben stroked his chin. "But maybe, if you learn to control that, you could do some cool stuff. C'mon."

He led me over to one side of the field. A large boulder jutted out of the ground. Ben slapped the rock's side and then turned to me. "We both know you could destroy this. Now let's see if you can change it, like you did with that car door and the plate."

I scowled at the rock. "I don't know if this is a good idea, Ben. We don't know what those powers can do."

"Exactly the reason why we have to practice. Remember how you and Dad used to goof off in the garage?"

I smiled. When my powers had first developed, Dad had been thrilled. He would take me into the garage and encourage me to practice destroying things, usually rocks we found in the back yard or in nearby parks. Although Mom didn't approve of it, it was those practice sessions that had taught me how to control my power. Most of the time.

"It's the same thing, Rob. Just give it a try."

He stepped out of the way. I stared at the rock. So what could I do to it? Melt it? Make it like taffy? Dr. Olympus thought I could turn my clothing into armor, but somehow, making a rock turn harder didn't seem like such a stretch.

I opened my palms toward the rock and summoned my powers. A tickle formed at the back of my head and spread over my skull. I flicked a finger at the rock.

The top two inches were sliced clean off and evaporated.

Ben clucked his tongue. "Try again."

I glared at him and took a deep breath. I closed my eyes and pictured the rock turning to liquid and flowing across the ground. I felt the same strange tickle at the back of my head. Mentally, I latched on to the sensation and encouraged it. Something shifted inside me.

I risked a peek.

Part of the rock had turned into a bubble and was floating free of the ground.

I gaped at it. "Hey, Ben, check this—"

The tickling sensation vanished, and the stone bubble popped, throwing rocky shards in every direction.

I snapped my hands up and shredded the projectiles. I blew out a long breath through my nose. "So what do you . . ." My voice trailed off as I realized that Ben wasn't paying attention.

He stared up at the sky, frowning. I turned to see what he was looking at. A small dot was zipping through the sky. An airplane? No, it was the wrong shape, and it didn't appear to be high enough. It almost looked like . . .

My eyes widened. A person. A person soaring through the air. And if I was seeing things right, he was heading right for us.

"Do you think he's spotted us?" I asked.

"Beats me." Ben shielded his eyes with his hand. "Are you sure he's even coming this way? He could just be passing through the area."

The flying man changed his angle and started descending. No, he was definitely heading for us.

"What do you think? Try to get out of here?" I asked.

"If he's really coming out here for us, he'll just follow the car," Ben said.

Good point. "Then we'd better get our masks, huh?"

I ran for DK. Thankfully I had left my costume in the back seat. I pulled the hood out of my duffel and pulled it over my face. Did I have enough time to get into my full costume? No, probably not, and if whoever was coming here proved to be hostile, I didn't want to have to fight him half naked.

Ben sauntered to my side. "I don't suppose you have a spare in there, do you?"

I rummaged around in my back seat and pulled out a bandana. "This will have to do."

"For what? Robbing a train?" Ben tied it on, hiding the bottom of his face. He looked up at the sky. "What do you think? Friendly?"

"We're about to find out."

A low roar built around us. Then the person fell out of the sky, smashing into the ground with enough force that the impact threw me off my feet. A tremendous cloud of dirt exploded, showering us with clods of dirt and rocks. The garage groaned and collapsed. I threw my arms over my head to protect myself.

When the smoke cleared, a solitary figure stood in a crater. He looked to be in his mid-thirties. He wore a bright green outfit and a simple mask that covered his eyes and nose. He was bald, but the stubble seemed to indicate that he'd shaved his head. Silver lines, like the patterns of circuits, wrapped around his skull and down along his jaw. I recognized him immediately.

"Downtime?"

The man smiled at me and nodded. "Glad to make your acquaintance, Failstate."

I couldn't believe it. Downtime was another licensed super-hero, but he was a veteran compared to me. He had been working in Seattle for the last fifteen years. He had a natural affinity for tapping into wireless communication and manipulating radio waves. When he wasn't fighting crime, he was developing new cell phone technologies.

Downtime glanced at Ben. "Are you in the middle of something, Failstate? Do you need assistance against this . . . person?"

"No, we—"

Downtime launched himself at Ben. Energy crackled across his body, and he slammed into Ben and sent him flying.

"No!" I shouted. "He's fine! That's Gauntlet!"

Downtime skidded to a halt and gave Ben a curious look. "That's not a new costume, is it? Because it's not very distinctive."

Ben stood up and dusted himself off. He glared at Downtime. "We weren't exactly expecting company right now."

"Ah, I see. I apologize if I've offended."

I let out a shaky breath and looked between my brother and Downtime. "What are you doing here?"

"Protocol. As I'm sure you've been told, it's only polite to check in with one another when arriving in a new city."

"Oh, right. Meridian told me. So what brings you to New Chayton? Better yet, how'd you even find me?"

He pointed at my pocket. "Your cell phone. Agent Sexton gave me your number, and I was able to track your signal. I considered it more prudent to appear in person. I trust that isn't a problem."

"Uh . . . I guess not. So what brings you to New Chayton?"

Downtime cocked his head to one side. "Isn't it obvious? The convocation."

I exchanged a look with Ben.

"The what now?"

"The meeting Agent Sexton called via the VOC for Tuesday evening? He's invited as many licensed heroes as could come to help solve your zombie problem."

CHAPTER 16

WHILE BEN CHATTED with Downtime, I dug out my cell and hit the speed dial button for Agent Sexton. The phone rang several times before clicking over to voicemail. So he had it on but wasn't answering. Not good enough. I hit the redial and waited. Still no answer. Again.

This time he picked up on the second ring. "What?"

"So am I invited to this big licensed hero get-together or was I going to hear about it after it was all over?"

He grumbled something I couldn't understand. "I suppose I would have told Meridian eventually. Maybe he would pass it along."

Fire bubbled through me. My fingers tightened on my phone and for a split second, I wanted nothing more than to transmit a burst of destructive energy through the cell phone to wherever Sexton was. "So let me get this straight. You don't believe me when I tell you about the zombies, but now you're bringing in other licensed heroes to do my job? What is wrong with you?"

"Not a thing. Let me break it down for you, rookie. I don't work for you. I serve my country. It's my sworn duty to make sure that heroes like you do their best to protect our citizens. And in spite of Chief Blackthorn's glowing recommendation, *your* best just won't cut it. So now I have to step in and make sure that New Chayton doesn't suffer because of it. Best way to do that is to bring in people to . . . help you."

Why did he make it sound like I didn't know how to tie my shoes?

"To help me with a problem you didn't even believe was real?"

"We'll discuss that at the conclave. So suck it up, meet with the other heroes, and follow their lead."

The line went dead. I realized that Sexton hadn't even told me where this big meeting was supposed to be.

I turned back to Ben and Downtime. The older hero leaned against DK and laughed at something my brother said. I was struck by the sight. Though he wasn't in his costume, Ben still looked like he belonged here, chatting with Downtime as if they were equals. Maybe he should have gotten the license after all. Maybe . . .

Downtime glanced in my direction. "My apologies for the surprise, Failstate. I'm sorry that I interrupted . . . whatever it was you two were doing here." His gaze shifted toward Ben. "Gauntlet wasn't all that forthcoming. Given your history on the show, it is odd to see the two of you together."

"I was just . . ." Ben shot me a worried look.

"He was auditioning to be my sidekick," I said. "I think he's got potential."

Ben's look darkened. I'd probably pay for that later, but it was so worth it.

Downtime nodded. "Of course, I should have known. So, Gauntlet, will we see you Tuesday?"

"Is this whatever-it-is open to non-licensed heroes?" Ben asked. His eyes gleamed.

"Sadly, no. Only the licensed and their deputies."

"Then I'm afraid I'll have to pass."

"Unless I make you my sidekick," I said. Couldn't resist. I turned to Downtime. "Speaking of which, can you tell me where it's going to be held?"

Downtime gave me a curious look. "You mean you don't know?"

I stammered for a moment. Of course I should know where it was. But would admitting my ignorance make me appear weaker? I had no idea. But if I didn't know, I couldn't go.

Downtime chuckled. "I see the VOC is as forthcoming in New Chayton as they are in Seattle. We'll be meeting in a penthouse in Magnus Tower. Do you know where that is?"

I smiled. Even if I didn't, at least I knew the landlord. "I'll be there."

"Excellent. I shall see you then. Since I have arrived early, I am available to patrol the streets. With your permission?"

I stammered for a moment. Who was I to deny another licensed hero? "Please, feel free."

"Excellent. Until Tuesday, then." Downtime crouched for a moment and, in a blast of thunder, rocketed into the sky before vanishing into the dusk.

I turned to Ben. "Want to tag along? I bet I could have the deputy paperwork done by Tuesday night."

"I'll take my chances on my own. But can you at least give me a ride home?"

I sighed. It would have been nice to have someone in my corner. Also, I didn't like the thought of skipping youth group on Tuesday. Hopefully this "convocation" would actually turn out to be helpful. But knowing my luck, I was about to step into a hornet's nest, and I was going to be smeared with honey.

CHAPTER 17

BEN AND I drove home in silence. He spent another hour chatting with Mom before returning to his apartment. I decided to stay in the garage. But I didn't touch my laptop. I wanted a break from being a hero. Too many thoughts swirled through my mind, chased by uncountable doubts. Even if I could sleep, there was no way that I would. My mind simply refused to shut down. But I knew that if I continued my search for answers about the zombies, I'd torment myself further. Instead, I only wanted to lose myself in a mindless task, something I could do without much conscious thought.

That left me with one option: sculpting.

I pulled a wooden crate out from under the tool bench and selected a large chunk of granite. I dropped it onto the rough wooden table with a satisfying *thunk*. With my power, it was easy enough to create elaborate sculptures. I just used my destructive powers to shave away the unneeded stone. Normally I sculpted for money. I had set up a web page that allowed me to take orders from all over the country. But I didn't want to do any orders, either. I simply wanted to create.

The only thing stopping me was the necklace. I pulled it free and winced as the transformation swept over me. I braced myself against the table and reigned in my power before it could spike. Once I was sure I had things under control, I blew out a shaky breath. Time to get to work.

Without conscious thought, I ran my hand over the rock. My power nibbled away at the edge, chunks vanishing from the stone. Normally, I would pay closer attention to what I was doing, but I wanted nothing more than to let my mind drift and empty itself.

What was I going to do? On the way home, I'd received two phone calls from other licensed heroes, letting me know that they were in town. I had managed to be polite, even though I wanted to tell them all to leave it to me. But as much as I didn't want to admit it, I needed the help.

But Sexton! Here I had always been led to believe that the VOC was there to help the licensed heroes, and yet it felt like every time I spoke to Sexton, we were engaged in some sort of hand-to-hand combat. I didn't need a best friend. But if he was supposed to be my liaison officer, shouldn't he be more willing to liaise? And why was he calling this convocation about zombies if he never believed me about them? Was he going to take credit?

I cocked my head to one side and examined the hunk of rock. It still didn't look like much, but I had smoothed away the rough edges. It looked kind of like a bird taking flight. The two lumps on top could be wings, maybe. Why not? It felt right. Using the tip of my finger like a paint brush, I stroked the excess rock away. Soon the general shape of the bird appeared, its wings cupped and its head twisted down. I frowned. It almost appeared as though it were trying to fly but couldn't. I kept at it, slowly working down toward the rock's base. I once again let my mind wander a bit, curious to see what would happen.

So what was my next course of action? Go to the conclave, obviously. But after that? I had no idea. I had no leads on where the zombies were coming from. Thanks to Sexton—I jabbed at the stone, drilling a whole straight through the base—I'd have plenty of help.

I leaned against the toolbench and looked at what I had created. Again, the shape of the rock's base was rough and unfinished, but it appeared as though I had carved a number of channels and grooves into it. It almost looked like . . . a bush? Whatever it was, the bird was apparently entangled in it. I frowned. Not the cheeriest sculpture I had ever made, but it still felt right. I hunched over the rock and set to work on the finer details.

By the time sunlight filtered through the garage's windows, I had finished. Sure enough, a bird—a hawk, maybe—was trying to fly, only it couldn't because its legs were caught in a thick bush. Or were those arms? It kind of looked like tiny hands grasping at the bird's legs and feet. Maybe it wasn't a bush but a horde of zombies pulling the struggling hawk down to tear it to pieces. I shuddered. And here I wanted to get my mind off work!

I straightened and rubbed the small of my back. How long had I been working on this? I glanced at my watch, and my eyes widened. It was close to ten in the morning!

I snared my necklace and tied it back into place. The throb between my eyes exploded into a wave of needles that swept over my body, only to fade into a dull ache that seeped through every muscle, every fiber. My stomach growled. Breakfast, then a quick run through the shower. And then . . . well, I'd have to see.

I turned to leave the garage, but I nearly jumped out of my shoes. Charlene stood in the open garage door.

Ice rushed through my veins. How much had she seen?

She froze. "I'm sorry. Your mom said you were out here in the garage, and I—"

Okay, she wasn't asking about my disfigured face. That was good. I tried to answer, but my mouth had gone completely dry. She was here, in my garage! I couldn't take my eyes off of her, drinking in her beauty.

Her hair had been pulled back into a tight ponytail. She wore a loose plaid coat over a pink t-shirt with a pair of khakis. She frowned and pointed to the sculpture. "Did you make that?"

I stammered but nodded. "Well, yeah."

Charlene walked past me to the workbench and leaned over to take a closer look at the bird. "This is . . . wow. This is incredible."

My cheeks burned, and a wave of tingles swept down the back of my head. "Thank you."

"How long did it take you to make this?"

My mouth snapped shut. I had no idea how to answer that. There's no way she'd believe me if I said overnight. "I . . . really didn't keep track. A while?"

She straightened up and looked over the workbench. "But how did you make this? I don't see any sculpting tools."

I didn't even know what kind of tools I'd need to make a sculpture like that. "I already put them away. Uh . . . why don't we go inside?"

We headed into the kitchen. Mom was seated at the center island. She smiled at Charlene, then grabbed her coffee mug and slipped out of the room, leaving me alone.

With Charlene.

I peeked at her out of the corner of my eye. She sat at the counter, and her gaze roamed over the room. It looked like she was studying the recipes Mom had hung over the stove, old favorites we had made so many times that we really didn't need the reference.

"Are you hungry?" I asked. "I haven't had breakfast yet."

Charlene smiled. "I could eat."

I retrieved a big pan from a cabinet. Next: eggs, cheese, and milk. I would have loved to make something more than just scrambled eggs, but I didn't trust myself to concentrate while Charlene was here. Half a dozen eggs should do it, maybe. Or would that be too many? Would it be insulting to imply I expected her to eat a lot? I was out of my depth and sinking rapidly.

Best to just forge ahead and hope I didn't mess up too badly. I cracked the eggs open in a bowl and added the milk and cheese. I stirred the ingredients and turned to Charlene. "Would you mind putting some bread in the toaster?"

She went to the cupboard I indicated and got out a loaf of bread. I greased the pan and poured the eggs in. They sizzled and popped. I grabbed a spatula and stirred.

Charlene turned to face me. "Can I be honest with you, Rob?"

Uh-oh. No conversation that started with that phrase ended well.

She wouldn't meet my gaze. "I'm . . . I'm not good at stuff like this. I've never . . . This past summer, when I met Mike, I thought that . . . well, he and I . . ."

My head felt like it had fallen off and was slowly spinning through the kitchen. This wasn't happening. No way.

"But I realized that he was just a friend. And . . . well, he kept talking about you, how I had to meet you, that he thought we would be . . ." Her cheeks flamed red. "And then in that alley, you saved me from those men. You were my knight in shining armor, and when I met you again at church and you asked me for my number, I thought . . ." She gestured wildly, almost as if she were fighting an invisible opponent. "And then, yesterday, I know I had to leave church early, but I thought you'd at least call me to see what was wrong."

The spatula slipped out of my hand. I stared at Charlene, my mind refusing to process what she was saying. That she was interested in me? Was this real? The last time I had been in this situation, it hadn't turned out well for me at all. But Charlene seemed so earnest. Could it be true?

Charlene shook her head, creating a flurry of red hair that obscured her face. "I shouldn't have said any of that. If you could just forget it. Better yet, I was never even here." She started for the door.

Before she could escape, I snared her arm. She spun and looked at me with wide eyes. Her mouth worked silently, as though she were trying to find the right words to say. I wished I could think of the right thing to say too, but nothing came to mind. Instead, I did the only thing I could think of.

I kissed her.

Her lips were soft against mine, but she was so frozen I thought I had made a major mistake. But then she softened and melted against me. Her arms snaked around my neck and pulled me closer. Her scent, honey on the wind, overwhelmed me. My heart slammed against my rib cage, and I just knew that if I wasn't wearing my necklace, my power would flare out of control and probably destroy most of the kitchen.

Just as abruptly as she'd pulled me in, she pushed me away. "No." She shook her head. "No. This . . ."

My heart turned to lead. How had I misread the entire situation? It didn't seem possible, but—

". . . this is good. And maybe someday we could . . . yeah." She smiled, a brilliant flash of teeth that blinded me. "But we barely know each other. We haven't spent any time together. I want this. At least, I think I do. But can we . . . can we take this a little slower?"

Absolutely. I nodded. "I'd like that." Actually, what I would've liked was to kiss her again, and going slow sounded like a terrible idea. But if going slow or not going at all were my only options, then I really liked the idea of going slow.

She giggled, and her smile grew even larger. "I think breakfast will be a good start."

I turned to my cooking.

At the same moment, the smoke alarm in the hall sounded. I groaned. It looked like we'd have to start over from scratch.

CHAPTER 18

MY STOMACH CHURNED as I walked into the lobby of Magnus Towers. The dark marble floors gleamed, so polished that I could see my own reflection in the surface. A veritable forest of plants filled the lobby, standing over conversation nooks. Men and women dressed in high-priced clothing stood in small knots and conversed quietly. I walked further into the lobby. To my left, water trickled across rocks and grooves embedded in the wall.

The conversation that ricocheted off the walls died. Everyone turned to look at me.

I shifted nervously, tugging my sweatshirt straight. Apparently they didn't have heroes show up in full costume all that often. Or, if they did, they were better dressed than me.

A doorman in the stereotypical floor-length red coat trotted up to my side. "Ah, Mr. State, is it?"

"No, just Failstate."

The doorman ushered me toward the elevator with a large sweep of his hand. He then snared my arm as we walked toward the elevator. "The next time you need to come here, sir, I suggest you use the service entrance around back. It's more . . . discreet. No need to give our tenants reason to worry."

"Should they?" I asked.

The doorman laughed, the strain obvious in his voice. We stepped to an elevator, and almost immediately, the doors opened with a ding. I stepped inside and looked around the interior. Shiny metal, like standing in a mirrored box.

The doorman reached inside to punch the topmost button on the panel, then he leaned back out. "Enjoy your stay, sir."

The doors shut with a soft click. With a rumble, the elevator started its ascent, the numbers scrolling by on the display over the doors. I idly scratched at my leg, wondering what would happen if the elevator stopped to pick up another passenger. I was probably the last thing they'd want to see on a Tuesday night. Or any night, really.

But the elevator didn't even slow, not until it reached the 72nd floor. Then a soft bell pinged and the doors opened onto another room with marble floors. The walls were made of dark hardwood. I took a careful step out into the foyer, a small room attached to a hallway.

Large bouquets of flowers the size of bushes flanked the elevator door. On my right was a black-and-white photo of New Chayton's skyline from the 1940s. On the other was a picture the same size, a fanciful painting of New Chayton, only this one appeared to be a prediction of what the city might look like in the future. There were at least a dozen new skyscrapers, all lit by searchlights from below. What could only be described as UFOs floated over the city. I peeked at the plate at the bottom of the frame: "New Chayton—circa 1996." I swallowed a laugh.

Soft classical music floated down the hall. I followed it deeper into the penthouse. The hallway opened into a large room. The walls were cream colored with rows of four foot panels. Pillars made of dark wood were evenly spaced throughout the room, the centermost containing a small fireplace. Leather furniture was pushed up against the pillars. Chandeliers that looked like inverted pyramids hung from bronze pipes. A bar filled one corner of the room. But the most stunning feature were the windows. They filled one wall completely and overlooked downtown New Chayton. The city sparkled beyond the glass.

My heart thudded against my ribs. Suddenly my doubts didn't seem so important. Sure, maybe I wasn't the best of the licensed heroes. But I was fighting for something important. No way was I going to let anyone overlook me tonight.

"Failstate! There you are!" Meridian appeared at my side, once again dressed in a black suit and mask. He threw an arm around me and steered me deeper into the room. As we walked, he whispered to me, "Stay on your toes here, kid. I've been to these things before. Feeding frenzies are friendlier than VOC conclaves."

We rounded a corner, and I stumbled to a halt. At least a dozen people in brightly dressed costumes were scattered in small knots through the room, sipping drinks and conversing quietly. I recognized a few of them. Downtime nodded to me in silent greetings.

Standing over by the bar was a man in jet-black body armor, his face almost completely covered by his mask. Raze from Los Angeles. He had a small glass of amber liquid in one hand. His gaze slithered over the women in the room. He was probably looking for his next date to a Hollywood premier. That seemed what he was best at nowadays rather than fighting crime.

I even spotted Dr. Olympus. The rest were strangers. I knew I had seen most of them on the news or in magazines, but I couldn't place match all the costumes with their superhero names. Even if I didn't know their aliases, though, they all had one thing in common. They were all living legends. I felt puny in comparison, an ant among gods. I rubbed my arms and wished for a moment I could retreat. But I couldn't, not with Meridian's arm around me.

"Let's make the rounds, okay?" Meridian steered me through the crowd. "You've met the Doc. And Downtime said he had a chat with you two days ago. Over there's Raze. Don't talk to him. Trust me." He led me over to a woman in blaze red tights with a long brown cape that pooled on the floor around her feet. Her mask covered the top half of her face and was divided into four quarters, each one a different color: brown, red, blue, and white. "Elemental from New Orleans, have you met Failstate yet?"

Elemental flashed me a large grin. "Not yet, but I've heard great things about you. Great things."

I scanned what she said for sarcasm. I didn't hear any. "Did you watch the show?"

She laughed. "Heavens, no. That so-called reality nonsense rots your brain from the inside out. But my protégé did watch the show, and now she won't stop raving about you. Isn't that right, Kyn?"

I turned around. An African-American girl, maybe around my age, smiled at me. She wore bright red tights that appeared armored across the shoulders, arms, chest, and legs. A simple domino mask bordered her eyes. Her hair was long and silky, bound in a ponytail that reached halfway down her back. Her smile was dazzling, and her large brown eyes raked over my body, leaving a trail of fire in their wake. I suddenly wished I could take off my hood, just long enough to breathe some cool air. But that would only ruin the party.

"The name's Kynetic, but my friends call me 'Kyn.' You can call me whatever you want." Kynetic's voice was little more than a purr. "What say you and I go find someplace more private and get to know each other better?"

My mouth went dry. How was I supposed to respond to that? "I-I-I think we have to stay here and find out what's going on."

She pouted, but the hunger didn't leave her eyes. "Too bad, F. But your choice."

"So, Meridian." Raze's rough voice, like broken glass getting scraped across a chalkboard, sliced through the music. "You in charge of this shindig? Can we get started or what?"

"Wish we could." Meridian opened his arms in an expansive shrug. "But Agent Sexton called this 'shindig.' Until he arrives—"

"The wait is over, folks." Sexton breezed into the penthouse, pausing long enough to shoot a dirty look in my direction. "I trust you're enjoying our hospitality?"

Raze signaled to the bartender for another drink. "So we ready to go or what?"

"Almost." Sexton glanced at his watch. "We're still waiting on one other hero."

Raze snorted and downed his drink. "So who are we . . ." His voice suddenly strangled and he winced, almost as if he had been poisoned. His eyes widened. "Oh, no. You gotta be kidding me."

Others in the penthouse reacted similarly, wincing and retching. Even Meridian staggered a little, placing a hand against his head. The only one who didn't appear affected was Elemental, but I could read the concern in her eyes.

Before I could ask what was happening, a dizzy sensation slammed into me. It felt as though I were falling down a deep pit, or as though I were about to vomit. A buzzing sound built in my ears, and the throbbing between my eyes grew worse. Was my power about to spike? Nothing like this had ever happened before. I looked for Dr. Olympus, to seek her help, but she was doubled over and moaning.

Then one of the large windows opened. Shadows like dark liquid poured through the opening, creeping along the floor and clawing up the walls. A dark figure stepped into the room, a man wearing a flowing cape that seemed more illusion than real. Even though his face was wreathed in darkness, I knew who it was immediately.

"Etzal'el."

CHAPTER 19

ALTHOUGH I COULDN'T SEE his eyes, I could feel Etzal'el's gaze sweep over the penthouse. During the brief moment that he looked at me, the churning in my stomach intensified. I felt the distinct urge to flee. But the sensation faded. Then Etzal'el glided into the room, and the window shut behind him as if closed by unseen hands.

"Oh, great, the Boogie Man has deigned to join us." Raze's voice was a bare growl, but it carried a hint of fear.

"I was invited, as were you." Etzal'el's voice was little more than a whisper, but each syllable sent shivers marching across my skin. "I have come to help in this dangerous time, as have you. Rather than resort to petty insults, let us instead turn to the matter at hand."

"Sounds good to me." Sexton clapped his hands together, wearing an obviously fake smile. "Ladies and gentlemen, thank you for—"

"It is not for you to speak," Etzal'el said.

Sexton blinked several times, sweat appearing along his upper lip. "What?"

"You may have summoned us, but it is not your place to lead this discussion. You are only here to liaise with us, not command." He turned to me. "This is your city, yes? What is the situation?"

Was he actually talking to me? I mouthed a few words, but the sounds wouldn't come out.

Raze snorted and pushed himself away from the bar. "Oh, this is rich. First we get Tall, Dark, and Terrifying crashing what could have been a great party. And now, we gotta listen to some wet-behind-the-ears kid? What a joke! I'm out of here—" He collapsed to his knees and moaned, his fingers digging into the sides of his head.

"Your tone is counterproductive." Etzal'el seemed to swell larger, his cloak billowing out like storm clouds. "It would be wise to cooperate fully."

Raze growled. A tremor wormed beneath my feet, but soon the entire room shook. Raze's eyes burned as he pressed his hands to the floor. A large crack snaked from his palm toward Etzal'el.

Etzal'el was tossed off balance.

Raze smiled, a feral and predatory grin.

Etzal'el regained his balance. "You dare to challenge me?" Darkness erupted from his cloak, overwhelming Raze.

Raze thrashed against the attack. The entire room shook, and it wouldn't have surprised me if he were rattling the entire building. Glasses tumbled and shattered behind the bar.

Meridian charged forward, light building around his body. "No brawling! Especially not in here!" Blinding flashes ripped through the air, so bright that I felt more than saw them.

Large swaths of the shadows surrounding Etzal'el vanished and, for a split second, I saw him as just a man standing in a simple white shirt and black pants, a floor-length cape and cowl covering most of him. A small amulet glowed at his neck. His face showed that he was young, maybe only in his twenties, which was surprising given the length of his career.

And then, just as quickly, darkness swarmed out of the folds of his cape and obscured him once again. He held up a hand and made a fist.

It appeared as though Meridian slammed into an invisible wall. He reeled away and clutched at his head.

"You should know better than to trifle with me, Meridian." Etzal'el's voice carried enough venom to blister paint from the walls.

"*Enough!*"

Who said that? And why was everyone looking at me?

Oh. I guess that had been me.

Etzal'el turned to face me. Two cold blue coals burned beneath his hood. Intense pressure built at the back of my skull, but it didn't grow beyond an annoyance. I stood my ground. If Etzal'el wanted to vaporize me, it wouldn't be because I attacked first.

Etzal'el seemed to shrink slightly. Instead of a towering demigod, he appeared more human, less threatening. "I apologize for my demeanor. I . . . forget myself at times. Please, let us begin our discussion." He glided away from the window and stood in a corner of the room, his head bowed.

Raze got up from the floor and dusted himself off. He guffawed. "Well, look who's ready for his big-boy pants." He grabbed the front of my shirt. "Don't ever interfere in one of my fights again, got it?" He shoved me away, not hard enough to knock me over but enough to make his point.

I straightened my shirt and looked around the room at the other heroes. None of them met my gaze, instead turning to talk to each other or examining their drinks. Why hadn't they intervened? For a moment, I wondered if I should stay. Why subject myself to the aggravation?

Then I saw Kynetic. Her eyes shone with a hungry light, her lips turned up into a smirk. Warmth spread through my cheeks. Maybe I could stay for just a little while longer.

CHAPTER 20

NOW THAT I'D TAKEN the lead at this superhero conclave, I thought I would be the one to do the talking. But the
moment everyone settled down, Sexton stepped forward with a
wide false grin on his face.

"Thank you all for coming," he said. "I'm pleased to see
that so many of you took time out of your busy schedules and
traveled so far to help us with this situation."

Apparently he wasn't going to let me lead the conclave,
after all. That figured.

"You make it sound like a church picnic," Raze grumbled.
"Get on with it."

Sexton cleared his throat. "Yes, well . . . In the past several
months, we've had reports of zombie attacks."

Wait a minute! "'Past several months'?" I asked. "It's only
been a week since . . . You mean . . . Why didn't you tell
me?"

Sexton glanced at me out of the corner of his eye. "You were out of town all summer, remember? On your big victory tour, obviously too busy to bother with your actual duties."

A retort clawed up my throat, but Meridian subtly shook his head. I clamped my mouth shut. Maybe this wasn't the right hill to die on, but Sexton's constant abuse was starting to rankle.

Sexton turned to a large, blank wall. A projection screen descended from the ceiling and the VOC logo appeared, replaced a moment later by a picture of a small house with rough wooden siding surrounded by yellow crime scene tape.

"The first incident happened this past July in Rosen Heights. Mrs. Bernice Laue was woken up in the middle of the night when she heard someone on her front porch. When she went to investigate, she found what she described as a zombie trying to get in her front door."

One of the heroes snorted.

Sexton's face twisted, but he blew out a breath through his nose. "After calling 911, she used her cell phone camera to take this picture."

A snarling face appeared, the flesh waxy and pallid. Part of one cheek had rotted away, exposing the creature's teeth. Its eyes were milky and vacant.

Some in the crowd gasped.

"Photoshopped!" Raze shouted.

"That's what the police thought, as well," Sexton said. "They searched the neighborhood but found nothing. They wrote it off as a prank of some sort. Three weeks later, the police in Tarransville received a similar call. Some kids saw a zombie shuffling down their road. Thing is, they had been watching that zombie show on cable just a few hours before. It was assumed that their imaginations had run away with them.

"A full month later, another zombie was reported in Rosen Heights. This time, the police were able to respond in time to catch a glimpse of the creature. But they lost track of it when it ducked down an alley. They found a scrap of clothing. They believed it to be medical scrubs."

I raised my hand. "Did any of these zombies have superpowers?"

Sexton shot me an annoyed look. "Not from what the witnesses said."

Huh. I drummed my fingers against my leg. So something had changed between then and now. They were growing stronger. But how and why?

Etzal'el growled from his post in the corner. "Minions of darkness."

Raze snorted. "Minions of what?"

"These zombies are animated by dark forces, make no mistake."

"This isn't Narnia, Etzal'el," Downtime said. "I'm sure there's a perfectly logical and scientific explanation for what's happening."

"And your science has never been made to serve dark purposes?" Etzal'el returned. "Never once?"

Sexton cleared his throat. "What I propose is that—"

Etzel'el turned toward Sexton, and his eyes blazed red beneath his cowl. "Why do you still believe that you are somehow in charge? This is Failstate's city, his responsibility. It is his plan we will follow."

Meridian reached over and patted my shoulder. "Go on, kid. Show 'em."

"I suggest—" My voice cracked, and I winced. "Now that you're all here, I suggest we establish patrols for the next several nights. We can cover the whole city better than I can on my own."

Raze sneered at me. "Oh, great plan. Patrol. None of us would have thought of that."

"I wasn't done yet. While it's important that we stop the zombies from hurting people or destroying property, I think it's just as important to determine their source. So unless the zombies are actually a threat, I suggest that we don't engage them but merely follow them instead. See where they're going. Not only that, but I also suggest we enlist the help of the unlicensed heroes in the city. I've worked with several of them in the past, and the extra help would—"

"Oh, that is ridiculous," Raze said. "I didn't come here to babysit undead morons, and I certainly didn't come here to hang with a bunch of amateurs!"

"Some of the finest heroes I've met have been amateurs," I said. "As a matter of fact, I would have rather been with them tonight than with you."

Raze burst out laughing. "Oh, I'm hurt. Really. The reality show winner doesn't want to play with me. Whatever shall I do?"

"If all you came to do is 'play,' maybe you should go back to Hollywood and hang out with your supermodels," I said. "That seems to be all you're good for nowadays."

Raze's eyes narrowed to slits. "Let me make one thing perfectly clear. I do not take orders from you. If I see zombies, I'm taking them out!"

Several of the other heroes nodded.

"And how does that help?" I asked. "If we're going to stop this problem—"

Sexton stepped in front of me. "Instead of arguing, why not plan what we'll do? If you'll come with me, please, I have a map set up over here. Let's discuss our strategy."

I tried to object, but most of the heroes followed Sexton into the next room. Only a few lingered with me.

I sighed and shook my head. Even if they weren't listening to me, it was probably best for me to know what they were planning. I followed them into a formal dining room.

Low-slung chandeliers filled with hundreds of crystal teardrops hung overhead. A long wooden table was pushed up against one wall, underneath a large painting of sailboats out on a lake. In the center of the room was a table big enough to seat at least thirty. Spread out over it was a map of the city.

Sexton walked around the table. He leaned over it and spread his hands on the map. "As you can see, ladies and gentlemen, I've taken the liberty of marking where the zombies have been spotted so far."

I glanced over the map. Sure enough, the correct locations were circled in red.

Dr. Olympus stepped forward, stroking her chin. "No pattern to their appearances. Truly random occurrences. Problematic to diagnose, even more difficult to treat." She crossed her arms. "Perhaps Failstate's plan is correct. Finding the source would be paramount."

I swallowed a chuckle. I wanted to hug Dr. Olympus.

Sexton shook his head. "We've been lucky so far. No one has been seriously injured. But given what happened in the warehouse district with the superpowered zombie, we may not be so fortunate next time. Raze's plan is the best. You see zombies, you take them out." He pointed to the map. "This is what I suggest. Each of you will be assigned overlapping territories to patrol. Your primary goal is to stop any further zombie outbreaks—"

I started to object, but Sexton held up a hand to cut me off.

"—and to find the ultimate source if possible. Of course, if you see other situations that require your assistance, please do so. Downtime, I was hoping that you could use your powers to help coordinate our efforts."

Downtime nodded. "Of course, but I do have a question: How long are you expecting us to remain in New Chayton? While we're here, the rest of our cities are left undefended."

Etzal'el glided forward, and his shadowy form swelled until he appeared ten feet tall. "This plague takes priority over anything we may find in our respective protectorates."

Downtime took a step back. "I understand, but from what I've seen, this isn't anything that Failstate wouldn't be able to handle on his own. How long do you expect us to stay here?"

Sexton's brows twitched into a frown, but then he smiled. "Not long. I suspect that this will all be over in a week. Two at the most."

I frowned. How could he know that?

Downtime seemed satisfied with the answer. "Two weeks. And then I go back to Seattle."

The others murmured their agreement.

Sexton's smile grew broader. "Excellent. I'd say we have our plan. Be sure to leave your contact information with Downtime. Please feel free to stay and enjoy the hospitality. We'll get to work tomorrow night."

Raze stomped back to the bar. He hip-checked me out of the way. I sighed. It was always nice to make a friend.

I stepped over to Downtime. "My cell number is—"

"I know," he said. "I've already got you entered." He turned to the other heroes and beckoned them to line up.

Well, that was that. I started for the elevator.

Etzal'el appeared before me, as if he'd flowed from his corner to block my path. "Do not lose heart, Failstate. Your plan is in the right. They simply do not realize it yet. I will do as you suggest."

"Really?"

The larger man nodded. "Indeed. And I shall begin right away. If I encounter the undead, I shall let you know."

With that, he soared across the room and out a window.

"I thought he'd never leave."

I whirled, only to find myself face-to-face with Kynetic again.

She smiled coyly at me. "I liked how you stood up to the others. Etz is right, you have the better plan. Count me in."

"You have my support as well," Elemental added.

"And mine," Dr. Olympus said.

I looked at them. Five of us who would try to track the zombies rather than destroy them, as opposed to the dozen who had sided with Raze and Sexton. Not the greatest odds, but they would have to do.

"Why don't we follow Etzal'el's advice and get started, then?" Elemental beckoned to her sidekick. "Kyn, you coming?"

Kynetic glanced at her mentor for a moment, then smiled at me. "No thanks, E."

Elemental's eyes flashed. "Kynetic. Now!"

"Okay, okay." Kynetic pouted, but then she winked at me. "See you around, F."

Elemental and Kynetic headed for the elevators.

I let out a long breath. If I hadn't felt in over my head before, I certainly did now.

CHAPTER 21

WHEN MORNING BROKE the next day, I swung by the house to get my school bag. I wished I could have stayed home, but skipping the second day of my senior year seemed like a poor choice.

My cell phone buzzed. I groaned. Probably Agent Sexton to heap even more scorn on me. I punched the answer button. "What?"

"Rob?"

I froze. The melodious voice sent shivers down my back. "Charlene?"

"Are you okay?"

I swallowed my anger. "Yeah, sorry. I was just heading out the door to school. You?"

"Second day of senior year. Wouldn't miss it for the world."

I smirked at the sarcasm in her voice. "This call is making my day better."

"I'm glad. Actually, I was hoping we could brighten each others' days some more. What are you doing after school?"

I didn't even want to think that far ahead. After school meant putting my plan into action, trying to track down the zombies and find their source. As much as I knew it needed to be done, I wanted a distraction. "What did you have in mind?"

"Well, I'm not expecting a lot of homework today. But we'll probably have a little. I figured the time might go faster if I had a partner to study with. Interested?"

My heart shot into overdrive. I swallowed a nervous giggle. Interested? That was putting it mildly. "Your place or mine?"

She paused, and my heart seized. Second thoughts already? No, I was being ridiculous.

"We'd better make it your place. Will that be okay?"

Now I hesitated. Last year, Mom had instituted a strict rule when it came to visitors of the opposite gender. She had to be home. So far as I knew, she would be. I'd have to double check. And even if Mom wouldn't be home, Charlene and I could always go to Krakatoa, a nearby coffee shop. "I think that should work. I'll text you at lunch, okay?"

Thankfully, it turned out that Mom would be home. She was having a rare day off from the hospital. And while I could hear the barely restrained excitement in her voice, she promised to be on her best behavior when Charlene arrived. When lunch came, I texted Charlene and then prayed for the afternoon to wrap up quickly.

Before I knew what was happening, I was racing back home. I had so much to do to get the house ready. When I'd swung by the house in the morning, the living room had been trashed, there had been a pile of dishes in the kitchen sink, and I was pretty sure that my laundry was creeping out of my room and into the hall. I had to get everything squared away before Charlene arrived.

As soon as I parked DK in the garage, I dashed up the back steps into the kitchen and into the living room.

I skidded to a halt and looked around. It was clean. Sparkling, even. It hadn't been like this when I'd left. Well, I could always do the dishes. I went into the kitchen, only to find a gleaming and empty sink.

I frowned. Had I gone into the wrong house?

Mom came into the kitchen and stopped short. A smile twitched at her lips. "Just FYI, I closed the door to your room. I'm not touching your laundry."

I looked around the kitchen again. Even the countertops appeared to be scrubbed clean. I turned back to Mom. "Today was supposed to be your day off."

She shrugged. "It was. But you like this Charlene, right?"

"Well, yeah."

She nodded. "Then this is important to me."

I couldn't believe it. She had spent the whole day cleaning the house? For me? I stepped forward and gave her a hug.

She hugged me back then gently nudged me toward the refrigerator. "Get a snack ready, okay? And I'll make myself scarce while you two study."

I did as she suggested, pulling out some cheese. I found crackers in the pantry cupboard. Not a great snack, but it'd be good enough.

A half hour later, the doorbell rang. My heart leaped up my throat, almost strangling me. I rushed to the door and opened it.

Charlene smiled at me. "Hi."

She was wearing a tight white shirt with a denim button-down shirt over it along with black jeans and a black cowboy hat. A blue backpack was slung over her left shoulder. Just the mere sight of her was enough to render me breathless.

"Hi." I stepped out of the way so she could enter.

Mom waited at the end of the hallway, a grin tugging at the corners of her mouth. Then she quietly slipped up the stairs to the second floor.

I led Charlene into the living room. She settled in on the couch and smiled at me expectantly.

My mouth went dry. What was I supposed to do next? I was in unfamiliar territory here. "Do you . . . Should we . . . . Um, is it okay if I turn on some music?"

She shrugged. "Sure."

"What do you like?"

"Nothing in particular. Do you have any Christian stuff?"

I fumbled with the MP3 player plugged into the stereo. I had some Christian stuff, but I couldn't be sure what to pick. Lost and Found? No, they were an acquired taste, and Charlene might not like them. I settled on Tangled Blue, a Christian folk rock group I'd recently discovered.

The music filled the living room, and I winced. Too loud! I cranked down the volume and turned to Charlene. She smiled and started pulling books out of her backpack.

"So how was your day?" I asked, wincing once again. Lame!

"Not too bad, I guess. I almost didn't make it to school, though."

"Why not?"

She snorted. "Two superheroes caused a traffic jam."

"What?" That got my attention. "Who were they?"

"I don't know for sure. I think one of the guys at school said they were Dr. Olympus and—what was the other one's name?—oh, the Bronze Basher. I think."

I swallowed, trying to keep myself calm. "Wh-what were they doing?"

She shrugged. "I have no idea. Looked like they were trying to help after an accident, but they were only making things worse."

"What do you mean?"

"I only got a glimpse of them, but it looked like that Basher guy was ripping the doors off a car that had smashed into another one. I suppose he was trying to get the driver out, but he almost hit my Jeep when he tossed the doors over his shoulder." She snorted. "Typical."

I froze. "What do you mean?"

She grimaced. "Oh, you know. Superheroes mean well, I guess, but they usually make a mess of things."

"You don't think they help make things better?"

"I suppose they try. But if they really wanted to make a difference, why do they need to wear a mask?"

My hand twitched for my necklace. "Maybe some of them need to."

"Oh, I'm sure. After all, you get more press if you 'do good' while wearing a flashy costume."

Heat nibbled at my cheeks. I bit back a sharp answer. I shouldn't take this so personally. She had no idea about my secret identity. And she was entitled to her own opinion, no matter how wrong it was.

She glanced at me, and her expression froze. "Is everything okay?"

I forced a smile. "Yeah. I guess."

She scooted closer to me on the couch. "What is it?"

What could I say? That superheroes had saved my life once? It was true, but if I said that, she'd want details, and I didn't trust myself to lie to her.

Her eyes widened. "I know what's going on here."

I froze. "Y-you do?"

She nodded. "I should have known."

Oh, shoot. Agent Sexton would love this!

"You like the superheroes, don't you?"

I couldn't process what she said. Then my head started bobbing. "Yes. Yes, I do."

She shook her head. "I should have known. A lot of people in New Chayton do. I'm sorry. I have this argument with my dad all the time. He loves superheroes too. Forget I said anything."

I pulled out my physics book and rifled through the pages for a moment. Then I looked up at her. "So why don't you like them?"

"I don't know exactly. I mean, they mean well. And if some crazy person has hatched a plot to take over the world or whatever, I'd want someone there to stop him. But most of the time, it's like they're only in it for the fame. Take Raze, for example. When's the last time you heard a story about him that didn't involve a Victoria's Secret model? Or . . . that Failstate joker. A winner of reality show? Really?" She shook her head. "I just wish the people who make a genuine difference got as much press, you know?"

Ouch. I opened my physics book. And yet, try as I might, I couldn't concentrate. It wasn't just Charlene's presence. That was intoxicating enough. But I couldn't shake her words. I'd have to do better. I'd have to show her that at least one super-hero could make a genuine difference.

CHAPTER 22

CHARLENE STAYED FOR ANOTHER HOUR. I think she got most of her homework done. At least one of us did. We chatted a little, and then I walked her out to her Jeep. She hugged me, kissed me on the cheek, and was gone. I watched her drive away and then jogged back into the house. I would go out on patrol and make a difference. For her.

After supper, I excused myself and headed out to the garage. I checked my cell phone. For the past several nights, Downtime had texted me a location to patrol, one "suggested" by Sexton. Sure enough, a new message waited for me, one that informed me that I was responsible for the warehouse district and Club Row.

I parked DK in an alley and found a low-hanging fire escape. I clambered up to the top of the building and looked over the neighborhood. The warehouses stood like large cement boxes with black ribbon weaving between them. Most of them were dark, although a couple had lights burning in high windows.

A few cars wound through the area. A warm spring breeze ruffled my hood, and I sniffed the air. Mostly car exhaust and . . . what was that? Rotten vegetables? I shuddered. Someone needed to take out the trash more often.

Gravel crunched behind me. Someone else was on the roof? I clenched my hands into fists and then whipped around, ready for a fight.

Kynetic smiled at me. "Fancy running into you here, Failstate. Why are you up here?"

"J-j-just looking for some . . . uh, inspiration, I guess."

"Same here." From the way she was devouring me with her eyes, I wondered what kind of inspiration she wanted. "Great minds think alike, don't they?"

I had no idea what to say to that. Kynetic's mere presence was scrambling my thoughts. I paced the edge of the roof. If I kept moving physically, that might translate to mental movement as well.

"Shouldn't you be with Elemental?" I asked.

Kynetic shrugged. "I guess. She wanted me to stay with her in Rosen Heights, but we weren't finding anything there. So I texted Downtime to find out where you were." She looked out over the roof's edge. "This is where you, Vertigo, and Gangrene fought the superpowered zombie, right?"

"Veritas and Gauntlet," I said.

"What?"

I shook my head. "Never mind. That's right."

Kynetic leaned on the half-wall bordering the roof and looked out over the neighborhood. Her forehead scrunched into a frown. "Well, nothing to see here. Why don't we get out of here, go look somewhere else?"

"'We'?"

"Absolutely. I think we would make a great team."

I laughed. "That's not really something I can judge, seeing as I barely know you."

"There are ways to correct that, you know." Her voice was low and husky.

I coughed, my throat suddenly dry. I was keenly aware of her body next to mine, almost as though I could feel her heat bleed through my costume and into me. She wasn't touching me, but she might as well have been. I turned to her and was arrested by how warm her eyes were, how open and inviting. A pleasant fog descended on my brain and snared my limbs.

"All you have to do is ask." She took a step closer to me, and the fog in my brain turned to molasses. "So what is it you want to know?"

Words collided in my throat, a dozen potential questions, most of them half-formed and idiotic. A tingle wormed down my spine. At first, I thought it was a nervous reaction to Kynetic's presence. But then, my power surged and flared.

Instead of destroying my surroundings, I caused a section of the roof to bubble and steam, as if the material were boiling away. I ground my teeth and tamped down on my power. The smoke rising from the roof instantly reverted to its original state, creating a delicate, branching sculpture. It appeared like a burning bush anchored to the roof.

Kynetic gaped at it for a moment. I shifted on my feet, wondering how she would react. The last thing I wanted to do in front of an ally was show off my glitchy powers.

Then Kynetic turned to me with a smile. "For me? And I didn't get you anything."

I parsed her tone for sarcasm and, surprisingly, found none. The same warm fog started to nibble at my thoughts. I shook my head to clear it. Best to beat a quick retreat. I quickly crossed to the fire escape and slid down, hoping to put at least a little bit of distance between us.

No good. She followed me down, her eyes bright and expectant. I ducked down an alley between two of the smaller warehouses. It was the fastest route to DK, but hopefully the walk would dissuade Kynetic. Instead, she fell in step with me.

I finally snared a question and forced it out of my mouth. "So what kind of powers do you have?"

Her lips pulled down in a scowl. But then she smiled again, and any hint of disappointment vanished. "I'm what you could call a kinetic sponge." She walked over to a dumpster and retrieved a long 2x4. She handed me the wood. "Here. Hit me with this."

I stared at the board in my hands. "No way! I can't do that."

"It won't hurt. Me or you. I promise." She set herself, widening her stance and shaking out her hands. "C'mon! Clock me right over the head. Or hit me in the stomach or across the legs or whatever. It doesn't matter."

She obviously wasn't going to drop it. But I still didn't like the idea of whacking her, so I barely swung the club and lightly tapped her in her side.

She rolled her eyes and batted the 2x4 away. "Really? I know you can do better than that!"

I gritted my teeth and swung again, a little harder but still not enough to do any real damage.

"That's pathetic. Why'd they give you that license again?" Kynetic grabbed the end of the 2x4 and shook it hard enough she almost ripped it out of my hands. "I'm not made of glass, F. Hit me!"

I didn't like it one bit, but if she insisted . . . I wound up and swung the 2x4 as hard as I could, closing my eyes the moment before it hit Kynetic in her side. But then the wood came to a sudden halt, almost as if it had frozen in midair. The stop wasn't jarring. It was as if I had been standing in that posture the whole time. I risked a peek. The wood was touching Kynetic's side. I had hit her, but I hadn't felt the impact at all.

She smirked. "See? Do it again, if you want to."

I frowned. What happened? I swung the 2x4 back and hit her again. The club came to a halt in the same spot, but I couldn't feel the impact at all. I chuckled. "That's pretty cool." I swung again, this time aiming for her head. The 2x4 stopped the moment it would have caved in her skull. I probably could've kept doing that all day.

"That's half of my power," Kynetic said. "Here's the other half."

The fourth time I tried to hit her, she touched the 2x4. With a loud crack, the wood disintegrated. I fell forward, my momentum carrying me off balance.

Kynetic stepped in close and tapped me in the chest.

It was like getting hit by a truck going at highway speeds. I was blasted off my feet and rolled end over end until I came to rest against the dumpster. Ow! I touched my chest, only to find that my shirt had turned rigid and hard, sort of like body armor. But then, a moment later, the fabric turned soft again. So Dr. Olympus had been right after all.

Kynetic ran to me and knelt down, her eyes wide. "I'm so sorry! I didn't realize you were hitting me that hard!"

I winced as an ache sliced through my chest. "Well, you told me not to hold b— Wait, what?"

"I told you, I'm a kinetic sponge. Whatever kinetic energy is directed at me, I absorb and then store up. And then I have that much energy available to me the next time I strike. But I can't hold on to it forever. It has to be released soon."

Her hands pressed against my chest. Then they roamed a bit, up to my shoulders and down my arms toward my hands. "Are you okay?"

"I think so. Just give me a minute." I sat up. "That's a really cool power."

Her hands snared mine. I looked down at them, then up at her eyes. She was so close, so tantalizingly . . .

"So is this what passes for adolescent mating rituals nowadays? If so, I am relieved that my age exempts me from such activities. It looks painful."

I sat up, startled.

Dr. Olympus walked over to me. Instead of wearing her lab coat, though, she was wearing a set of black tights, one that almost looked like a diving suit. But the tights were covered in armor plates. The few places that were exposed seemed to be made of a finely woven metallic mesh. Her hair was pulled back into a tight bun on the back of her head and what looked like extremely fancy night-vision goggles perched on her head, only these had two extra lenses.

"Dr. Olympus!" I scrambled to my feet and knocked Kynetic's hand away. "We were just . . . uh . . . Kynetic was just showing me what her power can do."

"When I hit you with the sledgehammer, you weren't nearly as understanding."

Kynetic gave me a look, one of her eyebrows quirking upward. Heat sliced through my cheeks.

"Have you encountered any zombies?" I asked.

Dr. Olympus shook her head. "No, and neither have any of our colleagues. Truth be told, Failstate, many of us are beginning to wonder what the fuss is about. I have experiments waiting for me in Fargo, and I'm sure Raze would like to get back to . . . whatever it is he does. But never fear, we will continue the hunt regardless. Actually, I'm glad I ran into you. I had a thought about your physical deformities."

My eyes widened. Why didn't she just get out a megaphone and announce it to the whole city? "We don't have to talk about that right here, do we?"

"I have a colleague at New Chayton University: Dr. Monica Weathers. She's doing research into some new plastic surgery techniques. Skin grafts for burn victims, reconstructing faces after traumatic events, that sort of thing. If you want, I could arrange a meeting. She might be able to help."

I became acutely aware of Kynetic's gaze on me. I shook my head. "That's . . . uh . . . it's an interesting offer, Doctor."

"Think about it. You might be able to dispose of the necklace."

Would this woman never stop? Why not just say my name—and scream out my Social Security number while she was at it?

Dr. Olympus snapped her fingers. "Speaking of which, I had additional thoughts about that, as well. I'm working on something back at the lab. Not sure how well it will work at this time, but it could be an improvement on your existing solution."

I forced a smile to my face. Sure, the doctor couldn't see it, but hopefully it would carry through to my voice. "Thank you. I can't wait to see what you come up with."

She waved away my words. "Enough chatter for now. I plan to head to the northern suburbs. Perhaps I will find some zombies there. If not, I'm sure there will be plenty to occupy my time." She tugged a pair of goggles over her eyes and walked away, scanning the walls.

I didn't want to look at Kynetic. I knew what was coming next. She would undoubtedly have questions about my necklace, my deformities, all of it. That, or she was trying to think of a way to get out of there quickly. Not that I could blame her.

"So now what, F?" she asked. "Where do we go next?"

I turned to Kynetic, stunned. She smiled sweetly at me, her hands tucked behind her back. That was it? No questions? No hesitation?

"Aren't you . . . Don't you want to know what she's talking about?" I blurted the words out and immediately regretted them. The last thing I wanted to do was invite her to look under my hood.

She shook her head. "None of my business. Not yet, anyway." She stepped in close and grabbed the front of my shirt. "Besides, I like mysterious guys." She released my shirt and smoothed it out, her hands lingering for a few moments on my arms. "Now let's go out there and make a difference, okay?"

Sounded like a great idea to me. "I'll drive."

CHAPTER 23

THE POLICE SCANNER chattered quietly in the background as I drove. I had DK in patrol mode. It had taken on the appearance of a badly dinged up Camaro with tinted windows. If anyone looked at us, they'd have no idea who was inside.

"Nice car, F," Kynetic said.

I grimaced. "Thanks. DK is pretty cool."

"'DK'?" Kynetic's mouth twisted into a wry smile.

My cheeks burned underneath my hood. "It's a long story."

"I see." She patted the center console. "Nice to meet you, Deek."

Deek? My fingers tightened on the steering wheel. Why had I agreed to have her come along?

"So where to, F?" she asked.

"Things seem pretty quiet here. Why don't we head over to Club Row? Even if there aren't any zombies, some of the clubbers might be getting rowdy."

"And if not, you could always take me dancing," Kynetic replied.

I laughed. "I don't dance."

"That's okay. I'm a good teacher. And I think we'd both enjoy the lessons."

I resisted the urge to look at her. I needed to keep my mind clear as I drove. But it was nice, all of her attention. For a moment, I let my mind drift, imagining what it might be like to take Kynetic into one of those clubs. All eyes would be on us—on her especially. All the guys would be jealous of me as we took our place on the dance floor. A slow song would come on, I would draw her close and . . .

But instead of seeing Kynetic in my mind, I saw Charlene.

My stomach twisted in a tight knot. What was I doing? As flattering as Kynetic's attention was, pursuing her didn't feel right. Sure, I hadn't been leading her on, but I hadn't been discouraging her either. I couldn't let this continue.

"Look, Kynetic—"

"I told you. My friends call me 'Kyn,' and I definitely want to be friendly with you."

Oh, boy. "Okay, Kyn. I think I'd better be honest with you: I'm flattered by the way you're treating me, but the thing is . . . there's someone else."

"Oh." She fell silent and laced her fingers together in her lap. "Girlfriend?"

"No."

She frowned at me. "You two have been dating for a while, then?"

"Not exactly."

Her frown deepened. "Passed notes to each other in study hall?"

My fingers tightened around the steering wheel. "It's complicated."

"Oh, sure." She smirked. "Does the Little Red-Haired Girl even know you're alive, Charlie Brown?"

My fingers tightened on the steering wheel. How could she know that Charlene had red hair? No, wait, I was panicking over nothing. She was trying to get a rise out of me and sadly, it was working.

We rode in a silence occasionally punctuated by the muted squawking of the police radio.

But after fifteen minutes, I shifted in my seat. I couldn't take the quiet any longer. "So how long have you been working as a superhero?"

Kynetic glanced at me, then she blew out a long breath through her nose. "Since I was thirteen. You?"

"Fourteen. Have you had any chances at a license at all?"

She laughed. "No, not really. I grew up in New York. And you know how well Etzal'el plays with others."

I had gotten that impression, yes. "Wait a minute. If you grew up in New York, why are you in New Orleans with Elemental?"

"More opportunities."

"What about your parents? Did they move or something?"

She shook her head. "No, they're still back in New York. I think. I haven't spoken to them in over a year, so I can't say for certain."

I looked over at her. She glanced at me, and it was almost as if she could read the confusion through my mask. "I was legally emancipated from them six years ago."

"Why?"

"I made some money when I was a kid. And no, I'm not telling you how. Anyway, 'Mommy and Daddy' treated me like their own private piggy bank and wasted most of it. A friend saw what was happening and convinced me to get out from under them. Best thing I ever did. Now my money is my own, and no one can tell me where to go or what to do."

I couldn't imagine that. Sure, my life with Mom and Ben had been rough up until six months ago, but even in the darkest days, I never would have considered leaving them. "Doesn't that get lonely?"

She shrugged. "Sometimes, I guess. But this way, I get to go where I want to and work with who I want. I've been a deputy to a dozen different licensed heroes. Downtime, Bronze Basher, even a disastrous two weeks with Raze. And now you, maybe." She reached over DK's central island and squeezed my shoulder.

I couldn't think of what to say to that. I came to a stop at a light and looked out the windshield. That's when I spotted her. A young woman was standing by a car with what looked like a bent coat hanger. She was trying to force the wire past the window into the car. She wore a white blouse and a green skirt, one held up by colorful suspenders covered in buttons. If she was a car thief, she'd picked the wrong costume.

I parked next to the other car. I opened the door and stepped out. "Ma'am? Is everything okay?"

She looked up at me. Black trails of mascara ran down her cheeks. She took a step back and waved the bent hanger at the door like it was a sword and she was fending off a dragon. "I'm gonna be late for work, and I locked my keys in the car and—" She sniffled loudly. "This sucks!"

"Don't waste your time on this," Kyn said from inside DK. "I'm sure there's other things happening that need our attention."

I frowned. "Hang on a sec."

"No, we gotta go—"

I shut the door and stepped around DK and looked over the woman's car. It was a newer model, a Chevy Malibu. A few plush animals peeked out the rear window at me, jammed between the glass and a toddler's booster seat. Thankfully, the kid wasn't locked inside the car.

"Do you have remote locks?" I asked.

The woman nodded.

I smiled. This, I could fix. I summoned my power and focused my attention on the car's locks. It felt as though my heart shifted two inches to the right.

With a muffled click, the locks opened.

The woman gaped at me. Then she laughed and ran around the car. She threw her arms around me and hugged me tightly. "Thank you so much! You don't know how much this means to me!" She released me and climbed into her car. It growled to life and pulled away from the curb.

I got back into DK.

Kynetic smirked at me. "Well, aren't you the hero?"

"Isn't that what we both are?" I started the engine again. "She needed help. I was able to give that help. No big deal."

Before Kynetic could reply, the police scanner squawked. "All units, we have a 10-76 at Eighth and Chestnut. The NCFD is requesting assistance."

The computer screen in DK's dash lit up with the details. A fire. It was halfway across town. If the fire department was already there, they wouldn't need our help. Best to just keep . . .

"All units, we have a second 10-76 at First and Washington. The NCFD is— Correction, we have another 10-76 at Smith and McKinley. And . . ." The voice of the dispatcher was muddled, almost as if she were arguing with someone. "All units, we have five, repeat five, 10-76s in progress at: Eighth and Chestnut, First and Washington, Smith and McKinley, McKinley and Waverly, and Houston and Sixth Ave. All units, please assist NCFD as needed at these locations."

I stared at the computer screen. The map of New Chayton glowed with amber light as the data scrolled by. The fourth fire, at McKinley and Waverly, was just three blocks from where we were. I frowned at the map. Five fires, at once? What were the odds? For all I knew, this could be a trap of some kind. A supervillain could have set the fires, hoping to draw heroes in. I'd be a fool to rush in.

Additional data popped up. The fire at McKinley and Waverly was in an apartment building. I nodded to myself. Even if this was a trap, people needed our help. It made the decision a no-brainer. I turned to Kynetic. "Call Downtime. Let him know we're heading to McKinley and Waverly."

I reached into the center island and set the vehicle for suppression mode. DK swelled around us and, as soon as the transformation was complete, I stomped the pedal to the floor, and we rocketed forward. "Feel like playing firefighter?" I asked.

Kynetic hooted and slapped the dashboard. "That's more like it, Deek! Let's go get 'em, F!"

CHAPTER 24

DK ALMOST WENT UP on two tires as we roared around the corner onto McKinley. There, right before us, was the fire, bursting out of the windows of a four story apartment building. A pillar of smoke rose high into the night sky. A small cluster of people stood across the street, dressed in their bathrobes and pajamas. Others came out of nearby buildings, the curious coming to see the show.

No sign of the fire department or the police yet. Understandable, given the mini-epidemic of fires throughout the city, but I would have felt a lot better if they had been here. I wasn't exactly equipped for putting out fires. Not unless there were features in DK that Magnus hadn't told me about.

"Any word from Downtime?" I asked.

Kynetic stashed her phone. "Sounds like he and some of the others are trying to contain the fire at Houston and Sixth. He sounded kind of distracted. He hung up on me."

I nodded. That was understandable. Well, best to assume we'd be on our own for this one. Time to get to work.

I got out of DK, Kynetic mirroring my moves. We jogged across the street to the apartment's residents.

"Is everyone okay?" I shouted to be heard above the roar of the blaze.

A man in a faded blue bathrobe nodded. "I think so."

"Do you know everyone who lives in the building?" I asked him.

"Most of them, yeah." He turned around to look over the crowd, mumbling names as he pointed at the different people. Then he frowned. "Hey, where's the girl from 4G?"

A high-pitched scream rent the air. I whirled around and saw a young woman stumbling out of the burning building. Her hair was a mottled mess, and black soot streaked her face. She was wearing a pair of sweatpants and a t-shirt. She screamed again and collapsed.

I was at her side before my thoughts caught up with my body. I knelt down next to her. Her hands were blistered and red, badly burned. But she shrieked and cried.

"Calm down, ma'am, you're okay." I wrapped an arm around her and tried to get her to stand. "But it's not safe right here. Let's get you across the street and—"

She jerked against my arm as if she were trying to break free. "No!"

Why was she fighting me? I tightened my grip and tried to steer her across the street, but it was no good.

She wouldn't calm down. She sobbed hysterically and dug in her heels.

"My baby! I was visiting a friend on the third floor, but I couldn't get up to my apartment. Please! You have to help me!"

Though I was standing fifteen feet away from an inferno, my body felt encased with ice. A baby? Trapped in a burning building? The woman kept fighting me to get back inside, but I dragged her away from the building. As I did, I strained to listen for the wail of approaching sirens. I could hear them, off in the distance, but I had no way of knowing if they were coming to this fire or one of the others. By the time we knew for certain, it would be too late. This woman needed a hero. And I was it.

"Kyn!" I motioned for Kynetic to come over. I passed the woman over to her. "Get her out of here and try to get her to calm down."

"What are you going to do?" Kynetic asked.

I answered by turning for the fire and running for the front door. Kynetic shouted my name, but I ignored her as the intense heat slapped at me. I took a deep breath and shielded my face with my arm. Then I dove through the door and into hell itself.

Smoke billowed across the ceiling. I coughed as the acrid air clawed up my nose. I should have dipped my mask in water or something before going in. Too late now. I paused for a moment and listened, hoping to hear the baby crying or something. Nothing.

I headed for the stairs and took them two at a time. My chest heaved by the time I reached the third floor. The crackle of the fire overwhelmed me, as did the smoke.

When I rounded the corner to go up to the fourth floor, I saw the problem. The fire blazed at the top of the stairs, cutting off my path. I looked around for a moment, wondering what I could do about that. I didn't see any fire hoses or fire extinguishers. At least, nothing that I could use. Why weren't there any sprinklers?

I shook my head to clear it. I had to keep moving. A plan formed in my mind, incomplete and wildly desperate, but it was the only thing I could think of. I ran down the hall, looking at the apartment doors. If I was lucky, each floor shared the same layout as the other three. If that was the case, then apartment 4G would be right above . . .

There! Apartment 3G. Its door hung open, revealing a smoky interior. I ran through the living room, which was furnished with a neon sign from a beer company, a futon, and a rickety entertainment center crammed with videogames. On the opposite wall, though, was what I was looking for: a balcony. I sent out a wave of destructive energy, obliterating the glass, and I jumped through.

I glanced down at the street below. Maybe the fire department had arrived and I wouldn't have to go through with this. The residents still milled around across the street, but that was it. Wonderful. Well, here went everything.

Summoning my power around my hands, I drove my fingers into the building's wall. Using the carved impressions as handholds, I pulled myself up the side, climbing up to what I hoped was Apartment 4G's balcony. Someone shouted at me from the ground below. I ignored it, focusing on what I was doing. If I faltered, even for a moment, I could fall to the ground below.

Once I reached the balcony, I pulled myself up and over the side. I peeked through the glass. I couldn't see much thanks to the smoke, but I thought I spotted some flames licking at the wall next to the door. I strained against the glass, trying to listen for the sound of a crying infant. Nothing. I ground my teeth. Hopefully I wasn't too late.

I took a deep breath and closed my eyes. *Lord, this is stupid. Bless my stupidity and let it work. Please!*

I braced myself and then lashed out, shearing through the glass door.

With a *whump,* the fire blasted through the apartment right for me.

I threw my hands over my face. The heat of the fire roared over me, but it felt muted, as if it were bleeding through a layer of concrete. I risked a glance at my arms. The sleeves of my shirt burned in two places, but I didn't feel it, not really. I frowned. What did I do this time?

No time to puzzle that out. I slapped out the flames and stepped into the apartment. The fire had spread to the couch and had started to work on the kitchen cabinets. I ducked my head and ran through the apartment. Where would the baby be? Not in the living room, thankfully. The bedrooms?

I came to a closed door. I slid off my glove and tapped the door knob. It felt cool. Good. At least the fire hadn't reached there. I gave the knob a twist and dove inside, bracing myself for the worst: a baby, lying still in a crib, unmoving.

Instead, I tripped over a pile of laundry and crashed to the floor in front of a large aquarium.

I picked myself up and looked around the room. A queen sized bed, the covers in disarray, sat beneath a large poster of a woman painted to look like a geisha. A small dresser was pushed against another wall. And in the aquarium . . .

I groaned. An iguana perched on a branch, staring at me through the glass.

"Baby, I presume?"

The lizard adjusted itself on the branch and regarded me with its bulbous eyes.

Well, as long as I was here. I opened the tank and reached inside. The iguana tried to escape, but I snared it and pulled it from its branch. "Settle down, Baby. I'm getting you out of here."

As soon as I had a good enough grip on the beast, I dashed out of the room. A quick check of the other bedroom, the bathroom, and the kitchen revealed that the whole apartment was empty. I ran back into the living room. The apartment door was engulfed in flames. No way I was going out that way. I ran for the balcony. Once outside, I peeked over the railing. It was a long way down. I wasn't sure if I could make the climb, not while holding a squirming iguana.

Kynetic darted across the street and stood underneath the balcony. "Jump! I'll catch you!"

Was she kidding? Apparently not. She spread her arms wide and urged me to do it. Well, she *was* a kinetic sponge . . .

A glance back into the apartment was all that I needed. I hugged Baby close to my chest and then threw myself over the ledge.

I closed my eyes and braced myself for impact. Maybe my powers would turn my clothes into impenetrable armor again. Would that keep me from getting injured when I hit the ground? I guess I would find out when—

I stopped falling. There was no sudden jerk, no blow to my back or head. One second I was falling, the next, I wasn't. Arms held me at my back and knees.

Kynetic smiled at me. "Hey there, handsome."

She set me on the ground. Then she stepped over to a nearby tree and punched it. Bark exploded with a large crack. "Ah, all better now."

The woman from the building ran over to me and took the iguana from me. She was crying even harder than before. She threw her arms around me and practically choked me as she repeatedly thanked me.

I turned to the crowd. "Is anyone else missing anyone? Is everyone out safely?"

The residents looked at each other, as if taking a quick inventory.

The man in the bathrobe spoke up. "I think that's everyone."

Fire trucks, their lights painting the buildings around us, roared up to the curb, and firefighters poured out.

Their captain ran up to me. "Is everyone out of the building?"

I nodded. "I'm pretty sure. I got . . . Well, I got the last one out myself."

The captain glanced at the iguana, his skepticism plain. Then he patted me on the shoulder. "Thanks for the help. I really appreciate it."

I went over to the man in the bathrobe. He seemed the most talkative. Maybe he could help shed some light on what happened.

He offered me his hand to shake. "Hey, thanks a lot, man. I really appreciate it."

"No problem. So tell me, Mr . . ." I waved my hand expectantly.

"Vince. Or Vinnie."

"What happened here, Vince? How did the fire get started?"

Vince blew out a long breath and rubbed the back of his neck. "Search me. I live up on the top floor. So there I am, sound asleep, when there's a loud bang from the roof. Next thing I know, my ceiling's on fire."

"Any idea what the bang was?"

He laughed. "Are you kidding me? I didn't look out the window or nothing. I just got outta there."

I nodded. "Very wise. Thanks."

I conducted a quick poll of the other residents and heard similar stories. No one knew how the fire had started. The people who lived on the top floor all reported the same thing: Something had hit the roof, and then the fire had started. Not a lot to go on.

Still, no one was seriously injured, and it looked like the fire department was going to be able to contain the blaze. I blew out a long breath. Not exactly what I had hoped for tonight, but sometimes even the small victories were good.

CHAPTER 25

KYNETIC SLIPPED AWAY shortly after the fire was put out without saying good-bye. That was odd. By that time, a few reporters had caught up to us. A camera crew shot some video for one of the local stations, and a photographer managed to catch a shot of Kynetic and me talking quietly.

After Kynetic left, I went around to the other fires, but they were all under control. What few witnesses I could find all had the same story: Something had hit their building, and then the fires had started. As I sat in DK at the site of the first fire, I called up the map of New Chayton on the computer screen. I frowned at what I saw. Instead of being scattered randomly through the city, all five fires were in a straight line four miles long.

I considered searching along that line. Maybe I could figure out where the arsonist had come from or gone. But I shook my head. Why would the arsonist keep traveling along a straight line? It'd be more likely that he or she would try to vanish. It'd be a waste of time.

Instead, I wound up patrolling around the line. I figured that the cops were probably busy assisting the fire department. I didn't want anyone to take advantage of their distracted state. I didn't see anything out of the ordinary. I would have thought that whoever had set the fires would have used that time to strike somewhere else. But I couldn't find anything amiss in the surrounding neighborhoods, and the police scanner was unusually quiet. Perhaps the fires had everyone spooked. When the sun started to poke over the horizon, I headed for home.

I parked DK in the garage and went inside. The thick smell of smoke followed me. Mom would not like that. I went into the basement and tossed my costume into the washer. As I did, my stomach rumbled. Best to eat breakfast before I headed out to school.

Once in the kitchen, I switched on the TV and set to work putting together some breakfast. While the weatherman joked with the anchors about some charity drive coming up, I pulled out a box of cereal and a large bowl. I settled in at the center island and started munching the crunchy puffs, washing it down with a bit of orange juice.

As soon as the weather report wrapped up, the anchors announced local news. I perked up and leaned forward.

"Last night, a series of fires broke out in New Chayton. The New Chayton Fire Department was assisted by other departments from surrounding communities and by members of the superhero community. Holly Anderson has more. Holly?"

The image on screen changed from the studio to a reporter standing in front of a burned out building. It looked like a small mom-and-pop grocery store. The sign on the front of the building had melted off completely, leaving a long trail of plastic down the red bricks. The reporter, a perky young woman in her mid-twenties, put on her best "serious face."

"That's right, Tom. New Chayton fire officials aren't commenting on the outbreak of fires that struck New Chayton last night, but sources within the fire department suggests that they suspect that the cause was arson."

I leaned forward in my chair and shoveled in another scoop of cereal. Maybe she would say something about the fire department's suspicions, but the reporter mostly went over what I already knew: five fires, spread through the heart of the city. Nobody was seriously hurt, thankfully, just a few people with smoke inhalation.

"The fire department has released a statement thanking a number of superheroes for their help. We've obtained some footage of one local hero who made quite the difference."

The screen shifted to a shot of a burning building. I frowned. It didn't look like the apartment building I had been at. Then someone, little more than a flash of blue and gold, burst through a lower level window. Gauntlet rolled across the lawn and came to a halt right in front of the camera, clutching a small girl to his chest. He set the girl down next to her parents, who gathered their daughter into their arms. Then the mother launched herself at Gauntlet and hugged him tightly. Even though he had been thrown off balance, Gauntlet still managed a brilliant smile for the camera.

I chuckled. Good for him. I bet he was loving every second of this.

Then Holly the reporter appeared on screen again. "But Gauntlet wasn't the only one working last night. Reports suggest that a team of licensed heroes, led by Raze, fought a villain that they believe was responsible for last night's fires."

My head snapped around as if I had been struck. They did what?

Once again, the picture on the TV shifted to a blurry video, one shot at night. Fires blasted through the darkness, silhouetting at least half a dozen people from behind. I couldn't recognize anyone, but given the way that two of them were hovering over the city streets and the rest were charging toward the flames rather than away, they had to be heroes.

"This amateur footage we've obtained show parts of the battle that raged through the back streets of Overton. Nobody we spoke to got close enough to see what happened exactly, but they said that after a battle that lasted about half an hour, the heroes defeated their enemy and then took off into the night.

"I caught up with Raze earlier this morning to find out what happened."

The image shifted to Raze sitting in a retro diner, all red vinyl and bright chrome. He still wore his costume, but I could easily spot the burned patches on his chest and arms. He perched on a tall stool at the counter, nursing a cup of coffee. He glanced at the camera out of the corner of his eyes and sneered.

"I can't say much. It's an ongoing investigation." He snorted. "I sound like a cop. But I can tell you that a bunch of us took on some sort of—" He frowned and took another sip of coffee. "A bad guy. We think he was responsible for the fires. Don't have to worry about him anymore, though, okay?"

"And what about Failstate? Was he with you last night?" Holly asked.

Raze turned to the camera. "No, he wasn't. I got no idea where ol' Failstate was. Maybe he was making an audition tape for another reality show."

The camera cut back to Tom the Anchor in the newsroom. "So have you found out where New Chayton's latest licensed hero was, Holly?"

Back to Holly in front of the burned-out building. "He was in action last night as well, assisting at one of the fires." She smirked at the camera. "According to what I've heard, he was instrumental in rescuing a salamander."

"It was an iguana!" I shouted at the TV. I shut it off before the camera could show Tom's reaction.

I glowered at the silent TV. The entire situation was spiraling out of control. My so-called liaison officer wasn't going to help me. Now there was an entire crowd of licensed heroes in my city, doing my job. And my older brother was getting better press than me.

Even as the bitter thought twisted in my mind, I recognized it for what it was. Petty. Unhelpful. Sin. If I had become a hero for the fame and publicity, yeah, then maybe I'd have a reason to be upset. But that wasn't why I put on a costume. That wasn't why I'd fought for the license six months ago. I got into this to help people. As much as it rankled, as much as it bothered me to hear the snideness in Raze's voice and the mockery in the reporter's voice, I had helped last night. I had. Sure, all I had saved was a lizard and helped a woman who'd locked her keys in her car, but those things helped in small ways.

But I couldn't rest. An idea nibbled at the back of my mind. Had Raze and his team fought a superpowered zombie? It certainly sounded like it, given how hesitant he was to speak to

Holly. Maybe . . . The fires had all been on a straight line. If
Raze's fight was on the same line, then maybe, just maybe, if
I backtracked, I could find where these zombies were coming
from.

So how could I find out for sure? Who would have been
with Raze last night? Some of the heroes in the footage were
flying. I smiled. Maybe one of them was Downtime. And while
Raze had been stand-offish, Downtime had been cordial, maybe
even a little friendly. He could give me the info I needed.

I retrieved my cell phone and checked my contacts. I
laughed. Even though I had never asked for it, his name had
been entered into the list. I hit the dial button.

The phone didn't even ring. "Hi, Failstate. What can I do
for you?"

"Were you with Raze last night?"

He hesitated. "As a matter of fact, I was. I take it you saw
our colleague on television just now?"

"I did. Where did this fight take place?"

"We were in a suburb named Overton, corner of Hillside
and Crescent."

"Thanks for the intel. Is there anything I can help you with
today?"

"Not that I know of, but if something comes up, I will
contact you."

I clicked the phone off and frowned. Best to get to work
and see what I could learn.

I went out to the garage and rummaged through some of
the boxes along one wall. I thought Dad used to have a map
of just New Chayton. I probably should have hung that up at
some point or another. Once I found it, I spread it over DK's
hood. Using a red marker, I put Xs on the map where the fires

had been. I added another X where Downtime, Raze, and the others had had their fight. As I might've guessed, the fight's location fell on the same line as those of the fires.

Was it possible that whoever it was had just traveled in a straight line from fire to fire until the heroes had stopped him, her, or it? I scratched the side of my head and squinted at the map. Maybe. But that was assuming an awful lot. Maybe they had fought a zombie. Maybe the zombie was somehow responsible for the fires. Maybe it traveled in a straight line the whole way. Maybe, maybe, maybe.

I sighed. Well, I had only one option, then: I'd have to track down the rest of Raze's team and see what they could tell me. I'd probably have to call Fire Chief Thompson, as well. That wouldn't be a fun conversation. And then I'd have to check out the location of each fire, see what clues I could find, and . . .

Wait a minute. I frowned at the map. According to it, the line passed close to Peregrine Field, a football stadium that had been torn down twenty years earlier. Mom used to tell us stories about going to games there with Dad. How old was this map? I glanced at the information box. Printed in . . . 1982? I snorted. I'd have to get a newer one at some point.

But the name Peregrine Field sparked a thought in the back of my mind. It wasn't just that the stadium had been torn down . . . What had happened to the land? I booted up my laptop and jumped onto the Internet. I read the wiki file about Peregrine Field. According to the article, after the stadium had been torn down, the land had been sold to New Chayton University. The University had built a series of new classroom buildings and lab facilities on the land.

Lab facilities?

Huh. It wasn't much of a lead, but it was enough for now. Maybe I'd have to go and meet Dr. Olympus's colleague, after all.

CHAPTER 26

AFTER SCHOOL THAT AFTERNOON, I headed for New Chayton University's campus. I found a parking spot six blocks from campus and set out to cover the rest on foot. Hopefully, I would blend in with everyone else. At least my necklace made me look relatively average. I never thought I'd be thankful for that. My route took me past the fraternities and sororities. A few of the girls glanced in my direction. I tried to walk taller, but my attempts only set them to rolling their eyes.

Fraternity row bordered the main campus. The school's buildings were an eclectic combination of architectural styles. One was a glass box that shimmered in the morning sun. Next to it was a building made of stone that almost resembled a Greek temple. All of the buildings faced a large open area, a well-manicured grass field. Students lounged against trees or sat on the grass. Some of them were playing frisbee golf. I frowned and looked around. So where had the stadium stood? I should have brought the map with me. I felt completely lost.

"Rob?"

Surrounded by at least half a dozen young men his age, Ben walked over to me. "What are you doing here?" he asked.

Clearly Ben's friends wanted to know the same thing given the way they were eyeing me.

My mind scrambled but then latched onto an explanation. "I'm here as a prospective student."

Ben's eyes narrowed. A predatory glint flashed through them. Clearly he saw the lie.

One of his friends laughed. "Then where's your admissions counselor?"

Shoot. I hadn't thought of that.

Ben whirled on his friend. "I think the better question is, where's that girl you claimed flirted with you in the caf yesterday?"

The others hooted. The one who questioned me fell silent, his face blazing. Ben offered me a half-smirk. I bit back my own smile. It felt good to have my brother on my side, a definite improvement from a few months back.

"So, this is what we're gonna do," Ben said. "You guys keep hunting and let me know what happens." He smacked one of them on the chest. "Get video on your cell this time, okay? I'm going to help my brother out, and I'll catch up with you."

The other guys headed off toward one of the buildings.

Ben watched them go before he turned back to me. "So what's the deal? For real this time."

"I think those zombies have been coming from here."

Ben frowned. "Rob, they're actually kind of smart once you get to know—"

"Not your friends, moron. The actual zombies." Over the next ten minutes I laid out my suspicions.

Ben pursed his lips and crossed his arms. As I wrapped up my thoughts, his frown deepened. "That's not a lot to go on."

"I know, but it's a lead. That's why I'm here."

"Okay. Well, let's see what we can dig up. Let's go."

He led me along the sidewalk toward a pair of gleaming buildings, some of the newest on campus. One was a massive theatre complex with an attached art gallery. And the other . . .

The Henry Newman Center for Biological Research.

That had to be it! I punched a fist into my palm and bounced on my heels. Ben glanced at me, and we headed for the building.

The initial rush I felt quickly faded as we approached the building. The Research Center looked intact. So did the rest of the campus. If the zombies had indeed come through the campus, there should have been more damage. Broken windows, scorched trees, something. But unless the New Chayton University maintenance staff was quick on cleaning up, there was nothing, not even a hint that anything had gone wrong. My shoulders slumped. It looked like I would have to go searching along the line after all.

Ben must have caught my disappointment. He jostled my shoulder. "Let's go take a look, okay? You never know what we're going to find."

We entered the building and were immediately assaulted by the tang of antiseptic in the air. The floor of the entryway consisted of baby blue tile. In the center was a statue of a DNA double helix crafted out of bronze that seemed to spin apart at the top. A few students sat on vinyl benches, working on their laptops or reading thick textbooks. Ben smiled at them, and they turned back to their studies. He jerked his head toward an office directory.

Once again, my heart sank. This was a waste of time. Unless there was a "Zombie Making Department," there was no way we were going to find anything useful. Still, I took a look, running my forefinger down the list of names. There was one that I recognized: "Dr. Monica Weathers." If I really wanted to take up Dr. Olympus's offer to get my true face fixed, at least I knew where to go.

Then my finger came to rest on another familiar name: "Dr. Floyd Ayers." I frowned. The guy from Charlene's zombie attack? According to the directory, he was a professor of microbiology. My skin puckered as if a cold wind blew over it. No way this was coincidental.

Ben leaned in close. "Got something?"

"Maybe." I tapped the directory twice. "Should we see if the good professor has office hours?"

According to the directory, Ayers's office was in 2417. We jogged up the stairs and down a narrow hallway, one dotted with plain metal doors every ten feet or so. The office marked 2417 was halfway down the hall. I peeked through the narrow window in his door. I couldn't see much. A large bookcase was crammed full of books on the opposite wall. A half-dead plant strained toward the meager sunlight that drifted through a narrow window. Apparently when they built the Research Center, they hadn't put in much thought about professor comfort.

"What do you think?" Ben whispered. "Want to sneak in and take peek around?"

My eyes widened. Was he crazy? It wasn't like I was in my costume or anything. Besides, while the rules of search and seizure were a little more lax for a superhero, I'd still have to outline my reasons for breaking into Ayers's office in a report to Sexton and the VOC. There was no way that Sexton would buy a mere coincidence as a reason.

But still . . . it was tempting. My fingers drifted up to my necklace. I wouldn't have to take it off for long, just long enough to send a blast of destructive energy into the door's lock. While Ben stood watch, I could take a quick peek inside. It was doubtful I'd find anything incriminating, but there was always that possibility. I grabbed the doorknob and rattled it. Maybe Dr. Ayers left it unlocked. But no such luck. Fine. Then I'd have to do it the hard way.

"What are you two doing?"

I spun around in time to see a very angry looking young woman storm down the hall at us. She was tall and gangly, her t-shirt and jeans hanging loose on her. Her hair, brown and stringy, was cropped short.

I jumped away from Dr. Ayers's door, which I'm sure only made me look guilty.

"I asked you a question." She jammed her fists on her hips, blocking the hallway. "Why were you trying to get into Dr. Ayers's office?"

"Uh . . ." The last thing I had expected was to be caught by a . . . I had no idea who this girl was, let alone why she would be so mad.

"My little brother was hoping to meet some of the folks in the science department. He's thinking of transferring to NCU," Ben said. "Do you know Dr. Ayers?"

"I'm his TA for the fall semester." The girl's gaze didn't move from me, and her features didn't relax at all. "He doesn't look old enough to be in college."

"He did a lot of PSEO. Brilliant kid, but obviously a little behind . . . well, socially. But he loves science. Right, Rob?"

Who was he calling socially behind? Then Ben elbowed me in the gut, and I managed a quick nod.

"So we're just here trying to find out more about the profs. What can you tell us about Dr. Ayers?"

The girl still hesitated. She wasn't buying it. She would call campus police, we'd probably get run out of the building, and that'd be the end of that.

Ben smiled, a generous flash of teeth. "You know, you look really familiar. I know I've seen you before. Were you over at the student union yesterday?"

"No."

"Huh." Ben stroked his chin thoughtfully. "I know I've seen you before. Maybe at the Delta Chi party last night?"

She scowled at Ben. "The Delta Chi party is tonight."

Ben snapped his fingers as if he just remembered that fact. "You're right, it is. Are you going?"

The girl gaped at him. "Do I look like I'd be going?"

"Of course," Ben said. "Why wouldn't you? Maybe we can go together."

"Do you have an invitation?"

"No, I don't." Ben flashed his most charming smile at the girl. "But I'm sure to get in if a lady as lovely as you is with me. What do you say? Meet you at the party at eight?"

The girl sputtered but then nodded. "Okay, I-I-I guess that's okay."

"That is, unless you've got to work for Professor Ayers or something. That would be a shame."

"No, Dr. Ayers is a sweetheart. Why do you think he keeps his office up here with the grad students? He wants to be more accessible."

"What does he research?" I asked.

Please let the answer be zombies. Please let the answer be zombies.

"Telomeres."

My mind went blank. I had no idea what those were.

She must have sensed my confusion. "Telomeres are part of our DNA. They keep our chromosomes from unraveling."

That still didn't help. I knew I should have paid better attention in biology.

"And do you help him with his research?" Ben asked.

She shrugged. "Sometimes."

"Does he have a lab or something?" Ben ramped up the intensity on his smile.

For a moment, I considered warning him off. He was clearly putting too much effort into winning the girl over. Even still, she blushed and nodded. "You want to see?"

"Only if it's no trouble," Ben replied.

"No, not at all." She led us through the building to a set of double doors, which she opened.

I poked my head inside.

I didn't know what I'd expected or even hoped for. Maybe a big vat with a half-rotten zombie in it or something along those lines. But instead, the girl showed us a spacious room with a number of lab tables in the middle. Microscopes and other scientific devices were set up, seemingly at random. Bottles and beakers and test tubes were stacked in a set of shelves. One wall was filled with a bookcase crammed with papers and folders. I tried to hide my disappointment.

"Thank you so much." Ben produced a small scrap of paper and scribbled something on it. "Here's my number. Give me a call later, and we'll make plans, okay?"

The girl ducked her head and smiled. She escorted us back to the entrance of the science building and then scurried off, almost running away.

Ben led me back outside. "Well, that was almost a complete bust."

"Are you really going to take her to that party?"

Ben shrugged. "Why not? She's cute, and I can think of worse ways to spend a Friday night."

I shook my head and chuckled. This was why I needed Ben's help. He brought a whole different skill set to the table. If I had done this on my own, I would have been arrested for sure. And for nothing.

"Thanks for your help." I hesitated. Might as well try again. "You know, if you ever change your mind and want to make this partnership official . . ."

Ben shot me a dirty look. "No, thanks. See you around, Robin."

He strode off, most likely to find his friends.

I sighed. Might as well just head for home, seeing as how this lead didn't pan out. Maybe I should head for Overton and do some poking around there, see what I could turn up. I really wanted to learn more about Dr. Ayers. But it wasn't like I had an extensive database about criminals and their activities.

My steps faltered, and I came to a stop. I might not have a database, but I knew someone who did. I dug out my cell phone and hit the speed dial button for Mike.

"Hello?"

"What are you up to right now?" I asked.

He hesitated. "I'm at home. Why?"

"I need your help."

CHAPTER 27

IT FELT WEIRD returning to Magnus Manor, especially entering through a door. Usually I arrived through the secret entrance to Meridian's Lighthouse, which was in an alleyway behind a park across the street. But this time, I pulled up to the five car garage and jogged over to the back door. I rang the doorbell.

When the door opened, it wasn't Mike standing there. Instead, Magnus glared at me. "You've got a bunch of licensed heroes fighting crime in your city, and all you can muster is saving an iguana from a fire?"

At least he got the lizard's species right. "Actually, I think I may have a lead on the source of the zombies. I was hoping to use the Lighthouse's computers."

Magnus grumbled and stepped out of the way.

Mike was waiting for us in the kitchen. He nodded in greeting to me but didn't say a word as Magnus led us deeper into the mansion. He led us into his study, a long room bordered with ceiling-high bookshelves that led to a large wooden desk that overlooked a huge window. Magnus walked over to the desk, which was empty save for a glass enclosed display of a prism. Magnus gave the display's base a twist, and one of the bookshelves to my left popped open. Mike hauled it open, revealing a staircase that descended into darkness.

Magnus stepped into the staircase and raised a hand. Brilliant light erupted from his fingers, driving back the shadows. "Let's go."

We walked down the stairs, which went down at least four stories. When we reached the bottom, we walked down a long hall that served as a makeshift museum. Tucked into alcoves were relics of Magnus's career as Meridian. Weapons confiscated from supervillains, bits and pieces of killer robots, and even a tank full of water. I stared at that. Why hadn't I ever noticed that before? That was a story I'd have to ask about at some point.

After the museum, we emerged in the Lighthouse itself, a room easily the size of an aircraft hangar. Chest-high walls divided the space into different rooms: a kitchenette, a chemistry lab, a sparring arena. Magnus led us to a wall filled with computer screens. The whole system came to life as we approached, filled with a mosaic of Meridian's starburst emblem.

Mike came to a halt and stared at the system. "Dad, where'd the keyboard go?"

"I got rid of it." Magnus gave his son a pointed look. "A month ago. I upgraded the system with a prototype our tech division developed." He turned to the wall of screens. "Computer, on."

The screens flared, the screensaver replaced with an interface I didn't recognize.

Magnus turned to me. "So what have you uncovered?"

I laid it all out: meeting Dr. Ayers in Club Row, my theory about the straight line, and the visit to NCU. Magnus frowned through all of it, stroking his chin thoughtfully.

When I wrapped up my thoughts, he turned toward the computer screens. "So why do you need my help?"

"I was hoping you might have something in your files on this Dr. Ayers."

Magnus studied my face, his face pinched in a frown, and turned to the bank of monitors. "Computer: records search— Dr. Floyd Ayers."

Data whizzed across the screens, bits and pieces of it coming to a halt at various points on the monitors. It looked like research papers, newspaper articles, online videos of his lectures. Within a few seconds, the entire wall had filled with information on Dr. Ayers.

Magnus squinted at the information. "Dr. Floyd Ayers, fifty-five years old. Did his undergraduate work at Harvard, did a stint overseas at Oxford, then at Georg-August-Universität Göttingen. He was one of the first graduates with a degree in biological engineering from MIT. Right now he's mostly researching telomeres at New Chayton University." He glanced at me. "Following me so far?"

"I'm good."

"Let's focus on his personal life . . ." Magnus waved a hand at the screen. Half of the data disappeared. The rest became larger. "No arrests, never been under suspicion for any crimes, but that doesn't mean anything. The same could be said for me. No outstanding debts, nothing unusual in his bank accounts. Still owes a few thousand on his house. If he's dirty, I'm not seeing it in any of this. Was married to a woman named Gail—"

"Was?" I asked.

"According to this, his wife died six years ago." He looked at me. "Why?"

I frowned. "Dunno. Seems important."

Magnus snorted. "If you say so, kid." He waved his hand again. "I don't know. I've tangled with plenty of 'mad scientist' types, and this Ayers doesn't fit the pattern. If you took this to the VOC, they'd never buy it."

Especially with Sexton in the mix.

"We still have that straight line of fires," I said.

Magnus snorted. "I'll give you that it's unusual, but it's not enough either."

"Can we look into the research center? I'm sure that's on the line."

"It's a waste of time, but fine." Magnus cleared his throat. "Computer: Acquire data on the Henry Newman Center for Biological Research." He shook his head. "There's nothing unusual about the research center at all. I should know. I donated a quarter of the money and—" His head snapped up, and he reached out and made a grabbing motion. The data on the screen came to a halt. Another gesture from Magnus brought up a large graph. "We may . . . uh, we may actually have found something."

I took a step forward and looked over the graph. According to the title, it was a record of the research center's electrical consumption for the past two years. The first half undulated gently. But then, six months ago, there was a huge spike, followed by another. And another. Each time, the power consumption quadrupled.

Magnus waved at the screen, enlarging that portion of the graph so we could see the spikes in greater detail. Each burst didn't last very long, just a few minutes, but the timing of each was what caught my attention.

"Those last two," I pointed to them, "happened six hours before the zombies showed up. That can't be a coincidence."

"I agree." Mike's eyes seemed to glaze, as if he were looking through the computer screens instead of at them. "There's definitely a connection."

"Well, then, I'd say you boys have a job to do tonight." Magnus crossed his arms. "You two feel like checking out New Chayton University?"

From Mike's sour expression, I could tell he wasn't thrilled at the idea. A thrill ran through me. I knew we'd find the answers there. Hopefully, we'd be able to handle whatever we found in the research center.

CHAPTER 28

NEW CHAYTON UNIVERSITY clearly knew what it was doing when it came to campus security at night. That was going to be a problem.

The research center was bathed in a pool of light, either from the multiple fixtures on the side of the building itself or from the numerous streetlights that dotted the campus. Not only that, but I could spot at least a dozen closed-circuit cameras perched on building corners and mounted on poles. And then there were the campus police to contend with. While Veritas and I watched from DK, the same patrol car drove by the building at least three times in a half hour.

"Think we should wait?" I asked. "See if we spot any openings?"

Veritas sighed and settled into the seat next to me. "Sure. Why not?"

I glanced over at him. He was almost pouting, slouched in the chair with his arms crossed over his chest. "What is your deal lately? I thought you promised to help me when I needed it after I got the license. But now, I have to drag you along."

Veritas looked out his window. "Things change."

I snorted. "Could you be any more vague?"

"Circumstances change. People change. You were gone for how long? Six weeks? Eight? A lot can happen to people during that time, you know, stuff that you weren't around to see."

The sheer venom in Veritas's voice rocked me. Once again, I had apparently messed things up. Here I had come back from the big victory tour and I just assumed that everything would remain the same. I hadn't taken the time to see how Mike was doing. He had gone through some traumatic times before I'd left. Some friend I was turning out to be.

"Bad stuff?" I asked.

Veritas sighed and shook his head. "No, not really. Well, kind of. I guess it depends on who you ask. For the first time in my life, I feel like I'm finally figuring out who I am. On my terms. It's like . . . like there's this magnet in me, drawing me along. And I don't know where it's taking me, but I know it's the right place."

"A place away from your father?"

"Kind of. You don't understand, Failstate. This," he waved a hand over his costume, "was never really my idea. This was all for Dad. His dream, his vision. Lux and Veritas, following in his footsteps. Lux would have the license and I would be her sidekick. And then . . . well, you know."

I did, all too well. For a moment, I was back in the vacant lot in Hogtown, watching as Lux's life bled from her.

Veritas fell silent, and I didn't want to intrude.

Ten minutes later, Veritas spoke again. "The thing is, Dad never asked if this was what I wanted. He just assumed that

I was fine with this. And so long as I was with Lux, I didn't mind. But since her death, since the way my life has changed because of Christ, I see things differently. I think I'm being called to walk a different path. One where I won't need to hide under this mask when I want to do what's right."

I had never imagined he would feel that way. For as long as I could remember, I had wanted to be a hero, to have my official vigilante license. I had always assumed that the other amateur heroes, especially Veritas, had felt the same way. "I'm sorry that I dragged you out here."

He shook his head. "No, don't be. You're right. I made a promise to you and, regardless of my feelings, my word will always be good."

We both fell silent. I looked out of DK and frowned. "Have you seen the security patrol car recently?"

Veritas leaned over to look out my window as well. "Not for the last twenty minutes. Think we should risk it?"

"Let's wait just a little longer and see."

Another twenty minutes crept by. During that time, I exchanged a few texts with Charlene, just checking on her day. Apparently she had gotten hit with an assignment to write a five-page essay on Hammurabi's Code for honors history.

For whatever reason, the security car didn't show. We had to take a chance. I found a place to park DK near the research center and engaged its patrol mode. DK's exterior shifted and turned a mottled brown, as if it had been exposed to the weather for too long. Hopefully no one would give it another glance.

We left DK and jogged across the street, diving into some bushes. I waited for a moment or two, trying to keep my breathing under control. I had no idea what would happen if we were caught trying to break into the research center. Maybe I'd get away with it because of my license, but I figured it was better to not find out the hard way.

When I was sure that no one was approaching, I dashed for the research center. Veritas followed me. We crept around the side of the building and found a set of stairs that led down to a basement entrance. According to the building plans that Magnus had found for us, this lower entrance led to the basement, which contained a boiler room and maintenance storage areas. As near as he could tell, security would be somewhat lax down there. It was easy to see why. The double metal doors didn't have a handle or a doorknob. There was no way to open it from the outside.

Unless you had a "master key"—like me.

I pressed my pointer finger against the flat metal plate screwed to the door where the knob should have been. A little burst of my power drilled through the metal and into the lock behind it. I managed to slip my fingertips into the door's seam and pulled, hauling the door open. Veritas slipped past me inside, and I followed suit. I pushed the door shut again and stacked some crates against the door to keep anyone else from breaking in. I'd have to do something to replace the lock later.

The research center's boiler room was a mass of shadow, filled with twisted pipes that snaked overhead and dove in and out of large tanks and other machinery I couldn't hope to identify. I stifled a groan. If I was this lost in the boiler room, how would I make sense of anything I found in Ayers's office or lab? I should have contacted my friend, an amateur hero named Blowhard. He was a molecular biologist in his secret identity. He would have been great for this. The only problem was that Blowhard lived in Santa Fe.

Thankfully the door that led to the rest of the basement level was unlocked. I glanced up and down the long concrete hallway and didn't see anything to worry about. Veritas and I snuck down the hall to the nearest stairwell.

"Where to first?" Veritas whispered.

"I'm thinking the lab," I whispered back. "It's on the ground floor. If we don't find anything there, we'll move on to his office."

Once we reached the first floor, I poked me head out again and glanced up and down the new hall. We still appeared to be alone. I motioned for Veritas to follow me. We jogged past a number of closed doors until we came to the lab that Ayers's TA had shown Ben and me earlier. I prepared to blow the lock, a numeric keypad, when Veritas knocked my hand away. His eyes went slightly unfocused and his hand jerked up. He tapped at the keys, an unsteady pecking motion, but the lock whirred and clicked. The door popped open.

"After you," he whispered.

I stole into the lab and pulled a small flashlight from my pants pocket. I swept the beam of light over the racks, the shelves, the cluttered tables.

I motioned for Veritas to join me. "You take that side of the room, I'll take this side."

We split up, and I walked along the shelves, studying the bottles. The labels were incomprehensible to me, covered in molecular symbols and names with way too many letters for me to read aloud. I did find a stack of scientific journals, but again, the titles were incomprehensible.

I shouldn't have been surprised. If this was where Ayers taught his students *and* where he created zombies, there'd be no way he'd leave incriminating evidence lying around for the morning class to find. I pursed my lips. I guess we'd have to check every drawer, every nook. Hopefully he'd have left something . . .

The door lock clicked and whirred.

I froze and turned to Veritas. He slid under one of the lab tables. I followed his lead and found refuge under the main desk. I pulled the single chair back in place and hoped that'd be enough.

The door to the lab popped open and a woman's voice drifted through the room. "You really want to see this place again?"

I frowned. It sounded like the girl Ben and I had met earlier.

"Well, I'll confess, I had an ulterior motive. I just wanted to get some alone time with you." Ben's voice.

What was he doing here? I wanted to peek from my hiding place but, at the same time, I figured it was safer to not know, especially given the way the girl was giggling.

"So what is it that Dr. Ayers is researching again? Telo-something-or-other?"

"Telomeres. It's really a fascinating subject. Dr. Ayers believes that it could hold the key to extending our lives by decades, maybe even centuries."

"Get out of here." One of the chairs scraped across the floor. Hopefully it wasn't anywhere near Veritas's hiding place.

"It's true! I mean, first he has to determine how to clear up the connection to certain types of cancer, but if anyone can do it, I'm sure Dr. Ayers can." Another chair scraped across the floor, the sound sending jags down my back. "But I hope you didn't bring me here just to quiz me on Dr. Ayers. Why did you want to get me alone?"

Ben chuckled, deep and throaty. "C'mere."

Oh, this had to be a joke! My fingers dug into my thigh, and I closed my eyes tightly, wishing I could do the same with my ears. Whatever they were doing, the sound wasn't making it into my hiding place, but I did hear the girl's disappointed groan.

"What are you doing?" she asked.

"It sounds like you've got a little crush on Dr. Ayers, huh?" Ben's teasing voice came closer.

"I do not!"

"Oh, I think you do. So do you sit in here and cast longing gazes at him?" Closer still.

I tensed. What was he doing?

The chair that blocked my hiding place pulled back, and Ben's legs appeared. "I can just imagine it. You sit there and you think, 'Oh, Dr. Ayers, if only you'd look at me the way you look at your telomeres.'"

Ben sat in the desk chair. He scooted forward and, though I tried to twist out of the way, his foot still caught me in the knee. His toes nudged my leg once, twice, and then he tried to kick me out of the way. I grabbed his foot and gave it a good yank.

The chair scooted back, and he peeked under the desk. His eyes widened, and I was sure he was about to cry out, but I held a finger up against my mouth, willing him to keep quiet.

"What is it?"

Ben's eyes blazed at me angrily and he sat up. "Nothing. I'd just rather get you someplace more romantic. Unless you find test tubes a turn-on?"

"No. Let's go."

"Great." Ben shielded his body from Tricia's vision, reached into his back pocket, and pulled out his wallet. He chucked it under the desk, hard enough that it bounced off my forehead.

Footsteps faded, and the door opened. The lights overhead turned off, and I let out a long sigh. Although they had left, I still waited a few seconds to make sure that they weren't going to come back. After counting to sixty, I picked up Ben's wallet and crawled out from under the desk.

Veritas emerged from his hiding place as well and adjusted his mask. "What was he doing here?"

"I have no idea."

The lock clicked and whirred again. I started for my hiding place, but before I could make it, the door popped open and Ben slid inside.

"What are you two idiots doing?" he demanded.

"I could ask you the same thing." I threw his wallet back to him.

He snatched it out of the air. "I thought I could get Tricia to tell me something about Ayers's research, something that could help you."

"Where is she?" I shot a glance at the door. "We don't have to worry about her—"

"Nah, I told her I lost my wallet. She told me the lock's code so I could get it. You're welcome, by the way."

"You two aren't going to start brawling again, are you?" Veritas asked. "Because I don't want to be in the middle if you do."

His softly spoken question cut through me. He was right: I was being stupid.

The lock whirred once more. Ben rushed to the door and caught it before Tricia could open it the rest of the way.

"What's taking you so long?" she asked.

"I couldn't find it in here. I really hate to say it, but I think I'm going to have to cut this short so I can go find it. Walk you back to your dorm?"

"Oh. Sure, I guess."

"Great." Ben slipped through the door.

I counted to thirty and then risked a peek into the hallway. They had disappeared. I turned back to Veritas. "Let's keep looking."

He nodded and went back to his side of the room. I focused on the desk, pulling open the drawers and looking through the contents. The center drawer held paper clips, pens, and random scraps of paper with notations on them. I pulled out my cell phone and snapped pictures of them. They probably wouldn't be helpful, but at least now I'd be able to look into them. The other drawers held syllabuses, corrected tests, and reams of lecture notes.

A half hour crawled by, but Veritas and I didn't find anything helpful. Then the door opened.

Ben slipped back in. "Sorry I took so long. Tricia . . . well, she didn't want to say good night just yet."

"Did she tell you anything?" I asked.

Ben shook his head. "Nothing helpful. I was being half-serious when I accused her of having a crush on this guy. She wouldn't shut up about what a genius he is. Going on and on about how smart he is and how brilliant his theories are." He looked at us both. "I assume you two found something more interesting."

"We may have, yes, but not from looking around here." I explained about the power spikes.

Ben listened to it all, his lips pursed. "Well, you're obviously looking in the wrong place. Do you see anything in here that would gobble up electricity like that?"

He had a point. "So we should go check out his office."

"That's where I would start." He started to unbutton his shirt. "Hang on a sec."

I stared as he stripped off his shirt and pants. He wore his Gauntlet costume underneath. Sure, he didn't have his shoulder armor or greaves, but he was still identifiable. He reached over his shoulders and pulled his mask up and over his face.

"Good to go. Lead on, Failstate."

I opened the door and peeked down the hall. Still empty. We dashed down the hall to the nearest stairwell and took the steps upward two at a time until we emerged by the graduate students research cubbies. I easily found Dr. Ayers's office again. Unfortunately, this door didn't have a keypad, so I sent a quick spike of destructive energy into the knob and slid the door open.

There was barely enough room in Dr. Ayers's office for all of us. Three of the four walls were dominated by bookshelves stuffed full with papers, journals, and textbooks. A tiny metal desk filled the rest of the space with an office chair behind it. A docking port for a laptop sat on one side of the desk, but the computer was missing. Otherwise, the desk was filled with papers, scraps of notes, and three open textbooks. Pushed to one side was the picture of a woman, probably in her mid-thirties. Her eyes sparkled as she smiled at the camera, her hair cascading down to her shoulders in blond waves. Most likely his wife, given the sheer size of the photo.

"Well, isn't this cozy?" Gauntlet asked. "So what are we looking for?"

"I have no idea," I said. "Anything about the zombies, anything about . . ."

The doorknob rattled. I looked at the door and then at my friends. Where were all three of us going to hide this time?

"You've got to be kidding me!" Veritas muttered.

Before we could move, the door swung open, and I blinked in surprise.

"Well, well, well," Kynetic said. "Looks like this is my lucky night."

CHAPTER 29

"WHAT ARE YOU DOING HERE?" I asked.

Kynetic squeezed into the office and pulled the door closed behind her. "Following up on a lead. Earlier today, I noticed that the fires from last night were on a straight line. I tracked it back to this building. I thought I'd poke around and see what I could find." She smiled at me. "You must have had the same idea, F."

"If I would have known, I would've had Tricia stick around," Gauntlet said. "We could've doubled."

Veritas elbowed him in the gut.

Kynetic turned to Veritas and Gauntlet. "Pleasure to meet you two. I'm fans of both your work." A worried expression flittered across her face. "So are you two sidekicking for Failstate?"

Gauntlet snorted. "As if."

Veritas shook his head as well.

Kynetic's radiant smile returned. "Then the position is open still. Good!" She turned back to me. "So what's the plan, boss?"

I squeezed past Veritas so I could stand behind Ayers's desk. "We check out everything in this office and hope we find something. With four of us, it shouldn't take too long."

"Not unless we waste time trying to breathe," Gauntlet said.

I ignored his complaint and sat down in Ayers's chair. I looked over the papers on his desk. A class schedule, a list of names along with student ID numbers, syllabi for his courses. Nothing about zombies. Huh. Maybe I'd have to check his desk drawers.

I tried to scoot the chair back so I could open one of the drawers but found that the chair wouldn't move. I frowned and tried again, digging in with my feet and pushing. Nothing. I twisted around to peek at the floor. The chair was bolted down.

"Hey, look at this, you guys!" I said.

Gauntlet tried to get around the desk at the same time as Veritas. The two of them wound up wrestling for a moment and in the process, they jostled the picture of Ayers's wife. The frame pitched forward. I tried to grab it but was too late. I winced at the sound of glass breaking.

But then I paused. A thin wire ran from the picture frame's leg and into the desk.

I frowned at it. What was this about? I picked up the frame and tugged on it. The wire didn't have a lot of give to it. I turned the frame over and ignored the long crack that ran across the woman's face. It wasn't a digital picture frame, so the wire wasn't a power source. What was it?

There. A series of roses had been carved into the frame's pewter, but in the middle of one bud was a small button. I tugged off one of my gloves and poked the button.

With a soft hiss, the desk chair sank into the floor.

The sudden move threw me off balance. I dropped the frame, and my arms pinwheeled. Gauntlet reached out and snared me. He helped me step over the hole in the floor. I peered down it. The chair had disappeared into darkness below.

I looked up at Gauntlet, Veritas, and Kynetic. "Do you think every professor on campus has a secret elevator like this?"

"If they do, they neglected to mention it on the orientation tour," Gauntlet said.

Kynetic smirked at him and stepped over to the hole. "Let's see what's down there." She stepped into the hole and tucked her arms at her sides.

Veritas shouted as she dropped.

I looked over the hole. "You okay?"

No answer. But then, Kynetic's voice drifted up from below. "Come down here! You have to see this!"

"You'll catch me again?" I asked.

"I'd never drop you."

I looked up at Gauntlet. He quirked a brow at me. "Catch you again? Something you're not telling me?"

"It's a long story," I said.

"I'll bet." Gauntlet glanced at Veritas. "And he got mad when I showed up with a date."

My cheeks burned underneath my hood. At least I could escape him quickly.

Sucking in a deep breath, I stepped over the hole and dropped. I fell down the shaft and then came to a sudden halt.

Kynetic had caught me. She smiled and set me on my feet. Then she looked up again. "Come on down, boys. I won't drop you either."

A second later, Veritas fell from the hole in the ceiling. Kynetic easily snatched him out of the air. Her knees didn't buckle or anything. Instead, Veritas came to an absolute stop in her arms. She set him on the ground and patted his shoulders.

"Okay, Gauntlet, your turn."

"I'm good, thanks."

My brother floated down through the hole. He passed over our heads before touching down as if he were stepping off a low stepstool.

Kynetic crossed her arms. "Show off."

"Look who's talking," Gauntlet said.

I glanced at Kynetic. "Do you need to release the energy?"

She shook her head. "I'd rather hold on to it, just in case. But if I start getting twitchy in a half hour, find me something to break, okay?"

"So what do we have here?" Gauntlet asked.

Dim lights flickered in the shadows. I could see a wavering glow, like a wall of glass with water behind it. I pulled out my flashlight and shone it around the room. Glass glinted at me, and I spotted computers, more racks of vials, lab equipment. In many ways, it looked like the lab upstairs. But this time, I couldn't shake the feeling of an oppressive weight bearing down on me.

"Let's find a light, okay?" My voice was little more than a whisper.

We spread out, and I found a light switch. A second later, the overhead lights snapped on. Several computers were pushed up against one side of the room. Another wall was nothing but a cabinet filled with vials, beakers, and test tubes. Up against the third wall were half a dozen metal cylinders, each large enough to hold a person, all of them submerged in a thick liquid. In the middle of the room was a machine, a seventh cylinder connected to it by a series of metal hoses. There was a thick metal door on a roller track on the wall opposite the glass one.

"Failstate, look at this." Gauntlet waved at me from by the shelves.

I stepped over to him. He pointed to a rack of test tubes on a head-high shelf. I couldn't identify what was in them, some sort of viscous liquid and grey tissue. Each one was labeled with red letters written in the same handwriting. But instead of chemical symbols or other data, each one bore a name: "IRISA," "X-CUTION," "NOMAD." Huh. What was this about?

"And look at this!" Gauntlet pointed at a lower shelf.

Another rack of test tubes, much smaller. There weren't that many, and these appeared to contain blood samples. This time, the labels didn't have names but long strings of letters and numbers. An encrypted ID of some kind? What was he trying to accomplish?

Kynetic waved me over to one corner of the lab. She had found a rack of clothing, dull grey pants and shirts that looked like hospital scrubs, just like what all the zombies had worn.

"This is it, folks. We've got it." I turned around and spotted Veritas seated at one of the computers. "You have anything over there?"

He nodded. "Dr. Ayers may be a genius, but he's lousy when it comes to computer security. His password was 'Gail.' His wife's name."

I jogged over to his side. "What'd you find?"

"Not much yet. Lots of research notes I can't decipher. References to molecular engineering, cellular regeneration. I can't make heads or tails of it right now, but—"

A whir cut through his words. I turned in time to see the office chair rise back through the hole in the ceiling.

"Did you do that?" I asked Kynetic.

"I wouldn't know how even if I wanted to. Maybe it's automatic?"

"Then how would you get out again?" Gauntlet asked, looking up at the ceiling.

I heard footsteps above us, and then an ominous click. That couldn't be good.

A second later, the chair started descending. As it did, a voice floated down from the top floor. ". . . don't know what set it off. My office is trashed. Probably a frat prank. They like to break into the science building every year and steal something. Last year it was a skeleton . . . I don't know what they'd want of mine. Hey, the lights are on."

The chair dropped into view. Sitting on it was Dr. Floyd Ayers. He was wearing a trench coat over a pair of jeans. He had a cell phone held to his ear, but he stopped talking when he saw me. His jaw dropped open, and his hand fell limply into his lap.

I stepped forward and jammed my fists onto my hips in what I hoped looked like an intimidating pose. "Dr. Ayers? We have some questions for you."

Ayers froze, his eyes as wide and round as the lenses in his glasses. "What are you doing here?"

"I think that's a question *you* had better answer, Doctor." I jerked a thumb over my shoulder at the device in the center of the room. "That thing wouldn't be for growing zombies, would it?"

Before I could reach him, Dr. Ayers pulled a device from his pocket, a small box with a series of buttons and switches on it. He mashed his hands on the buttons. An alarm ripped through the lab, and with a loud gurgle the fluid behind the glass wall began to drain through a grate in the floor.

That was all the time Dr. Ayers needed. He hit another button, and the chair started to ascend back for the ceiling. "I'm sorry." His words were drowned out by the sound of rushing liquids.

I lashed out with my power and tried to slice through the chair's base. A large gouge appeared in the metal, but it wasn't enough to stop it. At the same time, Kynetic rushed the chair and slammed into it, setting the entire column rocking. But it was too late. The chair disappeared into the ceiling.

"Failstate!" Gauntlet pointed toward the glass wall.

The liquid had drained completely and with a ponderous groan, the glass wall opened. Then, with a hiss, the metal tubes dropped into the floor, revealing three zombies.

Sort of.

All of them were obviously human, and their skin was patchy and mottled. But unlike the zombies I had faced before, these seemed more normal. Almost human. Instead of slouching and shambling, they stood erect. Their skin didn't seem quite as decayed. And a definite intelligence shone in their eyes. These were no mindless drones.

The moment they saw us, they recoiled and hissed, baring mouths full of teeth. One of the three, a young woman, clapped her hands together, and her body erupted in blue flames.

The second looked a lot like the strapper that Gauntlet, Veritas, and I had fought a few nights earlier—all muscles and long arms.

The third zombie's body rippled and expanded, as if it were made out of water. His lips twitched back into a feral snarl.

Three superpowered zombies. This was going to get ugly.

CHAPTER 30

BEFORE I COULD REACT, the water zombie exploded from his platform, racing at me. His body expanded into a large sheet as he ran, stretching out to envelope me like a damp towel. I tried to dodge, but he still caught me by the arm. His hands wrapped around me, twisting up my limbs like a python. I thrashed and, in my panic, my power spiked.

The floor beneath us turned gelatinous and rippled like a wave, throwing the zombie off balance. He slipped and fell. I shoved away from him and scrambled for the others.

Gauntlet, Veritas, and Kynetic ran to me, and we stood back-to-back. The other two zombies crept from the platform, their mouths working as they clacked and hissed at us. While they definitely appeared smarter than the previous zombies I'd faced, apparently the good doctor hadn't hooked up their vocal chords yet. Or maybe he didn't want to.

"Any ideas?" I asked. "Do we run?"

212

"That might be wise. It took three of us to take out the big guy last time." Veritas dropped into a relaxed ready position, his hands up and clenched into fists. "But it's your call."

"Forget running." Gauntlet tensed next to me. "Let's see what these freaks can do!" With a roar, he charged the strong man zombie and slammed into him.

The sound of the impact was almost deafening. But the zombie didn't go down. Instead, he drew back his arms and boxed Gauntlet on the sides of his head with his fists. Gauntlet stumbled and collapsed to one knee. The zombie cocked back his fist.

Gauntlet held up his hands. The air in front of him shimmered. Was he trying to erect a telekinetic shield? If he was, it didn't help: The zombie punched through and caught Gauntlet across the cheek. Gauntlet fell to the floor, unconscious.

"No!" The scream ripped from my lips, and I leapt forward. I charged my fists with my power and punched the zombie in its stomach.

The pain in my knuckles was excruciating, but the creature grunted and stumbled backward. Before I could press my advantage, though, the burning girl cupped a hand and threw a massive fireball at me. I ducked but still felt the heat slice over my head.

Veritas backed away from three of the other zombies who were steadily advancing on him. "With all these chemicals, we're lucky we haven't been blown to bits yet!"

"I'm not hearing any ideas!" I shouted as another gout of flames roared past me.

"How about we take this fight out of the lab?" Kynetic ran to one end of the lab and pulled back on a large metallic door on a roller track. It revealed a long tunnel beyond, one that disappeared into darkness.

"We have no idea where that thing comes out!" Veritas said.

"True, but at least it won't be here," Kynetic countered. "Your call, boss!"

I looked down the tunnel. Better the scary unknown than getting blown up, I figured. "Let's go!" I snared Gauntlet's hands and dragged him across the floor toward the door.

But the Strong Man apparently wasn't done with us yet. He stomped after me and swung at my head.

Kynetic darted around me and caught the punch on her open palm. She didn't even flinch. The zombie glared at her and swung again. Once again, she parried the blow and apparently absorbed the energy.

She laughed. "I can do this all day, honey!"

Strong Man punched the floor and charged. He slammed into her but she didn't even falter. He pushed and shoved but it was like Kynetic was an unmovable pillar. She actually fake yawned, as if the whole encounter bored her. She turned to me and smiled.

But then Water-Boy rose up behind her, his arms snaking out like long tentacles. Before I could warn her, the zombie lashed out and wrapped his arms around her neck.

Kynetic gasped, her eyes wide, and her hand snared the zombie's arm, trying to pry it off. But Water-Boy's arm was too much like taffy. For every bit she pulled away, more of the arm flowed back to choke her. She thrashed and kicked. One of her blows connected with Strong Man and blew him off his feet, almost as though a train had collided with him. But as much as she struggled, she couldn't break free.

"No!" I dropped Gauntlet's arms and charged forward, marshaling my power.

But what could I do? My powers had never been good at destroying organic material, and the zombies qualified. Was there some way that I could . . .

My powers spiked, and the wall behind Water-Boy boiled. One bubble popped, releasing a jet of steam that sprayed concrete shards into Water-Boy's back.

The zombie howled and dropped Kynetic. I bent down next to her, frantic. Was she okay? Was she even breathing?

Her chest heaved, and she coughed. She nodded at me.

I wanted to yell at her, hug her, do something. But Flaming Zombie Girl wasn't about to allow me a breather. She threw more fiery bolts in my direction. I ducked and dodged, but one of them burst on my sleeve. The heat ripped through me, and I yelped, frantically patting it out. What hadn't my clothes turned into armor that time?

Gauntlet groaned and wobbled to his feet. "I miss anything interesting?"

"We're getting out of here." I shoved him for the tunnel.

I glanced at Veritas. The fiery zombie hadn't touched him yet, but she was getting awfully close.

"Veritas, down!" Gauntlet clapped his hands together.

Veritas dropped to the ground just as a wave of telekinetic energy rippled through the air. It slammed into the burning zombie and knocked her off her feet.

"Get Kynetic out of here!" I shouted.

Veritas grabbed Kynetic and led her for the door.

I turned to face our opponents. The flaming girl was climbing to her feet. Strong Man had regained his balance. He slammed his fists together in a deafening bang. And Water-Boy looked about ready to tear me apart.

I backpedaled for the open door. Strong Man pounded the ground with his fists and then, with a gurgling bellow, charged at me.

I stomped my foot on the floor, sending out a wave of ripples through the cement. One of them caught Strong Man as he ran, and he stumbled, pitching headlong into a metal cabinet.

I had made it into the tunnel. I looked above me, unsure of what the tunnel ran under. Had I made it out from under the research center? I had no idea. Best to keep moving.

The zombies apparently had decided to be a little more cautious this time. They didn't charge me, but they didn't give up either. They crept forward, snarling and gnashing their teeth at me. Strong Man really appeared furious. I kept backing up, ready to counter any attack that came my way.

Then I backed into what felt like a solid object. I glanced over my shoulder and found Gauntlet standing next to me.

"You coming or what?" he asked.

I smirked. "Actually, I could use your help here. Think you can give the ceiling a good telekinetic blast when I tell you to?"

He peered up at the ceiling. "Sure, but what good will that do? Looks pretty solid."

"Leave that to me. Get ready." I braced myself.

The zombies paused. Water-Boy cocked his head to one side, regarding me with wide eyes.

"Now!" As I shouted, I lashed out toward the ceiling with my power. I tried to picture hundreds of little blades made of invisible destructive energy, chased by my ability to warp matter. Hopefully, coupled with a good blast from Gauntlet, we could—

The ceiling overhead groaned and, in a shower of concrete and dust, it collapsed, blocking the tunnel.

I scrambled away from the debris as quickly as I could. Gauntlet pulled me the last several feet. As soon as it was clear we weren't going to get pulverized by falling debris, he clapped me on the shoulder.

"Good thinking, little brother. Now what?"

I turned around to look down the tunnel. "Let's go."

The tunnel curved toward the right. We found Veritas and Kynetic waiting for us. We kept going for what felt like half a mile. The tunnel itself was empty, the only features the occasional bare bulb set in the middle of the ceiling. Eventually the floor started to slope upward, and we finally found ourselves in front of a set of garage doors with a large control panel next to them.

I glanced at Veritas, who shrugged. May as well try it. I hit the button marked "Open" and took a step back.

With a roaring clatter, the door rolled into the ceiling. I took a cautious step through the opening and into some sort of alley. I didn't recognize the neighborhood, but we clearly hadn't gone far from the NCU campus.

"Any idea where we are?" I asked.

Gauntlet turned around slowly but then shook his head. "None."

"Is everyone okay?"

Veritas patted his stomach. "They never laid a hand on me."

Gauntlet chuckled. "You're lucky."

"Kyn, how about—?"

Before I could finish my question, she launched at me, catching me in a massive hug. I blinked in surprise, but then she pushed up my hood just a little and kissed me. The movement caught me off guard, especially since she didn't seem at all repulsed by my natural lips. I froze, but then, without really thinking about it, my arms wrapped around her, and she melted into me. Her heady aroma, sweet and slightly spicy, washed over me and—

Veritas cleared his throat.

My eyes popped open. What was I doing? I gently disentangled myself from her and took a step back, tugging my hood back into place. She smiled at me and winked.

My cheeks burned, the heat reflected by the fabric.

"Well, now that we know everyone is okay, what's our next step?" Gauntlet asked.

I pulled out my cell phone and hit the speed dial for Downtime. "Now we bring in the cavalry."

CHAPTER
31

WHILE I EXPLAINED the situation to Downtime over the phone, Gauntlet and Veritas scouted the neighborhood and returned.

"We're just a few blocks from Club Row," Veritas reported. "There's a parking garage just down the block. Maybe we can have everyone meet us there?"

I relayed the suggestion to Downtime, who promised to summon as many other heroes as he could. I knew it would be a hard sell to some of them, like Raze, but maybe the lure of the zombie lair would be enough to get them there. I hung up the phone and motioned for Veritas to lead the way.

The four of us jogged down the alley and out onto the street. We came out by the parking garage, a four story structure. We took the stairs and emerged on the upper deck. Thankfully the top level, open to the night sky, was mostly empty.

Kynetic stroked my arm and smiled. "I'm going to go keep an eye out for the others, okay?"

She slunk away, an extremely obvious wiggle in her hips.

The moment she was out of earshot, Gauntlet turned to me. "So . . . anything you want to tell us?"

I stammered for a few moments. "Not really, no."

"Is there something you should be telling Charlene?" Veritas's voice was laced with venom.

"No!"

Veritas's eyes narrowed, and I could practically feel his mental probe ram into my brain.

I tried to wave the sensation away, but it only intensified. "Will you knock it off? I'm not lying! Yes, Kyn seems to like me, but—"

"'Kyn'?" Veritas asked.

"'Seems to'?" Gauntlet added.

I growled. "This wasn't my idea."

"Maybe not, but you didn't seem all that upset by it either." Gauntlet chuckled and lightly punched me on the arm. "I always knew you had it in you. Following in your big brother's footsteps, you heartbreaker."

I knocked his hand away.

"Oh ho! I seem to have struck a nerve." Gauntlet laughed.

"I don't think this is all that funny," Veritas said. "What do you actually know about her?"

I mouthed a few half-answers, not really speaking, before I shrugged with one shoulder. "She's really nice."

That only made Gauntlet laugh harder. Veritas shook his head.

I didn't need this abuse. I turned and stomped away. Gauntlet called my name but I ignored him. Hopefully the other licensed heroes would show up soon, and we could get down to business and end this ridiculous business.

"Problems?" Kyn leaned against the edge of garage's wall, her head tipped down and a seductive smile on her lips. Her soft, inviting lips . . .

I shook my head. "No, not really. They're . . . They mean well."

"I'm sure they do. I'm sorry if you found that awkward back there, but I wanted to thank you properly for saving my life." She regarded me with a coy expression. "So did you like that?"

My mouth went dry. Without really thinking about it, I nodded.

"I thought so." She took a step forward. "You know, I'm really the best one to be your sidekick. There's a lot we could learn from each other."

A pleasant haze rippled through my mind. That sounded like a really great idea. I'd be able to spend more time with Kynetic, which would be awesome. With her at my side, I could get some really positive press. And the long nights on patrol wouldn't be quite so lonely. Besides, it wasn't as if Charlene and I were exclusive or anything.

I had an awesome thought: Could I have Charlene as my girlfriend when I was Rob and Kynetic as my sidekick/girlfriend when I was Failstate?

Wait, what was I thinking? I shook my head, trying desperately to clear it. I couldn't do that! I barely knew Kynetic! I had no idea if she'd make a good sidekick, though her prowess would definitely be useful. And what about Charlene? Okay, so we hadn't become anything official, but sneaking around with another girl, even if I was in my alter ego, didn't seem like the right thing to do.

"Kyn . . . I . . . I . . ." And yet the words wouldn't make it out of my throat.

She sighed and her head dipped. "You don't have to say anything. I get it. I—"

"I trust I am not interrupting anything, am I?"

Kyn winced and doubled over. A wave of nausea roiled through me. And suddenly, a tower of darkness stood next to me, a cloak whipping in the wind.

Etzal'el stared down at me and, even though I couldn't see his eyes underneath his hood, I had a feeling he didn't approve.

"I was wondering if you were still in town," Kyn grumbled.

"I do not answer to you, temptress." He turned to me. "I have received the summons. Where are those foul abominations?"

"In a lab not too far from here," I said.

"Then why do we delay? We must go and smite these blasphemous creations before they have a chance to escape." The vehemence in Etzal'el's voice sent a flood of ice down my back.

"D-d-don't you think we should wait for the others?" I turned to Kynetic, hoping she'd back me up, but she was look-ing positively sick.

"If you wish. But I shall scout ahead and assess the situa-tion. If I believe it warrants my intervention, I shall not wait." Etzal'el seemed to flow from the garage floor onto the wall. Then he simply stepped off the edge.

I started to call out for him to stop, but instead of drop-ping, he rushed through the night sky, soaring off into the darkness.

The moment he left, Kyn straightened and took a few deep breaths. "I hate when that guy is around. Always make me feel like I'm going to spew all over the place." She regarded me with curious eyes. "Doesn't he affect you the same way?"

"Not really." I mean, sure, he creeped me out, and I had felt unsettled both times I'd seen him, but nothing as bad as Kyn was describing.

"Huh. I wonder why that is?"

A figure dropped out of the sky with sound of rushing winds. Elemental smiled at me. "Good to see you again, Failstate."

"Ma'am." I nodded in greeting.

She laughed, a quick chortle. "Failstate, we are colleagues. There is no need for such formality." Elemental eyed Kynetic for a moment. "I hope you're staying out of trouble."

Kynetic smiled sweetly at her mentor, but I could see the venom lurking in her eyes. "Of course."

"I am glad to hear that." Elemental's tone was too guarded, though, as if she didn't really believe Kyn. "Well, I can't wait to hear what you've found." She smiled at me once again and headed over to greet Veritas and Gauntlet.

"What was that all about?" I whispered to Kyn.

Kyn rolled her eyes. "Elemental and I haven't always seen eye-to-eye when it comes to 'proper conduct' as heroes. That's why I was hoping I could find a more willing licensed hero. Someone who could really help me make a splash." She traced a finger across my chest. "We could be really good together."

"I told you, I have a girl already . . ."

"You'd forget about her easily enough. Believe me. I can be very persuasive."

I took her hand and tried to move it from my chest, but it felt as though it were glued in place. "Kyn, I just don't think that's a good idea."

She snorted. "Oh, come on. What can that other girl offer you that I can't? You're exactly what I need."

Her words lodged in my mind. "I'm what you need? Really?"

"Sure. We need each other. I scratch your back, you scratch mine. And we'll have some fun along the way." Her arms twined around my neck, and she pressed herself up against me. "What do you say?"

"You just can't take no for an answer, can you?"

Kyn smiled, but now there was a sharpness to her expression. "Not when I see something I want."

I paused, comprehension dawning on me. "My license. That's it, isn't it? You want a license too. You couldn't get it with the other heroes, and now you don't think you can get it by teaming with Elemental, so now what? You upgrade to me? Think you'll get your license that much faster?"

Kyn looked away and scratched behind her ear. "That is not the case."

I snarled. "I don't need to be Veritas to know when someone's lying to me."

She glared at me. "I don't need to take this from you! I'm out of here!" She stormed away.

For a moment, I wanted to go after her, apologize for my harsh words. Then I realized how stupid I was being. That's exactly what she'd want. I turned and walked back to the rest of the group.

"Problems?" Elemental asked.

I nodded.

Elemental sighed. "I'm sorry. I should have warned you about Kyn. She means well, really, but she's a little ambitious."

I didn't doubt that at all. I once again tried to find the right words to say, but never got the chance. Downtime dropped from the sky just as Raze came up from the lower levels of the garage, followed by Dr. Olympus and the half dozen other heroes who had sided with him at the conclave.

"So what'd you find, kid?" Raze asked.

I fought the urge to glare at him. Or gloat. "I've found the source of the zombies. There's a secret lab under New Chayton University, and a man named Dr. Floyd Ayers is the one creating them."

"Dr. Ayers," Dr. Olympus said. "I know Dr. Ayers. There's no way that he would—"

"Why don't you just listen to what Failstate has to say?" Gauntlet asked.

"Who's this kid?" Raze's gaze swept over Gauntlet from boots to mask.

"This is Gauntlet," I said. "And that's Veritas. They helped me in the lab and—"

"They your sidekicks?" Raze asked.

"No!" Gauntlet and Veritas answered the question simultaneously.

Raze snorted. "Then what are they even doing here? Get lost, brats. There are adults working here."

Gauntlet bristled. "Now hold on just a minute!"

Raze shooed him with a dismissive wave. "Go on, beat it, cream puff, before you get hurt."

Several of the other heroes nodded and murmured in agreement. That portion of Gauntlet's skin that peeked out from under his mask reddened, and his hands clenched into fists.

Uh-oh. I had seen that look before. If I didn't step in and stop this, we'd have a brawl on the roof of this garage, and that wouldn't help anyone.

"All right, let's settle down," I said, hoping I'd injected enough steel into my voice. "They may not be my official sidekicks, but I've worked with both Veritas and Gauntlet before, and I value their input." I tried to stand as tall as I could. "So if you've got a problem with them, you take it up with me."

Raze appeared to consider it. He clenched and unclenched his hands several times before he laughed. "Fair enough, rookie. Let's keep going."

I breathed a sigh of relief. "So like I was saying. There's a lab—"

"—under New Chayton University," Raze motioned for me to hurry up. "We got that part. What I haven't heard is why this doctor would be making zombies in the first place. Any ideas about that?"

"Not really, but he did lose his wife. Maybe he's trying to figure out a way to resurrect her somehow?"

"Oh, please," Raze rolled his eyes.

"You might be surprised," Veritas said quietly. "There are some people who'd be willing to do just about anything if it meant they could bring back someone they love."

I looked at him and wondered what things *he* had contemplated, if it might mean bringing back his sister. "At any rate," I said to Raze, "when we escaped there were three zombies left in the lab. We had them trapped, but there's a chance they could escape."

A car squealed around the corner of the garage and came to a stop right next to us. I frowned at it, wondering who would be crazy enough to drive like that in the middle of the night and approach a group of superheroes in such an aggressive fashion.

Agent Sexton kicked open the car's door and stormed out of it, making a beeline for me. "You want to explain yourself, Failstate?"

"I'm discussing the situation with everyone right now. We're going to—"

"Do you know what you've done? You've stirred up some sort of hornet's nest over at the campus. There are zombies everywhere!"

What? "Define 'everywhere.'"

"According to campus police, dozens of zombies have come out of the research center and are tearing up the campus." He poked me in the chest. "So what are you going to do about it?"

Raze stomped a foot, and the whole parking garage shook under the impact. "I'll tell you what we're going to do! We're going to go after them and take them out! Who's with me?"

The other heroes roared their approval. Raze pointed in the direction of the campus and they surged forward. Downtime and Elemental took to the air, and the others either raced for the stairs or simply jumped over the edge of the garage wall.

Gauntlet nudged me. "Let's go, Failstate. We've got work to do."

I nodded absently. I'd have to figure the rest of it out later.

CHAPTER
32

THE OTHERS HAD A GOOD HEAD START on us, but we were able to catch up with them. The entire group charged down the middle of the street, apparently not caring that oncoming traffic was having to stop or swerve to get out of the way. But then, if half a dozen superheroes were charging down the street, I'd get out of the way too.

Dr. Olympus offered me a feral grin. "I look forward to doing battle at your side, Failstate! We are sure to win the day!" With a loud war cry, she charged forward.

Off in the distance we heard the sounds of screams, followed by loud booms and explosions. I tamped down on my power before it could spike.

"Okay, folks, here's the drill," Raze shouted. "Strappers up front, as always. We'll take the fight to the zombies and do our best to take them out. Boosters, you focus on rescuing the civilians. Cognits . . ." He snorted. "Just try not to get in the way. That goes for you too, Failstate."

My throat constricted to keep me from saying something I knew I'd regret. I'd show him. I'd show all of them.

"Stay focused, call for help when you need it, and—" Raze grunted and gasped. He fell to one knee. "Oh, no. Not now!"

Etzal'el dropped out of the sky, darkness rippling out of him like a burst water balloon. "It is good that you are all here. The situation is dire!"

"Will you get out of here, Spooky?" Raze grunted. "You're not exactly helping."

Etzal'el growled, which sounded like broken glass grinding together, but he launched into the air, disappearing into the night.

Raze shook his head and started running again. I could still hear his profanities just fine.

The campus looked like a the set of a disaster movie. Three cars had been flipped and were burning. Zombies shuffled through the streets, banging on the doors and windows of the nearby buildings. A city bus careened down the street, the exterior covered in the undead, and slammed into a fire hydrant.

"All right, let's end this! Go!" Raze took off into the midst of what looked like a zombie scrum.

Then bodies flew through the air, almost as if a bomb went off, revealing Raze in the epicenter. Elemental swooped down from on high, and large jets of flame burst from her hands, cutting through the ranks of the zombies and turning them to charcoal. The smell of roasted meat washed over me. I gagged.

I looked around. The other heroes joined the fight, all of them except for Veritas and Gauntlet. I glanced at them. "What are you waiting for?"

"You," Gauntlet said. "Raze may think he's in charge, but I don't answer to that jerk."

Veritas nodded. "I agree. What's our next move?"

Before I could answer, Etzal'el dropped out of the sky next to us. Veritas and Gauntlet didn't seem affected all that much by his presence either. Weird.

"Come, I must show you something." He charged the nearest cluster of zombies and lashed out with his cloak. Zombies were knocked off their feet and tumbled in every direction.

I followed in Etzal'el's wake, ready in case he missed a zombie. But I didn't have to worry. The undead didn't stand a chance against him. We went deeper and deeper into the campus, Etzal'el clearing the way while the others ran after me, until we were only half a block away from the research center.

Etzal'el leveled a finger at the building. "See for yourself."

It was like ants coming out of an anthill. Zombies boiled out through the doors and windows, charging off into the night. New ones emerged every second. I didn't have to do the math to see the problem: Dr. Ayers was somehow pumping out more zombies than we could destroy. Unless we could all fight indefinitely, we would eventually be overwhelmed.

"That's a lot of zombies," I said. "How's he cranking out that many?"

"I believe I may have part of the answer. Observe." Etzal'el whipped out the edge of his cloak. The shadow rippled out and snared four passing zombies, lassoing them together into a writhing mass. Etzal'el flicked his arm, and the knot of bodies was yanked back to us. "Look at their features."

I winced. Unlike the superpowered zombies we had fought in the lab, these were definitely dead creatures. Their faces were decayed and broken, the flesh barely holding together. I groaned and swallowed the bile that threatened to crawl up my throat.

"Disgusting!" Gauntlet said.

"Look closer." Etzal'el shoved the writing mass toward us.

I took a step back. What was so special about these zombies? They snarled and clacked at us, their flesh mottled and their hair stringy. Their hair . . .

I took a closer look. Etzal'el had caught two men and two women. The men both had the same auburn hair while the women had black hair. But that wasn't the only similarity. While different parts of their faces had rotted away, it was pretty clear that the men shared the same facial features. So did the women. Twins? Maybe.

I looked at some of the other zombies. They all wore the same faces. All the males looked the same, and all the females looked the same, as if these zombies came from only two models.

"Clones?" I whispered. Why would anyone want to clone zombies?

Etzal'el snapped his cloak out, and the zombies he held tumbled end over end onto the ground. "I do not know. But one thing is clear: Unless we make it into the lab and stop whatever process is creating these abominations, we will—"

"Look out!" Gauntlet shouted.

The zombies Etzal'el had just freed charged him. Etzal'el whirled and threw open his hands. Shadows erupted from his fingers and rushed across the ground, blasting through the zombies until nothing remained but bits of bone and flesh. Those remains crumbled to dust and vanished.

But that attracted the attention of the other zombies. At least two dozen veered off from their rampage and headed straight for us.

I prepared for the fight, but Etzal'el stepped between them and us.

"Go! I will hold them off. You three, find a way into the lab and stop Dr. Ayers."

Etzal'el launched himself at the zombies. Shadows erupted from his cloak and rushed across the ground, enveloping a mass of zombies. The darkness swallowed up a large chunk of the streets.

"You heard the man!" Gauntlet said. "Let's go!"

"How are we supposed to get in there?" Veritas asked. "A frontal assault on the research center would end badly for us."

"True," Gauntlet said. "It's a shame you brought down the tunnel. We could have used that to get—"

"That's it!" I whirled on Veritas. "Do you think you can find where the tunnel is?"

Veritas looked around and nodded. "It's not far from here. Come on."

He led us through the carnage. Gauntlet worked to clear the way, knocking aside the zombies that emerged from the research center as Veritas searched the ground. Finally, he found a large part of the campus green that had collapsed in on itself, as if whatever was underneath it had vanished. It had to be where I had caved in the tunnel.

"Here goes everything," I muttered.

I stood between the cave in and the research center and summoned my destructive energy. I imagined it turning into a wedge with the point digging into the earth. Then I pushed it downward. My powers slowly ate away at the ground beneath me.

A zombie gurgled a challenge and charged at me. My concentration faltered, and the field fell apart. I raised my hands and lashed out with my power, but it was no good. The zombie tackled me out of the divot I had dug, and we rolled across the ground. I pressed my forearm into the zombie's throat. In spite of that, he kept snapping at my face.

"Someone get him off of me!" I shouted.

Gauntlet snared the zombie by the back of his neck and tossed him into the side of a building. The zombie collapsed to the ground, its body broken and twisted, then it burst into dust. "You keep going, I'll watch your back."

I nodded my thanks and stepped back into the divot. It took a few moments to settle my breathing, but soon I was back to digging. Slowly but surely, the hole in the ground descended, my power chewing up the dirt beneath. At one point, I must have hit the power lines because the lights in the nearby building switched off. I winced. Sexton wouldn't be happy when he learned about that. I shook my head to dislodge the ridiculous thought.

While I worked, Veritas and Gauntlet did their best to keep the zombies at bay. Gauntlet managed to construct a circular barrier around us using wrecked cars, but even then it was a fight as the zombies scrambled over the makeshift wall.

I couldn't worry about that. I kept my focus on what I was doing. It couldn't be much more. I had to be . . .

Suddenly the ground beneath my feet opened up into darkness below.

I flailed my arms, trying to grab the edges of the hole I had created, but it was no use. I fell. As I did, my power spiked.

Instead of hitting solid concrete, I landed on a floor that had suddenly turned springy. It roiled like a waterbed beneath my feet, and I rolled out of the way. "I'm in!" I shouted up the hole.

Gauntlet lowered himself into the hole using his telekinetic power. As soon as he landed, he helped Veritas land safely too. "So what's the plan, Failstate?"

"You and I will be the assault team. Any zombies in there, we take them out. Veritas, your job is support. Secure some evidence, knock that remote out of Dr. Ayers's hands if he's there—that sort of thing."

Veritas nodded.

"We ready?" I asked.

Veritas and Gauntlet both nodded. We ran down the tunnel, slowing only when we approached the lab. The last thing we needed was to be ambushed by the superpowered zombies. But we didn't see them. Perhaps they were distracted by the commotion in the lab.

The lab had changed. The hole in the ceiling for the office chair had been enlarged into a gaping maw bordered by ladders. The glass wall was open, and the tubes opened and closed at a steady rate, pumping like pistons. Each time they opened, more of the zombie clones scrambled out. As soon as they were free, they scrambled up the ladders. I could only imagine what the horde was doing to the inside of the research center.

Strong Man, Flaming Girl, and Water-Boy tromped around the center island, almost as if they orbited Dr. Ayers, who was hunched over the console. He wasn't working the controls, but was only observing the readings. In spite of that, sweat had plastered his hair and stained his shirt. He looked about ready to keel over.

"Okay, so let's—" I started to say.

"F, get down!"

Kyn blasted past me as if she were being shoved from behind by a train. She launched into the air, streaking over the central console and Ayers's head and then slammed into the metal tubes. Sparks erupted from the center console, and the lights overhead flickered. An enormous cloud of steam rushed from the chamber and filled the lab then blasted down the hallway. It smelled like a mix of gasoline, dead leaves, and, oddly, peppermint.

"Kyn!" I darted forward.

I sent out a blast of destructive energy to clear the air. Ayers rose from his crouch and stared at the wreckage. The lights overhead flickered. Fires guttered in the remains of the tubes, half of which had shattered as if they were glass. The others had been caved in and twisted. The zombie-making device tried to continue functioning, but the tubes couldn't move. The metal moaned and screeched in protest. Then, with one final gurgle, the entire device went dark.

Kyn stumbled out of the wreckage. She took a few steps but then collapsed against the wall, sliding down to the floor.

"Plan B?" Veritas whispered.

I nodded grimly. I charged the rest of the way into the lab until I stood in the center. The large device separated me from Ayers.

"Kynetic has taken out your zombie-making machine, Dr. Ayers, and now it's time for you to face justice!" I said. That actually sounded pretty heroic!

"No!" Ayers shouted. "I can't let you stop me. Not now, not when I'm so close! Get them!"

Strong Man, Water-Boy, and Flaming Girl turned on us, but I laughed. We were ready for them this time.

But then the zombies that had climbed out of the lab started scuttling back in. They crawled down the ladders. Some of them even managed to scrabble across the ceiling like spiders.

I fell back a step. Our advantage had just crumbled.

Strong Man charged with a gurgling bellow. I lashed out with my power and sheered through part of the ceiling. A chunk broke free and smashed into him from above, knocking him to the ground.

Gauntlet blew past me and landed a solid punch into Flaming Girl, hitting her hard enough that her permanent halo of flames winked out. She smashed into the far wall, and her body crumbled into dust. Then Gauntlet tackled Water-Boy and started tying his limbs into knots. Within minutes, the zombie was a writhing mass of twisted limbs, unable to go anywhere.

That took care of the superpowered zombies, but at least a dozen of the normal kind had climbed back into the lab. I looked over the ceiling, At any moment, they could charge and overwhelm us. And yet they only clung to the walls and the ceiling, glaring at us with dead eyes. A few moaned, a sound that rippled through the entire crowd like a call and response. Maybe they wouldn't attack unless they were provoked.

The console in the center of the lab dinged and hissed, steam jetting from the long cylinder.

They must not have liked that sound, because with a shrieking howl, they charged us.

Gauntlet darted forward and threw his hands open at the horde. The zombies slammed into an invisible barrier and ricocheted off. They tumbled into each other and went down in a tangle of limbs.

Veritas leapt over the tangle of zombies and ran for Dr. Ayers, only to be taken down by three zombies. He disappeared under a pile of the undead.

"Enough!" I shouted.

As near as I could tell, there was only one way for me to end this. Normally, my powers couldn't destroy organic material. Time to see if the undead counted. I closed my eyes and offered up a quick prayer. I sucked in a deep breath and drew my hands up to my chest. Then with a shout I flung open my arms and lashed out with my power, unleashing a wave of destructive energy at the zombies.

The creatures stumbled backward as if they were being buffeted by a high wind. They tried to push against it, but as they did, their bodies disintegrated. I sought out each zombie and blasted it until they were all gone. I took another shuddering breath and ended the flow of destruction. My legs felt like rubber, and I stumbled. A wave of dizziness swept over me. I shook my head and stumbled over to Veritas. His attackers had torn and ripped his costume, but he didn't appear otherwise injured. Good. Time to finish this.

I turned to face Dr. Ayers. "This madness ends now, Doctor!"

"Agreed."

I froze. Dr. Ayers had disappeared. Instead, a man I didn't recognize stood at the console. He was tall and well-muscled, wearing only a pair of silver bicycle shorts. His hair was a mass of tightly curled brown rings. His face looked like it had been carved from a piece of solid steel, his eyes two green chips of emerald.

"I don't quite know what's going on here," the man said, "but I know an unfair fight when I see one. Hold on a tic. Let's see what we need to know."

He walked over to the zombie-making device and pressed his hands against it.

I paused, glancing at Veritas and Gauntlet. Who was this guy? And where had Dr. Ayers gone?

The man stopped touching the device and turned to me. "Near as I can tell, those ugly things have a short fuse. And since the contraption that makes them was taken out by that dame, we shouldn't have any new ones to deal with."

Dame? Kyn! I whirled around and ran to her side. She was slowly sitting up, holding her head.

"Are you okay?" I offered her a hand.

She smiled shakily. "I think so. I think I got banged up more than I expected." She hauled herself up and then looked at the newcomer. "Who's that?"

The new guy turned and looked at Kynetic. And then he flinched. He reacted as though he had stepped into something disgusting.

But he recovered quickly. "I suggest I get some new trousers and we go up and see how your allies are doing, okay?" He went over to the rack of grey scrubs and started flipping through them. "Boy, they don't give a fella a lot of choices, do they?"

Veritas and Gauntlet came over to me.

"Any idea who that is?" I asked.

Gauntlet shook his head.

"He . . . looks familiar, doesn't he?" Veritas asked.

I looked at the man again. He was stepping into a pair of grey scrub pants. Now that Veritas said something, yeah, he did. But I couldn't place the face.

"Excuse me," I said, "but would you mind introducing yourself?"

The man paused in the middle of pulling a shirt over his head. Then he finished tugging it into place. "Oh, I get it.

238

Name, rank, serial number? No dice, Charlie. At least, not yet. Not until I see someone with a bit more clout than you, okay? I can tell grunts when I see them."

Gauntlet bristled. "Now wait just a moment here. I'm no—"

I held an arm across Gauntlet's chest. "I understand. Whenever you're ready."

The man nodded and continued to get dressed.

Gauntlet grabbed my arm and spun me around to face him. "What are you doing? We don't have any clue who that guy is."

"That's exactly why I think we should take it easy. He's a complete unknown. We don't know how strong he is or what he's capable of. As long as he's peaceful, I figure we let him do his thing and we don't confront him. At least, not until we have a little more backup." I jerked a thumb at the ceiling.

Gauntlet's eyes widened, and he nodded. "Gotcha."

I turned to Veritas. "We'll go upstairs with our new friend here. Why don't you take a look at that console and see if you can't figure out what Ayers has been doing? Maybe find out where he might have gotten himself to."

Veritas nodded. I glanced at the newcomer. He had finished getting dressed and was waiting on the bottom rung of a ladder.

"You ready?" he asked.

"Whenever you are."

Gauntlet, the newcomer, Kyn, and I climbed up the ladder. The research center had been destroyed. Dr. Ayers's office had been ripped to shreds, and its walls had been blown out. It appeared as if every door in the building had been smashed and every window broken. Debris from other offices was strewn through the halls. Thankfully, there were no zombies here now. We picked our way through the wreckage and finally found a busted-out exterior door.

The newcomer strode out into the night air. He stumbled to a halt.

I couldn't blame him. The area around us was ruined. Cars had been overturned and several were on fire. Trees and bushes had been uprooted and tossed around. The green space that bordered the science building had been churned into mud. Thankfully, there were no signs of any more zombies. Either they had all crumbled, like the newcomer had suggested they would, or the other heroes had dealt with them. Helicopters buzzed overhead, and sirens wailed in the distance. It was like a war zone.

And yet, the newcomer didn't seem to be focused on any of that. Instead, he gawked at the buildings. "Where are we?" His voice had dropped into a whisper.

"New Chayton University," I answered.

He staggered. "No. It couldn't be."

"About time you guys showed up!" Raze jogged across the campus toward us, a scowl on his face.

The other heroes followed in his wake. Downtime skidded to a halt, his gaze locked on the newcomer. He immediately snapped to attention, saluting.

Huh?

Raze looked between Downtime and the newcomer, frowning. But then recognition spread across his face, and he took a step back. "No way."

A similar reaction spread through the other heroes. Many of them saluted.

I looked between them and the newcomer several times. "Okay, I give. What am I missing?"

"Don't you recognize him, Failstate?" Dr. Olympus asked. "He's the greatest licensed hero who ever lived. That's Sarge."

CHAPTER

33

FOR A MOMENT, my mind refused to understand what Dr. Olympus had said. Sarge? Yeah, I had heard of him. Who hadn't? He was the greatest hero the early twentieth century had known. I'd even seen a picture of him at the VOC headquarters. Sarge had risen to fame during World War I, had gained even more prominence during the Temperance War of the '20s, and then had given his life to stop a Nazi supervillain in the early days of World War II. His career had been the inspiration for dozens of heroes, and the modern VOC was patterned after suggestions he had made. If my licensed colleagues were living legends, then Sarge was a titan, a god of sorts.

This had to be a joke. Sarge had died decades earlier. There was no way that this guy could possibly be . . .

But the newcomer didn't deny it. Instead, a tight smile tugged at his lips. His hand snapped to his forehead in a salute. "Good to see that there are so many of you fighting the good fight. What's the situation?"

I should have answered his question, but my words gummed up my throat. Instead, Raze stepped forward, his hands tucked at the small of his back. He looked like a soldier. "The perimeter is secure, sir. We were able to pulverize most of the zombies. You must have dealt with their source, right, sir?" Raze's face shone with expectation, like a little kid on Christmas morning.

Sarge—if that's really who this was—laughed easily. "No, soldier, I'm afraid I can't claim responsibility. Instead it was this man who took out the apparatus down in that cellar." He clapped me on the shoulder and gave me a tight squeeze.

Raze's open surprise was simply delicious. So were the admiring looks that the other heroes gave me. But guilt quickly chased away any sense of satisfaction or accomplishment. I hadn't done anything.

I turned toward Kyn. "Uh, actually, it was—"

"But even though the fight may be over," Sarge said, "there's still a lot of work to be done." He pointed at some nearby buildings that had been trashed by the zombies. "I want a team to go through there and check for survivors. I can see a few—are those cars?—well, whatever they are, they're on fire, and they shouldn't be. Two more of you, find ways to get those blazes under control."

"Why should we take any orders from you?"

Every eye turned toward me. I froze, ice shooting through my veins. Had I actually said that out loud? Raze glared at me, looking about ready to rip my head off and stuff it down my neck. The other heroes didn't look much happier.

"I mean . . . uh . . . no offense, sir, but while you look like Sarge, we can't be sure that you are. You've been—inactive?—for over seventy years now. Even if you are who you say you are, don't you think you should get caught up with the rest of the world first?"

Now Raze really looked ready to murder me. He took a step toward me, "Failstate, you and me are gonna have a long talk."

Sarge stepped between us. "No, he's absolutely right. I have been gone for a long time." His gaze roamed over the buildings. "Everything looks different. I can only imagine how things have changed. I guess some habits are hard to break. Forgive an old soldier for his impetuous behavior." He turned to me. "What do you suggest I do?"

Oh, boy. This was going to be tricky. I didn't want to antagonize the others but, at the same time, we really didn't know who or what this person was.

I motioned to Dr. Olympus. "Why don't you go with Dr. Olympus? She can give you a quick medical exam so we can make sure you're in good health." I winced when I said it. Sarge looked fine, but I figured if there was anyone who could figure out where Sarge had come from and what had brought him back, it was Dr. Olympus.

Dr. Olympus stepped forward, and her demeanor changed. Instead of standing tall and proud, she jutted out her hips and her lips somehow became fuller. "Sarge, it would be an honor to give you a thorough physical." Uh-oh. I'd seen her do this before.

Sarge actually blushed. "Well, miss, I'd ask you to go easy on me." He clapped me on the shoulder again. "It's good to see that our world is still in good hands, even now. With any luck, I'll be able to rejoin you all on the front lines very soon."

Dr. Olympus slipped a hand around Sarge's elbow and led him away, a definite shimmy in her hips.

"Well, look who thinks he's ready for his big boy pants." Raze glared at me.

"If you'd pull your head out of the clouds, you'd know I did the right thing," I shot back.

"Whatever. No matter who he is, he still had the right idea. Downtime, you and I will check the buildings for casualties. Elemental, you try to put out those fires."

"Do you guys need any more help?" Gauntlet asked.

Raze snorted at him. "From you, junior? Not a chance. You stay here with Failstate and try not to mess anything up, okay?"

Raze and Downtime set off for the buildings.

Elemental stepped over to Kynetic and looked her over. "Kynetic, are you all right?"

Kynetic offered her a shaky smile. "I think so. I just need a moment to catch my breath."

"Good. Then maybe you can explain what happened on the battlefield. Didn't I say you were supposed to stay with me?"

"You did," Kynetic said.

"And yet you emerged from the science center with Failstate. Were my orders somehow unclear?"

"No. I just thought that . . ." Kynetic shrugged.

"I see. Come with me." Elemental's voice was stern, reminding me of a disappointed parent.

Kyn didn't meet my gaze. Instead, she walked over to Elemental's side. Elemental gave me a disapproving look and then jogged toward the nearest burning car.

"Kyn?" I said.

She paused but didn't face me.

"Good job in the lab. I couldn't have done it without you."

She just ran after Elemental.

I turned to Gauntlet. My brother scowled at the ground and kicked at some loose pebbles, scuffing at them with his boot.

"You okay?" I asked.

"Why wouldn't I be?" Gauntlet returned, his tone making it clear he wasn't. "Just because nobody's taking me seriously."

"Welcome to my world."

I wanted to relish Gauntlet's anger. For years, I had been the one to languish in his long shadow, struggling to be noticed and fighting for the chance to be taken seriously on my own terms. It felt kind of nice to see the shoe on the other foot for once. But I shook my head to clear out those thoughts. That problem had been dealt with. Forgiven, forgotten, over. I couldn't backslide into old habits, not now.

"We both know what you did," I said. "And you know how much I appreciate it."

Gauntlet snorted. "If this is going to turn into another commercial for becoming your sidekick, forget it." He sighed. "See you later."

So what did that leave me with? I could help look for survivors, but I doubted Raze would want my help. The same thing was true with Elemental. Go see how pseudo-Sarge was doing with Dr. Olympus? I shuddered. Something told me I was safer if I stayed away. That left me to check on Veritas. I started back for the research center.

I'd made it halfway there when a large black Suburban screeched to a halt by the curb. The doors burst open and VOC agents streamed out, weapons drawn and ready. Sexton was at the front of the pack, with Kensington at his heels.

"Is the situation under control?" he asked.

I waved around at the empty campus. "See for yourself."

"Is it true?" Sexton demanded. "Is . . . is Sarge back?"

"That's who he claims to be," I said.

Sexton's face lit up with a genuine smile. "Excellent." He looked around. "Well, where is he?"

"Dr. Olympus is checking him out." I jerked a thumb in the direction that the doc had led Sarge.

Sexton charged off, presumably to find them. I sighed. So much for asking how I did or what I did. At least he hadn't chewed me out, for once.

Kensington fell in step with me as we walked to the science center. "Just so you know, we have ambulances inbound to help with any wounded civilians. The fire department is on the way also, although it looks like Elemental and Kynetic have that under control. Our After Works Team will be in here within six hours to assess the damage and start the rebuilding process. Mayor Reilly will likely want to be briefed in the next few hours, so I'd be ready for that if I were you. Is there anything else you need?"

I shook my head. "No, but thanks for all that." I gestured in the direction Sexton had run. "Don't you want to go see Sarge too?"

Kensington shook his head. "I see the pictures every day I go into work."

"There's a big difference between a picture of a hero and the genuine article."

"True, but the way I figure it, I'm talking to the genuine article right now." Kensington's lips twitched into a smile. "I have a sister who attends NCU. Because of what you did here tonight, I know she's safe. Thank you."

My mouth went dry. I stammered a response, but Kensington clapped me on the shoulder and started barking orders to the other VOC agents.

I picked my way back through the wreckage of the science center and slid down a ladder. The secret lab was more of a garbage pit now. The wrecked zombie-making machine still sparked and smoked but looked like a twisted sculpture. What few overhead lights still worked flickered, causing the shadows in the room to dance. The racks of chemicals had been smashed. The air didn't smell much better than it had. The gasoline smell was gone, replaced by the odor of rotten eggs. The only thing intact in the room was the central device. It had somehow escaped all of the damage. But its central cylinder now stood open, revealing a large pool of brackish water inside.

Veritas sat by the main console, data streaming by on a computer screen. But my friend wasn't looking at the computer at all—his gaze was fixed on a blank spot on the wall.

"You okay?" I asked.

He blinked and turned toward me. "I . . . Yeah, I think I'm okay. That is—" He waved at the computer. "There's just a lot . . ." He cleared his throat and rubbed at his eyes. "There's a lot to process here."

I frowned. There was something about his tone that bothered me. "What's going on?"

Veritas sighed. "It's complicated."

"Then start at the beginning." I knelt down next to him.

Veritas blew out another long breath. "Dr. Ayers has figured out how to resurrect dead people."

I whistled. "How is that possible?"

"Have you ever heard of a villain who called himself Kudzu? He was from Alabama."

I shook my head.

"Kudzu died while fighting a group of heroes forty years ago. Well, sort of. See, Kudzu's power was that he could regenerate himself when he was injured."

"So how did he die if no one could kill him?" I asked.

"From what Dad told me, it took a lot of firepower. And truth be told, the heroes really didn't kill him. Well, they did, but parts of his body refused to die. Some tissue samples of Kudzu got sent here to NCU. Dr. Ayers got his hands on them and was using them for his research into telomeres and life extension. As near as I can tell, he decided to do some experiments with the samples to see if he couldn't use them to resurrect dead people."

"You're kidding."

"I'm not. His research notes are gibberish to me. But as near as I can tell, Ayers developed some sort of serum from Kudzu's tissue samples. If he injects it into even part of a dead person, that starts a process that brings that person back to life."

"Yeah, but how?" I asked.

"Apparently the serum temporarily transfers Kudzu's power to the subject, allowing the tissue to regenerate the same way Kudzu would."

"Where did Ayers get tissue samples for the zombies?"

Veritas shrugged. "According to his notes, the medical school had plenty of cadavers lying around. And he didn't need much for his experiments."

"But why zombies?" I asked. "None of them looked truly alive."

"Early test runs of the serum weren't entirely successful, hence the rotten flesh and poor motor control. That's why they crumbled after a while: The Kudzu formula wasn't stable enough. When the power wore off, that was it. Game over. But now . . ." Veritas rubbed his eyes again. "It seems to be the real deal, Failstate. With a few drops of this serum, you could bring someone back from the dead. That's what Ayers was planning on doing with his wife. It's all right here."

My stomach dropped into my boots.

"Just think about it, Failstate," Veritas whispered. "We could fix things and set them right. We could . . . She'd be back."

My head snapped around. I knew what he was going to suggest. "Veritas—Mike—we can't resurrect your sister."

He whirled on me. "Why not? It wasn't her time, and we both know it, Rob! If you were to ask my dad, he'd say the same thing! We could bring Elena back!"

"We don't know if this process is safe or not! What if there are side effects? And even if we could do it, would it really be her? Her soul—or something else? What if she came back as one of those zombies and we had to kill her? Not to mention that you'd have to exhume her body!"

"But we know it's safe!" Veritas stabbed a finger at the computer screen. "According to Dr. Ayers's notes, he was running one final test, and he was confident it would work. That had to be Sarge! Then he was going to use the serum to resurrect his wife! If he was sure enough in the results that he was willing to use it on his own wife, I'd say that means it has to be pretty safe!"

I couldn't argue with that. Sarge did seem pretty normal. At least, he hadn't clacked his teeth at me yet. But even still, the idea didn't sit well with me. "Mike, it just isn't right. Do you really think it'd be right to play God?"

"But we have to! We have to—" He collapsed against the console, his shoulders heaving. He choked and started crying.

I took a tentative step toward my friend and put a hand on his shoulder. "What's going on?"

"Don't you get it, Rob? This is my chance to make things right."

"What are you talking about? Mike, it's not your fault she died."

"I know that."

"Then what's—"

Veritas whirled on me. "She wasn't a Christian!" Tears pooled in his eyes and soaked into his mask. "Don't you get it, Rob? My sister died outside of the faith. She's lost for all eternity! But now . . . now I can bring her back. I can share with her what I've learned, what P.G. has been teaching me, and . . . and . . ."

"You don't know for sure that she'd listen," I whispered as gently as I could. "Or even if it would really be her."

"But I don't know that she won't listen, either. I have to make this right. I have to at least try—can't you see that?"

"Mike . . . that isn't your call."

He knocked my hand off his shoulder and glared at me.

And then the VOC team found us. Kensington was the first one down the hole. The rest slid down the ladders and spread out through the lab.

Kensington smiled at me again. "All right, Failstate, we'll take it from here."

I tried to say something, anything, that would comfort Veritas some more.

He swiped away the tears. "I won't get in your way." He scrambled up one of the ladders and disappeared.

For some reason, I had a feeling as though he had disappeared forever.

CHAPTER 34

I SUSPECTED I should have followed Veritas to make sure he was all right, but I wound up spending the rest of the night at the campus, assisting as much as I could. Mainly what I wound up doing was destroying debris. By the time the sun was peeking over the eastern horizon, most of the mess from the previous night's battle had been loaded onto trucks or disintegrated by me.

Just as the sun was starting to peek over the buildings, Kensington found me near a large pile of broken masonry. I held out my hands and sent a wave of destructive energy through them. Within a matter of moments, they had dissolved.

"Failstate, Mayor Reilly, Chief Thompson, and Chief Blackthorn would like to meet with you," Kensington said.

I nodded and followed. He led me across the open space to a large semi. The truck's trailer looked like a mobile home bristling with antennas and satellite dishes. Large black letters, "VOC," were stenciled onto the silver exterior. Two agents stood guard at the base of the stairs. They nodded to me as I walked up the steps.

The interior of the trailer was filled with video monitors, computers, and half a dozen agents. Every surface gleamed in the surprisingly bright lights. I followed Kensington as he wove through the cramped space until we came into a small conference room toward the back of the trailer. A good-sized table with a large monitor embedded into its surface took up most of the space. The monitor displayed a map of the surrounding neighborhood. Data about the destruction scrolled by, indicating where the worst damage had been inflicted.

Mayor Reilly, Police Chief Blackthorn, and Fire Chief Thompson were seated around the table. The mayor was nursing a cup of coffee. Thompson looked so tired I almost mistook her for a zombie. Blackthorn nodded to me in silent greetings.

Mayor Reilly looked up at me and smiled. "Failstate, thank you for joining us."

"Of course, Mayor Reilly." I slipped into a chair at one end of the table.

Heavy footsteps tromped through the trailer behind me, and Agent Sexton appeared at the head of the table. He gave me a condescending look and turned to the others.

"Let's get started," Mayor Reilly said. "Failstate, why don't you get us caught up on what happened last night?"

I outlined the events as best I could: my suspicions about Dr. Ayers; how Veritas, Gauntlet, Kynetic, and I had found the lab; how the battle had unfolded; and Sarge's return. I made sure to emphasize the help that Gauntlet, Veritas, and Kynetic had given me, if for no other reason than to spite Raze.

Mayor Reilly listened to the whole story without taking another sip from her coffee. When the tale wound down, she frowned. "And Dr. Ayers? I assume he's in custody?"

I glanced at Agent Sexton. "Uh, no, Your Honor. He . . . somehow escaped."

"Escaped?" Thompson demanded. "How is that possible?"

"I can answer that," Kensington said from his perch by Sexton. "Our team has sifted through the rubble in Ayers's lab, and we found a secret exit behind one of the consoles. He must have fled while Failstate was destroying the zombies."

"I see." Mayor Reilly turned to Blackthorn. "George?"

Blackthorn grunted. "I've already got a BOLO out for Ayers. His picture is at the airport, the bus terminal, and the train station. Every cop in New Chayton is looking for him. And, I suspect, so are the superheroes."

"That's just great," Thompson said. "So we have a madman out there who knows how to create a zombie horde. What if he has a second lab somewhere in the city?"

"That's unlikely, ma'am," Kensington said. "It looks like Ayers was working with some highly specialized equipment. I suspect he'd have a hard time setting up another lab like this one."

"But it's still possible, isn't it?" Thompson shot back.

Kensington blanched. "I suppose."

Mayor Reilly held up a hand. "What about Sarge? Is it really him?"

"It looks that way, Your Honor," Sexton said. "Dr. Olympus has commandeered one of the biology labs over at Concordia University and is running a series of tests on Sarge. But based on the data we've recovered from Ayers's lab and her preliminary results, it does appear as though Sarge is back."

Reilly's eyes widened. "Wow."

That was an understatement.

"So what's the procedure for this?" she asked.

"Quite frankly, Your Honor, we don't have one," Sexton said. "This sort of situation is unprecedented. We're all flying in the dark here."

"There's one thing I don't understand." Blackthorn fixed Sexton with a hard gaze. "From what Failstate said, this 'Kudzu-serum' can only work if Ayers had a sample of the person he wanted to resurrect, right?"

Though he didn't seem to be asking me, I nodded anyway.

"Sarge was interred at Arlington National Cemetery, right?" Blackthorn asked. "So how did Ayers even get a tissue sample or whatever he needed? Did he take a D.C. vacation to go grave robbing?"

Sexton paled. He looked at Kensington, who could only shrug. Sexton turned back to the Chief. "That's . . . uh, that's an excellent question, sir, and we'll investigate that immediately."

"So in the meantime, what will happen with Sarge?" Reilly asked.

"Until Dr. Olympus completes her tests, nothing," Sexton said. "But provided she clears him, I suppose he could return to active duty. Perhaps his license could be reissued as well."

Mayor Reilly brightened. "That would certainly help our current situation, at least until the Hoplite returns."

Sexton nodded. "Yes, ma'am, it could."

I looked between everyone, feeling as though I had suddenly turned invisible. I cleared my throat. "Your Honor, is there anything else you need me for?"

Reilly blinked at me, then smiled sympathetically. "I'm sorry, Failstate. Please, go home and get some rest. Thank you."

Blackthorn nodded. "If you don't mind, Your Honor, I'll walk out with Failstate. I need to get back to headquarters and make sure everyone's doing their duty."

"Of course, George. Thank you for your time."

Blackthorn motioned for me to follow him. We wound through the cramped trailer and out into the cool morning air. Blackthorn led me across campus toward a large sedan parked nearby.

Once we were out of earshot of the trailer, he paused and looked at me. "How are you holding up, Failstate?"

I chuckled, thinking of what had happened between Kynetic and me, the hurt in Veritas's voice, Gauntlet's frustration. "Truth be told, sir, I've been better."

"I don't doubt it. But from what I've heard, you did good last night. Just like I knew you would."

My cheeks warmed at the praise. "Thank you, sir. But if you don't mind me asking, what do you know about Sarge?"

Blackthorn smiled. "He was a little before my time. Not by much, mind you. But both my father and his father were cops in New Chayton. Grandfather used to tell me stories about Sarge." He looked down at the ground. "From what he told me, Sarge was good at what he did. Grandfather really appreciated the hard work he did. As a matter of fact, my dad tells me he only saw Grandfather cry three times: at my father's wedding, at my grandmother's funeral, and when Sarge was reported killed in World War II. On the whole, I'd say it's a good thing he's back."

"Yes, sir."

"But that doesn't let any of us off the hook." He patted my shoulder. "Stay vigilant, Failstate. Like I told you before, we need heroes. We need you. This isn't over yet." Blackthorn climbed into the back of his sedan, and the car drove away.

I stood up a little straighter. Even if Sarge was as great as everyone said, I was going to do my best not to let Chief Blackthorn down.

CHAPTER 35

I PULLED UP the driveway and tumbled out into the garage. I tried to slam the door to punctuate the night's events, but I barely managed a weak bang. Maybe I would try to sleep, even a little. I probably wouldn't be able to get more than an hour, but maybe that would help me calm my roiling thoughts.

I shuffled up the back steps and into the kitchen.

Mom was seated at the center island, sipping a cup of coffee. She smiled. "Rough night?"

I sighed and collapsed on one of the stools. "You could say that."

"I bet." She nodded toward the TV.

I looked over. The 24 hour news channel was running footage from the night before, showing the other licensed heroes battling the zombie horde. Raze in particular looked like a vengeful god, obliterating every enemy who dared cross his path.

"Wonderful," I muttered.

Then the image on screen shifted to the reporter, a well-groomed blond man in a dark suit. "But while the city is still reeling from a 'zombie apocalypse,' perhaps most shocking of all is the news that one of our city's greatest citizens has returned."

The TV cut to a grainy sepia toned picture of Sarge. He wore what looked like a wool coat and pants with odd bulges at his hips. "Many of are familiar with the exploits of Sarge, the man who singlehandedly won the Temperance War. But now, it would seem that we can look forward to even more exploits from New Chayton's legendary defender."

From that picture, the screen jumped to footage labeled *Earlier This Morning*. Sarge, still dressed in the grey scrubs from Ayers's lab, was hustled through the NCU campus to one of the VOC's black vans. As the footage played, the reporter's voice supplied the commentary. "While the VOC wouldn't comment on Sarge's presence at the battle, they have revealed that they will be holding a press conference later today."

I snared the TV remote and shut it off.

Mom eyed me. "You okay, Robin?"

I laughed mirthlessly. "Not really, no."

"Want to talk about it?"

I glanced at her. "What about your 'I don't want to know what you do' policy?"

She shrugged. "I'm your mother. I can change the rules when I want to. Now what's got you so upset?"

I hesitated. It actually would be nice to talk to someone who wasn't a hero and didn't have a stake in any of this. But at the same time, I didn't feel right dumping it on Mom either. I mean, it was probably hard enough to know that both of her sons were going out and risking their lives as heroes. To make her my confidante didn't seem particularly smart or safe.

"I'm fine, Mom. Really. It's going to be okay."

She watched me for a few moments longer then shrugged. She clearly didn't buy it, which was okay since I didn't buy it either. "Well, okay, but if you change your mind, you know where I live, got it? Make sure you eat something." She breezed out of the kitchen for the driveway.

I retrieved a toaster pastry from the kitchen cupboard and munched on it as I went up to my room. I paused for a moment to look in Ben's former bedroom. Although his furniture was still in place, the room felt empty and hollow. I realized how much I missed him. Maybe that was why I was trying so hard to get him to be my sidekick. If we had to work together, we wouldn't drift apart again.

I shook my head and crossed the hall to my room. I sat down at my desk and booted up my desktop computer. I figured I might as well do some research.

There were a lot of fan sites dedicated to Sarge's memory. They were all filled with the same photos: Sarge as a young man in World War I, mugging for the camera with his comrades-in-arms. Sarge, his signature uniform covered in mud after the Second Battle of Somme. Sarge raiding a speakeasy in Chicago. Sarge posing with President Roosevelt after the U.S. entered World War II. Sarge's body lying in state in the U.S. Capitol, surrounded by flowers and mourners.

I finally found what I was looking for on one page whose author had tried to dissect Sarge's career and abilities. As near as I could tell, Sarge was a cognit, like me, only they didn't use those terms back in his day. More specifically, he had a power called "psychometry," the ability to gain mental impressions from touching an object. I recalled how he'd touched the zombie-making device and had seemed to learn something that way. That power, combined with a keen mind capable of almost supernatural tactical decisions, had made him a force to be reckoned with. The way one web article put it, "If Sarge knew his opponent, he was well nigh unbeatable."

I called up his biographical information and scanned it. There was no mention of his life before his military career, which had started in 1917 when he'd enlisted. Apparently his powers had kept him one step ahead of the enemy troops, allowing him to lead his comrades to several decisive victories. He'd never arisen beyond the rank of sergeant, hence his nickname. When he'd returned to the States after the war, he'd disappeared.

That had changed during Prohibition. A criminal master-mind named the Blue Duchess had put together a network of villains to flout the Volstead Act. But controlling the nation's rumrunners had turned out to only be Act One in her scheme. Within a few years, her operatives had infiltrated most government agencies. On top of that, she'd bribed enough people that she had been close to overthrowing the government and installing herself in its place.

But then Sarge had intervened. He had been doing his best to prevent the rumrunners from working in New Chayton. Then he had learned about the Blue Duchess's scheme, and he'd vowed to stop her. That had led to the disastrous five year Temperance War, which had pitted the Blue Duchess's people against Sarge and what few allies he could find to oppose her. I had read about the Temperance War in school. It was required learning for kids in New Chayton. The war had practically leveled our city in 1926. Few people had believed that Sarge could win, but he did, finally defeating the Blue Duchess in 1931.

Sarge had gone on to help revamp the Vigilante Act, the law that allowed superheroes to do what we did. His influence had led to the founding of the Vigilante Oversight Commission and their myriad rules and regulations.

Then, when World War II broke out, Sarge had gone back to the front lines. Unfortunately, he died in the early years due to a Nazi supervillain named Übermensch. After lying in state at the U.S. Capitol building, he was buried with full military honors in Arlington National Cemetery in 1942.

I mopped a hand over my face. While the article helped fill in some of the blanks about Sarge, it only dredged up more questions. If Sarge's body really was in D.C., how did Dr. Ayers get a tissue sample? How was Sarge going to change things now that he was back? Given Sexton's almost fanboy-like behavior at the NCU campus, I had no doubt that he would do his best to reinstate Sarge's license as soon as possible. Even if the Living Quark were incapacitated and Nightsilver and Shadowfall were still gone, I doubted Sexton would want my help once Sarge was back in the field. I could almost hear Sexton drawing up the papers to revoke my license.

"Rob!" Mom's shout caused me to jump. "Can you come down here, please?"

I shut down the web browser and headed out of my room. Now what? I hadn't dirtied any dishes for breakfast. So what was going on?

I got my answer when I came down the steps.

Charlene was waiting for me.

She looked particularly haggard and tired, almost as though she hadn't slept the night before. Mom excused herself, leaving Charlene and me alone in the entryway.

Charlene offered me a wan smile. "Hi." Her voice barely registered.

"Hi. What are you doing here?"

"I don't know. When I heard about those zombies, I just wanted to make sure you were okay."

Cold sweat erupted along my brow. How did she know I had been involved in that? Had I dropped some hints? I didn't think so. Magnus had been right: This was a lot trickier than I thought it would be!

She laughed nervously. "I know it's silly. I mean, why would *you* be down at NCU, right? But I just had this feeling all night that I should . . . well, pray for you. It kept me up all night. And then this morning I just had to make sure . . ." She blushed furiously, her cheeks almost matching her hair. "I know I sound ridiculous."

Anything but. I was excited to see Charlene, but then I remembered what had happened between Kynetic and me last night, how Kyn had kissed me, and how I hadn't really minded. I felt like I was going to be ill.

"But it's more than that," she said. "I was wondering . . ." She gritted her teeth, an almost-there smile, and shook her head. "Would you like to meet my dad?"

I blinked. "Absolutely."

Her smile widened just a little. "Can you come now?"

"What, right now?"

She nodded.

I shrugged. "Let's do it."

She grabbed my hand and squeezed. "C'mon, I'll drive."

"Mom, I'll be back later, okay?"

Mom poked her head out of the kitchen and smiled. "Have a good time. Call if you're going to be late."

I followed Charlene out of the house, offering a silent prayer that I'd be able to make up for the mistakes I'd almost made.

CHAPTER
36

CHARLENE'S JEEP WAS PARKED at the end of our driveway. I climbed into the passenger seat and paused. The interior was pristine. The black vinyl seats seemed to glisten in the early morning light. A large stereo system was set in the dashboard, blinking with multicolored lights. An MP3 player was plugged into it. This thing must have cost a small fortune.

Charlene slid into the driver's seat. "I know, it's a bit much. Dad insisted on buying it for me on my sixteenth birthday." She started the engine, and loud praise music blared from the speakers. Charlene lunged for the MP3 player and fumbled with it, finally killing the sound. She blushed. "Sorry." She pulled out of the driveway and started for the freeway.

I watched the neighbors' houses slip by us.

"So have you ever been to New Kidron before?" she asked.

I froze. I had, but only as Failstate. The Valley Correctional Facility, a federal prison designed to hold supervillains, was located in the suburb of New Kidron. Once again, I had no idea what I could tell Charlene without causing her to ask more questions. I decided to stumble forward and do my best. "Not really, no. Isn't there a prison there?"

She rolled her eyes. "Valley. Ugh. Don't get me started. I mean, how stupid is it to take the most powerful, the most violent, and the most sociopathic people in the world and house them all together under one roof? That won't turn around and bite anyone, especially not with Failstate watching the city."

I turned away so Charlene wouldn't see my cheeks turning red. "I guess you're right."

There was a long pause. Then Charlene spoke up. "I'm sorry. I know you're a fan of superheroes."

"At least they were around last night, right?" I asked. "Beats having to deal with zombies on your morning drive."

"I guess." Charlene blew out a long sigh. "So how was school yesterday?"

We filled the rest of the ride with stories from the week. I winced when I realized I hadn't called her as often as I should have. Some potential boyfriend I was turning out to be!

We eventually exited the freeway into New Kidron. Unlike the area around Valley, Charlene live in a nice neighborhood of stately brick homes and well-manicured lawns. It was still morning, but the nearby small park was filled with joggers and dog walkers.

Charlene pulled into the driveway of a two story house—no, mansion—made of red bricks. White-bordered windows gleamed in the afternoon sun. An gnarled oak tree dominated the front yard. I couldn't help but gape a little.

Charlene smiled sheepishly. "I know, it's a bit much."

"I've seen bigger."

She favored me with a lopsided grin. She must have thought I was kidding, but I was being serious. Her house would have easily fit in a corner of Magnus Manor. Better to let her think I was joking.

Charlene led me around the house to a side entrance, one that led into an expansive kitchen. All of the appliances were stainless steel, the counters all made of granite. A large rack filled with pots and pans hung over a sleek, black stove. Charlene tossed her keys onto a small ledge by the door and led me deeper into the house.

"Daddy?"

We walked through a large archway into the dining room. A large glass-fronted cabinet was filled with figurines of children and puppies and other cute scenes. The table, which could seat six, was buried with papers, books, and boxes. Then it was through to a living room.

A large screen TV hung on one wall. Opposite that was a brick fireplace. Most of the furniture, a matching set of two recliners and a couch, seemed shoved toward the corners. Dominating the far wall was a hospital bed. A frail man lay on it, his jaw lined with red stubble. His eyes were lined with heavy bags. A clear plastic tube snaked around his ears and down to his nose. He had a large scrapbook open on his lap, the pages filled with curling and yellowed newspaper articles.

I stopped short, unsure of what was happening.

Charlene crossed to the bed and sat down on its edge. She hugged the man and kissed his forehead. "Hello, Daddy."

The man smiled, a series of wrinkles creasing his skin from his mouth. "Hi, baby. Who's your friend?"

She smiled in my direction. "This is Rob Laughlin."

The man's eyes widened. "Oh, you mean . . ."

She shot him a look and poked him in the chest.

He offered me a hand. "Glad to meet you, Rob. You can call me Steve."

Charlene frowned and looked at the book in his lap. She rolled her eyes. "Daddy, what are you doing?"

Steve smiled. "Just taking a walk down memory lane. I mean, can you blame me? Sarge is back!"

I glanced at the scrapbook. Most of the articles appeared to be about Sarge. Many of the photographs were the same ones I had found online. Were these original newspaper articles? I let out a low whistle. "That's an impressive collection."

"Thanks." Steve shut the book and ran a hand along the cover. "I inherited this from my dad. He collected most of these articles. After he passed, I kind of picked up where he left off. I've got close to forty books like this, with articles from all over the world about all the big heroes. And now, with Sarge back, I think I'll be needing to get some more." He chuckled. "How great would it be to actually meet him!"

"You're into superheroes?" I asked.

Steve nodded. "Absolutely. I can't get enough of them."

"That's something that you two have in common, Daddy," Charlene said. "Rob likes superheroes too."

"Really?" Steve smiled at me. "Did you catch *America's Next Superhero* last spring?"

You could say that. I nodded.

"I loved that show. It's a shame they cancelled it. I was really hoping that Gauntlet would win the license. That kid was great." He reached up and ruffled Charlene's hair. "I tried to get this one to watch it with me, but she was always too 'busy.'"

"There's more important things in the world than running around in tights," Charlene said.

Steve chuckled. "I suppose you're right, but still." He patted the scrapbook. "These men and women are living legends. They're icons. They change the world with what they do."

My stomach curdled. So far, since receiving my license, I hadn't done anything worthy of legend. Sure, there was that business six months ago, but that didn't really count. I had lucked into that more than anything. If I wanted to live up to what Steve said, I'd have to step up my game.

Steve took a few deep breaths. "I hate to break this up, but if you two will excuse me, I'm getting a little tired."

Charlene kissed her dad on the cheek, and she escorted me out of the room.

She didn't say a word until we were back in the car. "So that's my dad." She tucked a stray lock of hair behind her ear.

"Is he okay?" The words escaped my lips before I could think about them.

"No." A frown creased her brow. "He used to smoke five packs a day. As he says, it caught up with him."

"I'm sorry."

She winced and wiped away a few tears. "Do you mind if we not talk about it?"

"Sure. It was good to meet him, though." I buckled up. "So now what?"

A smile flitted across her lips. "Well, I'm not doing anything today. Feel like hanging out?"

I smiled as well. "Like you have to ask? Let's go."

CHAPTER 37

I HAD CHARLENE DRIVE us to the Hawkeye Mall, which was near my house. Usually, when I went there, I was haunted by memories of Elizabeth and my brother, especially how Ben and I had almost killed each other here six months earlier. But this time, the memories remained dormant.

We wound up shopping for most of the afternoon. Normally I didn't like clothes shopping. I preferred to get into the store, get what I needed, and get out again. But with Charlene, it was enjoyable. She tried on a few cute outfits that sent a funny flutter through my stomach. She even insisted on buying me some new clothes as well, a polo shirt she claimed would make my eyes "pop," whatever that meant. She suggested that, sometime in the near future, we dress up and go out to a nice restaurant, which was more than enough to get me on board.

As we walked out of a clothing store, Charlene threaded her fingers through mine, and a pleasant tingle washed over me. It felt better than how I felt when I was with Kyn. Sure,

Kyn seemed into me, but it felt more like she wanted to devour me. With Charlene, I didn't feel any pressure. Well, beyond the pressure to not trip over my own feet. But I knew she wanted only to spend time with me, nothing more.

Charlene pointed to the movie theater. "What do you say? Have enough time to take in a movie?"

"With you? Definitely."

She blushed at the compliment. "So what should we see?"

I looked over the posters. The Hawkeye Theater had only four screens. One was a movie in the genre I thought of as "torture porn." The poster promised lots of blood, guts, and graphic violence. Not a good choice for a first date, I figured. The second was a kid's movie about talking cheetahs. That was a maybe. The third was a definite chick flick starring the latest Hollywood heartthrob, some guy named Chris Kolmorgen. And the fourth . . . I swallowed a wistful groan. *By Darkness Hid*, an epic fantasy I had been looking forward to seeing for the past six months. I knew what I would pick if I were by myself, but I doubted that Charlene would go for a movie about young people learning how to control their telepathic powers.

I braced myself for long, lingering looks and romantic sap. "Why don't you pick?"

She smiled mischievously. "Well, maybe we could see *By Darkness Hid*."

"You—what?"

She nodded. "Unless you want to see that romantic comedy."

"No! I mean, *Darkness* would be fine."

"Great! I read the books three years ago, and I nearly died when they announced they were making it into a movie!"

She grabbed my hand and dragged me to the theater.

As we went, I looked up to heaven and mouthed a silent prayer of thanks.

The movie was great, if a bit uncomfortable for me. I wanted nothing more than to put my arm around Charlene, snuggle in with her, and enjoy the action. But I had never been to a movie with a girl before, so I had no idea how to do this. The only thing I could think of was to do the clichéd "yawn and stretch" move, but even I knew how corny that would be. Finally, a half hour into the movie, I risked reaching over and taking her hand again.

She glanced at me, and her smile melted my brain. She then guided my arm up and over her head. She lifted the armrest between us out of the way and settled in, pressed up against my side. There were only two downsides. My arm went to sleep with an hour left in the flick, but I was not about to move it. More problematically, our position somehow caused my necklace to dig into my neck. That got painful after a while.

By the time the film ended, it was close to dinnertime. "Why don't we get some food?" I suggested.

Charlene nodded, and we went into the mall's food court. As the smells of grease and meat washed over us, Charlene looked around at the shops. "Did you hear about what happened here last spring? The news said that there was a gas explosion that nearly demolished the whole mall."

Heat clawed at my cheeks. I had heard that explanation as well, although I knew what had really happened. "Yeah. Crazy, huh? So where do you want to eat?"

She picked a pizza restaurant and ordered a slice of cheese pizza. I got pepperoni, and we found a table for two in one corner of the food court. We didn't talk about much, just enjoyed the food and watched the passersby. Truth be told, I didn't want the date to end.

But after we had eaten, Charlene glanced at her cell phone and smiled sadly. "This was great, Rob, but I have to get home. Mom will be wondering where I am."

"Oh, absolutely."

She drove me home and let me out of the car at the curb. But she surprised me by getting out of the car too. She came around the car, stepped in close, and pressed her lips against mine. It wasn't nearly as intense as the kiss we'd shared in my kitchen earlier in the week, but it still sent my heart jackhammering against my ribs.

"Call me, okay?" she whispered.

"Absolutely."

She squeezed my hand and got back into her car. I stood at the curb and watched as she drove off, not daring to move until she disappeared around a corner. Then I turned and headed back into the house.

The bubbly feeling in my head slowly turned to lead. As wonderful as the day had been, I knew that the memories would make the next time I saw Kyn that much harder.

CHAPTER

38

I SUPPOSE IT shouldn't have surprised me that I found it so difficult to concentrate as I went out on patrol. What Steve had said about heroes being legends tumbled through my brain, colliding with memories of Charlene's body pressed up against mine in the movie theater and the soft kiss at the end of our date. It was a good thing that I didn't find anything worth my time during the patrol. The police scanner reported a few cases of b-and-e plus a domestic dispute in Overton. I swung by each site to see if the cops needed my help but they had each situation well in hand. By five the next morning, I had had enough, and I went home.

It was Sunday morning, so at nine I went to Mount Calvary, hoping to see either Charlene or Mike. Neither of them showed up. Before the service started, Charlene texted me that Steve was having a bad day and she couldn't make it. But where was Mike? Where was *Veritas*?

I found a seat by myself and tried to lose myself in the singing and in P.G.'s lesson, but my mind kept drifting to my missing friend. Maybe I'd have to call him when I got home.

But when I returned home, I noticed the sleek black Mercedes in our driveway. As soon as I had parked DK, Magnus stepped out of the vehicle. His face was drawn into a somber scowl. Uh-oh. Clearly this wasn't going to be a pleasant visit. He motioned for me to follow and stepped into the garage.

"Mr. Magnus, is Mike okay?" I asked.

Magnus scowled for a moment. "I have no idea. He spent all day yesterday moping in his room. Wouldn't tell me what's going on either." He looked around, eyes peering up at the rafters and then down at the oil-stained cement floor. "I haven't forgotten about getting you a better lair, kid. The VOC's being stubborn, as usual, but I'm not giving up on that."

"That's a nice thought, sir, but I don't think we can dig out something like your Lighthouse under this house without people noticing."

Magnus grunted. "You might be surprised. I did just that without my wife ever noticing. The VOC has some wizards when it comes to stealthy construction, folks who can keep their mouths shut. But I didn't come here to talk about Mike or construction projects. Things are about to get a lot more complicated." He waved for me to take a seat on the couch. "I take it Sexton hasn't called you since . . . the incident at NCU?"

"No." I sank into the cushions and tried to keep my stomach from twisting down into my shoes.

Magnus snorted and ran a hand through his hair, the same way that Mike often did. "Figures. It seems that this 'Sarge' character is the real thing. At least he is according to every test that Doctor Olympus could dream up. That threw the VOC hierarchy for a loop. This sort of thing is unprecedented. So this is what they've come up with . . ."

I braced myself.

"Sarge is going to back on active duty. And they want you to partner with him for a while."

Wait, *partner* with him? Why? "As what, his sidekick?"

Magnus shook his head. "No, I made sure of that. I know that a lot of folks at the VOC don't have a high opinion of you, but as far as I'm concerned, you earned that license fair and square." He ground his teeth, and his fingers dug into his knees. "I had to call in a few favors to make sure they didn't demote you, but there we go. So far as the VOC is concerned, you two are equal partners. For now."

I'd begun feeling better . . . right up until he added those last two words. "What do you mean?"

Magnus sighed. "Technically, New Chayton is only supposed to have five heroes. And I know, Living Quark's out on medical, the Hoplite is otherwise engaged, and so on and so forth. But they're still on the books, and until the VOC decides to change their statuses, New Chayton has one hero too many."

I fought the distinct urge to throw up. "So after this 'partnership' is over . . ."

"They could easily ask one of you to move to a different city. And given Sarge's stature and reputation . . ." Magnus waved his hands as if inviting me to finish the thought.

Right. Well, leaving town was better than what I thought he was going to say, which was that they would just take my license back. New town, huh? Hmm. Maybe Maui needed a superhero, although my costume would get awfully stuffy in the tropics.

Still, leave New Chayton? Really? I looked around the garage. Granted, I didn't know what I was going to do next year when I went away to college, but I hadn't ever thought of leaving New Chayton. I had finally started feeling comfortable in my own home. Starting over again in someplace new. Finding a nice girl . . .

"Listen, I didn't mean to scare you," Magnus said. "It very well could be that Sarge will want to go somewhere else. He did most of his work in Chicago, what with the Temperance War and all that. For now, just do your best, okay? Sarge will probably want to go out on patrol with you tonight, so be ready to show him how the city has changed and how well you can protect it, all right?"

"Sure. But what about Dr. Ayers? I was thinking maybe I should try to find him and bring him in."

Magnus shook his head. "That's not what the VOC wants you to do. Sexton was very clear on that point. He wants you to stick with Sarge for now. That kid—what's his name? Kensington?—he's heading up the investigation into Ayers. Now, if you happen to come across the doctor at some point, I don't think anyone would complain. But for now, just babysit Sarge. Okay?

I swallowed and nodded. Magnus clapped me on the shoulder and walked back to his car. I headed back to the house. Better check in with Mom and then start getting ready. This would most likely be an interesting evening.

CHAPTER 39

SO WHERE WAS I supposed to meet Sarge? I had tried calling Agent Sexton all afternoon, hoping that he would have that information or an idea as to how I could contact the recently resurrected hero—to find out if Sarge even did want to be on patrol with me tonight. But once again, I couldn't reach him. I talked to Downtime, but as it turned out, he had returned to Seattle. He was friendly but not helpful either. I wondered how many of the other heroes had gone home. Most of them, probably.

Finally, when it became clear that no one would help me, I set out toward Hogtown. The Blue Eclipse Boys or the HazMats would likely give me something to do.

I pulled off the freeway and into the streets of Hogtown. To say that the buildings had seen better days was an understatement. Most were on the verge of collapse, their brick and mortar fronts a mass of cracks and chips. Many of the windows were covered with bars or plywood. At least a third of the streetlights didn't work, and the few that did cast long and dark shadows through most of the streets.

I was tempted to switch on DK's suppression mode but then realized that wasn't the best move. True, it might be enough to discourage new crime when I drove by, but I wouldn't be able to really help people from inside a mini-tank. I found a discreet parking spot and turned on the camouflage mode. DK transformed itself into a Camaro with two flat tires and no hubcaps. Hopefully that would discourage anyone from taking a closer look.

I set out through the shadows, sticking to the alleys. Cars roared in the distance, folks sticking to the freeway and not venturing down into Hogtown itself. The sounds of TV shows drifted down from the apartment buildings I passed. It sounded like most people were watching the New Chayton Locusts' preseason game against the Bears. Based on the angry outbursts, it sounded as if the Locusts were doing their usual best to lose the game. I glanced at my cell phone. Still before midnight. If I didn't find any crime here, maybe I'd head over to Club Row before last call. There was bound to be trouble there.

Someone dropped down from a fire escape, landing in front of me in a low crouch. I jumped back, and my powers flared. A nearby dumpster burst like a wet paper sack, spewing garbage all over the alley. I dropped into what hopefully looked like a defensive stance. If I was lucky, my attacker would think I'd destroyed the dumpster on purpose.

Whoever it was rose and stepped forward into the weak light. It was a man, dressed in olive green wool with dull brass buttons. Three stripes—I think they were called "chevrons"— were sewn onto his sleeves closer to the wrist. The pants had odd lumps toward the hips, something I would have expected to see on someone who rode a horse. Topping it all off was a dull metal helmet, little more than a disc with a small bulge in the center for the head. Just the uniform was a giveaway, but when the man stepped fully into the light, I recognized him.

Sarge glanced down at the trash strewn across the alley and raised one brow at me. "Tactical diversion?"

"Sure." I sent a blast of destructive energy across the alley's surface, instantly destroying the refuse.

Now both of Sarge's eyebrows climbed his forehead. "Impressive."

I frowned. From his tone, Sarge didn't consider it the least bit impressive. But I had to play nice with him, if for no other reason than to avoid giving the VOC a reason to move me. "How'd you find me?"

Sarge knelt down and ran a hand over the rough cement then looked at his fingertips and rubbed them together. "I've done a little reading up on you. I figured this part of town would have significance to you because of what happened with the girl—Lux, right? Given the layout of the streets and the most likely entry points to this neighborhood, I assumed you would leave your vehicle near here and set out on foot. I established a recon position," he pointed toward the top of one building, "and waited. You did show up six minutes earlier than I expected."

I ground my teeth. I didn't like his clinical tone. "So now what?"

He straightened up and dusted his hands on his pants. "I think it best to talk about the chain of command, don't you?"

Oh, great. Here's where he'd pull rank on me. I braced myself for the worst.

"I had a long talk with that Agent Sexton earlier today about what I can expect out here. He seems to think that my mere presence in the city will turn this burg into some type of utopia. Somehow, I doubt it, but it's a nice thought. But still, from what I understand, Sexton seems to think I'll be taking charge tonight, and since he's the VOC liaison officer, we'd best keep him happy, right?"

I wanted to scream in frustration, but I managed to nod.

"Good. But don't worry, I'm a fair man. You have a suggestion, make sure you pipe up. Now, let's go see what crimes we can thwart. Unless you have an objection?" He didn't wait for me to answer. Instead, he turned and walked out of the alley.

I took several deep breaths before setting out after him. *Lord, help me tonight. Keep me calm, keep me cool, and please, help me to not make a fool out of myself.*

CHAPTER 40

I DECIDED TO LET SARGE LEAD the way. Actually, it was more like he took the lead and I didn't argue. Maybe if he got himself lost, he'd actually ask for my help, and I'd be able to step up and show him how valuable I could be. Failstate, the human GPS.

And yet it didn't seem like that would happen. Sarge didn't even hesitate as we walked through the neighborhood. It was as if he were being guided somehow, led deeper and deeper into Hogtown. Instead of sticking to the alleys, though, he marched right down the streets. That caused ice to twist down my back, and I had to tamp down on my power. I felt exposed, as if dozens of eyes were burning into me from every building we passed.

After ten minutes of walking, though, Sarge came to a halt outside a rundown storefront. He looked it over and shook his head.

"What's the matter?" I asked.

"This used to be Old Man Davis's hardware store," he whispered. "I did odd jobs for him when I was growing up. Sweeping floors, stocking shelves, that sort of thing. He was a good man." Sarge clenched his jaw for a moment. "A good man."

Were those tears pooling in the corners of his eyes? For a split second, I was sure that I saw actual pain sweep across his features.

Of course he didn't need my help finding his way: These were his old stomping grounds. "So what happened to him?" I asked.

Sarge snorted. "He opened a speakeasy in his back room. I shut him down and sent him to prison." He turned and marched away. "Don't let yourself be fooled, Failstate. Give a person an excuse, and they'll do their best to flout authority. It's up to us to make sure they submit."

I fell in step with him. "So did you grow up in Hogtown?"

Sarge gave me a sidelong glance. "Is that what you're calling this place now? It seems disrespectful. Yes, the slaughterhouses were unpleasant if you were downwind from them, but they provided jobs for the entire community." His gaze roved over the buildings again. "Hard to believe that they're gone, that so much has changed." Once again, his face hardened. "But some things never do. Come. I've seen intelligence from the police that suggests we may find criminals nearby."

Two blocks later, he ducked down an alley. I had little choice but to chase him, breaking into a jog.

He knelt down in the alley's opening and signaled for me to hang back. "There we go," he whispered.

I peeked around the corner. Three young men stood under a broken streetlight, chatting and pacing in tight circles. Two of them, a white man and a Latino, were huge, looking like they had been carved out of boulders. The last, though—a black man wearing a purple-and-gold Locusts jersey—leaned against the streetlight and took long drags from a cigarette.

"Watch," Sarge said.

After a few moments, a nervous-looking young woman walked up the sidewalk. The man who was leaning against the light post motioned for her to come with him. They stepped inside the nearby building. A few minutes later, the woman left and skittered up the street. The man resumed his post. As he did, he adjusted something in his jeans pocket.

"I assume that what is happening is illicit," Sarge said, almost asking me a question. "They look like rum-runners to me."

My mouth popped open. I worked on finding the right words for a few moments before I said, "Something like that. But we don't know for sure they're doing anything illegal, so—"

"Then let us find out." Sarge disappeared down the alley, heading back the way we came.

I followed. He jogged through the shadows before he darted down an opening and out into the streets, jumping out in front of the woman from the street corner.

She was a mess, little more than skin and bones. Her t-shirt, torn in several places, was dirty and grungy. Her eyes were sunken and bloodshot, and her hair was a stringy mess. She yelped when she saw us and tried to get away.

Sarge didn't let her. Instead, he sprinted around, cutting off her escape.

She turned back toward me and whimpered. "What d'ya want? I didn't do nothin'."

I held out my hands, hoping to keep her calm.

Sarge didn't seem quite as concerned. "We know better. And so do you. Now, my young colleague and I could take you to the local precinct and tell them what we saw. I can't say for certain what will happen to you, but I suspect it won't be pleasant." He stepped closer, and she shrunk back. "Or you could hand over whatever it is you purchased, and we will let you go. Which will it be?"

The woman looked between us for a moment or two. Then she dug in her pocket and tossed a small baggie of bright blue powder at Sarge's chest. She turned and scrambled past me, almost tripping over her own feet.

Sarge caught the bag out of the air. He held it up to the meager light and frowned at it. He tossed it between his hands for a moment, his eyes distant. He tugged off one of his gloves and opened the bag.

"What are you doing?" I asked.

He glowered at me and then stabbed an uncovered finger into the dust. He gasped for a moment and swayed, almost as if he were about to collapse. But then he shook his head. His frown deepened. "Some sort of narcotic. I don't understand its chemical properties, but one thing I do know: It's tainted. If that woman had used this, she would have been dead within a week."

Of course. His psychometric powers. I grimaced. "It's called 'Blade.' Nasty stuff. There's a lot of that in Hogtown, especially since the HazMats moved in."

He frowned at me. "The what?"

"It's a gang, the HazMats. The term originally meant 'hazardous materials.' They deal in this sort of stuff."

Sarge's hand tightened into a fist around the baggy. "Then we shall stop them. Now."

I laughed. "That'd be nice, but we don't know where the Blade is coming from."

Sarge looked at the bag again. "Part of it came from South America. The rest is from a chemical supply company in New Jersey."

I blinked. "That's . . . interesting—but that's not what I meant. No one knows where they make the Blade or who's supplying it."

"So we need to find the Big Cheese?" Sarge smiled grimly. "No problem."

Once again, he set off. I jogged after him. He took us through the back alleys in what seemed like a random pattern before we emerged from a nearby alley just half a block from the men on the corner. Thankfully, they didn't spot us as we peeked around the corner.

"So do we have a plan?" I whispered.

Sarge nodded. "You make sure that the one leaning against the lamppost doesn't get away, then incapacitate one of his gorillas. I'll take out the other heavy."

I stared at Sarge, not sure I heard him correctly. "Sarge, I'm not a strapper. I'm not sure—"

He clapped me on the shoulders. "Neither am I, Failstate. That's never stopped me in the past. Now let's do this!"

He strode out of the alley and headed for the corner. I scrambled after him.

Sure enough, the men on the corner had spotted us. One of the "gorillas," as Sarge described them, nudged the other and jerked a thumb in our direction. The man leaning against the light post straightened and turned to face us.

"Good evening, gents," Sarge said, his voice remarkably calm. "Nice night to loiter."

The leader's gaze swept over Sarge. "What are you supposed to be? Halloween ain't for another few months."

His friends laughed.

"Who I am is the one who's shutting you down." Sarge's voice was still cool and collected.

The laughter stopped.

The leader's eyes narrowed. "Is that a fact? We ain't done nothin' wrong here."

"That's not what your last customer told us. Now, we can do this one of two ways: the easy way or the fun way. In the easy way, you hand over whatever you've got in your pockets. The cash, the drugs, all of it. Then you'll tell where I can find your supplier. And last, we'll all go down to the local precinct and you'll turn yourselves in and sign a full confession."

The leader sneered at us. "Ain't happening."

"Oh, good. I'd hoped you'd pick the fun way."

Sarge leapt toward one of the bodyguards, fists flying. The smaller man shouted and yanked a gun from his waistband. I lashed out with a blast of destructive energy and sliced the weapon in half. Then I ran for the leader and tackled him into the lamppost.

He struggled, trying to push his way free of my arms. I latched onto the post and did my best to hold him back, but beyond that, I wasn't sure what I could do. It's not as though I carried handcuffs.

Then I had an idea.

I pressed my palms onto the lamppost firmly and willed it to turn to taffy. The metal turned soft, then bendy, and the whole structure drooped. I quickly twisted it around the leader, using the metal like rope. He gaped down at me for a moment. I then released the post and allowed it to return to its metallic state.

It worked! The leader struggled against the now bent post and stared at me, his eyes wide with fear.

With a roar, the other gorilla charged me. I spun and charged my fists with destructive energy. I ducked the body-guard's punch and landed a superpowered right cross to his jaw.

He reared back, his agonized shrieks echoing off the nearby buildings. I waded in, landing two more quick punches to his gut, then I slammed a fist down across his cheek. He dropped to the pavement and didn't move.

How was Sarge doing? The other gorilla had backed him into a wall, raining punches down on him. Sarge had his hands up to protect his face. He tried to ward off the blows, but it was clear that he was overwhelmed.

"Hey!" I shouted and charged after the larger man.

He turned just in time to catch my fist across his temple. He yowled and fell back, clawing at his face. I landed two more punches, pouring as much energy into them as I could. I gave him a brutal uppercut, and the big man quickly crumpled and lay still.

Sarge stared at me, anger flashing in his eyes. Then he swallowed hard. "Good job." He strode over to the leader, who was still struggling against the makeshift restraints. "Tell me what I want to know."

"No way," the leader said. "You ain't getting nothing from me."

"That's where you're wrong," Sarge whispered. He pulled the bag of blue powder out of his hip pocket. "This has already told me a lot about where it came from. But I want more. I want your boss."

Some of the man's original cockiness returned. "I ain't got a boss. I'm an independent contractor."

Sarge snorted. "Please. You're nothing. A foot soldier. You're nothing. It's all you people are suited for."

My eyebrows climbed my forehead at that one. Racism from an iconic superhero?

"So I'm going to ask you again. Who is your boss?"

The man clamped his mouth shut.

Sarge sighed. "Have it your way, then." He clamped his hands on either side of the man's head.

For a moment, nothing happened. Then the drug dealer jerked and spasmed inside the twisted metal. He whimpered, begging in broken sentences for Sarge to let go. Then he jerked and went rigid. His eyes popped open, and he stared at Sarge. His whimpering turned to a full-throated wail, and it looked as if he were about to melt. Every blood vessel in his face turned a sickening black, the discoloration spreading from the spot where Sarge held him.

I darted forward and knocked Sarge's hands away. He stumbled back and wobbled for a moment. The drug dealer collapsed, sagging in the lamppost's embrace and moaning softly.

"What were you doing?" I demanded.

"Learning everything I could about our friend here." He smacked the drug dealer on the back of his head, hard enough that the man whimpered. "Isn't that right? I know quite a bit . . . including where to find his boss. Let's go." Sarge walked away.

I looked around at the mess. The two bodyguards were still unconscious. And the drug dealer still whimpered where he was tied up in the lamppost. I shaped my destructive field into a blade and sliced through the metal. The dealer dropped to the ground with a *thud*. I pulled out my cell phone and dialed the local precinct to come pick them up.

I ground my teeth. If this was what my future here looked like, maybe getting transferred to another city wasn't such a bad idea.

CHAPTER 41

"ARE YOU SURE?" I asked.

Sarge looked through DK's windshield and nodded. "Oh, yes. That scumbag knew our target's whereabouts. He'll be here."

The Katana Club's neon lights bathed the area in a strange green and pink glow. A long line of people snaked around the block, hopeful partiers who were stopped by the large bouncers that worked the door. I knew Katana only by its reputation. It was New Chayton's most exclusive club, nestled in the heart of downtown. Only the most famous and popular were allowed inside.

And, according to Sarge, the man responsible for bringing Blade into New Chayton was in there, as well.

"So what do we do?" I asked. "They're not going to let us through the front door since we're not on 'the list.'"

Sarge snorted. "I was never on any 'list' at the speakeasies I raided."

"But you went into those situations with a battering ram and backup," I countered.

"Not always. And what are you if not backup? But you're not wrong about a frontal assault."

Frontal assault? I was thinking about asking to go in, not breaking down the doors. Was he crazy? If the rumors were true, Katana was a hive of underworld activity, a neutral ground for the different gangs to hammer things out without violence.

We wouldn't be the first heroes who had tried to get in. There had been an epic confrontation here between Meridian and his archnemesis, Mind Master, back in the early '80s. I would have to ask Magnus about that story. I almost suggested calling him right there, if for no other reason than to try to regain some control of the situation. After all, Sarge had promised to listen to me.

"So the front door is out." Sarge rubbed his chin. Then he smiled. "Let's try the back."

I found a parking spot for DK, and we set out through the alleys once again. Sarge led the way, darting from one hiding spot to another. As we approached Katana, I snared Sarge's arm. He scowled at me.

I wished for a moment I could scowl back and he'd see it. I jabbed a finger up toward the side of the building. A tiny white security camera whirred back and forth, its glassy eye sweeping the alley. Clearly they wanted to make sure they saw who was coming. I concentrated on the camera and with a loud snap, sparks erupted from the device.

"What was that?" Sarge demanded.

Did he mean my power? Didn't he know what I did? Or did he mean— "The camera?"

Sarge looked between me and the wrecked camera. "That was a camera?"

Uncertainty rippled across his face, and I suddenly realized how lost he must be. To find himself suddenly eighty years in the future, in a place that should be home but wasn't.

I reached out and put a hand on his shoulder. "Look, if you need a moment or two—"

Sarge knocked my hand away and his scowl deepened. "No time to be maudlin. Let's get inside."

"How will we know when we find their boss?" I asked.

"I'll know."

I swallowed my retort and followed him as we trotted to the rear entrance. The alley behind the club was surprisingly clean. There were two dumpsters pushed up against the opposite building, along with a truck parked off to one side. The back of Katana wasn't much to look at, a large brick wall with a few small windows cut into the sides. The ones closest to the ground were too small to shimmy through. The larger ones were two stories up, and even if we moved the dumpsters, I still wouldn't be able to reach them. Somehow I didn't think that Sarge was likely to give me a boost.

Sarge ran to the only door, a simple metal door without a window and a large metal handle attached to a numeric keypad. Sarge rattled the handle for a moment or two, then frowned at the keypad. "Now what is that?"

I sighed and pointed at the device. It sizzled for a moment and then the door popped open. "It's unlocked."

He once again glared at me, but I thought that just maybe I saw a flicker of respect in his eyes. But he didn't say anything and just yanked the door open and stepped inside.

We found ourselves in a back hallway with an office on our left and some sort of employee break room on our right. Sarge jerked his head toward another door at the end of the hall. He practically kicked the door open. I chased him.

Sarge had come to a halt in the doorway, his eyes wide. Rhythmic music pounded the air, the vibrations rattling my chest. We'd emerged into the main area of the club. Young men and women gyrated on the dance floor, a large pit carved out of the middle of the room. Given the way some of the ladies were dressed, I felt the need to look away. They weren't leaving much to the imagination.

Surrounding the dance floor was a waist-high railing with tables and chairs pushed up against it. Bars stretched across the walls to our right and left, lit from underneath by a series of neon lights. It seemed as though all the people here had a drink in their hands as they shouted at each other to be heard over the droning music.

Sarge stepped over to one of the dancers, a young lady grinding against a man in a tight shirt and pants. "Excuse me, miss, you wouldn't happen to know where the—?"

She took one look at him and burst out laughing. So did her dance partner. They disappeared into the crowd.

Sarge frowned. He walked up to another man and tapped him on the shoulder. "Excuse me. Could you please—"

The man glanced at Sarge and rolled his eyes. "Oh, just what we need. Why don't you two masks blow? Nobody's doing anything illegal here."

"The fact that you felt the need to tell me that suggests otherwise," Sarge said.

The man thumped Sarge in the chest. "I told you, get lost."

"Not until you tell me where the VIP Lounge is."

"Why? You hopin' for a free drink?" He chortled. "Well, the beer's on you!"

The man upended his bottle and dumped it onto Sarge's shoulder. Sarge's eyes widened as the man laughed and walked away. I snared his arm to keep him from going after the other man. He glared at me, so I pointed to another end of the club. A large man with muscles so huge that they strained against his suit stood at the entrance of stairs that went up to a second floor. Sarge barreled into the crowd, knocking people out of the way.

The bouncer held up a hand as Sarge approached. "This isn't a costume party, gentlemen. As a matter of fact, I'm pretty sure neither of you are—"

Sarge struck the man in his neck. The bouncer choked and keeled over. Sarge snared the sides of his head and kneed him in the nose, tossing him aside. I gaped at the fallen man long enough that it barely registered that Sarge had started up the stairs. I dashed up after him, not wanting to face any additional security on my own.

The VIP lounge was quieter, but there seemed to be just as many people packed into the room. Flatscreen monitors pulsated with lights and color. Once again, women and men danced together in the center of the room, but that was before Sarge elbowed his way through them. From the way his shoulders were hunched and his hands were mashed into fists, I guessed that he had spotted his target.

Seated in a plush couch at the back of the room was a young man, maybe in his early thirties, dressed in an impeccably tailored suit, black with silvery pinstripes. His shirt was black and he wore a red tie. His hair was slicked back with some kind of oil. Two young ladies lounged next to him. No, more like on top of him, different parts of their bodies draped over or entangled with his. As pretty as they were, my eyes were drawn to the pair of burly men that stood at either end of the couch. More likely private bodyguards.

The young man in the suit glanced at us through narrowed eyes. He took a sip of his drink. "I don't know you."

Sarge took a step toward him, only to be blocked by the bodyguards. Sarge rose to his full height. "We have business with your boss."

"No, you don't," one of them growled.

I groaned. This could only lead to more violence. Given how crowded the club was, a lot of people could get hurt. I flicked a finger at the two bodyguards and sliced through their belts and zippers. Their pants dropped. They looked down at themselves, then turned to me, murder in their eyes.

I crossed my arms. "I could do worse. You want to risk it? All we want to do is talk."

At least, I hoped that's all Sarge wanted to do. The guards glanced at their boss. He sighed but nodded. The bodyguards hauled up their pants and stepped out of the way.

The young man disentangled himself from the girls and leaned forward. "If it isn't New Chayton's oldest and newest vigilante. What, they filming a buddy cop movie here?" He laughed.

A split second later, his friends did too.

"Are you Weston Sanderson?" Sarge asked.

I wondered how Sarge knew— Oh, right, the dealer and the light post.

The man nodded.

Sarge pulled out the bag of blue powder and tossed it onto Sanderson's lap.

Sanderson poked at the bag. "Hey, if you wanted to party, you came to the right place. But while this is generous and all, I'm really not into this stuff. Besides, Katana has pretty strict rules about what you use to get buzzed."

"We took that off one of your customers tonight," Sarge said. "Your bag man sends his regards, by the way."

Sanderson froze, his glass at his lips. Then he raised his eyebrows and lowered the drink. "One of *my* customers? I don't have any customers. Besides, I've been here all—"

"Cut the malarkey." Sarge leaned over Sanderson. "I was busting clowns like you when your *dad* was nothing but a sparkle in Grandpappy Sanderson's eye. I'm putting you on notice, Junior: I'm going to bring you down."

Sanderson glared at Sarge, his face contorted in a snarl. But then, just as quickly, the smooth smile returned. He leaned back and took another drink. "Good to know. I hate to say it, though, but it looks like you've worn out your welcome."

He pointed over Sarge's shoulder. I turned around and saw three more bouncers glaring down at us. Sarge looked them over and snorted. But thankfully, he didn't make it a fight. He shouldered his way past them. I followed, tensed and ready in case he did something stupid.

The bouncers steered us through the crowd on the main floor. Several of the club's patrons jeered as we passed. Instead of taking us to the front door, they hustled us out into the club's parking lot.

I started to say something, but Sarge headed off down the alley. I ran after him.

"What was that all about?" I demanded.

"We put Sanderson on notice," he said. "He knows we'll be coming for him now."

"Yes, he will!" I said.

"That's how you do it. You let the other man know you intend to fight him so that you can face him in a fair fight."

I gaped at Sarge. "What about those pushers we took out?"

Sarge waved away my objection. "Foot soldiers. Besides, the rules only apply to our equals, not our lessers like them."

My stomach twisted into another knot. "You've never seen me without my hood. How do you know I'm not one of your 'lessers'?"

Sarge froze. His gaze snapped to my hood, then roamed over the rest of my costume. His face contorted into a sneer. "That's not the point, and you know it."

No, it wasn't. "Look, maybe that's the way things worked when you were active, but times have changed."

"You think I don't know it! What I saw in there was absolutely scandalous! I mean, I lived through the '20s, son. I saw the flapper styles and the new dances and all that. But such open . . . debauchery!" He pulled at the shoulder of his uniform, still wet and stinking of beer. "And did you see what that moron did to me? You'd think we were the enemy, after all that I've sacrificed for them. Three wars, dying so they could act like animals!"

"That's . . . that's not fair," I said.

"Oh, no? Here I've been brought back, and for what? To protect a bunch of ingrates?"

I stared at Sarge for a few moments. "Look, it's not that bad."

"If we were to search everyone in that den of iniquity, how many of them would be carrying little bags of Blade?"

"I have no idea, and neither do you."

Sarge pursed his lips and glared at the back of the club. He paced a tight circle for a moment, looking as if he were getting ready to charge back into the club. As he walked, he reached out and touched one of the cars in the parking lot. He frowned, and his eyes went unfocused for a second. Then a smile flitted across his lips.

"Why don't you go get the car?" he asked. "I'll stay here and cover our withdrawal."

I frowned. His mood shift seemed rather sudden, but if he was calm . . . I jogged down the block and slid into DK. Just to be on the safe side, I activated suppression mode. If Sanderson or his thugs tried anything, maybe they'd think again if I rolled up in a tank.

Good thing I did. When I arrived back at Katana, a small crowd had gathered in the parking lot. I thought for sure that Sanderson's goons had jumped Sarge. But when I got out, I realized that it wasn't Sanderson's men at all. Instead, the man who had dumped beer on Sage was being held back by three other men. The man looked ready to murder Sarge, who smirked at him while standing at parade rest.

"What's going on here?" I demanded.

The man glared at me. "Look at what that freak did to my car!"

The car that Sarge had touched was a wreck. The headlights and windows were busted in, and numerous dents dotted the exterior. A small length of pipe lay on the pavement near the car's wheels.

I turned to Sarge. "Did you do that?"

Sarge shook his head. "Me? Why would I do this? While you were off getting the car, some hoodlums came in and did this." He looked at the man from the bar. "You know how hoodlums can be."

The man tried to charge again, but his friends held him back. "It was you, and we both know it!"

Sarge took a step forward and sneered down at the man. "Did you see me do this?"

The man stopped fighting. He actually took a step back. "No."

"Then I suggest you stand down before I have to shut your mouth for you."

The man shook off his friends' hands. He looked angry enough to spit, but he swore under his breath and stomped back into the club. The man's friends gave us both hard looks and followed him in.

I turned to Sarge. "Funny. I didn't see any 'hoodlums' running from the parking lot just now."

Sarge shrugged. "Maybe you need to get your eyes checked, Failstate." He stepped closer to me. "Or are you doubting my word?"

I quickly shook my head. "No."

Sarge smiled. "Good. Then let's call it a night, shall we? I think we've made some great progress cleaning up New Chayton." He clapped me on the shoulder and marched out of the parking lot.

I stared after him then looked at the damaged car. Guilt pressed down on me. For some reason, I had the feeling that we had left New Chayton a little messier. Hopefully tonight was just a fluke.

Hopefully.

CHAPTER 42

I NEVER THOUGHT I'd look forward to a day at high school. But after the previous night's insanity, I figured that, if I could only lose myself in the assignments and lectures, I might be able to temporarily forget about what had happened with Sarge.

But try as I might, I couldn't escape it. The thoughts chased me into class. Mr. Richards's civics lecture conjured up images of Sarge taking out his frustrations on that clubber's car. At one point, I was sure I saw Kynetic flirting with the captain of the football team near my locker, but when I looked again, it was only the head cheerleader. Every time the intercom crackled to life, I was sure it would be Agent Sexton calling to bawl me out. Instead of finding the day a relaxing escape, I wound up more keyed up than when it had started.

When the final bell rang, I quickly escaped the school. Maybe I'd drive over to Charlene's and surprise her. Hopefully, she'd be free. And even if she wasn't home, maybe I could spend a few moments to talk to Steve about Sarge. I couldn't go into specifics, obviously, but any insight would help.

I exited the school building, and my cell phone chirped. A smile tugged at the corner of my mouth. Maybe it was Charlene calling to invite me over. I fished it out of my coat pocket and glanced at the screen. My eyebrows rose. According to the caller ID, it was Agent Kensington on the other end. He shouldn't be calling me here! I hit the answer button. "Um . . . this is . . . Uh, what can I do for you?"

"Hello, Failstate!" Kensington's voice blared in my ear loud enough that I worried my classmates would be able to hear him. "I just wanted to touch base with you."

"Do you have some new information?"

"As a matter of fact, we do. We asked the people in the D.C. office to check Sarge's grave at Arlington to see if it had been disturbed. According to them, it appears as though someone drilled through the concrete and then sealed it again," Kensington said. "We have them checking the security footage to see if they can determine when this happened. I don't suppose Sarge said anything to you last night, did he?"

I checked both ways then crossed the street to the student parking lot. "Not about Dr. Ayers, no."

"That's too bad."

"Have the police said anything about finding Dr. Ayers?"

"Nothing."

I slowed to a walk as I approached DK. Ben sat on the hood and scowled at me. Two cardboard boxes sat on the ground next to him. For a moment, I was mentally transported back to our childhood. That was the look he wore right before he administered a "much deserved" beatdown.

"Thanks for the call," I said into the phone, my gaze locked on Ben. I hung up, and my fingers twitched toward my necklace. If this was going to turn into a brawl, I wanted to at least level the playing field.

"About time." He slid off the hood and jabbed a finger at the driver's side door. "Get in. We need to talk."

So we weren't fighting. Thank goodness. I did as he said, climbing into the driver's side. He shoved the boxes into the back, dropped into the passenger's seat, and glowered out the window. A few girls waved at him, giggling to each other. He didn't even wink at them.

Oh, this was going to get ugly.

I pulled out of the parking lot, trying to keep one eye on the road while staying alert for some sign of what was bothering Ben. "So are you going to say anything?" I asked.

"Drive to the farm, Rob. I think we both need to get some practice in."

Ah, so the boxes probably had more plates in them. He said nothing else on the whole drive to the farm where we'd practiced before. Once we were there, he dragged the boxes out of the back and dropped them on the ground so hard I was sure the plates were going to break.

He whirled on me. "Do you want to tell me what you were thinking?"

"Um . . . about any topic in particular?"

Pressure built around my head. Was he trying to crush my skull telepathically? This time, I did take off my necklace. He did say we were going to practice, after all.

"What were you and Sarge doing at Katana last night?" Ben stabbed his hands into the boxes and pulled out a stack of plates.

I blinked. Was he following me? "What business is that of yours?"

Ben threw the plates at the ground. Instead of shattering, though, they jerked to a halt and started to orbit Ben. "Just answer the question, Robin!"

"We—we took out some drug dealers in Hogtown. Sarge figured out that they worked for Weston Sanderson, and he decided we should confront him."

Ben once again growled, his fingers clenching and unclenching. The halo of plates picked up speed. "Do you realize what you've done?"

I fell back a step. If Ben launched those plates at me, I wouldn't have a lot of time to take them out.

Ben reached out, and one of the plates dropped onto his outstretched finger. It continued to spin, picking up more speed as it did. "You remember how I told you I was working on something big? Something that could get me my own license?"

I vaguely remembered that, sure. I nodded.

"A few weeks back, I busted a black market weapons sale in the warehouse district. The Blue Eclipse Boys were trying to buy some nasty stuff. Once the dust settled, I asked one of the Boys some pointed questions about why they needed the tech." He reached out and another plate landed on his other hand. "Turns out that they've been losing a lot of territory to the HazMats since you took out Pyrotrack."

He fired the plates at me. I lashed out and shredded them in the air. I wanted to smile, and not just because I got both plates. The fact that the Boys were crumbling because of something I did felt pretty cool. But then Ben glared at me and any sense of satisfaction fled. Two more plates dropped onto his fingers.

"Anyway, he started spilling his guts about everything that the HazMats have been up to, and it's nasty. Not just drug dealing: human trafficking too. Bringing in little girls from Asia and making them—" Ben snarled and clenched his fists. The plates shattered into dust. "You get the idea."

"So what happened?"

"I did some digging. You know, turned on my charm." He snared two more plates out of the air and set them to spinning on his fingers. "I found out that the next shipment of girls was coming in last night."

He fired off the plates at me. I managed to clip one, and the other sailed off down the field.

My stomach churned. Ben was right. This was huge. If he rescued those girls, it would propel his career forward, maybe even get him a license.

"I take it things didn't go as planned?"

Ben clenched his jaw. "You could say that. I got to where the shipment was going to be delivered, but the truck never showed up. Instead, about a half-dozen HazMats armed to the teeth ambushed me and tried to kill me!"

It felt as though a glacier had parked itself on my chest. "Are you . . . that is, are you—"

He waved away my words. "I'm fine, don't worry. It wasn't easy, but I survived. Even managed to get some one-on-one time with one of them to find out what went wrong. Turns out, two superheroes confronted their boss in a nightclub, and he got antsy. Changed the schedule for the delivery and sent his boys just in case you and Sarge showed up. They found me instead."

He flicked his hands, and the rest of the plates in the air shot toward me.

I lashed out with a destructive field and shredded all of them at once. "Ben, you've got to believe me. I had no idea that that would happen! Honestly!"

He glared at me, but his features softened. He nodded. "Okay. But Rob, this is a problem. Those girls are still out there. I want to make sure they're okay, y'know?"

I grimaced. I understood all too well. "Tell you what: Why don't you go on patrol with us tonight? I could use the help with Sarge anyway."

Ben arched a brow at me. "Problems?"

I rolled my shoulders. "Maybe. I don't know. He's just . . . a little off."

"Well, you've gotta cut the guy some slack, Rob. He has been dead for somewhere around eighty years now."

"Yeah, I know. Still . . ." I glanced over at my brother. "So what are you up to now?"

"Nothing. Why?"

I tied the necklace back on and winced as my face transformed again. I started back for DK. "Why not come home and surprise Mom? I bet she'd like to have you home for dinner tonight."

Ben smiled and nodded. "That sounds awesome. Thanks, Rob."

I smiled. "Anytime."

CHAPTER 43

"SO WHERE IS HE?" Gauntlet demanded, pacing by DK.

I looked up at the nearby buildings. "That's a good question. Last night, he kind of found me. And we didn't make any arrangements for where we'd be tonight."

Gauntlet groaned and kicked at the ground. "That's just perfect!"

I sighed. Dinner with Mom had gone well, but Ben's dark mood had come back the closer we'd gotten to the time to go patrolling. I could practically feel the tension radiating from his body as we'd suited up. As we'd driven into Hogtown again, Gauntlet had become more and more restless. And now it looked like a wild animal in a cage.

"Will you settle down?" I said. "If he doesn't show in five minutes, we'll deal with this on our own. We'll find some HazMats and lean on them."

Gauntlet snorted. "Like that will happen. They've probably all gone to ground because of what happened last night."

He had a point. While we hadn't gone very far into Hogtown, I could already feel the difference in the air. The neighborhood felt quieter, more peaceful.

The fire escape next to us clattered, and someone slid down the ladder to the pavement. Gauntlet dropped into a ready stance, but I turned, fully expecting to find Sarge. After all, that's how he'd greeted me last night.

Instead, Veritas rose from a crouch and dusted himself off. "Hey."

I stared at him, my jaw slack. "What are you doing here? And where have you been? I've been looking for you for days."

Veritas shifted on his feet. "I had a lot to think about. I was hoping to tag along tonight. Is that okay?"

I glanced at Gauntlet. "That okay with you?"

"Why ask me? You're the one with the license." Gauntlet kicked at a nearby trashcan.

"Welcome aboard." I motioned for Veritas to sit next to me.

He sat on DK's hood. "So what's he like? Sarge, I mean."

How could I answer that? I mean, I knew what Sarge's reputation was. He was one of the greatest heroes who had ever lived. And yet, given what I'd seen of him, I didn't much care for him. But should I really share my thoughts about him?

"Well, he's . . . That is to say, he's . . ."

"Why don't you ask me yourself?"

Sarge stood behind us, his feet slightly apart and his hands tucked into the small of his back. He regarded the three of us coolly, his head cocked to one side. Though my hood covered my face, I still looked away, studying the top of my boots.

Sarge strode forward until he was toe-to-toe with Veritas. Veritas didn't even blink. Instead, he stared back at Sarge, his gaze darting over his face and costume.

Then Sarge stuck out a hand for Veritas to shake. "They call me Sarge. I recognize you both, but I don't believe we've been formally introduced. What's your name?"

Veritas clasped hands with Sarge. "Veritas."

"Ah, a truth-seeker, are you? Then what truth about me do you want to know?" Sarge asked.

Veritas hesitated, his eyes narrowed.

I had seen that look before. He was mentally dissecting Sarge, pulling out truths that possibly Sarge himself didn't know. But then, Sarge had touched Veritas as well. His psychometry had probably teased out all sorts of information.

"Two questions: What do you know about Dr. Ayers or where he went?"

Sarge shrugged. "The VOC asked me the same thing. Aside from that small glimpse I got of him in the lab, I don't know anything about him."

Veritas's gaze sharpened. "I see."

"And your other question?"

"What is death like?" Veritas asked.

Sarge's eyes flickered for a moment. "You could die and find out for yourself."

"I'm not asking for—" Veritas closed his mouth.

"Ah, I see," Sarge said. "This isn't idle curiosity, is it? You . . . want to know what happened to someone you lost."

Veritas swallowed hard. "You were gone for decades. You must remember something."

"Someone close to you. And you want to know if she can come back too."

"Can you answer my question or not?"

Even I jumped at the fire in Veritas's voice.

Sarge hung his head and smiled. "I'm afraid I can't. I remember landing with the troops in Dieppe. I remember fighting Übermensch and the way he . . ." Sarge's face twitched into a frown. "And then I remember waking up in that lab. But what I may have seen or experienced between then and now . . . No, son, it's all a blank."

Veritas's shoulder slumped. "I see."

Sarge moved on, stepping closer to Gauntlet. Gauntlet straightened up and threw his chest out, but he kept a wry half-grin on his face. No way was he taking this seriously. If Sarge picked up on that . . .

Sarge stalked around Gauntlet, eyeing him from every angle. Then he came to a stop in front of Gauntlet and placed his hands on his shoulders. He stared deep into Gauntlet's eyes. "I've known many heroes in my day, so I know quality when I see it. And you, son, have that indefinable aura of greatness. I can tell you're destined for glory, to do things that most men have only dreamed of."

Gauntlet faltered, his gaze flicking from Sarge to me and then back again. "Uh . . . thank you, sir."

"Are you ready to find your destiny?" Sarge asked.

"You make it sound so fatal," Gauntlet said.

"Trust me: Death isn't everything it's cracked up to be. Shall we go?"

We piled into DK, Sarge taking the passenger seat. I glanced over my shoulder. It looked like my brother was about to eat his own knees in the back. He glared at me. All I could do was shrug.

"So what's the plan tonight?" I asked.

"I believe I know where to find the facility that produces New Chayton's Blade supply," Sarge said. "We're going to take that still down."

"Even though we've already warned Sanderson that we're coming?" I asked. "Won't we be walking into a trap?"

"That very well could be, but now it will be a test of our mettle, a battle for the ages." Sarge leaned forward in his seat. "Glory awaits."

I cast one more nervous look over my shoulder at my friends before I started the engine and we slipped out into the night. I didn't know if "glory" awaited us, but I did offer up a quick prayer asking God to watch over us. I had a feeling we'd need the extra help.

CHAPTER 44

"SO WHAT DO YOU THINK?" I whispered to Veritas.

He closed his eyes, and his head tipped forward. He shook his head. "Nothing helpful. How about you?"

I chuckled. "You mean besides my usual feelings of impending doom?"

Veritas's eyes twinkled, but I could still see the tension in them.

I peeked up and over DK at our target, the supposedly abandoned Blackthorn Meat Processing plant. Sarge had led us here with a singular determination. Even when I showed him data from DK's onboard computer that listed the building as vacant, he had insisted that we were in the right place.

It sort of made sense. It made the perfect headquarters for the HazMats. Even though the signs were faded and most of the windows broken or covered over with plywood, the factory still looked mostly intact. Its red brick exterior was scuffed and dirty, and the doors looked ready to collapse, but the frame looked solid. The facility filled a whole city block and towered over us, at least four or five stories high, meaning it was large enough to hold several Blade labs with room to spare. Although there were no lights in the windows and no cars in the parking lot, that didn't mean anything. If Sanderson had been running his drug cartel out of this site, he had been doing so for months without anyone catching on. He obviously had been careful.

I allowed myself a grim smile. Hopefully his luck would run out tonight.

Gauntlet dropped from above, floating to a halt a few inches above the pavement before landing. He too glanced over DK's hood at the seemingly abandoned building. "Anything?"

I shook my head. "You?"

Gauntlet shook his head. "Nothing from up top either. Where is Sarge?"

I poked my head up and looked around. When we had arrived at the processing plant, Sarge had sent Gauntlet out to check out the situation from above while he did some on-foot reconnaissance, leaving Veritas and me to "hold the fort" by DK. He had said he'd be gone for only ten minutes, if that. But now it was verging on twenty . . .

I turned to my left and realized that Sarge was crouching right next to me. I nearly leapt out of my skin. "Okay, how do you guys do that?"

Sarge smirked at me. "It's not difficult if you're willing to do the hard work." He turned to Gauntlet. "So what do we have?"

"Nothing. The roof is empty, so far as I can tell."

"Overconfident. That will work to our advantage. Let's go."

He led the charge, darting out from behind DK and across the street. I scrambled after him, vaguely aware that Gauntlet and Veritas fell in with me. We sprinted across the street. As we approached the chainlink fence around the lot, I lashed out with my power, carving an opening for us to shimmy through. Another mad dash across the vacant parking lot and I crashed into the building's wall. I froze and tried to stretch out with my hearing. Had anyone heard or seen us? I didn't hear anything out of the ordinary.

Sarge touched my shoulder and beckoned for me to follow. We edged along the side of the building to a set of double doors. Sarge made a slashing motion at them. Although I couldn't be sure, I guessed that he wanted me to get the doors open.

I glanced at Gauntlet and jerked my head at the doors. "I'll cut, you catch?"

He nodded.

With a quick flick of my wrist, I sheared through the doors' hinges. They fell outwards, only to float gently to the ground.

Sarge didn't wait for the doors to settle. He stepped through the open doorway. I followed.

We stood in a large open room, one with a stained cement floors and metal pillars that soared into the darkness overhead. The room had to be at least the size of a football field, and its ceiling was fifty feet up in the air. Chains hung down from the ceiling at random points. Most of the room was dark, but across the room was a bank of windows. Some sort of office maybe?

Sarge moved silently but quickly across the open space. Gauntlet brushed past me, his usual cocky half-grin firmly in place. I could practically see the hunger shining in his eyes. He was obviously already dreaming of the promised glory. I risked a peek at Veritas. He shrugged and set out after the other two. With a sigh, I took up the rear.

As we walked, a nagging sense of wrongness clawed at the back of my brain. From what I understood about Blade, the process for making and refining it was complex. It wasn't like a meth lab that could be set up in a kitchen. The process required extra ventilation, at least a rack or two of very specific chemicals, and special equipment to cook and strain and refine the chemicals. As near as I could tell, there wasn't any of that here.

Wait, what was that? I froze in place and held my breath. It sounded like . . . girls whimpering off in the shadows. I frowned. Where was the Blade lab? And why would there be girls in here?

Cold fingers danced up my back, and my eyes widened. We had to get out of the warehouse. We had walked into—

Bright lights blazed on, temporarily blinding me. Doors banged open around us, and men poured into the room, each one armed with an automatic weapon. They quickly surrounded us.

One of them, a large man wearing a garish red-and-black suit, stepped forward, an immense walking stick tucked under his right arm. He smirked at us. "So glad you could make it, gentlemen!"

—a trap.

CHAPTER
45

THE LARGE MAN clapped his hands together, a broad smile on his face. "Finally! Do you know how long we've been waiting for you morons to show? I was startin' to think you was gonna stand me up."

I dropped back in a defensive crouch. My gaze swept over the gun-wielding gang members. We were out-numbered at least four-to-one, and there might've been snipers we couldn't see in the darkness overhead. Not the greatest odds, but we'd probably do okay. I could still hear the girls crying. Or maybe it was small children? Where were they?

Sarge rammed his fists into his hips and cocked his head to one side. "Sorry to keep you waiting. Where's Sanderson? I thought he was the big boss here."

"Nah, he's just the public face. Me, I'm the brains."

"Nice of you to show up in person. You're that eager for us to defeat you?"

The larger man laughed. "Is that what you think is gonna happen here? Not even close. See, I've been dreaming of this moment for a long time. A very long time. I been laborin' in the shadows for too long now, always comin' in second. But no longer. Tonight, I'm takin' all four of ya down on my own."

"Says the man with all the backup," Sarge retorted.

"What, these guys? They're only here to make sure that this goes the way I planned. Y'know, be prepared?"

"Somehow I doubt you were a Boy Scout."

"Actually was, now that you mention it. Ditched the troop when I got a better offer."

I looked around. Most of the gunmen had their weapons trained on Sarge. Good. While Sarge kept them distracted, I'd act.

I glanced at Gauntlet and Veritas. They both nodded. I took a deep breath and tensed, ready to launch into action. Gauntlet shifted ever so slightly to his left. Keeping my arms straight at my sides, I extended five fingers and counted down silently. Four . . . three . . . two . . .

"Hey, you three!" The boss pointed in our direction. "Knock it off! You think I don't know what you're up to!"

Half of the guns swiveled in our direction. I relaxed and, a second later, so did Gauntlet and Veritas.

The large man shook his head. "Ah, yeah. Failstate. I gotta say, I been doin' my research on you, kid. You had potential, you really did. But right now, you're too much of a small fry for what I've got planned. Same thing goes for the other two yutzes. Nah, this is between me and the Sarge here. You've made a big splash here in New Chayton, Sarge. Everyone's buzzin' about how you're back from the grave. The way I figure it, if I'm the one who puts you back in the ground, then everyone's gonna buzz about me, right?"

"You make it sound like we're not going to fight back," I said.

"That's 'cuz you ain't."

The boss pulled a remote control out of his suit coat and flipped a switch. Motors whirred overhead, and a large cage descended from the ceiling until it hung thirty feet over our heads. Inside were a dozen girls, some looking as young as thirteen. They wore filthy rags and stood huddled together. They looked down at us, and their eyes radiated fear. I could imagine their voices, pleading with us to help them somehow.

I turned to Gauntlet. These had to be the girls he had been trying to rescue. Fury flashed through his eyes, and his hands balled into fists.

The boss chortled. "Like my insurance policy? Here's the thing: I got the chains holdin' up that cage wired to blow. You guys so much as make a wrong move, and they go splat. Now get over there."

One of the gang members walked around behind me and shoved me in the back with his gun. I stumbled forward. Gauntlet and Veritas fell in with me, and we were forced to one side of the warehouse. Half of the gunmen turned to aim at us while the other half kept their weapons trained on Sarge. On the one hand, this would work better for us since the gunmen were clustered together. But if I acted, the girls would likely die.

"It's nothin' personal, boys," the man continued. "But you're just gonna be three more overlooked victims. The real news will be that Sarge was taken out by Doomstone."

The way the boss said his name, it was clear he thought I should be impressed.

"Am we supposed to know who you are?" Gauntlet asked. "Maybe you should hire a PR guy."

Doomstone growled. "I won't need one by tomorrow morning. Boys, shut him up. Permanently."

The gunman behind me clamped down on my shoulder, pressing down hard enough that I got the message. Two others motioned for Gauntlet to step up against a wall while the rest formed an impromptu firing squad.

Gauntlet's eyes met mine. Although he looked calm, I could read a hint of fear behind his eyes. What could I do? Could I use my power to turn his costume into armor? No, I barely knew how to do that with my own outfit. I had no idea if I could project that effect over any distance. How about destroy the guns before they could fire? Sure, a blast of destructive energy would do the trick, but Doomstone would just drop the cage. What was I going to do? Why wasn't Sarge trying to intervene?

The gang members raised their weapons and took aim. It felt as though my entire body had been flash frozen. An intense chill wrapped around my arms and legs. Gauntlet's Adam's apple bobbed, and he closed his eyes.

"No!" The word ripped out of my throat.

A body dropped out of the darkness above and landed in front of Gauntlet. The gunmen shouted in surprise but opened fire anyway. It took a moment for the identity of the newcomer to register. Kynetic! She stood tall in front of Gauntlet, her arms wide open.

Bullet after bullet slammed into her. And yet, the only indication that something was wrong was the slight twitch of her upper lip and a small bead of sweat that trickled from her brow down across her mask. But her costume didn't shred, she wasn't knocked backward, and I didn't see any blood.

Within a few seconds, the hail of gunfire stopped. Kyn smirked at the gunmen and raised her hands, palms down. Dozens of bullets poured from her fingers and clattered across the cement floor.

Then she disappeared in a blur of motion. My head snapped around, trying to follow her, but I couldn't. She must have unleashed the collected energy of the bullets all at once. But why use it like that?

Then I understood why. Doomstone stared at his empty hand. The remote for the cages had vanished.

Kyn reappeared next to me. She handed me the remote. "Your move, gentlemen."

I didn't have to be prompted again. I let out a blast of destructive energy that tore through the crowd of gunmen. Patches of their clothing dissolved away, but more importantly, their guns crumbled in their hands. Gauntlet waved his arms, and several of his executioners were thrown off their feet. Veritas had already taken out his guard and had ran to my side.

I tossed Veritas the remote. "See if you can disarm this. Gauntlet, try to get the girls out of those cages. Sarge, Kyn, and I will handle the rest. Right, Sarge?"

I whirled on Sarge. His face appeared to be carved out of stone, his eyes wide and staring and his mouth hanging open ever so slightly. But he recovered quickly. "Absolutely! Leave Doomstone to me!"

Oh, great, so that left about sixteen for me to handle on my own. Piece of cake.

Doomstone laughed. "Then c'mon, creampuff!"

He flexed his arms and squatted down, his face twisting into a rictus of pure rage. He roared, a gurgling sound that quickly turned into a loud bellow. As he did, his clothing swelled and angular shards of stone ripped through the material. Within a matter of seconds, Doomstone was encased in obsidian stone armor, all sharp angles and jagged spikes. Only his eyes, which blazed with red light, were visible through the solid piece of rock that covered most of his face. With another roar, Doomstone charged Sarge and slammed into him.

Sarge rolled across the floor, end over end until he somehow managed to pop back up on his feet. His eyes narrowed, and he darted forward, landing two quick blows across Doomstone's chin and then a kick to his stomach. Doomstone's rock armor cracked under the assault, and he stumbled backward. When had Sarge gotten strong enough to do that?

Doomstone regained his footing and backhanded Sarge, knocking him down.

Blood trickled from the corner of Sarge's mouth. He rose from the floor, but it looked as though his legs could buckle at any moment.

Doomstone chuckled, the sound of boulders grinding together. "That's right, little man. Now you'll learn to fear me. Boys, finish the others."

The supervillain stomped toward Sarge.

With a roar, the gang members rushed toward me. I snapped out of my reverie and charged up my fists with destructive energy.

I punched the nearest gang member in the chest, and he went down tearing at his shirt and howling. I ducked another punch and swept that attacker's feet out from under him, then I rolled and lashed out with my power. I carved a divot under the feet of another HazMat. He lost his balance, allowing me to tackle him to the cement.

Kyn waded into our opponents, not even trying to block their kicks or punches. Given the way she was sending them flying when she punched them, it was clear she was using their own strength against them by absorbing the force of their attacks.

"I would have thought you'd be gone by now," I said.

She smirked at me, even though one of her attackers clocked her across her forehead. "I thought about it, but I didn't feel right leaving things the way they were between us. I wanted to come back and say I'm sorry."

So far as I was concerned, saving my brother was a pretty good apology.

One of the gang members swung a length of pipe at my head. I spotted it too late, but then my power flared. The pipe ricocheted off my hood with an audible clang. I kicked the HazMat goon in the knee, and he went down.

I took stock of the HazMats. Kyn and I had taken most of them out. Kyn picked up the last two and cracked their heads together. I looked over to see how Gauntlet was doing. He had leapt up onto the cage and crawled to the chain.

"Veritas, how's it going?"

He had removed the back of the remote and was fiddling with its innards. "I think I've almost got it. I . . ." His eyes widened. "Oh, no."

Fire burst from the chain holding up the cage, and it started to drop.

Gauntlet's arms pinwheeled, and it appeared as if he might tumble off. But then he dove for the chain and caught it in his hands. Even though the cage fell away from him, he hovered in midair and hauled back on the chain, his arms and back straining.

The cage dropped two feet but then stopped sharply. The girls shrieked and screamed, but they didn't fall any farther. Then Gauntlet lowered it the rest of the way and collapsed on top of it. He rolled off the top and dropped to the floor. He ripped the side of the cage off and waved for the girls to come out. They burst past him and ran for the exit.

Gauntlet collapsed, his hands on his knees. His chest heaved, and he gasped for air.

I stood up a little taller. I wanted to whoop. I wanted to give him a hug. I wanted—

A loud boom echoed through the empty space, and Sarge came to a rest at my feet, his body limp. My head snapped up, and I saw Doomstone stomping toward me.

"One down." He cracked his knuckles. It sounded like redwood trees snapping in half. "It's better that my boys didn't kill all of you. I'm going to enjoy this."

CHAPTER 46

I BACKED AWAY from Doomstone, trying to keep as much distance between him and me as possible. As I did, I glanced at Sarge. Was he breathing? It looked like it, but I didn't think he'd be waking up anytime soon.

I glanced back at my friends. They too were retreating. The problem was, we really didn't have anywhere to go. The empty room didn't provide much by way of cover. We could maybe make a break for the offices on the opposite end of the building, but I doubted that Doomstone would let us get very far. "Any suggestions?" I asked.

"Just one." Kynetic whirled to Gauntlet. "Hit me. As hard as you can."

"What?" Gauntlet turned to me, a question on his face.

"Just do it!" I said. "She'll be okay. Trust me."

Gauntlet reared back and smashed Kynetic as hard as he could.

Kyn didn't so much as flinch at the impact. "Thanks, big guy. I've got this." She whirled and charged at Doomstone. She slammed into him so hard that I was sure the resulting crack was loud enough to shatter glass.

Doomstone skidded across the cement floor fifteen feet before he came to a halt. Cracks radiated through his chest armor and flakes of stone dropped to the floor. He laughed. "Not too bad, little girl."

Then he charged and snared her by the arm. He tossed her to one side. She hit the ground hard and rolled.

Gauntlet charged in, his fists hammering like pistons onto the cracks. Once again, Doomstone fell back, trying to block some of the punches. Most of them struck home. Gauntlet let loose a battle cry that grew louder and louder with each punch.

As impressive as it was, it soon became clear that he actually wasn't hurting Doomstone. Instead, the villain laughed and then smashed a giant fist across Gauntlet's head. With a groan, Gauntlet crumbled.

I turned to Veritas. "Make sure those girls are safe and bring help. Paramedics, SWAT team, army, whatever. Go!"

Veritas hesitated and then darted out of the room. I turned to face Doomstone. "Just you and me now, Doomstone."

He guffawed. "Am I supposed to be intimidated? Dumb kid in a Halloween mask and ratty old clothes? You've got absolutely no chance."

"We'll see, won't we?" I offered up a silent prayer of thanks that my voice didn't crack.

Another bellowing laugh. "Your funeral."

He charged and swung his arms like scythes.

I ducked the blow and ran to one side. Doomstone turned and punched again, another blow that I easily sidestepped. He was obviously toying with me.

Doomstone punched again, his fist slicing the air over my head. I marshaled my power around my fist and darted in, landing a solid punch to his chest.

Apparently enough of the destructive energy made it through the thick rock armor because Doomstone fell back with a grunt. He rubbed his chest, the sound of stone grating on stone enough to set my nerves on edge. "Neat trick. Maybe under other circumstances, I'd give you a real fight. But as it is, I gotta finish off Sarge yet, and I can't let you distract me anymore."

His punches came in faster and faster. How could a man that big, encased in stone, move so quickly? I felt as though I were dancing as I juked and wove, trying desperately to avoid his punches.

Then a blow grazed my temple, and stars exploded in my vision. My arms flailed as I tried to stay on my feet. I tripped over my own boots and landed with a thump on the floor.

Doomstone's foot whistled down at me, and I rolled out of the way. It slammed into the cement hard enough that cracks snaked out from the point of impact. Doomstone laughed and stomped after me.

I kept rolling until I had put enough distance between him and me that I could risk getting to my feet. My legs felt like water beneath me, and I staggered. This wasn't good. I could barely touch him through that thick armor. If only there was some way for me to get rid of it.

My eyes widened. There was! My power had trouble destroying organic material, but rocks fell outside that category. At least, normal rocks did. Hopefully Doomstone's armor did too. Only one way to find out. I fell back, stumbling over my feet as I went. I retreated farther and farther from the inert bodies of my fallen friends.

"Where you goin', Failstate?" Doomstone tromped after me. "There's nowhere you can hide."

With a roar, he charged. I dodged to my left and he barreled past me. As soon as he was clear, I unleashed my power, channeling it into one large blast in front of me.

Doomstone staggered as wave after wave of destructive energy slammed into him. He threw up his hands over his face, but the stone armor on his forearms boiled away under my assault. The cracks in his chest widened, and more chunks fell away, disappearing before they could hit the floor.

Sweat poured down my face. Keeping this high-powered blast going and focused was taking everything I had. I could already feel my control slipping, the throb behind my eyes turning painful and sharp. It felt as though all of my strength were draining down through my legs and into the floor underneath me. But I couldn't stop. Not now.

Doomstone took a step toward me now. He peeked over his arms at me, and I realized that most of his stone helmet had been destroyed. A look of genuine panic flitted across his face. But still he kept coming.

I poured it on, trying to wring every last ounce of strength from myself. If I could only finish the job, completely destroy his armor, maybe then I could . . . I could . . .

My legs buckled beneath me, and I fell to one knee. It felt as though lead were coursing through my veins, tugging at my arms and head. Grey nibbled at the corner of my vision, and a warm fog enveloped my brain. I couldn't keep this up anymore. My power sputtered and then stopped.

My hands dropped, and I fell to all fours. My body heaved as I sucked in air, trying to put out the fire in my lungs. Then the strength went out of me, and I fell to the floor, hard enough that my head ricocheted off the cement.

Something scraped across the floor and nudged me. Then a strong hand rolled me onto my back. My eyelids flickered and then drifted open.

Doomstone stood over me. Most of his stone helmet had been sheared away. Only small clumps off rock jutted out of his body at random points. There was a small stone rosette embedded in his chest, and enough rocky armor to pass for shorts on his legs. He looked just as tired as I felt, but triumph still gleamed in his eyes.

I soon understood why. He lifted up his right hand to strike—it was still encased in stone.

"A good try, kid." His voice was hoarse and little more than a whisper. "But I win. And once I've had a moment to catch my breath, I'm going to end your friends as well."

He drew back his fist, and I braced myself.

But then someone vaulted over me, a blur of olive drab, and slammed into Doomstone. I managed to summon enough strength to prop myself up on my elbows to see what was going on.

It was Sarge. He looked like an avenging angel as he pummeled Doomstone. The villain tried to defend himself, but Sarge simply knocked his hands away. Sarge landed two quick blows across Doomstone's jaw and then gave him a blow to his stomach. The crimelord dropped back and fell to his knees. Sarge grabbed him by the front of his shirt and lifted him up, then landed one last blow across his face. Doomstone dropped to the floor.

Sarge paused, his chest heaving. He turned to face me, and his lips peeled back in a sneer.

I clambered to me feet. My head swam, and my surroundings went out of focus, but I didn't want to stumble in front of Sarge. Gauntlet and Kyn were still out, but so were the gang members, thankfully. I rushed to Gauntlet's side and leaned down to check on him. He was still breathing, and he groaned a bit. His eyes fluttered open, and he grinned at me ever-so-slightly.

Sarge was right there next to me. He grabbed Gauntlet by the hand. "Good job, soldier. You did yourself proud by rescuing those girls. I was glad for your help."

I stared at Sarge. What was this nonsense? Had I somehow turned invisible? No, that wasn't right. I tamped down on my frustration. That everyone was alive and breathing was the important part, not who got the credit. Besides, my brother *had* been pretty heroic in how he'd caught that cage.

What about Kynetic? I turned around.

She had sat up and was rubbing her head.

I rushed to her side. "Are you okay?"

"Now that I've seen you, yeah. I forgot how much it hurts when someone hits you."

"How was he even able to do that?" I asked.

She grimaced. "My power isn't permanently turned on, F. I have to be ready to 'catch' the kinetic energy. I messed up. Sorry." She mouthed a few words and then smiled. "I'm glad I came back."

"So am I." I helped her to her feet.

Sarge clapped Gauntlet on the shoulder and then made a beeline for the exits. Now what? I turned to Kyn, but she nodded and motioned for me to go. I jogged after Sarge.

Veritas was leaning next to the exit. I stopped to check with him, but he waved me through the door.

I emerged into a pool of bright light. Half a dozen police cars filled the warehouse's parking lot. Officers jogged past me and into the warehouse, followed by a swarm of EMTs. Not only that, but a number of reporters had set up their cameras and were shouting questions at Sarge. He once again stood at the ready, hands tucked behind his back and his feet slightly apart.

". . . and as I said, I will not be answering any questions at this time. Instead, I will hold a press conference in two days on the steps of City Hall. Thank you." He turned to walk away but paused when he saw me. His lip twitched into a snarl for a moment, but then he marched back into the building.

"Failstate!" Several reporters called my name and waved for my attention.

"Do you have any idea what Sarge is going to announce at his press conference?" another yelled.

"No." But I really wish I did. I sighed. There was really only one way to find out.

CHAPTER
47

SO SHOULD I HAVE BEEN IN COSTUME for Sarge's press conference? I toyed with the idea but decided against it. Sarge hadn't invited me to attend. Clearly he wanted the spotlight to himself. There really wasn't any reason to antagonize him. Not only that, but this gave me a chance to blend into the crowd and disappear. Maybe I'd notice something new about Sarge if he didn't know I was watching.

The drive into downtown was uneventful, although the Friday afternoon traffic snarled some of the roads. But the real obstacles appeared when I approached City Hall. Apparently, the cops had set up a perimeter around the building and were refusing to let traffic through. I found a parking spot a few blocks over and pumped a bunch of quarters into the meter. Hopefully, Sarge wouldn't go longer than an hour.

I dropped into the river of humanity that flowed through the sidewalks and headed for City Hall. It was a towering skyscraper made of brown stone and silvery glass, soaring up among the office buildings with what appeared to be a large crown made out of steel posts. At its base was a large plaza with a wide reflecting pool in front of the entrance. Someone had set up a platform off to one side of the plaza, and reporters were clustered in front of it. But a good-sized crowd of on-lookers had formed as well, forming an outer perimeter behind the reporters. I stepped up to the edge and glanced at my watch. Almost four o'clock. I hoped Sarge wasn't running late.

My cell phone chirped in my pocket. I pulled it out and answered. "Hello?"

"Failstate? This is Agent Kensington. You got a second?"

"Uh, sure. What's up?"

"I just wanted to update you on what we've learned about Sarge's grave."

There was a large roaring sound that partially masked his voice. "Where are you right now?" I asked.

"Waiting for Sarge to show up for his press conference."

I turned toward the stage set up near the entrance to City Hall. Sure enough, I spotted Agent Kensington standing on one side of the platform, his gaze scanning the crowd.

"Why? Where are you?" Kensington asked.

I stammered. A nearby police car fired off its siren once, a loud whoop that sounded like it was right next to me.

"Are you here at the press conference too?" Kensington asked.

I risked a glance at the stage. He stood straighter and scanned the crowd. I quickly ducked behind another man. True, there were a lot of people on their phones at the time, but I didn't want to take the chance of being spotted. "You were saying about Sarge's grave?" I said.

"The VOC office in D.C. has reviewed all the footage, and they think they know when the tissue sample was taken."

"That's great!"

"Not exactly. Someone erased a two hour block of footage from July 29th this last summer. It must have happened then."

"So we don't have evidence of what Ayers did."

"That's the thing," Kensington said. "I'm not sure it was him. I've been going over everything we've found about Dr. Ayers: his financials, interviews we've conducted with his colleagues at NCU, even his Facebook account. As near as I can tell, he's never been to Washington. As in ever."

"Maybe he has an accomplice who helped him."

"We're looking into that, but we're not turning up much. Well, I've got to go. I think Sarge will be out here soon." He hung up. I stashed my phone in my pocket and let out a sigh of relief. One minor disaster averted.

"Hey, you!"

Charlene? I turned and there she was, her smile dazzling. She rushed over to me and hugged me tightly.

"What are you doing here?" I asked.

"Dad sent me," she said. "He wanted to be here himself to see Sarge in the flesh, but he's . . ." Her head dipped. "He's having a bad day. Can't get out of bed. So he sent me with the video camera and instruction to not miss a thing." Her smile faltered. "What are you doing here?"

"I was in the neighborhood and thought I'd . . ." My voice trailed off as I realized now I'd have to come up with an excuse as to why I was in the neighborhood to begin with.

Thankfully, she wasn't able to press me. The doors to City Hall opened, and several people walked out. Mayor Reilly led the way. Chief Blackthorn and Chief Thompson followed her out onto the platform.

Behind them were men and women in dark suits and sunglasses. I pegged them immediately as VOC. Sure enough, bringing up the rear was Agent Sexton, a tight grin on his lips.

And then Sarge appeared, dressed in his usual army uniform. The crowd around me erupted into cheers, several people shouting welcome to him. Sarge didn't acknowledge any of it, although he did touch the edge of his helmet in a salute as he approached the platform.

Soon the entire group had assembled on the platform, and Mayor Reilly stepped up to the podium. She smiled at the crowd and waited for the noise to die down. "When I heard that New Chayton's own Sarge had returned to active duty, I could hardly believe it. Like many of you, I'd heard the stories of how he dedicated his life to protecting the United States of America and her citizens in the early part of the 20th century. While I don't totally understand what's brought him back, I know I'm not the only one who's grateful for his return."

The crowd erupted in new cheers. Mayor Reilly smiled warmly and waited until the noise died down.

"Sarge," Mayor Reilly said, "I know I'm sleeping a little better at night knowing that you're patrolling our streets."

Even more cheers echoed through the plaza. I glanced at Charlene, but she had raised her camera and was engrossed in what she saw on its miniature screen.

Mayor Reilly moved to one side and motioned for Sarge to step forward. The crowd continued to shout. This time, Sarge did smile, waving to the crowd as they shouted his name.

Finally, after three or four minutes, the people around me fell silent.

"Thank you all for this homecoming. In many ways, I too am having a hard time believing that I'm here, standing before you all, in this strange new world in which I find myself. But the support I've received from so many of you, including the men and women of the Vigilante Oversight Committee, has been wonderful. You have made this transition much more painless."

Sarge gripped the edges of the podium. "I've spent the past few days getting to know our great city once again. There have been a lot of changes, a lot of things that I'm still trying to get used to. One thing that hasn't changed is you, my fellow citizens. I've always believed that New Chayton produces the United States' finest citizens, and that hasn't changed."

The crowd cheered even louder. I clenched my jaw. The man knew how to work a crowd, I had to give him that.

"But, like I said, a lot has changed. We aren't as united as we used to be. Maybe it was because of the War to End All Wars and the two that followed, but the America that I knew stood together. We were good people, decent people. Yes, there were a few bad eggs, but they were in the minority. Now, society seems to be crumbling around us. The wrong people are being idolized and held up as examples to our children. I fear that what once made America great is gone." Muscles in his neck seemed to clench. "I intend to change that."

No one cheered this time. Instead, I could hear the distant sounds of traffic, but even that seemed to grow quieter, as if everyone were sucking in a deep breath to hear what Sarge would say next.

"I intend to make a difference, not just here in New Chayton, but throughout this great country of ours. Some of you undoubtedly heard about what happened in Hogtown the other night, how the local gang who call themselves the HazMats tried to ambush me and several of my colleagues. I'm pleased to report that we were able to foil their plot and bust up their cartel."

The crowd applauded.

Sarge raised his hand. "And I wanted to share the limelight with one of them in particular. Gauntlet?"

I froze. The doors to City Hall opened once again, and Gauntlet stepped out. The sunlight glinted off of his shoulder armor as he waved the crowd. He walked up to the platform and took a place next to Sarge.

Sarge reached over and put a hand on Gauntlet's shoulder. "This young man is an excellent example of what's right with our city. He knows that there are problems, serious problems, and he has stepped up to help. Gauntlet was invaluable two nights ago. Not only did he help me dismantle a major criminal enterprise, but he also rescued a number of young ladies destined for a life of misery and abuse. I'm pleased to report that, with the help of the State Department, those gals are headed home, safe and sound."

A few of the young ladies in the crowd shouted Gauntlet's name. My brother shot them a wide grin and winked.

"And now," Sarge continued, "I'm going to call on his help once again.

"But not just him. With the help of the VOC, I am starting a new initiative, one that will start here in New Chayton and will spread across this great nation of ours. I am calling on not only those like Gauntlet and myself who have special abilities, but also on those of you who don't, to join me in reclaiming our country, in setting it on the right path again, and making us great again."

The audience roared their approval.

"In the coming days and weeks, I will be sharing more information with you on how you can help us achieve this great vision. I understand there's something called the 'Internet' where I'll be able to . . . put . . . the information you'll need. And you'll be able to find it, right?" Sarge smiled thinly. "Although I'll need help putting it there."

A few people chuckled.

"Thank you all, and God bless America!"

The crowd screamed their approval. The reporters started shouting questions at Sarge but he didn't answer them. Instead, he waved and started back for the City Hall entrance. The others filed off the stage, although Gauntlet did spend a little time mugging for the cameras.

Charlene lowered the camera and turned to me. "Wow."

"Wow" was right, but I didn't trust myself to say anything. Why had he invited Gauntlet to join him? Why not me? Yes, Ben was more photogenic, and sure, he needed the publicity more than I did, but it still annoyed me. What was Sarge trying to do?

"So are you busy now?" Charlene asked. "Do you want to maybe get something to eat?"

That brought a smile to my face. "Absolutely."

"Great."

My cell phone chirped in my pocket. I pulled it out and glanced at the caller ID. It had better not be Kensington again.

I froze. According to this, it was Downtime.

I flashed a smile at Charlene, hoping that it somehow masked my nervousness. "I'm so sorry, but I have to get this." I hit the button and pressed the phone hard against my ear. I took a step away from Charlene and hunched over. "Hello?"

"Greetings, Failstate!" Sure enough, it was Downtime. "I presume you saw Sarge's announcement just now?"

"Uh . . . yeah. I did."

There was a momentary hesitation. "Am I to take it that you're not able to speak openly at this moment?"

I glanced at Charlene again. She smiled. I turned ever so slightly away from her and tried to shield the phone with my body. "Something like that, yes."

"Very well, I will make this brief. I am calling on behalf of Sarge. He wishes to have another conclave with as many licensed heroes as can attend. The same place as before, this Saturday. Will you be able to attend?"

I looked back at City Hall. When had Sarge done this? And why didn't he consult with me about this? He was picking up some bad habits from Sexton. "I should be able to, yes."

"Very good. We will see you then."

The line went dead. I tucked the phone back into my pocket and turned around.

Charlene brightened. "So are you ready to go eat?"

"Sure," I lied. Suddenly I wasn't all that hungry anymore.

CHAPTER 48

STEPPING INTO THE PENTHOUSE of Magnus Towers was like stepping into a museum. Or a mausoleum. Once again, everything shone and glinted in the soft light. A table of hors d'oeuvres filled one wall and some light jazz drifted through the room.

Much to my surprise, I was the first one to arrive. I had expected to have found Meridian, at least, seeing as it was his building. But as near as I could tell, I had the penthouse all to myself. I wandered past the hors d'oeuvres, running my hand along the table top, before I stepped up to one of the large windows that overlooked the city.

New Chayton looked peaceful and calm. Lights threaded through the streets, the sounds muffled through the glass. I pressed my hand against the glass. From this perspective, it was hard to believe the city needed any heroes at all.

What was going to happen here tonight? The news outlets had been buzzing since Sarge's announcement. Some of the talking heads had even gone so far as to theorize that the VOC as we knew it was coming to an end. That wasn't entirely bad, not from my perspective, but where would that leave me? My stomach curdled, and I rubbed a hand over it. Maybe I was just hungry. Well, so long as no one was here to peek under my hood, I might as well grab a snack.

I turned around and practically ran straight into Etzal'el.

"Failstate." His voice ground over me, leaving numb tingles in its wake. "A pleasure to see you."

"So I take it Downtime got in contact with you as well?" I asked.

Etzal'el growled, a low rumble that sounded like a distant earthquake. "He did indeed. I felt it best if I attend and see this . . . abomination for myself."

"So you don't trust Sarge?" I asked.

"I do not." Etzal'el seemed to grow taller, swelling up before me. "He has been animated by dark forces."

Oh, great. That's just what we needed to keep everything running smoothly tonight, more of Etzal'el's paranoia. "You can't know that for certain."

"Do you think me a fool? Tell me, Failstate, how did Dr. Ayers construct his secret laboratory beneath NCU's campus without anyone noticing? Where did he find his resources?"

"Well, I—"

"And the return of this 'Sarge'—it is not the miracle so many claim. I fear it serves a darker purpose."

I blinked. That . . . that actually made sense.

"That is why I am here tonight," Etzal'el said. "I must be ever watchful, for I know that Sarge's return does not bode well."

"For who?"

Etzal'el's cloak billowed around him like a cloud of doom. "For the living."

A chill swept through me.

The elevator pinged, and Raze sauntered into the penthouse. "Lucy, I'm home!" He stopped when he saw Etzal'el. "Oh, great. You're here too. And I thought tonight might actually be fun."

Etzal'el only growled.

I stepped between them. "So do you have any idea what Sarge wants to talk about?"

Raze snared a plate and started piling food on it. "No idea. But I guess we'll find out, won't we?"

"We shall see." Etzal'el glided over to the corner and took up position, probably so he could watch the whole room.

Slowly but surely, more licensed heroes arrived, even more than the last time we'd met. I was impressed. Clearly Sarge still commanded a great deal of respect. When Meridian arrived, he nodded in greeting to me and then spent several minutes welcoming everyone else.

Sarge arrived, and the room fell silent. He stood at parade rest, looking over the assembled heroes. Then he smiled. Well, not really "smiled," exactly—more like his lip twitched in a smile-like direction. But based on what I had seen in the past week, it was the most warmth he was likely to show.

"It's good to see you all here. I've been reading dossiers on all of you, and I am humbled by the sheer might gathered in this room tonight." He looked over us all. "But I must say I am disappointed in your collective failure."

It was as if the heat had been sucked out of the room. Raze froze, a mug of beer raised to his lips. The glass shattered in his hand. "What?"

"You heard me. In my generation, we fought a war to end all wars, and we won. I personally safeguarded this country from a coup by taking on the Blue Duchess myself. I even sacrificed my life to stop the Nazis in the Second World War. And what do you all do?" Sarge stalked over to Raze. "You date pin-up girls and attend motion picture premieres." Sarge turned to Downtime. "And you spend more time inventing doo-dads for the phone company than patrolling Seattle." His burning gaze swept over each one of us. "There are many who find you nothing more than dilettantes. And I agree."

Raze snarled and took a step forward, jabbing a finger at Sarge. "I don't care who you are, zombie-man. No one talks to me that way!" He clenched his fists, and a rumble shook the room.

"No brawling!" I started forward, my arms out.

Raze charged at Sarge, a roar building in his throat.

Sarge raised a hand. A blast of rainbow-colored light erupted from his palm, creating a shield in front of Sarge. Raze slammed into it hard and fell to the floor. Sarge dropped his hand, and the shield vanished. Sarge lunged and pressed his forearm on Raze's neck.

I gaped at him behind my hood. An energy shield? This didn't make sense. How had Sarge upgraded himself?

Sarge looked up at us. "You see what I mean? Vain. Easily distracted. A joke. Well, I am going to change that. Starting tonight with all of you."

Downtime cleared his throat. "Wh-what did you have in mind?"

"When the Blue Duchess set up her organization, she had the right idea for the wrong reason. Her criminal syndicate very nearly overthrew the government. I intend to emulate her tactics, just not her goal." Sarge spread out his arms as if inviting us to hug him. "I want you all to join me."

A low rumble filled the room. For a moment, I thought Raze had recovered, but it wasn't him. Instead, Etzal'el had moved from his post in the room's corner. He slipped through the room and towered over Sarge. Sarge didn't back down. Instead, he cocked his head to one side and looked up at Etzal'el's hidden face.

"I will not be a part of this." Etzal'el's voice, while just a whisper, was enough to back me up three steps. "Mark this one well, friends: He will only lead you to disaster."

Shadows erupted from Etzal'el's cloak, rushing through the room and devouring the light. Much to my surprise, no one reacted. Then a light flared, not so surprisingly, from Meridian. It wasn't much, just enough to reveal that Etzal'el had disappeared.

A moment later, the light returned fully. Sarge looked over the remaining heroes. "Anyone else wish to leave? I won't hold it against you. But for those who stay, you will help me usher in a glorious future, first for New Chayton, and then for the rest of the country."

The other heroes didn't answer. They didn't head for the door either.

Sarge smiled, an expression that would be better suited for a lizard. He clapped his hands together. "Excellent. Then let us start discussing how we will reshape our world."

Meridian stepped closer to me and grabbed me by my arm. He steered me out of the room and toward the elevator.

"Don't you want to hear what Sarge has to say?" I asked.

"Oh, it's tempting." The sarcasm in his voice practically burned me. "I normally wouldn't admit this, but Etzal'el's right. This whole thing stinks. Have you noticed that Sarge hasn't brought up Dr. Ayers at all?"

Huh. That was a good point. "Have you talked to him about this at all?"

Meridian snorted. "I tried to earlier today. He basically told me to mind my own business and that he had better things to do with his time." He fixed me with an intense glare. "If I didn't know any better, I'd almost think he didn't want Dr. Ayers found."

That made sense. If I were Sarge, I wouldn't want Dr. Ayers found either. He would be the only one who understood me and how I was put together. He might even know my weaknesses, maybe even some I didn't know about . . .

My eyes widened at the thought. I turned to Meridian. "I think I should look for the good doctor."

He nodded. "My thought, too. But stay here for now, okay? Play nice with Sarge. And then, after this is all done, see what you can do to find his creator."

CHAPTER
49

DK'S DATABASE HAD Dr. Ayers's address. I doubted he was hiding at his home, but it was as good a place to start as any.

His house was a sleepy one story rambler, beige siding with a two car garage to the left. The lawn was overgrown with dandelions. The flower beds were filled with weeds as well. Close to a dozen newspapers were strewn across the front step, and mail had been jammed into the slot in the door. It certainly appeared as though Dr. Ayers hadn't been home for the past week, but that could be a ruse.

I drove past the house three times before finally parking a block away. I sprinted into Ayers's backyard. Like the front yard, the back was a mess of weeds and out of control grass. A small deck extended from the house, with some well-worn plastic furniture and a rusted grill. I pressed up against the large glass door and tried to peer through it into the kitchen. It looked empty enough.

There was one way to know for sure. I shaped my destructive field into a blade and slid it along the door's lock. Hopefully that was all the security Dr. Ayers had. I gave the door a shove, and it slid open. Taking a deep breath, I stepped inside.

The first thing I noticed was the smell. Rotten eggs or . . . well, something rotten, that was for sure. Sitting on a wooden dining room table was a plate of moldy food. I gagged at the sight of it. I had no idea what it was supposed to have been. Next to the plate was a newspaper. I risked a peek at the date and saw that it was the day that Ayers had unleashed the miniature zombie apocalypse at New Chayton University a week earlier.

I backed away from the table and looked around the darkened interior. Aside from the disgusting plate, the rest of the dining room and kitchen area was pristine, if a little dusty. I risked a glance at the plate again. It almost looked as if Dr. Ayers had been in the middle of a meal when he had been called away, and he'd never returned.

I swung through the living room, another dusty cavern of worn furniture grouped around a brick fireplace. A hallway led to a cluttered office and a master bedroom with a king-sized bed. I pursed my lips and looked over the pictures on Dr. Ayers's dresser. Most of them featured the same middle-aged woman, obviously his wife, Gail.

So where could he have gone? Maybe he owned a cabin up north? Even if he did, I'm sure the cops or the VOC would have checked there already.

The house was seemingly a dead end. Maybe I should go and check the lab on campus again? By now, the VOC had probably cleaned it out. But maybe I could find something. Or if *I* couldn't . . .

I pulled out my cell phone and hit the quick dial for Mike. It rang twice and then clicked over to voicemail. I hung up and tried again. Still no answer.

"Mike, it's me. Can you meet me at the research center in a little bit? I need your help on something." I hesitated, wondering what else I should say. "Hope you get this soon. Call me when you do."

I took one more look around Dr. Ayers's home. I sighed. Hopefully I'd have better luck on campus.

I looked at my watch. It was coming up on 11:30 p.m., and there was still no sign of Mike. He obviously wasn't coming. I'd have to do this by myself.

The lab facility was little more than a hollowed out shell, its broken windows and doors boarded over with plywood and covered in yellow crime scene tape. I ignored the warnings and shoved open one of the makeshift doors. Maybe I could get down into the secret lab and sift through the rubble. Or see what remained of Dr. Ayers's office. There had to be a clue there somewhere.

I almost fell into a gigantic chasm. The floor of the lab facility had been ripped out to reveal the hidden lab beneath. Only the lab was empty. Apparently the VOC had packed away all of the wrecked lab equipment, leaving nothing but smooth concrete walls and floors.

Another dead end. I sighed. Maybe Meridian would have some ideas about what to do next. I'd call him, pick his brains, and—

I stepped out of the research center and found Sarge leaning against the wall.

"Out for a midnight stroll?" He pushed off the bricks and ambled toward me, a predatory look in his eyes. "Looking for the good doctor? I can't blame you. The man's clearly dangerous, Failstate. A threat to everything we hold dear."

I fell back a step and my arms started to rise into a defensive stance. It felt as though Sarge's voice was oozing over me.

"Your instincts are good. You know that, right? Dr. Ayers is not bold, and he is a creature of habit. While he's smart enough to not return home, he probably wouldn't go far. He's likely in the area . . . and perhaps continuing his experiments."

What? Hadn't Kensington said something about the lab equipment being too rare for a second lab? Sarge's suggestion made no . . . Wait. Yes, it did make sense. Dr. Ayers wouldn't give up, not now. He'd keep doing his work until he resurrected his wife, if that's what he hoped to do.

Something felt odd. My mind seemed to be having a hard time thinking clearly.

"He's a threat," Sarge said. "He needs to be stopped. Why, he could even be unleashing more mayhem right now. It's a good thing you're here. Those zombies would need to be stopped."

Of course they would. And I'd do it too.

"The people of New Chayton need a hero. They need you." With that, Sarge disappeared into the shadows.

I blinked and shook my head. What had just happened? Had Sarge actually been here? It felt as though I'd been moving through molasses, as if the whole world had slowed for a moment and then rushed to catch up with itself.

Well, I clearly wouldn't find any evidence here. Time to head out.

I started across campus.

Thirty steps along, I heard a girl's scream off to my right. Without thinking, I broke into a sprint. The girl screamed again, so I poured on the speed. I leapt over a bank of low bushes and wove between the cars parked on the street. I crossed over to fraternity row and skidded to a halt at what I saw.

Zombies. Dozens of them. Possibly even hundreds. They milled about between the fraternity and sorority houses, clattering and hissing at each other. They wore a variety of clothing, tattered remains of their former lives. A few broke off from the pack and chased screaming girls back into the houses. Others flowed up the steps and tried to break into the buildings themselves.

I fished my cell phone out of my pocket and tried to dial 911. The screen flickered and went black. Dead? How could my phone be dead? I needed backup. Despite my earlier bravado with Sarge, there were too many of them for me to fight on my own.

Three zombies turned and looked at me with their dead, milky eyes. They pointed at me and started shuffling toward me, picking up speed as they walked. I tossed my phone to the side and dropped into a ready stance.

More zombies had joined the slow-moving charge. If they reached me, I'd be overwhelmed. I smiled grimly. *If* they reached me.

I lashed out with my power and ripped open a rut in the pavement near the middle of their ranks. Several of the zombies tripped over the obstacle and fell, their limbs tangled together. The others slowed and turned toward their companions, almost as if they were confused. Good. I could use the distraction.

With a roar, I charged into the crowd, landing punches and kicks as I could. I managed to charge up my fists for a few of the blows. The zombies collapsed around me, falling onto their backs and seeming to have difficulty getting up again.

I nodded with satisfaction. True, it was only a small chunk out of the larger horde, but I was just getting warmed up.

More of the zombies had turned to face me now. They regarded me with their slack expressions, and I almost felt sorry for them. But I shouldn't. I'd plow through them all and find Dr. Ayers. He had to be nearby. Not in the sorority houses, probably, but maybe in another lab. I should have known he'd have more than one.

Four more zombies, all of them large enough to be line-backers for NCU, charged me. The rest of the horde, oddly, started to flee. I retreated two steps and unleashed a burst of destructive energy. It ripped through two nearby parked cars and set off their alarms. Gasoline spurted from their destroyed tanks and washed across the streets. A streetlight toppled and nearly took out two of the zombies, but they jumped back in time to avoid getting hurt. I frowned. How had they become so agile? The glass of the light shattered, and a spark hit the pooled gas. A wall of flames shot across the street.

Now all of the zombies were fleeing from me. I wanted to laugh and savor their fear. They were right to run. I'd take them down too.

Something tackled me from behind, striking my knees. I crumpled to the pavement. I flipped over and found a zombie holding me down. This one actually looked a bit familiar, what with its patchy blond hair, its chiseled yet decaying jaw, and its piercing green-gold eyes. It almost looked like . . . like . . .

It felt as though the world shifted around me. My vision shimmered. The molasses in my brain drained out.

I realized that it was Ben glaring down at me. Not a zombie or even a zombie version of Ben, but my actual brother.

I gaped at him. "Wh-what's going on?"

"I was about to ask you the same thing." His voice was a bare hiss.

I shoved him away and rolled to my feet. When I looked around, the horde of zombies was gone. No, not gone. They were still there, watching me. But they'd all been transformed. They weren't undead at all. They were . . .

I swallowed a moan. They were college students. Normal people. They all regarded me with open fear, and I couldn't blame them. The street had been torn up, two cars were on fire, and a dozen people lay groaning on the street around me. I'd done that. "What's . . . what is going on?" I repeated weakly.

"What does it look like? It's a college party. You know, Saturday night, time to blow off some steam. Why did you attack us?"

No, that's not what I did at all! "There were zombies everywhere. And my phone was dead, and so I had to . . ."

"Oh, really?" Ben scooped up my phone and held it out to me.

I stared at it. The screen was lit. I shook my head. "No, that's not right!"

"That's one way of putting it. What were you thinking?"

That was a good question and one that I was sure I'd be asked again.

• • •

Agent Sexton paced in front of me. I couldn't even look at him. I studied my gloves, the way my fingers were laced together.

The VOC had showed up shortly after Ben had stopped me. They'd taken charge of the situation, coordinating the fire-fighters and EMTs who had also responded. I stayed out of their way and, given the angry looks most of them gave me, that was for the best. I even considered retreating entirely, but I knew all too well that Sexton would hunt me down personally.

Sexton glanced at me and mumbled a string of expletives. Then he rounded on me with such ferocity that I worried he would shoot me. "Do you have any idea what you've done? You injured a dozen coeds and caused who knows how much damage to the area. Do you want to explain yourself?"

How could I? I knew how ridiculous it would sound, but I honestly thought everyone had been zombies. But why? True, I had been so jumpy since I'd seen Sarge . . .

Sarge! He must have done something to me, tricked me somehow. That had to be it. My brain had been foggy ever since I'd seen him.

"Well, Failstate? I'm waiting."

"It was Sarge. I ran into him by the lab building and he . . . did something to me."

Sexton frowned. "What are you talking about? Sarge is still at Magnus Tower."

My head snapped up. "That's not possible."

"It is. I just came from there. He and about half a dozen other licensed heroes are still poring over maps of New Chayton even as we speak."

I worked my jaw for a moment, trying to find my voice. None of this made sense.

Sexton shook his head and started pacing. "I should have known this was going to happen. We never should have given you a license in the first place. You're a screw-up and always have been."

That did it. "Maybe if you had actually supported me, none of this would've happened. Instead, you've withheld information from me, second-guessed me at every turn, called meetings behind my back, and tried to turn heroes against me. If you had been a better VOC agent, none of this would have happened!"

Sexton's lips peeled back into a snarl. His eyes blazed. "Don't think you're going to pin this on me! I've had it with you. Failstate, pending further review, your license is hereby suspended!"

CHAPTER 50

WHEN I PULLED into our driveway, DK's headlights revealed Magnus waiting for me in the garage. I groaned. I knew I'd eventually have to talk to my mentor about what happened. But I was hoping I could tackle that later rather than sooner. Might as well get it over with.

Magnus didn't move as I climbed out of the car. Instead, he leaned against my dad's workbench. It was only after I had come around the vehicle that he uncrossed his arms. "Well?"

I shrugged, unsure of what he wanted me to say. Were there any words that could make this better? I launched into an explanation of what happened with the college students. I wrapped it up with, "I screwed up."

Magnus laughed, a low chuckle. "Yes, you did. But I don't blame you."

"Why? Because of Sarge? I could have sworn he was on campus, but my mind seemed so screwed up."

Magnus frowned. "That is a puzzler. It almost sounded like what Mind Master was capable of, back when he was in his prime. But according to everything we know about him, Sarge never had powers like that before. It may have been a factor, sure.

"Look, F—Rob. We've all been there at one time or another. You get some bad information, you make a snap judgment, and stuff happens. As much as we want to convince ourselves otherwise, none of us are perfect. You may have caused some damage, but the VOC will clean it up. Thankfully, no one was injured too severely."

"What about my license?" I asked.

Magnus sighed and motioned for me to take a seat on the couch. "That one's going to be tougher. The fact of the matter is that you always had an uphill climb. There were some folks in the VOC who resented the way you earned your license—though you had nothing to do with the system we'd set up. They don't totally understand what you went through to get it, and because of that, they see you as a fluke. Add in the fact that Sarge is the current flavor of the month and, well . . ." He spread open his hands.

I frowned. "You almost make it sound as though you suspected this might happen."

Magnus's lips pressed into a thin line for a moment. "I did."

"Then why didn't you warn me?" Heat flashed up my spine.

"Because I didn't want to worry you. And their resistance would've come against whoever it was who had won the contest. It's nothing personal against you. Besides, would you have really done anything differently had you known?"

I thought over what I had done in the past few weeks. I eventually shook my head.

"I didn't think so. You've got a good head on your shoulders. You've proven that to me time and time again. And I knew that if you'd just be yourself, you'd show them how great you can be, and you'd win them over. That's still going to happen. I know it. Along the way, things just . . . Well, they went off the rails. That happens. We deal with it and move on."

"How do I do that, with no license? How do I move on after this?"

"I don't know," Magnus said. "We all deal with our disappointments in different ways. Me . . . I went out west. Met a woman and . . . Well, you know the rest."

Oh, I did. Mike was the result.

"So this is what I'd suggest you do. Find something that helps you feel at peace with what happened, and focus on that. Then lay low. Let the dust settle. Live your life outside of the mask for a while. At some point, you'll start feeling the itch to get out there again. When that happens, do it, but take it slow. I'll keep working on the VOC. Who knows? We may get this straightened out within a few days and you'll be fine. Okay?"

I nodded sullenly. "Sounds like good advice."

He patted me on the shoulder and started out of the garage. As he walked by DK, something occurred to me. "Hey," I said, digging in my pocket, "here are the keys."

Magnus looked over his shoulder and smiled. "No way. This car was a gift. She's yours still. And that reminds me, I'm going to get after the VOC about making sure you get what payment you've earned." He waved away my words before I could even object. "No arguments. Now remember what I said: find some peace, lay low, and wait for the itch, got it?"

"Got it."

Magnus left. I stood in the garage, fiddling with DK's keys. Thankfully, I knew just the place to find that peace.

Mike met me by the doors of Mt. Calvary's gym. He clapped me on the back. "I heard what happened. I'm so sorry. Are you okay?"

"Where were you?" I asked. "I tried calling!"

Mike grimaced. "I was with P.G. and the youth ministry team here. We were having a prayer meeting. No cell phones allowed."

I nodded, swallowing the flash of resentment I felt. He should have been there. How would things have gone differently if Mike had been with me as Veritas? But that was in the past. Dwelling on it wouldn't help me find peace.

Mike glanced at the sound board. "Look, I've got to take care of some business before this all kicks off, okay? But I want to talk to you about all of this soon." He sprinted back over to the soundboard and slid in behind it.

I waved at a few of the people already there for youth group. I must have caught P.G.'s attention, because he hurried over to me and slapped me on the back so hard that I staggered.

"Rob! Good to see you again! We've missed you." Concern flashed across his face. "Are you okay? I mean, I saw something on the news this morning about . . . Well, you know."

I smiled, knowing it would look fake. "I'm fine, really. And you'll be seeing a lot more of me from now on—not on TV, but, you know, here."

"Uh . . . good. Well, I'll talk to you later." P.G. hurried on to someone who'd just entered the door.

I wandered along the edge of the chairs, looking for a place to sit, when arms wrapped around my waist from behind. I turned and found myself face-to-face with Charlene. Now *here* was part of the peace I'd been hoping to find.

She smiled at me but broke the embrace. "I wish I could keep that up, but you know how P.G. is about PDA. Are you okay?"

I wanted to laugh. Maybe I should have come with a sign that said *I'm okay, really!* "Why do you ask?"

"You're just looking a little upset. Anything you want to talk about?"

I wished I could. But something told me that sharing my secret identity even now would be a bad idea. Best to keep it generic. "No, just stuff at school. You have a place to sit yet?"

She hesitated. "I need to make a few announcements before P.G. gets going, but as soon as I'm done, I'll be there. Save me a spot?"

"You got it."

She snared my hand and squeezed. Then she sashayed up to the stage. I found a spot with two empty seats on the fringe of the chairs. The band started up a song, calling the hundred or so participants to worship.

After singing praise songs for fifteen minutes, P.G. bounded up on stage and waved to the crowd. "Good to see you all here this morning. Whether you're an old returning friend or a new-comer, we're glad you could join us. We're going to have a lot of fun, but before we do, Charlene has to speak with us about something important. Charlene?"

Charlene walked on stage with a wireless handheld mic. She waved to the crowd. "I'm sure some of you probably saw the news about a superhero named Sarge. I don't know about you, but what he had to say about making the world a better place really resonated with me."

Someone hooted in agreement, and a few more people applauded.

"Speaking of making the world a better place, I want to remind you that we're doing a lot of other servant events. I know that going to a homeless shelter early on a Saturday morning or putting together care packages for women at the local crisis center isn't as flashy or exciting as fighting super-villains, but those 'little jobs' are just as important. We have a sign-up sheet over there for the next event. Please consider coming with us, okay?"

She descended from the stage and found me. She slid into the chair next to me and flashed me a smile that melted my feet. "I can count on you, right?"

"Wouldn't miss it for the world."

CHAPTER 51

I OPENED THE DOOR for Charlene and motioned for her to enter the restaurant. "After you, Miss Gardner."

"Why, thank you, Mr. Laughlin." She giggled. "I've been looking forward to this more than the servant event."

"Me too." I answered.

I followed her into the restaurant, a bar and grill decked out with odd knickknacks, posters of movies from the last three decades, and photos of the local high school sports teams.

The hostess, a college-aged girl, greeted us with a knowing smile. "Your usual table, guys?"

I chuckled. For the last four weeks, after Tuesday night youth group and the servant events Charlene organized, she and I had come to this restaurant for a late night snack.

The hostess led us past her podium and into the restaurant. A number of flatscreen TVs played softly in the background, most of them tuned to different sports channels, although the one near the bar was always kept to a 24-hour news channel.

The hostess showed us a small table for two tucked into a corner. We settled in. As we did, Charlene's smile grew just a bit more dazzling.

"What?" I asked.

She shrugged. "I don't know. It's . . . I'm just really happy. You're starting to spoil me, I think, with all this attention."

I managed to keep from grimacing. Ever since the debacle on the NCU campus a month ago, I had found myself with a lot more time on my hands. I was able to fill the empty, sleepless nights with schoolwork. That left plenty of time to go to youth group and servant events. And to spend time with Charlene.

My gaze flicked toward the TV showing the news. Not surprisingly, it was a story about Sarge and his coalition. I had to fight to keep from groaning. Sarge had been busy, first by claiming the meat packing plant from the HazMats and turning it into his own compound, then by taking back Hogtown from the gangs with the help of other heroes. Every night, the newscasters gushed about what he had done and what he was going to do to "transform America."

Charlene followed my gaze. "You know, Dad wants me to take him down to that guy's compound."

I blinked. "Why?"

"He's hoping to catch a glimpse of Sarge, I guess. Did you know they're actually giving tours?"

I gaped at her, not trusting myself to speak. After yelling at us for being glory hounds, Sarge had certainly changed his attitude. I forced myself to smile. "If you need any help with that, let me know."

"I will." She reached across the table and gave my hand a squeeze.

A young woman approached our table, dressed in the red-and-blue uniform of the restaurant. She flashed us a dazzling smile. "Hi, there, guys. I'm Cathy, and I'll be serving you tonight. Can I get you started on anything?"

Charlene placed her usual order: a slice of cheesecake and a raspberry lemonade. I stared at the waitress. She looked familiar, but I couldn't quite remember where I had seen her before. She wasn't our usual waitress. Belatedly, I realized she was patiently waiting for me to order.

"Rob? You okay?" Charlene asked.

I jolted out of my confusion. "Oh, sorry. Apple pie and a Coke."

"I'll be right back with that." She left.

My gaze flicked back to the TV, and I had to stifle a groan. Now, instead of Sarge, they were showing Gauntlet entering Sarge's compound. If my star had fallen, Gauntlet's had definitely risen. He was on the front line of every fight, at every press conference Sarge held, somehow in every picture the media released. Still, I was happy for Ben. This was what he had always wanted. He hadn't been given a license yet, but rumors were swirling that he would soon. Sexton would probably want to just give him mine. At the same time, though, it was a constant reminder of what I had lost.

I looked back at Charlene. She looked upset, scratching at the tabletop with her index finger. "What's the matter?" I asked.

She smiled, but it disappeared quickly. "I'm just a little disappointed with the turnout at our servant event tonight. I just wish we could have had more than five people."

I grimaced. "Well, you can hardly blame them. Picking up trash at Cesar Chavez Elementary wasn't all that exciting. No offense."

She sighed. "Maybe, but that's not the point, is it? The point of service isn't to be fun or wild or anything like that. Instead, we're supposed to be making the world a better place, even if no one notices. *Especially* if no one else notices."

"I suppose." I leaned back in my chair as the waitress arrived with our desserts and drinks.

"Isn't that what they're about too?" Charlene gestured toward the TV. "I mean, I don't totally get why Dad loves superheroes so much, but I do have to admit that they're trying to do the same thing. Make the world a better place."

The waitress laughed, a short bark. Her eyes widened. "I'm so sorry. I'm not laughing at you. It's just . . . well, have either of you been to Hogtown lately?"

Charlene shook her head. So did I. Was that where I had seen this lady before?

"I've got a cousin who lives there. He says that, yeah, the streets are safer from the gangs, but there are surveillance cameras everywhere. Plus those heroes patrol the streets day and night. He says it's like living in an occupied city."

"So you don't care for superheroes that much?" I asked.

The waitress smiled. "They're not all bad. I even met one once."

"Oh, yeah?" I asked. "Who?"

The waitress's smile grew wider. "Failstate."

So I had met her somewhere. But where?

"The guy who nearly destroyed NCU?" Charlene asked. "I wouldn't call him heroic."

I bit my cheek before I said something.

"I have to disagree. He saved my life," the waitress said.

"How?" I asked. Now I had to know.

The waitress hugged herself. "I . . . I haven't always had my life together. I was addicted to Blade for a long time. I nearly wrecked everything."

Charlene frowned. "What does this have to do with Failstate?"

"I'm getting to that. A few weeks back, I hit rock bottom. I saw how messed up my life was, and I knew I had to do better. But then I got locked out of my car. I was going to miss my shift again, and I just knew I was going to get fired. And if that happened . . ." Tears appeared in her eyes. "I'm sorry. I just knew that would be it. I'd lose my job, I'd lose my apartment, I'd lose everything."

She wiped away a tear. "And then Failstate came along. He popped open my car, and I just made it on time. And I realized that I had to do better. I enrolled in rehab, and I've been getting my life together ever since." She laughed. "Sorry, didn't mean to turn this into a twelve-step program. Can I get you guys anything else?"

Charlene shook her head, and the waitress walked away.

Wow. That thing with her car had seemed so insignificant at the time. I had no idea it would make that much of a difference.

"Huh." Charlene nodded absently, but then she turned to me. "See, that's what I'm talking about. It's kind of like what Jesus says in Matthew 25, y'know?"

I blinked at her. "What?"

She tipped her head to one side, her exasperation clear. "Haven't you been listening to the Bible studies at the servant events?"

I mouthed a few excuses, but she laughed and batted the back of my hand with hers.

"I'm kidding. But seriously, Jesus commends people for giving Him a drink of water, clothing Him, visiting Him, just little things like that. Nothing big and flashy. I think that's what He calls us to do. Change the world, one little thing at a time. So maybe Failstate got one right. It doesn't mean I like him now." She sighed. "Anyway, that's why I wish more people had shown up to pick up trash." She smiled coyly. "Besides, if there had been more people, then it wouldn't have taken so long, and I would have had more time to spend with you."

My cheeks warmed, but what she said ricocheted around in my brain. Here I had been beating myself up for not being a "legendary" hero, not making a large enough impact. Could it be as simple as that? Do what you can, big or small, and let God worry about the impact?

As I considered that thought, a sense of peace and calm, something I hadn't felt in a long time, settled on me. I felt a gentle prompting, an urge, an . . .

I grabbed my fork and dove into my apple pie, scarfing it down as quickly as I could.

Charlene gaped at me. "I didn't realize you were that hungry."

"Sorry." I sucked down half my drink. "I just remembered I have somewhere I have to be."

Charlene's face fell. "Well, okay."

I winced inwardly at her tone. I hated to disappoint her, and I really didn't like lying to her. But I had to get home.

I had finally felt the itch.

CHAPTER 52

I DROVE CHARLENE HOME and returned to mine. Once inside my room, I reached under my bed and pulled out my duffel bag. I winced at the collected dust. I brushed it off and started pulling out the pieces of my costume. The urban camo pants, the dark sweatshirt, the thick work gloves, the Halloween hood. Normally, seeing the tattered and worn clothing would have annoyed me, but this time, I couldn't help but smile. It was as if a long-lost friend had returned, a flattened Failstate just waiting to be inflated.

I double-checked the costume, looking for rips or tears, spots where my power had chewed through the fabric. I wanted to look my best. As near as I could tell, the clothing was intact. I folded each piece and stuffed it back into the bag. A cold chill swept through me. It almost felt as though I were going out on patrol for the first time.

That brought back memories: sneaking out in a simple costume when I was thirteen. Gauntlet and I partnering for the

367

first year until his vain attitude drove us apart. I wished he were going with me.

I shook my head. I was a licensed hero. Well, a formerly licensed hero, I guess. I had to do this. I had to get out there, even if I were an amateur once again. I slung the pack over my shoulder and headed down the stairs.

Mom was seated at the center island in the kitchen as I passed through. She sipped a cup of tea, reading a magazine. When I entered the room, her gaze darted to the bag and then to my face. She started to say something, but then she stopped. Tears glistened in her eyes but she nodded. "Stay safe, Robin. Okay?"

"I will."

I went out to the driveway and climbed into DK. I ran my hand over the dashboard and smiled. "Let's go find some bad guys."

A part of me really wanted to go on patrol in Hogtown, in defiance of Sarge and his team. But I knew that wasn't smart. There was no telling how they might react to an unlicensed outsider encroaching on their turf—Gauntlet notwithstanding. But no one said I couldn't check the perimeter. At the very least, it gave me something to do while I listened to the police scanner.

DK crept along the side streets. I kept one eye on the buildings that rolled by. Instead of being covered in graffiti with broken or boarded-over windows, the buildings of Hogtown looked clean now, almost fresh. I suspected that if I were to return during the daytime, the neighborhood would appear as pristine as a Hollywood set. I couldn't argue with Sarge's results, but the effect appeared almost surreal. Or more like unreal.

The police scanner chattered in the background, but nothing big. I blew out a long sigh. Looked like my first night back was going to turn out to be rather boring. Well, I supposed I had to crawl before I learned to—

A shadow darted through DK's headlights. It lurched and stumbled, almost like a . . .

My hands tightened on the steering wheel. No way. Not again.

I slammed on the brakes and craned my neck around to see where the shadow had gone. But I didn't see anything. At least, nothing that—

Another shadow darted across the road. Then another. And this time, the shadow paused long enough to allow me to get a good look at it.

A zombie, a young man with a drooping, half rotten face, turned into the light for a moment. He wore grey scrubs. He—it—paused before shuffling off into the darkness.

I quickly pulled over. By the time I got out, at least ten more zombies had crossed the street from Hogtown into the surrounding neighborhood.

Was I hallucinating again? The last thing I wanted to do was attack another group of coeds. Fool me once, shame on you—fool me twice, shame on me.

Then again, we weren't anywhere near the campus. At the very least, there were at least a dozen supposed "zombies" in a residential neighborhood in the middle of the night, up to who knew what. I should at least keep an eye on them.

I secured DK and sprinted after the zombies. Unfortunately, they had disappeared into the darkness, but I could still hear low moans in the distance. More than that, the unmistakable smell of rotting flesh clawed through my mask. These had to be the real deal. There was no telling what kind of damage they'd cause if they weren't stopped.

I finally spotted them converging under a streetlight at the end of a block. I frowned. What were they doing? They milled around in the middle of the intersection aimlessly. A few of them moaned, others clacked their teeth, but it almost looked like they were waiting for something. But what? Well, at least they had stopped. That would make what I had to do a little easier.

I took a few deep breaths and readied myself to move. I'd dart in and try to turn the ground to Jell-O. Maybe that'd be enough to toss a few of them off their feet. After that, I'd have to improvise. Ready . . . set . . .

A blast of rainbow light slammed into the zombie horde from above, disintegrating half of them in one burst. I threw up my arms to shield my face. The zombies' moans became louder, more animal-like, but they couldn't escape. Another blast took out even more of them.

Then a figure dropped into the center of the survivors. A tremor ripped through the street. While it was barely strong enough for me to feel through the bottom of my feet, it threw the remaining zombies off balance. Whoever had landed stood up. Even from this distance, I could tell it was Raze.

Sarge stood next to him and flung open his arms. Beams of rainbow light cascaded from his hands and scythed through the remaining zombies, turning them to dust.

I ducked behind a car.

Raze dusted himself off. "Thanks for the help."

Sarge snorted. "You're welcome."

"So tell me, was this at all ironic for you?" Raze smiled. "Taking out your own kind, as it were?"

"Don't be ridiculous," Sarge said, his voice ice. "These are nothing like me."

"Oh, of course not. Of course. Still, it has to strike you as a little unusual, right?"

"Will you shut up? Rather than annoy me, you should figure out how these guys escaped from their pens."

"Someone probably forgot to latch the gate. Happens all the time with dogs."

Sarge snared Raze by the front of his uniform. "Then go check on that, got it? I've got a meeting I need to get to." Sarge released him and stomped off into the darkness.

Raze grumbled something under his breath and headed out. I scrambled around the car as he passed, keeping it between him and me. As soon as he was halfway down the block, I darted after him. I suspected I knew where he was heading, but I had to know for sure.

I followed him out of the residential neighborhood and back into Hogtown. The transition was remarkable. I once again noticed how the graffiti had been cleaned from the walls, the way the buildings looked to be brand new. There wasn't even any litter, no blowing newspapers. The streets were eerily quiet, as if Raze and I were the only ones out and about.

Thankfully, Raze never stopped to see if anyone was following him. At one point, he did pause at an intersection. It looked like he was going to go left, but instead, he shook his head and went right. Even still, I stuck to cover as much as I could, not only to avoid him, but to also hide from the numerous security cameras mounted on poles and on the sides of buildings. There was no way that someone could monitor all of them at once, but they might have motion sensors that would draw someone's eyes. It was better to play it safe.

After walking for ten blocks, Raze finally arrived at Sarge's compound. Like the rest of Hogtown, the meat packing plant had been transformed. Instead of looking like a rundown den for drug dealers, it looked like a military fortress. A tall brick wall had been erected around the perimeter, topped with razor wire. Security cameras dotted the wall at regular intervals. Jutting up over the wall was the building itself, crowned with so many antenna and satellite dishes that I wondered if Sarge was using it all to watch TV and get caught up on the seventy-plus years of movies he'd missed.

Raze marched around the wall to the sole gate. He glared up at the nearest security camera and shouted something. The gate, a solid metal plate at least six inches thick, ground open, just wide enough to let Raze back inside. Then it rolled shut again.

I stared at the walls. Had the zombies come from inside there? It didn't seem likely, what with the wall. But this was the best lead I had. I'd have to infiltrate Sarge's compound.

That thought brought a smile to my lips. At least I had an easy way of doing that, especially since there were bright yellow signs on the walls that notified me that public tours started at 10:00 a.m. This looked like a job for Robin Laughlin. After all, I could blend in better as a tourist.

"Please, let them have left some incriminating evidence just lying out in the open, visible to passing tours," I whispered. A prayer? Not really, but it'd be cool if God said yes to that one.

CHAPTER 53

AS SOON AS SCHOOL LET OUT the next day, I ran out to DK and fired it up. I sent off a quick text to Charlene, assuring her that I missed her and was thinking of her. That was true, even if my mind was a bit overcrowded with zombies. Then I headed off for Hogtown.

Next, I called Alexander Magnus.

My former mentor answered on the first ring. "What's going on, kid?"

"I was just wondering if you could have your sources in the VOC check up on something for me." I explained about the zombies and my suspicions. "I just want to know what happened to Dr. Ayers's lab equipment and if they have any new leads on the good doctor's whereabouts."

Magnus snorted over the line. "I'll see what I can turn up, Rob, but I wouldn't hold my breath. Ever since Sarge built that fortress in Hogtown, the VOC has circled their wagons. I'm getting the royal run-around on just about anything. Like your missing compensation? I pointed out that they should have at least offered to build you a lair while you were licensed, but since they didn't, they should hand over a portion of the budget for that. They're claiming that they did build you a lair on the NCU campus. Can you believe their audacity?"

I waved away his words, although he couldn't see me do it. "Let's not worry about that right now. Just find out what you can about Ayers and his equipment."

Magnus was silent for a moment. "Yes, sir, Mr. Laughlin. Is there anything else I can do for you before I go back to running my multi-billion dollar corporation?"

My cheeks burned at his sarcasm. "No, that just about does it. Wait, one other thing. Do you know if Mike has any plans this afternoon?"

"I don't think so," Magnus answered. "But you better ask him yourself. I'll call you back when I learn anything."

The line went dead, and I dialed Mike's number.

"Hello?" From the background noise, it sounded like he was in his car. Good.

"Hey, are you doing anything?"

"Not really. I've got a ton of AP physics homework, but it's not due for another few days. What's going on?"

"I need your help with something. Not in-costume or anything, just as another pair of eyes."

Mike sighed but didn't answer.

"Look, I know how you feel, and I understand it. I just . . . I just really need your help on this. Especially, since, you know, you kind of stood me up last time. Not that it's a big deal or anything. But still . . ."

Another sigh, but this time, Mike spoke. "Fine. Where are we going?"

"Meet me at Sarge's compound. It's time we went on the tour."

Thankfully, the line outside the compound wasn't too long, just another fifteen or twenty people. Mike and I took up our spots at the end, and I glanced over the surrounding neighborhood. While it didn't look as creepy in the day, it still felt far too sterile. I glanced at my watch. According to the signs, the tours ended at 4:30. It was nearly four now. Hopefully there'd be enough time for one more tour. I patted my legs quietly as we waited.

"How are things going with Charlene?" Mike asked.

"Oh . . . good. Really good. How are things with your dad?"

Mike sighed and ran a hand through his hair. "Not as good. After what happened to you, he really put on the pressure for me to step up and take your place."

I winced. Mike had told me how much pressure his dad had put on him before. I could only imagine how bad it had become since I'd lost my license. "Sorry."

"Not your fault." He looked around. "So what, exactly, are we looking for here?"

I shrugged. "No idea. I just want a look on the inside."

"Fair enough."

We made small talk until the gate rasped open and the line filtered through the opening. As I stepped inside, I studied the area between the wall and the building. The pavement had been patched and was a uniform black, unmarred and uncracked. The building's crumbling bricks had been replaced so seamlessly that it was impossible to tell where the old bricks had been and where they had been repaired. I still felt as though I were facing a fortress of some kind. Thick bars covered every window, and even more razor wire topped the edges of the building. Cars of different makes and models were parked up against the wall in a makeshift parking lot.

Then the doors to the building opened, and a perky young woman stepped out. She had short brown hair and an infectious smile. She wore a pair of khaki capris and an olive drab t-shirt. She stepped up to us and waved.

"Well, hey there, everyone! My name is Clarissa, and I'll be your tour guide today. Now I know what you must be thinking. 'Clarissa, what possible superpower could you have besides your sunny personality?'" She laughed at her own joke.

No one else did.

"Well, not everyone here has superpowers, and that's okay. Sarge is recruiting a lot of people to join his movement. All of us share one thing in common: a desire to make the world a better place. If you'll follow me, we'll show you what we're up to and then, at the end, we'll explain how you can help."

Clarissa led us in through the doors. I let out a low whistle. Once again, the interior had been transformed.

A small dining area had been set up in one corner of the warehouse. At the other end was a full gym complete with a sparring area. Another part of the room was filled with banks of video monitors. Only four people sat in front of those monitors, although I spotted Downtime flitting from station to station, apparently tweaking the controls. Good thing he had never seen me as Robin Laughlin.

"As you can see, one of our friends, Downtime, is hard at work," Clarissa said. "Thanks to his efforts and those like him,

Sarge has been able to take back the streets of Hogtown. For the first time in eighty years, Hogtown has the lowest crime rate in New Chayton!"

One of the others people on the tour raised her hand. "Can we meet Sarge?"

Clarissa cocked her head and pouted, her expression exaggerated. "Unfortunately, no. Sarge is currently in a meeting with Her Honor, Mayor Reilly. But you never know who else may show up here! A number of other licensed heroes have taken up Sarge's call to arms, and they come and go as they perform important missions to protect our city."

I glanced at Mike. "Anything?" I whispered.

He shook his head. "Not really, no. She believes what she's saying, but aside from that, I'm not . . ." His voice trailed off, and he elbowed me in the gut.

I turned to see what he was looking at, and I froze.

Gauntlet had walked in from the back office.

Clarissa clapped and giggled. "Well, what did I tell you? Here's another one of Sarge's allies—Gauntlet!"

Gauntlet just nodded in Clarissa's direction and started over toward the gym equipment. I breathed out a sigh of relief. Once he started working out, he'd be too focused to see Mike and me standing in the room. I hoped.

"Could you come over and say howdy to these folks, Gauntlet?" She turned to us. "Wouldn't that be a treat?"

No, not at all. But the rest of the tour group made such a fuss that Gauntlet started over. He slapped on his biggest grin and began to shake each person's hand individually, sharing a few words with them. Everyone else seemed delighted. I felt nauseous. Maybe there was some way Mike and I could dodge him. If we stuck to the fringes of the crowd and did our best to scoot around the edge, maybe he wouldn't see us.

And then there he was, standing in front of me with his hand out.

For a moment, he stared at me, the surprise clear on his face. His smile turned brittle and fake. He took my hand and gave it a squeeze, adding a bit of a telekinetic boost to get my attention. He leaned in and whispered, "What do you think you're doing here?"

"Taking the tour," I whispered back.

A scowl flitted across his face. "What are you really doing here, Robin?"

"Can't tell you now. Folks will get suspicious, if they're not already."

Gauntlet looked around at the rest of the crowd. He smiled and nodded.

"Break some plates later?" I whispered.

"Sounds good. Two hours." Gauntlet released my hand and turned to the crowd. "Good to see you all. And I'll leave you in Clarissa's capable hands."

Clarissa squealed as Gauntlet strode over to the gym equipment. He set to work, doing squats. But he did manage to send one more dirty look my way.

"While I know we'd all love to stay here and watch him work, we do have to keep going," Clarissa said.

She led us from the main area into one of the outlying rooms, which had been transformed into a museum detailing Sarge's life and career. I tuned out Clarissa's chirpy narration. Clearly she had been given a script, and she was determined to follow it.

I pulled Mike back a bit so no one would overhear us. "Anything yet?"

Mike frowned, looking around. "Maybe . . . I don't know. I'm getting a faint impression of . . . I don't know what. Sorry."

Clarissa concluded her speech and took us to the final room. Inside were racks of clipboards. She handed one to each of us. I looked over the paperwork. It was an application for something called "Sarge's Auxiliary."

"By now, I'm sure you've seen how dedicated Sarge is to protecting us and making our lives better. But as powerful as he is, he needs all of our help. That's why we're asking you to join his Auxiliary. By doing so, you'll be agreeing to help him in his quest to make New Chayton a better place. It's completely optional, of course, but we are stronger together than we are apart."

I considered filling out the application, just to see what would happen. But I decided against it. No need to take that kind of a risk. Instead, I turned to Mike. "Feel like hanging out a little while longer? Maybe come talk to Ben with me and make sure he's staying honest?"

Mike sighed. "You don't really think that Ben is going to lie to you, do you?"

I didn't think he would. But right now, I figured it would be better to play it safe.

CHAPTER 54

I SAT UP as a motorcycle roared in the distance. Sure enough, Gauntlet drove the vehicle into the empty field. Good thing that Mike and I had changed into our costumes as well.

Gauntlet got off the motorcycle and stomped over to us.

"Mom would kill you if she found out you were driving that," I said.

"You going to tell on me?" Gauntlet scowled. "What were you two morons doing on the tour?"

"Just seeing how Sarge is settling in," I said. "How's that going for you? Is it everything you were hoping for?"

"Oh, yeah. Absolutely."

I glanced at Veritas. He shook his head, just enough to confirm my suspicion.

Gauntlet rounded on him. "Stay out of my head, Veritas."

"Like I needed him to tell me that you were lying," I said. "What's going on?"

Gauntlet rammed his fists onto his hips. "I asked you first."

Fair enough. I pulled a box of used dinner plates out of the back of DK, and I told Gauntlet about what I had seen the night before: Raze, Sarge, and zombies "out of their pen."

Gauntlet pulled one of the plates out and spun it on his palm. "That's ridiculous. Raze didn't mention anything when I relieved him this afternoon."

"Could he be hiding something?" Veritas asked.

Gauntlet shook his head, but once again, I could read the uncertainty in his eyes.

"What's going on, Ben?" I asked.

He sighed. "I don't know. Lots of little things. Sarge doesn't seem really interested in having me on his team. Not for doing anything important. It's like I'm arm candy or something. He and some of the others have these secret meetings that I'm not allowed to attend. And I'm not sure he really wants to make New Chayton better."

"Why do you say that?" Veritas asked.

"It's just an impression I get. Like, the other day, I suggested that if we really wanted to make a difference, we should organize a food drive. A big one. Or support the work of homeless shelters or something like that. Sarge said it'd be a waste of time, that we'd be helping the wrong people, that we had 'bigger fish to fry.'" Gauntlet cocked his arm back and fired the plate into the air.

I lanced out with my power and obliterated the plate. "Is it possible he has intel on a supervillain plot?"

"Maybe." Gauntlet retrieved another plate and spun it on the tip of his finger. "But whenever he hands out patrol assignments, he keeps all of us inside the Hogtown perimeter. The last couple of nights, we've focused on two buildings on the border of our territory, almost like we're guarding them."

"What's in the buildings?" I asked.

Gauntlet shrugged one shoulder. "I don't know. Sarge and Raze 'liberated' them from the Blue Eclipse Boys about two weeks ago, but he doesn't want anyone to go near them."

I glanced at Veritas. That might be something worth investigating.

Gauntlet must have realized what I was thinking. He fired the plate at me, and I barely had enough time to bring up a destructive field to shred it.

"Don't even think about it," he said. "He's made it absolutely clear that we're not supposed to go inside them."

"Good thing I'm not on your team then, isn't it?" I retorted. "I'm not even a licensed hero anymore, so who cares what I do?" I turned back to Veritas. "What do you say? Up for a little snooping around?"

Veritas hesitated. "I suppose. But we'll have to be really careful."

Gauntlet shook his head. "Are you not listening? Those buildings are Sarge's now. If he caught you—"

"And how's he going to do that? Are you going to tip him off?" I demanded.

Gauntlet stared at me, his eyes narrowed and hard. I could see the debate raging inside him. I held my breath. There was a chance he would do just that, if only to earn a few more points with Sarge.

With a sigh, he dropped the plate back into the box. "No, I won't. We're brothers."

I nodded. "Thank you."

"Don't mess this up, Rob," Gauntlet said. "And keep me out of it."

"I'll do my best. So where are they?"

Gauntlet kicked at the ground. "One of them is on Robert Street, just north of the freeway. The other is down by the river, near the Lewis Memorial Bridge."

A smile twitched at my lips. The building on Robert street sounded close to where I'd seen the zombies. "Thank you. You might want to stay away from those buildings tonight."

He nodded and got back onto the motorcycle. He gunned the engine and took off back down the dirt road.

I turned to Veritas. "So what time should I pick you up?"

Once again, Veritas hesitated. "I suppose around midnight. But then, after this, I'm done, got it? No more."

I nodded. "Absolutely."

CHAPTER 55

WHEN VERITAS AND I RETURNED to Hogtown later that night, we found the building by Roberts easily enough. It was a five story building, all grey bricks with wide windows on every floor. It had fallen into disrepair along with the rest of the neighborhood. Unlike all of the other buildings, which looked so pristine and uniform they might have been created by copy-and-paste, this one actually had a large hole that had been blocked with plywood. It appeared as if it had been a loading dock of some kind. The hole was raised three feet off the ground, and underneath it were large black rubber bumpers.

Veritas hung up his cell phone and tucked it into one of the pockets on his utility belt. "Okay, I had Dad check the data from the power company. He says the buildings are drawing a lot of power, three times what their neighbors are consuming."

From the building's exterior, I couldn't tell if the lights were even on. All of the windows were dark. Maybe they had been painted over from the inside? Hard to say. "Did he say anything else?"

"Just that he wished us good luck."

I grimaced. Something told me we would need it.

"So what's the plan?" Veritas asked.

"Well, the obvious way in would be that plywood patch, but I suspect they'll be watching for that."

Veritas nodded. "I know I would."

"So we need another way in. Thoughts?"

Veritas ruffed up his hair for a moment. "We could try the roof. If there's a staircase that goes up there, it'd probably be relatively insecure."

"That's a mighty big 'if,'" I said. "I don't know. Maybe."

"Psssst!"

Who was that? I turned around, and my heart jumped up my throat. Kynetic! She waved at us from a nearby alley. I pointed her out to Veritas, and we dashed to her hiding place.

She scowled at me. "I don't know whether to kiss you or punch you. Where have you been?"

"I've been . . . Well, I've been lying low, letting the dust settle . . ."

"Taking a class in clichéd excuses?" She rose from her crouch and beckoned us deeper into the alley. "While you've been off licking your wounds—there's another cliché for you, by the way—some of us have been keeping an eye on Sarge. So are you finally going to take that jerk down?"

"What are you talking about?" I asked.

"Look around you, Failstate. Don't you see what he's done to this neighborhood?" she asked.

Veritas and I exchanged a quick glance.

"He's cleaned it up?" I asked.

She snorted. "He's done more than that. The buildings, the people, they're all fitting into Sarge's very particular mold. And if they don't, they're taken care of. Have you ever heard of the Sixth Street Mission?"

I nodded. It was an organization that worked with the homeless who lived in Hogtown. Charlene and I had delivered some coats there three weeks earlier. "Sure."

"They're not open anymore, and that's thanks to Sarge."

I gaped at her. "What do you mean?"

"Three weeks ago, Sarge had a little 'visit' with the director and basically told him to shut down the mission. Held him by the throat, up against a wall. Even used the phrase, 'or else.'"

"You're kidding," Veritas said. "Do you have any proof?"

She glared at him. "Of course I do. I was videotaping the entire encounter on my cell." She pulled out the device, fiddled with it for a moment, and tossed it to me.

I thumbed the play button. The video played out just as Kyn had said. Sarge and Raze cornered a man outside a building. Sarge said something to him, his voice tinny over the speakers, and then, when the man shook his head, Sarge grabbed him by the throat and slammed him into the building's wall.

"The mission shut down shortly after that," Kyn said. "Then the homeless people in Hogtown disappeared."

I felt a little light headed. I handed the phone back to Kyn.

"Why didn't you show that to the proper authorities?" Veritas asked.

Kyn laughed, a hint of hysteria in her voice. "Now why didn't I think of that? What do you think I did? I brought the video to the VOC and showed it to them. The agent who met with me asked if I had given them my only copy. So of course

I told them, 'Yes.' They didn't do anything about what Sarge had done. So I sent a copy to the local TV stations and even a few national affiliates.

"Next thing I know, I hear from Elemental. She says that the VOC is asking some very pointed questions about where I am and how they can find me. So I went underground and hid out here, gathering as much information as I could in the hopes that someone," she glared at me, "would finally show up here to take Sarge down. I never realized I'd have to wait a whole month."

My cheeks burned. "So do you know what's in that building?"

She shook her head. "No idea. There was some sort of explosion last night, though. But by the time I got here, they had patched up the door already. But I might know a way in. Follow me." She led us farther down the alley, away from the building.

"Wrong direction," Veritas said.

"Not exactly, wise guy. That building used to be part of a bigger complex. According to my research, it used to rely on steam heat from a boiler that was stored in this building over here. There's a tunnel that runs from here to there."

"It's probably been sealed," Veritas said, but I could hear some doubt in his voice.

"I realize that. But I'm guessing that Sarge either doesn't know about the tunnel or doesn't think it's a problem. I'm also willing to guess it's the best way in. Besides, if three people with superpowers can't get through a sealed tunnel, we all ought to hang up our tights." She came to a halt outside another building. She gestured toward a set of stairs that led from the alley down to the building's basement. "Unless you have a better option?"

I glanced at Veritas. He didn't look happy, but he shook his head. I led the way down the stairs and, using my power, sliced through the door's lock.

Once we were inside, Kyn pulled out her cell again and used it as a flashlight. "C'mon," she said. "I'm pretty sure that the tunnel is over here."

We walked along one of the foundation walls. The paint on the bricks had turned dull and smudged with water stains and mildew. The exception was a door-sized section of unpainted cinderblocks.

Kyn smiled and gestured toward the wall once again. "After you."

I took a deep breath and pushed out with my power, driving a large wedge of destructive force into the wall. The bricks slowly vaporized. I ground my teeth and pressed on, trying to widen the hole. Sweat poured down my brow, and salt tickled my lips. What if Kyn was wrong? What if I hit a sewer pipe on the other side of the wall?

But then I punched a hole a foot across through the bricks, revealing a darkened space beyond. A musty smell flooded the room, and I gagged. Kyn held up her light and shone it through the hole. There was a long tunnel on the other side of the bricks, brown and rusted pipes lining the ceiling.

That was all the proof I needed. I redoubled my effort, pouring the destructive energy into the gap. I widened it until the unpainted blocks were gone.

"Nice tunnel." Veritas's voice was little more than a whisper.

"I accept your apology," Kyn said. "After you."

Veritas frowned at her. "Why me?"

"You've got the freaky truth-seeing voodoo powers, right? I don't want to get lost in there." She handed him her cell phone.

Veritas grumbled something under his breath, but he slipped through the hole. I followed, and Kyn brought up the rear. The musty smell grew stronger the deeper in we went. There were no signs directing us, but that didn't matter. Whenever we arrived at a fork or branch in the tunnel, Veritas wouldn't even pause. Apparently Kyn had guessed correctly about his power. At one point, we passed a stack of wooden chairs, slowly rotting in the darkness.

Eventually, we came up to another cinderblock wall. Kyn brushed past me and rapped against it with her fist. She turned to me, an expectant smile on her face.

I took several deep breaths and repeated the process. By the time I was done, I was sure I'd have to wash my costume a few times just to get the sweat smells out.

We emerged in another basement, but this one was much cleaner. While it was still dark and dank, someone had swept the cement floor. A large boiler roared in the corner. Kyn once again led the way past a collection of pipes that disappeared into the ceiling to a metal staircase, one constructed out of grating.

I tested the door at the top of the stairs. Unlocked. I carefully cranked the knob and slipped the door open.

We emerged into a wrecked hallway. Stained green tile lined the floor and crawled halfway up the walls. It reminded me of a hospital. The lights overhead buzzed and snapped as we crept down the hall past large windows that had metal wires crisscrossing through them. I glanced through the windows to my left. The room on the other side was huge, and the ceiling was supported by half a dozen pillars made of metal I-beams. But the room was empty, filled with nothing but shadow. I motioned for us to keep moving.

We passed by room after room. At one point, I found an old building directory hanging on the wall. Though most of the letters had fallen out of the black felt and had collected in the bottom of the case, there was enough left for me to figure out that this had been a medical clinic for the workers in the old slaughterhouses. That explained some of the large rooms. They would have been wards, probably filled with cots. So why would Sarge want an old medical building?

The first floor turned out to be empty. We didn't find anything in the rooms except for the old reception area near the front. A half dozen couches had been overturned and scattered throughout the room. I glanced at the others. Might as well keep going and see if we could find anything interesting.

We backtracked to the loading dock and found a staircase that led to the second floor. Like the first, the floors were covered in the same puke green tiles. Once again, I had to question why Sarge would bother with this building at all. It's not as if . . .

I peeked around a corner into the next hallway. This one was brightly lit and had at least three security cameras pointed toward a large metal door. Unlike the rest of the building, the door looked almost new. It gleamed in the light, casting reflections on the walls.

"I'd say we found what we're looking for," I whispered.

Veritas risked a look as well. "So what do you think we should do?"

"I'll kill the cameras. Then we find out what's behind door number one." I closed my eyes and pictured the cameras shorting out. Three soft pops sounded around the corner. I risked another look. All three were smoking. I motioned for my friends to follow. There was no telling how long we had before someone investigated.

Once I reached the door, I rapped on it. I winced at how solid it felt. It had to be at least six inches thick. Like a bank safe. There was no way I could chew through it quickly. I glanced at the keypad next to it, and then I looked to Veritas.

He nodded and stepped up to the keys. His eyes went unfocused, and his hand jerked up, as if no longer under his own control. He stabbed in a series of six numbers before hitting the enter key.

With a ponderous groan, the doors retracted into the walls, revealing a small office. It wasn't much bigger than my bedroom at home. A small desk was shoved up against an unpainted sheetrock wall. A stack of manila file folders sat on the left hand side, a simple beige phone on the right. On the opposite wall was a set of double doors. I motioned for Veritas and Kyn to go through them.

I flipped open the folder on top of the stack and scanned the contents. Lots of data, technical gibberish I couldn't possibly hope to decipher on my own. But at the bottom of the page was a list of names. Irisa, X-Cution, Nomad. Wait, those were the names on the tubes in Ayers's original lab! One name stood out: "Mind Master." He was a reformed supervillain serving multiple life sentences in Valley. Why did Dr. Ayers have his name written here? I scanned the page again. As near as I could tell, Ayers had somehow obtained a blood sample from Mind Master. But why?

Kyn popped her head back into the office. "F, you've got to see this!"

I stepped through the moment the opening was wide enough. I stopped short.

I was standing in a large room, easily sixty feet long and eighty wide. The exterior windows had all been painted black. Row after row of glass tubes filled the space, forming a long corridor. Each tube was filled with a blue liquid that occasionally bubbled.

More importantly, each tube also contained a sleeping zombie.

They were brutes, every one of them, so large that they barely fit in the tubes. Tubes ran down from the top of the cylinders and into the zombies' mouths and noses. A few of them twitched, their arms and legs spasming as if they were dreaming. The dreams of zombies . . . I'm sure I did not want to know what they dreamed of.

As I crept down the row of tubes, I couldn't help but whistle, low and soft. "There must be hundreds of them in here," I whispered.

"At the very least. And that's just on this floor," Kyn added. "We have no idea how many there are in the other two above us."

"Six thousand, seven hundred and fifty," a voice said. "And that's in this building alone."

A man stepped out from behind one of the tubes. He wore a long white lab coat and looked tired. Exhausted, even.

Dr. Floyd Ayers.

"And if you don't do something to stop Sarge and soon," he said, "he will unleash them on the world."

CHAPTER 56

"YOU!" I DROPPED into a defensive crouch. "What are you doing here?"

"What does it look like? Sarge captured me shortly after his rebirth, and now he's brought me here to make me build him an army."

"Why?" Kyn asked. "What does he hope to gain?"

"He doesn't share his plans with me. I'm just the hired help. I always have been." He removed his glasses and rubbed the corners of his eyes. "And I had such high hopes for my research."

"Making zombies?" I asked.

He glared at me. "No. Life restoration. Bringing back those that we've lost. Like Gail." He pulled out a picture. "I was devastated when she died. I thought that if I could just perfect my techniques, I'd be able to reunite with her. We'd be able to pick up where we left off."

"So why don't you?" Veritas asked. Hunger burned in his eyes. "You obviously have the technology."

"No, it wouldn't be right. It wouldn't—"

"But you could do it, right?" Veritas asked, his voice insistent. "You could bring someone back from the dead."

"Yes, I could. But I won't. Not anymore."

Veritas took a step forward. "But why?"

Ayers sighed and mopped a hand across his brow. "Because how can you know for certain that it's them? I mean, really? How could I ever be certain that it would truly be my Gail with her spark and her spirit and her . . ."

"Her soul?" I asked.

"Exactly." Ayers turned to Veritas. "How could I know that it was really her and not some pale imitation I created? No, I wish I had never created this formula. As sad as it is for me to admit, you cannot recapture the past."

"Oh, but that's where you're wrong, Floyd."

I whipped around. Sarge stood in the door behind us, Raze standing behind him.

"Don't you see?" Sarge took a step into the room. "With your help, we will recapture lost glory. America's lost glory. Do you know what I see when I look out there?" He gestured toward one of the painted over windows. "Lost sheep, desperate for a shepherd. They wallow in their own filth, ignorant of the people who have fought and died for them, and all the while this extraordinary country, one that I died for, slides deeper and deeper into the pits of hell. I intend to change that."

"With an army of undead soldiers?" I asked. "I'm not sure that'll be much of an improvement."

"Every war needs foot soldiers. Our dear Dr. Ayers has provided me with that. But I found some worthy lieutenants on my own. Isn't that right, Doomstone?"

No way.

Doomstone appeared behind Sarge, already covered in his rock armor. "Told ya, kid. I'm gonna make my mark, after all. We're going to go strictly big time."

"It won't work," I said.

Sarge snorted. "Who will stop me? You?"

I straightened. "Yes, me."

"That will be difficult, especially given the murder charges against you."

"The what?"

A sharp crack split the air. I jumped, then noticed a smoking gun in Sarge's hand. But I didn't feel anything—had he missed me? But then Kyn cried out. Panic seized my chest. Had he shot her? Was she okay?

No, she was fine. Her hands covered her mouth, and she stared down at . . .

Oh, no.

Dr. Ayers lay on his back in a spreading pool of blood.

I dropped to his side and pulled off my gloves so I could press two fingers against his neck. I thought I felt a pulse, but it was thready and erratic. Dr. Ayers tried to speak, but his voice came out in ragged gasps. Then he went still, and the pulse disappeared. I rocked back on my heels. He was gone.

Sarge threw the gun at me. Without thinking, I caught it out of the air.

"Failstate, how could you?" he demanded.

I looked down at the gun. "Nice try, genius." I summoned my power and shredded the gun. Once it had disappeared completely, I pulled my gloves back on. "So now what?"

Sarge scowled at me. "I have eyewitnesses. Raze, what did you see happen?"

Raze hesitated. He shifted his weight back and forth, almost looking like he had to go to the bathroom. "Well, I'm not so sure . . . that is—"

Sarge turned to him and clapped his hands on Raze's shoulders. "We've talked about this, son. I know we got off to a rocky start, but everything you want is within your grasp."

Raze nodded. He smirked at me. "It was Failstate, all right. I saw the whole thing." His voice had turned sing-songy.

Wait. I knew that tone of voice. I had heard it before, when people were being mind-controlled. More of the pieces were coming together.

Sarge smiled triumphantly. "You can't stop me, Failstate. You never could."

I gaped at him. What was he going to do to me now? Was he going to arrest me? Or would he let me go? He wasn't making a move toward capturing me. If anything, it looked like he was expecting me to run. Of course. It would make me look guilty and help support his version of events. He'd hunt me down—the dangerous rogue superhero who murdered Dr. Ayers in cold blood—and the public would love him even more.

"Hold on a second. Whatever happened to facing your foe head-to-head, issuing a challenge to him and then duking it out to see who's truly the best? Or was that all talk?" I took a step forward. "You claim to be the embodiment of a lost, better way, but it looks like you've been tainted by this world too. I should have known you'd turn out to be a coward."

Sarge bristled. "You take that back."

"Why should I? We both know it's the truth. Instead of attacking your problem—me—head on, you've been resorting to dirty tricks and traps. If you want a fight, I'll give it to you. Head-to-head, my team against yours, winner take all."

Sarge's face purpled for a moment, but then he laughed. "Oh, please, Failstate. You think I don't recognize a desperate gambit when I see it? There's no reason for me to give you this."

"So you *are* afraid," I said. "I should have known. No wonder the Nazis were able to take you out so easily."

It was as if all the air had been sucked out of the room. Sarge's eyes went cold, almost dead. His upper lip twitched, his features flickering into a rictus of pure rage. Then he slammed me into one of the large glass tubes. His forearm pressed against my throat.

"I should just end you now." His lips peeled back into a snarl.

"You could." It was a struggle to choke out the words. "But would that give you the victory you want? Think of the accolades, the press. Defeating a rogue hero would propel you over the top. You might not even need the zombie army anymore. It's possible that the country would let you take over."

Sarge's eyes narrowed. Then he dropped me to the floor with a smile. "Fine. You go and get a team together if you can. We'll meet on the field of battle on Sunday at the old railyard. High noon. Does that sound acceptable to you?"

"Terms?" I asked.

"What else? Life and death."

I should have figured. "Then I'll see you back here in two days. C'mon, Kyn, Veritas. We've got work to do."

As we passed Doomstone, the supervillain cracked his knuckles. It sounded like rifle shots. "I'm gonna smash you into little bits, kid. Might want to work up your last will and testament."

I wanted to stop and fight, strip him of his armor again, but Kyn pulled me down the stairs and out into the night air. She didn't stop dragging me until we had crossed out of Hogtown completely.

Once I was sure we were out of their territory, I blew out a shaky breath and turned to Veritas. "Now I need your help to—"

Veritas shook his head. "No."

I stopped and stared at him. "What?"

"You heard me. Failstate, I'm done. I can't . . . I can't do this anymore. I'm sorry." He backpedalled and then disappeared into the night.

I took a step after him but then stopped and turned back to Kyn.

She threw her arms around me. "I'm so sorry," she whispered. "I know you two were close."

My arms automatically wrapped around her. I stood there, numb. What was Veritas thinking? "Well, we still are close. We just . . . We'll work it out."

Kyn pulled away from me. "F, I know you don't want to hear this, but I don't think we can beat Sarge. There's no way. How many superheroes does he have on his team already? How many more could he rally to his side in two days? I know you have friends, but I don't think you'll be able to find enough."

I met her gaze. "What do you suggest I do?"

"Leave town. With me."

I gaped at her. Had I heard her correctly? "You want me to run?"

She shook her head. "Don't think of it that way. Think of it as . . . a strategic withdrawal. The city is Sarge's anyway. Let him have it for now"

I stared at her and, for a moment, I wanted to take her up on her offer. She was probably right. Sarge had Raze, Downtime, and dozens of other heroes, including Gauntlet. Even if I called in every favor I had, it wouldn't be enough. But if we put some distance between us and him, maybe we'd have time to rally, to gather our strength. Sure, New Chayton might fall under his control, but that had already happened . . .

Wait, what was I thinking?

I shook my head. "I can't. It's tempting, but I have to face him. It's the right thing to do. Isn't that what being a hero is really all about: doing what you can and trusting the rest to God?"

"Even if it means you'll be killed?"

"Hopefully not. But yes."

Kyn pursed her lips but then nodded. "Okay. I'm with you. But who else can we get? Sarge has so many licensed heroes on his side."

"Trust me: A license isn't all it's cracked up to be. And I intend to prove it." I pulled my cell phone out of my pocket. "I just have to call in the cavalry."

CHAPTER 57

I SPENT MOST of most of my free time over the next few days on the phone, calling in every favor I could think of. Most of the licensed heroes turned me down, of course. They probably wanted to see who won the fight. I tried not to let that rankle me too much. They were probably just as star-struck as the rest of the country was. I even tried calling Ben and Mike, but they wouldn't take my calls.

On Saturday morning, after my calls were done, I headed over to Charlene's house. I knew I couldn't tell her what I was going to do. I wished I could have. But I had to see her for what might be the last time.

When she opened the front door, my heart stuttered almost to a halt. She was radiant. Breath-taking. And that was just when she was in sweats. Tears stung my eyes.

Her smile, blinding in its intensity, disappeared. "What's the matter?"

C'mon, Laughlin, keep it together. "I just . . . I just had to see you. You're not busy, are you?"

She shook her head and stepped out onto the porch. "Never too busy for you." She hugged me tightly.

I closed my eyes and savored the way she felt in my arms. I wanted to freeze time, forget about zombies, Sarge, all of it. Just be here, her and me, for eternity.

"I love you." The words slipped out of my mouth.

She froze in my embrace. My eyes widened. What had I done? I hadn't meant to say that.

But I realized it was true. I did. I didn't know if it was a forever-type thing. In that instant, I loved her more than I could say.

She pulled away ever so slightly and stared into my eyes. "You . . . you what?"

I stammered, my heart turning to ice. "I'm sorry. I didn't mean—"

She kissed me, holding me tight against her. I pulled her in close and once again, I wished I could freeze time.

After a delicious eternity, she pulled away and smiled shyly at me. "I love you too."

I breathed out a sigh of relief. "I'm glad."

"Now," she patted me on my shoulders and disentangled herself from my arms, "what's bringing all this on?"

I stammered once again. How could I explain this? I'm about to fight a life-or-death struggle against an undead superhero tomorrow and wanted to see my girlfriend one last time. Yeah, that would go over well. I finally shrugged. "Nothing in particular. I was just out and about and wanted to see you. I won't be at church tomorrow."

"Then I'm definitely glad you stopped by. I won't be at church either."

"How come?"

She waved toward the house. "Dad. He's actually started to feel better, so he wants me to play chauffeur for him. He's got a whole big day planned out. As a matter of fact, that's why he's taking a nap right now. Resting up for the adventure." She smiled shyly at me. "You wouldn't want to go for a walk, would you?"

I would have rather kissed her some more, but a walk sounded great too. I nodded.

We ambled around her neighborhood, holding hands and talking about nothing really important. She shared what she had planned for the next servant events. I told her about my schoolwork. I tried to ignore the gloom that stalked my every step. I wanted this to be Charlene's last memory of me, a nice guy on a walk, no matter what happened tomorrow.

An hour later, we returned to her home. She squeezed my hand and kissed me again. "Call me tomorrow night, okay?"

"Of course," I lied.

With one last smile, she went inside the house. I watched her go and listened as the door shut with the sound of a coffin closing. I wanted to stay there longer, but I couldn't. I had another lady in my life to spend time with.

I pulled into the driveway and parked in my usual spot. When I climbed out of DK, I almost knocked over a motorcycle with my car door. Oh, no. Apparently I wasn't the only one who wanted to see Mom before tomorrow.

The kitchen door banged open, and Ben stepped out. He glanced toward the garage and then froze on the top step, surprise painted across his face. Then he scowled at me, his expression sour.

"You're lucky I don't run you in right now," he growled.

I gaped at him. "Are you telling me that you actually think I—" I caught myself and looked around at the neighboring houses. There was no way I wanted to have this argument in the open. There was no telling who would overhear. I jerked my head toward the garage and headed that way.

Ben slammed the door behind him. "He told me you murdered Dr. Ayers. And Raze says he saw the same thing."

I held out my hands in surrender. "Okay, take me in."

"What?"

"If you're so sure that I'm guilty, then take me in right now. I won't fight."

Ben scowled and kicked a cardboard box near the garage door. He sighed. "No. I'm pretty sure you didn't."

I should have been happy with how he answered, but the "pretty sure" still stung. "Then what's the problem?"

"I don't know what to do!" He threw open his arms. "Sarge keeps talking about a better world that we'll create together, but then he . . . Dr. Ayers . . . and I'm hearing rumors about what are in those two buildings and . . ."

He kicked the box again. Apparently he hadn't put his power behind the blow, because the cardboard only dented. Ben paced past the box and then collapsed into the couch. "What am I supposed to do, Rob? Sarge is expecting me to take part in the fight tomorrow. But if I do . . ." He gave me a meaningful look. "I don't want a repeat of last spring, y'know?"

I grimaced. Six months ago, Ben and I had nearly torn each other apart. I didn't want to relive that either.

"So I'm stuck."

"You're only stuck if you want to be. Ben, you know what's right in this case. Why are you having so much trouble with this?"

Ben's head snapped back, and his eyes flared. "Careful there, *little brother.* Don't assume you have all the answers right now. Sarge may be extreme, but he has good ideas."

"Like what? Forcing everyone to conform to his ideals? That's not right, Ben. You can't force people to have right morals. It's a transformation that has to come from within, a little bit at a time."

Ben scowled. "I suppose."

"So what are you going to do?"

He sighed. "I don't know. I'll think about it."

"Pray about it too," I said. "Ben, what if you do go out tomorrow? What will we do then?"

Ben studied his hands for a moment. When he looked up at me, his eyes appeared dead. "Stay away from me, and I'll keep clear of you."

"If that's what you think is best."

He nodded and rose from the couch.

"Don't take this the wrong way," I said. "But I hope I don't see you soon."

He paused at the garage door. "We'll see."

He left, and a moment later, the motorcycle engine roared to life and then faded into the distance.

I took one more look around the garage. I ran a hand along the tool bench's top. I reconsidered Kyn's offer. It would be an easy thing to run. We could hide out, rally more support, and strike back hard. I shook my head. No. What I had said to Gauntlet had been right: The little things mattered. But when a person could do something big, he had to stand up. I had to see this through.

But not on an empty stomach. I forced a smile on my face and headed to the house.

Mom looked up from the stove as I stepped through the kitchen. "I'm glad you're home! I was beginning to think I'd be eating alone tonight, especially since Ben left."

"I wouldn't miss this for the world, Mom."

"Good. I made chicken marsala. You set the table, okay?"

I nodded and went over to the cupboard. I pulled out two plates and headed for the kitchen's center island.

"Not there. Not tonight." Mom jerked her head toward the dining room.

Really? We never ate in there, not unless we had company visiting. Usually the table was heaped high with laundry or bills or any number of things. I stepped through the door and stopped short. The table was clean. So was the rest of the room.

"Well, don't just stand there," Mom said. "Dinner's almost ready!"

That got me moving again. Within a few minutes, I had the plates and silverware set out, then I helped Mom get the food onto the table. I pulled out her chair, and she sat in it.

I took my place and started the table prayer we always used. It was one that Mom had learned as a girl. "Come, Lord Jesus, be our guest—"

Mom put her hand on top of mine. "Not that one. Not tonight. Let me."

I looked at her in surprise.

She had folded her hands and bowed her head. "God, thank You for my boys. You did a great job when You created them, and I've been so blessed by them. Be with both of them in the coming days, Lord, and protect them. Bless the food we're about to eat. May it give us the strength to serve You in all we do and say. Amen."

She started dishing up some of the chicken and a pile of roasted potatoes. A wave of prickles swept down my back. Why would she have prayed for protection for both Ben and me? Unless—

"Mom, how much do you actually know?" I asked.

Mom paused, a scoop of carrots hovering over her plate. A smile played across her lips. "Rob, I'm a nurse. I've been trained to notice details. I know you've been making a lot of calls. I may not have heard what you were saying, but I could see how stressed out you were. And then Ben showed up tonight out of the blue, just to see me. Something is going on. Now, I still don't want to know the details of what you two are up to. I only want to know one thing: You're going to watch out for each other, right?"

I felt encased in ice. I wanted to lie to her, to promise her that both of her boys would come home after the battle. But I couldn't. I didn't know if Ben would be in the mix. I didn't know what would happen to me. At the same time, though, I didn't want her to be overly worried either.

"I will do my best, Mom."

Her smile grew. "That's all I ask. Now dig in before it gets cold."

I did as I was told, though I wasn't all that hungry. I could barely taste the food. Mom quizzed me on how Charlene was and how school was going. I told her about the calculus test coming up in a week and how I planned on asking Charlene to the upcoming Halloween dance. She told me about work. On the surface, it was like any supper Mom and I had shared.

Yet I couldn't help but feel like a convicted criminal on death row. At least my last meal was a good one since I had spent it with Mom.

CHAPTER 58

I SAT ON THE EDGE of my bed as the sun rose on Sunday morning. Bright beams filtered through my bedroom window, painting it in brilliant colors. I closed my eyes and let the sun's warmth bleed through my body. I didn't want to move. I didn't want to leave that spot, that safety. If anything, I wanted to wake up, to find out that the past two months had been nothing but a nightmare, a bizarre dream that was mercifully releasing me into a brighter day.

I knew that wouldn't happen. But the time had come. By the end of the day, either I would defeat Sarge and his cronies and New Chayton would be safe, or, more likely, I would be gone, and I wouldn't have to worry about their despotic plans. Either way, I had to get going.

I pulled the duffel bag out from under my bed and unzipped it. I pawed through the contents, double-checking that it was all there. Mask, clothing, gloves, boots. A few spots on my shirt had almost worn through. I fingered those spots, wondering idly if I shouldn't have bought a new uniform for the day. It seemed like a waste of money given my chances. I sighed and zipped the bag up again. There was no avoiding it. My team, such as it was, would be gathering soon. I wanted to be there first to greet them all and thank them for what they were going to do.

I trudged down the stairs and into the kitchen.

Mom bustled about, dressed in her Sunday best. She glanced at me. Her gaze flicked the bag and a momentary look of disapproval skittered across her face.

"Skipping church?"

I sighed again. "I have to, Mom."

She examined my face, and her features softened. "Well, okay. Just don't make a habit of this, all right?"

I swallowed a mournful laugh. If things turned out the way I expected, I'd be back to church only one more time—and I'd be the guest of honor. That thought alone opened up a pit in my stomach, a churning void that threatened to eat me from the inside out.

Mom turned back to the counter and poured herself a cup of coffee. I watched her as she worked. Things had been so much better between us, much better than I had ever dreamed, and yet, it still felt as though there were a chasm separating us. And I knew it was my fault. I had been so caught up in what I had to do that I had let things slide.

When Mom turned around, I stepped forward and hugged her. Tears filled my eyes. I wanted to say something, to tell her goodbye, to apologize for the ways that I had let her down, to ask her to pray for me and my team. But at the same time, I didn't want her to worry. More specifically, I didn't want her to stop me.

Actually, I did. I wanted someone to step in and stop all of this. But I knew that if she tried, I'd let her stop me, and that would only result in disaster. I had to do this. It had to be me.

"I love you, Mom."

"I love you too, Robin." She squeezed my shoulders. "I'm guessing whatever it is you're doing will take a while. Do you think you'll be home for supper?"

Now I laughed. "I hope so."

"Well, call me if you can't make it, okay?" She picked up her coffee cup and took a long sip, her attention fixed on the newspaper.

I slipped out the kitchen door and headed to DK. I tossed the duffel into the passenger seat and slid into the driver's side door. I cranked the engine and slipped out of the driveway.

As I drove, my hand came to rest near the center island. I smiled. Might as well turn on suppression mode. If this was going to be Failstate's final ride, I might as well do it in style.

I hit the button, and DK shifted around me. The engine's growl turned to a low hum, and I sat up a little straighter. Time to face my destiny.

I had suggested to the others that we meet in Quay Park. I didn't think that there'd be all that many people out and about on a Sunday morning, and it was relatively close to Hogtown. I found a parking spot for DK and quickly changed into my costume. I jogged over to the nearby picnic pavilion. As I ran, I checked my watch—coming up on 10:00, and apparently I was the first to arrive. I grimaced underneath the hood that covered my face. Hopefully that didn't mean I'd be the only one to arrive.

As the minutes ticked by, I paced in the picnic shelter, my footsteps echoing in the open space. I glanced around the park. Was I going to be the only one to show? If I was, then I had a bigger problem on my hands than—

"Hey." Kyn sidled around the edge of the pavilion and stepped close. "So it looks like it's just you and me, huh?" Her smile grew coy. "I could think of worse fates than standing side-by-side with you."

My cheeks flushed. "Kyn, I—"

She chuckled and shook her head. "Relax, F. I heard you the other night loud and clear. I wish things could be different, but I understand."

For a split second, I wanted nothing more than to hug her, hold her close, find some comfort before the others arrived. *If* the others arrived. I peeked at my watch again—closer to 10:15 now. Had I truly been abandoned by everyone else?

A feeling of cold slithered up my spine, and a wave of dizziness washed over me. Kyn groaned and took a step back, her hands darting to her temples. A mass of shadows oozed into the pavilion, quickly resolving into Etzal'el. He seemed to tower over me, the amulet at his throat blazing brightly.

"It is good to see you again, Failstate," he said. "It is appropriate that we make our stand this day. Just as the power of darkness was broken on a Sunday morn so many centuries ago, so too shall we drive it from your city."

"Uh . . . sounds good," I said.

Etzal'el nodded then turned to Kyn. "Young lady, I fear I have mistreated you. When first we met, I saw you as little more than a leech who would quail from serious conflict. To see you here, now, shows me how wrong I have been. I pray that you forgive me that transgression."

Kyn grimaced, a sickly smile, and shook her head. "No need. You were spot-on about me. You can blame this guy for the change." She slapped my arm.

"So this is the meeting of the Failstate Fan Club? I was beginning to worry I was in the wrong place."

I not only recognized the voice of the newcomer, but the whirring and clanking identified him all too well. Kid Magnum walked into the shelter, wearing his usual suit of armor bristling with weaponry.

I darted forward and shook his hand. "Thank you so much for coming. I wasn't sure if you'd want to."

"Are you kidding?" Kid said. "The chance to blow up zombies? Who wouldn't want that?"

I smiled. Kid and I hadn't always gotten along, especially when we'd competed against each other on *America's Next Superhero*. We'd been able to set aside our differences when we'd had to, but I hadn't been sure if he'd step up again. It turned out I was wrong.

"And I didn't come alone." Kid gestured behind him.

Three more amateur superheroes stepped into the shelter. Blowhard, an older man dressed in pirate regalia, touched his forehead in a subtle salute. Prairie Fire, a young lady dressed in a black jumpsuit with bright blue-white electrical jags stitched into it, smiled shyly at me. But the one who surprised me the most was the man who stepped into the shelter wearing a chrome helmet and what appeared to be a mechanic's beige jumpsuit. He smiled at me and slapped the sides of his helmet, producing an audible clang.

"I thought you retired," I said.

Titanium Ram smirked. "Are you kidding? When Kid called me, I begged him to bring me along. I said it before, Failstate: No way we're gonna let you twist in the wind. You've got my skull at your service. I'll even try to keep from getting stuck in a wall this time."

I laughed, a sound that was drowned out by the roar of jet engines. A large mechanical walker, at least ten feet tall and made out of gleaming metal, landed outside the pavilion. The frame opened up with a soft hiss, and Dr. Olympus emerged. She wore a tight black suit, her hair pulled back in a bun. Over her eyes she wore a pair of goggles that blinked with red, green, and blue lights.

Kid let out a low whistle. "I gotta get me one of those."

"The walker or the woman?" Blowhard asked.

"I'm not picky," Kid replied.

If Dr. Olympus had heard him, she didn't let on. Instead, she walked up to me and smiled warmly. "I stand ready to fight with you, Failstate. May we find glory on the field of battle together."

Her demeanor shifted ever so slightly. Instead of looking so tough and austere, the corner of her eye twitched, and she seemed to almost vibrate. "Of course, it's going to be a hard fight. I've been crunching the numbers, running projections on how the battle might progress, and the news isn't good. Given the numbers on Sarge's side, we're in for a hard battle. Any advantage we have will help. Speaking of which, I have something for you."

I hesitated. "You didn't bring those swords, did you?"

She shook her head and swatted at the air as if she were driving away an insect. "No, no, no. Of course not. Something better! Come!"

She led me out of the pavilion to the walker she'd arrived in. She stepped up to the machine's hip, which was at chest-height on her. She touched a control on her wrist, and a compartment opened with a soft click and hiss. She reached inside and pulled out a bag the size of a backpack and handed it to me.

"What's this?" I held the package out at arm's length, wondering if it would explode somehow.

"Open it."

I gritted my teeth and did as she said. Inside, I found a suit made of thick material. It almost looked like a SCUBA suit, except that there was a distinct honeycomb pattern woven into the fabric. The legs had been patterned to look like urban camouflage. The shirt had a series of grey lines shot through. There was even a hood with scrim sewn into the front. I gave the fabric an experimental squeeze, then I pulled on it. It felt sturdy.

"What's this?" I asked.

"A new uniform. Given what you said about how you destroy your clothes with your power, I figured you might need something a bit more sturdy. That's woven carbon nano-fibers, very durable, very tough. Made to take a lot of punishment before it wears out. Perfect for someone like you." She nodded at the bag. "But that's not all. Take another look."

I peeked in the bag and pulled out what appeared to be a digital watch. I frowned and held it up.

"Do you have your necklace on you?"

I pulled it out of my pocket.

Dr. Olympus took both and untied the crystal in my necklace from the hemp rope. She then twisted the watch's face. The back opened up, revealing a small compartment. She set the crystal inside and gave the watch's face another twist. The door slid shut over the crystal.

"When that door is open, the crystal will be pressed against your skin. You'll appear a normal human. Twist the watch face, the door shuts, and you can be Failstate. Much more elegant than a necklace." She handed me the watch.

I looked between the watch and the uniform. "But why would you do this for me? I'm not even a licensed hero anymore, and I was never a very good one."

Once again, the doctor waved away my words with a flick of her wrist. "Pshaw. As if we need a piece of paper to allow us to do what's right. Besides, in a fight like this, we need public opinion on our side. Our leader needs to look the part, yes? So go, put it on." She shooed me away.

I found a nearby restroom and quickly changed into the new costume. It was definitely snugger than what I was used to, but it felt good. Then I pulled the hood up and over my head, drawing the scrim material to conceal my true face.
I glanced at myself in the grimy mirror. A real hero stared back at me. A chill swept through me, and I felt stronger somehow. Hopefully I could live up to my new image. I emerged from the bathroom and headed back to the pavilion.

Kid Magnum whistled long and low. "Holy cow!" He turned to Dr. Olympus. "You have any presents for me, honey?"

"Just some advice." She stepped over and grabbed Kid Magnum's arm. She twisted it around his back. "Don't let yourself get distracted. By anything." Her facial features softened for a moment, her eyes narrowing into predatory slits. "And . . . call me after this is all done. I'd like to get a look under your helmet."

Kid stammered. Dr. Olympus released him and turned back to me with a wink.

"What about Gauntlet and Veritas?" Blowhard asked. "I would have thought they'd be here."

Kyn reached over and rubbed my back.

"They're not coming," I said. "Let's leave it at that."

Kid and T-Ram exchanged a look.

"That doesn't sound like Gauntlet," T-Ram said.

"I know, but he's still not coming," I said. "At least, I hope he's not."

T-Ram and Blowhard exchanged a confused look, but thankfully, they didn't press me further.

"So are we ready?" Kyn asked.

"Almost," I glanced at Kid, Blowhard, Prairie Fire, and T-Ram. "Thank you guys for coming. I can't tell you what this means to me that you're here. A couple of us were involved in a pretty nasty fight a few months back. Something tells me this one is going to be even worse. I think part of the reason why we survived last time is because we had . . . well, before we went into battle, someone prayed for us. I'd like . . . I'd like to do that right now."

Dr. Olympus looked surprised. So did Kyn. But Etzal'el rose up even taller and nodded.

I folded my hands and bowed my head. "God, right now we're all nervous. We're worried. We're weak—even with the superpowers You've given us. We're facing an enemy that outnumbers us. We're fighting people who used to be our friends. And we don't know what's going to happen. So we need You. Help us, watch over us, and if it is Your will, let us win. May we be a blessing and a help to others. Uh . . . in Jesus' name. Amen."

My cheeks burned as the others mumbled their own "Amens." Then a hand touched my shoulder and squeezed. I turned to see tears in Kyn's eyes. She nodded.

I swallowed. *God, be with me and, if I don't make it, bring me home.*

"Let's do this."

CHAPTER 59

AS WE WALKED through the streets of Hogtown, I couldn't help but look at the buildings that loomed over us, their windows like the eyes of angry giants glaring down at us. I wanted to wrap my arms around myself and disappear, but that wasn't an option. I forced myself to stand taller, to hide any hint that I was nervous. I was probably failing miserably.

A chill swept over my left side. I glanced over and saw that Etzal'el had fallen into step with me.

"Do not be discouraged, Failstate." His voice was a low whisper. "The coming battle may be difficult, but good will prevail."

"I wish I had your confidence. We're outnumbered, outgunned, and—"

"Numbers mean little. Gideon won with mere hundreds when he could have had thousands. David slew the giant with a single stone. Their strength came not in numbers nor in weapons, but because of Who stood at their side. That same one stands at our side even now. And in truth, we may very well fall this day. Sarge and his forces could succeed. But the ultimate victory belongs to the Lord. Rest secure in that."

I looked up at him. "You're just full of optimism, aren't you?"

"Failstate, I stand in shadows. Every moment, I see darkness that would cause most to flee in abject terror. I have known what it is to feel lost, dejected, and defeated. And yet I know that the victory is mine through Christ Jesus our Lord. That is what keeps me going." He looked down at me. I thought I caught a glimpse of his eyes, sad and haunted, underneath his hood. "Never let go of the foundation upon which you stand. It is what sets you apart from these others."

I wanted to say more, but we were approaching the rail yard. Etzal'el glided away from me, falling toward the back of our line. At the same time, Kid Magnum and Dr. Olympus jogged toward the sides in their mechanical suits, their weapons whirring and clicking as they readied them. I glanced to my right and left. Kyn nodded to me, as did T-Ram. Blue jags danced across Prairie Fire's arms, arcing to the ground. Blowhard adjusted his pirate's hat and offered me a weak smile. I drew in a deep breath. Ready as I was ever going to be.

Let this work out, God, please.

The fence surrounding the railyard had already been flattened. We stepped over it. At least half a dozen sets of tracks spread out before us. A few old and decaying railway cars dotted the area, each covered in faded graffiti. I swallowed. Sarge's forces could be hiding in any of those. I motioned for my team to advance. We moved slowly, carefully, weaving through the train cars.

We found Sarge in the center of the railyard. He stood at parade rest, his hands tucked into the small of his back, on top of one of the cars. Raze leaned against the side of the car, his arms crossed. I looked around. Where were the others? Where was Gauntlet? This didn't bode well. My gaze jumped from train car to train car.

"Noon, just as we said. Glad to see you're punctual, Failstate," Sarge called. "Nice threads, by the way."

"So now what?" I asked.

Sarge smiled. "Now I give you one last chance to stand down. This doesn't have to end the way we both know it will."

"Not going to happen," Kyn shouted.

"I wasn't talking to you, girl," Sarge roared. "This is a conversation between your betters. Learn your place!"

"My place is right here, where I can kick your—"

I held up my hand to cut her off. "Maybe I should offer you the same deal, Sarge. Surrender now, and no one has to get hurt."

Sarge laughed. "Why would I do that? Besides, you haven't answered my offer yet."

"True. I haven't. T-Ram? Why don't you give the nice man our answer?"

T-Ram chuckled and scraped a foot across the dirt. Then, with a roar, he bust forward, dropping his head down. He covered the distance to Sarge's train car within half a heartbeat. The wood and metal exploded. Sarge toppled from his perch, and Raze dove out of the way.

"Go!" I shouted.

My team advanced.

Just then, the train cars around us burst open. Sure enough, the rest of Sarge's team had been hiding inside them.

Kid Magnum and Dr. Olympus whirled around and opened fire on the newcomers. Etzal'el rushed into the fray, flanked by Blowhard and Prairie Fire. Kyn reached over and squeezed my arm before she darted off to find someone to fight.

That left me to take on my target: Sarge himself.

I started forward, marshaling my power. I lashed out, destroying big chunks of the wrecked train car. But then the ground bucked under my feet. I fell onto my back, pain exploding up and down my spine. I groaned and tried to sit up but a large boot clamped down on me.

An insane light burned in Raze's eyes. "Game over already, Failstate. I knew you couldn't hack it."

A vibration ripped through my chest. I gasped as pain lanced through me. Raze ground down his heel even harder, and another tremor ripped through me.

"That's what it feels like when your internal organs get shaken up," he said. "Not very pleasant is it?"

My fingers clawed into the dirt. I closed my eyes and did my best to block out the pain. A desperate plan formed in my mind. I summoned my power and let it build, even as Raze sent another quake through my chest. Then, when I was pretty sure my ribs were about to rattle to pieces, I let loose a destructive blast.

The ground beneath me disappeared, carving out a hole at least four feet deep.

I dropped backward. Raze toppled over the top of me. We slammed into the bottom of the hole, and I rolled, coming up on top of Raze.

I held him down with one hand and marshaled my power around my clenched fist. I rammed it into his chin, and he howled. I struck again, and then again. On the fourth blow, Raze went slack, whimpering quietly.

I clambered off him and out of the hole.

The battle raged around me. Kid Magnum had been backed up against one of the train cars by the Bronze Basher. Kid's bullets ricocheted off the Basher harmlessly.

Dr. Olympus charged to help him, but then she staggered and whirled. Downtime perched on her back, his hands glowing as he pressed them against her suit.

Etzal'el faced off against four opponents, all of whom appeared nervous to actually engage him.

Still no sign of Gauntlet or Veritas. I frowned. Where could they be? And if and when they showed up, whose side would they be on?

Someone slammed into my back, and I tumbled. My head bounced off a metal rail, and stars exploded in my vision.

Sarge rolled to his feet and appeared over me. The overhead sun wreathed him like a halo. He shook his head sadly and pulled out a service pistol. "No tactical awareness. Such a shame. I had hoped you'd put up more a challenge, Failstate, but I—" He frowned, and looked over his shoulder.

I frowned as well. Although my ears were still ringing from my impact with the rail, I could hear a distant sound. It was like a collective moan, underlaid with clicks or clacks or . . .

My eyes widened. Oh, no.

I sat up. A swarm of zombies moved through the streets of Hogtown, tearing apart everything in their path. Sarge gaped at the mass of teeming bodies as well.

Slowly our battle ground to a halt. The heroes all turned to stare as the zombies crawled through the streets. At least a hundred were headed our way.

"No!" Sarge pressed a hand to his ear. "Downtime! What is going on? Who authorized their release?"

Downtime dropped from Dr. Olympus's back. He said something, but I couldn't hear what it was.

Sarge roared in fury and dropped to his knees. "No! This is too soon! This will ruin everything!" He rose from the ground and flew off over the teeming horde.

My jaw dropped open. Yet another new power?

I backed away from the mass of zombies that shuffled toward us. There had to be hundreds, and those were just the ones right here.

"Failstate, what are we going to do?" Dr. Olympus asked.

Several of the other heroes chimed in asking the same question. I realized belatedly that some of them were the same folks who had been fighting us just a few moments ago.

"How many zombies are there, total?" I asked.

"Thousands," Downtime said. "Tens of thousands."

"And they're all loose now," Kid Magnum growled. "Way to go, guys."

"This was never part of the—" A female voice snapped.

"Knock it off," I said. "We've got a major problem here. My guess is that they're not coming just for us. A lot of people are going to get hurt or even killed if we don't stop them now. How do we do that?"

The other heroes fell silent. Then Downtime raised his hand. "The failsafe."

"No, it's Failsta— Oh, um. The what?"

"Dr. Ayers insisted on it. Each of the zombies has a microscopic device implanted into his central nervous system. There's a control panel in Sarge's command center that, when tripped, sets off those devices. They would kill the zombies immediately."

I ground my teeth. The device would have to be in the command center. And there were a whole mess of zombies between here and there.

"All right, this is what we're going to do: I need three of you to help me get through that horde to Sarge's command center. The rest of you, take out those zombies. That's the only thing that matters right now."

Etzal'el appeared at my side. So did Kyn and T-Ram

I turned to the others, making sure I included our former opponents in my gaze. "You're all heroes. It's time for all of us to start acting like it again."

I turned to Etzal'el, T-Ram, and Kyn. "Let's go. We've got a horde to stop."

CHAPTER 60

ETZAL'EL DARTED IN FRONT of me and threw his arms open wide. A blast of shadows scythed through a row of the undead. T-Ram charged forward, plowing open a long lane. Kyn and I jogged behind them.

So it went—the two of them clearing the way as we traveled deeper and deeper into Hogtown. The streets were choked with undead as the entire horde shuffled along, each zombie moaning and clacking.

We arrived at one intersection. The mass of zombies writhed in front of us. It was like a swarm of locusts devouring everything in front of them. They simply rolled over all in their path. Car alarms screeched as dozens of feet tromped over the vehicles. Newly planted trees along the streets swayed and toppled. The streets were clogged. It was like a constantly shifting seven foot wall.

Etzal'el stopped and whipped around in a full circle. His cloak snapped out and swept the nearby zombies off their feet.

He turned to me. "This is where Titanium Ram and I shall make our stand. You and Kynetic go ahead."

I looked over my shoulder. Sarge's compound was just down the block. "Are you sure?"

Etzal'el nodded. "We shall be fine."

"You heard 'im, Failstate," T-Ram rolled his shoulders for a moment, the sunlight dancing across his helmet. "Go. We got this."

I turned to leave.

Behind me, Kyn shouted, "Wait!"

I turned around to see what was wrong.

She looked at the compound, an uncertain look on her face. Then she turned to T-Ram. "Hit me. As hard as you can."

T-Ram's mouth dropped open. He looked at me, a question in his eyes.

I nodded. "Do it. She'll be all right."

T-Ram frowned for a moment. Kyn turned to face him, her stance wide and her arms open. She beckoned him, a frown on her face.

"I don't know," T-Ram said.

"She can handle it. It's part of her powers." At least, I hoped she could handle it. I knew how much force T-Ram could generate in one of his charges.

T-Ram finally sighed. He backed up ten feet and charged straight for Kyn.

I wasn't sure what I'd expected when he collided with her. A thunderclap, or maybe she'd make some sort of noise. That's not what happened. Instead, one moment, T-Ram streaked toward Kyn. The next, he had stopped, his helmet planted in her stomach.

He straightened, a confused look on his face. "What just happened?"

Kyn closed her eyes and let out a small giggle. "That's the stuff. Thanks, sweetie." She patted him on the side of the face.

"If you are done, I could use your assistance!" Etzal'el shouted. Half a dozen zombies climbed over him, pulling on his cloak.

T-Ram shook his head as if clearing it. "Go on, you two. I've got this." He dropped his head and, with a mighty bellow, charged into the ranks of the zombies.

I turned to Kyn. "You ready?"

"For anything."

We ran down the street. Thankfully, what few zombies there were seemed more interested in joining the fight against Etzal'el and T-Ram than in engaging the two of us. Within moments, we arrived at the compound.

I ran my hand along the wall and turned to Kyn. "Well?"

She frowned at me. "Well what?"

"That kinetic charge you're holding should do the trick. Knock it down."

She shook her head. "No way. I'm holding that for something special."

I frowned. "Like what?"

She shrugged. "When I see it, I'll know."

"Then I guess it's up to me."

I took a deep breath and summoned my powers. A fire built up within me, and I released it, directing it toward the wall. The cement in front of me sagged as if it were turning to taffy. Not quite what I was hoping to achieve. I sucked in another breath and shoved my hands outward, channeling even more destructive energy. Cracks ripped through the wall and widened as the entire structure collapsed. A hole ten feet across burst through the cement.

I tamped down on my power and bent over, my hands on my knees.

Kyn touched my shoulder. "Are you all right?"

My chest heaved. "Just give me . . . a second . . . to catch . . ."

A bullet ricocheted off the wall next to me. I winced and whipped around. Doomstone, once again wearing his rocky armor, marched down the streets. Behind him were at least two dozen thugs, each of them heavily armed.

"Well, well, well, lookie who we got here, boys. I was hopin' I might cross paths with you again, Failstate."

"Oh, really?" I asked. "Sarge was looking for you earlier, you know."

Doomstone waved a dismissive hand at me. "I ain't worried about that clown. He's just like everyone else, always underestimatin' me. I nearly took Sarge out a few months back. And now he goofed and got the party started too early. Those zombies are gonna make mincemeat out of you capes."

"And you'll be there to pick up where Sarge left off?" I asked.

Doomstone shook his head. "Nah, he always thought too big. Hogtown, then New Chayton, then the state, country, world. Me, I woulda stopped at Hogtown. And now, thanks to this mess, I can. When it's all said and done, me and the HazMats are gonna rule this neighborhood."

I leaned over toward Kyn. "So is this special enough for you?"

She tipped her head to one side and considered Doomstone. She shook her head. "Almost."

"What is going on here?"

I turned around. Gauntlet stood in the hole in the wall and scowled at us.

"What are you doing?" I demanded.

"Sarge told me to make sure that nobody got in here that didn't belong." He fixed me with an angry glare. "So you get in there."

I blinked, not sure I heard him correctly. "What?"

"Go. He's inside the building. I can handle these twerps."

"You think you can double-cross Sarge and get away with it?" Doomstone roared.

Gauntlet laughed. "I'm amazed you can say that without a hint of irony."

Doomstone stomped his foot, and cracks radiated through the street's pavement. "You seem to forget we have you outgunned."

"He's got a point," I said.

Gauntlet gave me a half-smirk. He made a beckoning gesture, and a small metal cart with four large slots carved into it, rolled up behind him. I peeked inside and had to swallow a laugh. Each one was filled with stacks of plates.

Gauntlet stomped his foot, and a dozen plates shot into the air and began to orbit him. He looked at me again. "Go take him down for me, okay?" Then he flicked his hand in the direction of the HazMats.

The plates shot forward as if launched by a cannon. They slammed into the thugs, knocking them off their feet. Kyn grabbed me by the hand and dragged me past Gauntlet.

"Stay safe," I whispered to him.

If he heard me, he didn't let on. Instead, he stomped his foot again, and more plates leapt into the air.

We raced across the open area of the compound and into the main building. The large meeting room was deserted, although papers were strewn about the interior as if someone had just rushed out of the room. Where was Sarge's command center? I jogged over to the old offices. The room was filled with cardboard boxes. No sign of Sarge at all. Where could he have gone?

"F? How about this?" Kyn pointed to the door that led to the basement.

That had to be it. I ran to the steps and raced down them.

A large bank of computer monitors filled one wall. They displayed a map of Hogtown. Red dots swarmed through the streets. Zombies, I guessed. Thankfully, it appeared as if they were all still contained within this one neighborhood. I had no idea how the others were managing that, but it was a good thing. Dominating the center of the room was a massive table. Sarge sat at the head of the table, hunched over a bank of controls. He cursed as he tapped at the keys.

"Something wrong, Sarge?" I called.

He whipped around, pulling out his gun.

I was ready for him this time. A spike of destructive energy demolished the weapon.

He looked down at it and laughed. He tossed it off into the darkness. "Nothing's wrong. Yes, this all started a bit early, but once I save the city from yet another zombie outbreak, they'll hail me as an even greater hero. And that's on top of stopping a cadre of jealous unlicensed heroes. This can still work into my plans."

"Think again," I said. "Your team has changed sides. They're working with my guys to clean up the mess you've made. Gauntlet seems to have come to his senses as well, and

Doomstone apparently wants you eliminated. All that's really left is you."

Sarge glared at me, but then he laughed and shook his head. "It's a shame, really. You and I could have made the world such a better place."

"Except you're not really interested in saving the world, are you? Just forcing it to fit your mold."

Sarge's eye flared. "You lack vision. I, on the other hand, will achieve everything I've ever dreamed of."

This had gone on long enough. I started around the table.

Sarge held up a hand. He snapped his fingers, and a gout of flame appeared around his hand. "And this is why. You see, Dr. Ayers did more than just figure out how to revive me. He also learned how to transfer one hero's powers into another."

"Yes, I know."

He frowned at me. "You couldn't possibly—"

"From what I understand, it's part of the revivification process that recreated you. You wouldn't be standing here if it weren't for Kudzu's regeneration powers. It explains how you were able to sway so many people to your side. And why I thought all those frat boys were zombies. You 'borrowed' Mind Master's powers, didn't you?" I nodded toward the flame engulfing his hand. "And Pyrotrack's too, obviously, plus who knows how many others. But do you really think that's going to change anything? You could have the powers of every hero on the planet, and I would still take you down."

Brave words, but with Sarge's plan crumbling around him, I knew I could back them up.

I started around the table again.

Sarge darted to two high-backed chairs that were turned away from me. "Perhaps you could, but you forget: I always like to have options. Did you know that we encouraged people to come and visit us here at the compound? Two of them decided to stay with us after the morning tour."

He turned the chairs around, revealing two people, a man and a teenage girl. The man I vaguely recognized. But the teenager had red hair and . . .

My blood froze. It was Charlene.

CHAPTER
61

IT FELT AS THOUGH I was in a dream. This couldn't possibly be real. Not the way the flames wreathing Sarge's hands cast ominous flickers over Charlene's skin. Not the way she trembled in the chair, her eyes wide and filled with tears as she pleaded with me over the piece of duct tape on her mouth.

What was she doing here? I realized that the man next to her was Steve, Charlene's father. He sat in the chair next to her, passed out. She had said he'd wanted her to take him on the tour, maybe even meet Sarge. I wanted to rip off my mask, show her that it was me. I wanted to beg Sarge to let her go. I wanted to kill him. I wanted—

Sarge brought his flaming hand even closer to Charlene's face. "That's right. You just stay over there. I'd hate to see something happen to such a beautiful face."

Did he know? Could he? Maybe he had picked up some impressions from me. "If you harm her—either of them, I mean—in any way . . ."

433

"You'll what?" Sarge laughed. "See, that's why you fail as a hero. You haven't learned the hardest lesson of them all: To be truly effective, you have to let go of your heart. You have to ignore that little voice inside you that tries to hold you back. You have to be willing to make hard sacrifices and do what you have to do.

"Like now: What will you do? You could stop me, you know, but it would mean letting this little honey die or at least get all crispified. So what will it be, Failstate? Will you finally be the hero?"

"Kyn?" I asked. "How about now?"

I turned around to look for her. Kyn was gone.

I turned back to face Sarge. His fingers danced beside Charlene's skin, so closely that I was sure he would touch her at any time.

"No one is here to help you, certainly not that brownie. You shouldn't associate with someone from such a filthy race. So what's it going to be?"

"You know, I think it's time I did something about your racism." Kyn's voice sounded from high above. Then she dropped from the ceiling, landing square in the middle of the table.

It was as if a bomb went off. With a loud crack, the table shattered. She must have released the blow she'd stored from T-Ram. Sarge was knocked off his feet and away from Charlene, who winced and tipped over in her chair. Kyn was already on the move, scooping up Steve and grabbing Charlene to pull them both out of the way.

"Get him, F!"

Sarge roared and threw open his palms. Instead of fire, he threw a wave of rainbow light at Kyn. It smashed into her and knocked her off her feet. Her head bounced off the concrete, and she went still.

"No!" I shouted.

Sarge laughed and clenched his fist. Once again, a gout of flames spread up his arms and danced across his entire body. He stepped over the wreckage of the table and approached Charlene. He opened his palms over her, and the light from his flames grew brighter and brighter.

God, help me! I need to stop him!

A sense of peace settled through me. I knew, right then, with absolute certainty, what I had to do.

I launched myself, leaping over the remains of the table, and slammed into Sarge with my shoulder, knocking him out of the way. Fire lanced through my shoulder and down my back. I clamped my mouth shut, swallowing the howl that threatened to tear me apart.

Sarge recovered his balance and opened his hand. "That was stupid, Failstate. So now you're going to burn."

The flames slammed into me and poured over my uniform. I winced, wishing for a moment that my new costume was fireproof. I hadn't thought to ask Dr. Olympus.

But maybe it was. I could see the flames cascading around my body, but I couldn't feel any heat. That was strange. Even if the clothing were fireproof, I would have thought I'd feel something. Maybe my brain was protecting me as I died. I reached out my hand toward the fire . . .

Only to snatch it away again. My fingers ached for a moment. Like a burn. I frowned. Maybe if I concentrated, willed my glove to be fireproof.

I tried again and this time, I was able to immerse my hand in the stream of fire.

I chuckled. Apparently that new wrinkle to my power would come in handy after all. I turned to look at Sarge and smiled. I took a step forward, then another.

Panic crossed Sarge's face. "What are you doing? Get back?"

It felt as though someone were tickling the inside of my skull. More mind control? I shook my head, and the sensation vanished. I laughed even more. "Sorry, Sarge. That one won't work either. What else you got?"

Sarge cocked his hands back and they began to glow with a burst of rainbow light. He threw them at me, and a wave of multicolored light shot toward me. I closed my eyes and imagined my costume turning into a sheet of mirrors. When I opened my eyes again, I laughed even harder. The rainbows had reflected off of me and turned into a harmless light show.

I closed the distance with Sarge and lashed out, catching him in the stomach. I channeled my destructive powers around my fist and landed another blow. Then another. Finally, I grabbed Sarge and, as I held him up by the front of his shirt, I imagined the floor behind him turning to liquid. Sure enough, a small pit formed filled with what looked like grey water.

"Tell me, Sarge. You didn't happen to steal anyone's super strength, did you?" I asked.

He mumbled something through quickly swelling lips.

"I'll take that as a 'No.'" I pushed him.

He dropped into the pit. He thrashed against the liquid, which easily came up to his neck. I let go of the transformation and, in an instant, the floor resolidified, trapping Sarge in concrete up to his neck. I sent a trickle of destructive energy down into the floor to carve a little wiggle room for him. I didn't want him to suffocate.

His head jerked back and forth. Finally, he glared at me. "Failstate! You release me right now!" He followed that demand with a string of expletives that caused heat to rise in my cheeks.

I looked around the room and spotted a mop bucket in one corner. I picked it up and carried it over to Sarge. "Language, Sarge. And you call yourself a role model." I tipped the bucket over and dropped it on his head. Granted, it wasn't enough to silence him, but at least his voice was muted.

Charlene! I raced over to her side and helped her sit up. I gingerly pulled the duct tape from her mouth.

"You saved me," she whispered. "Thank you." She threw her arms around my neck and held on to me. "I thought we were dead."

I wanted to hug her, kiss her, comfort her, but I knew I couldn't. Not as Failstate. At least maybe now she wouldn't rag on Failstate so much. I gently pulled her arms from around my neck. "How's your father?"

She whirled to look at him. "Dad!" She crawled to his side and checked him. "I think he's okay, but he needs an ambulance."

I grimaced. That might be hard to come by, what with a zombie apocalypse raging on the streets outside and all.

Kyn sat up and rubbed her head. "What happened?" Then she looked from me to Charlene and back. Her face fell, but then she nodded once and got up. "What about the failsafe?"

The what? Wait, that's right! I looked at the table. Sarge had been fiddling with a set of controls when Kyn and I had arrived. But they had been destroyed in the fight. If those had controlled the failsafe, then it was smashed beyond help.

The large screen on the wall flickered on. I frowned. Once again, I noticed that the sea of red dots, while somewhat thinner than when we first arrived, was still contained entirely in Hogtown. That didn't seem possible. What was—?

Then one of the screens blinked and shifted to a familiar mask. Veritas stared out of it at me. "So is Sarge taken care of?"

I looked over at the bucket, which rattled against the concrete floor. "You could say that. I take it the zombies were your doing?"

Veritas nodded. "I figured all those bickering heroes needed something to unite them. A zombie apocalypse seemed like the right way to go. Plus it was a great way to show the rest of the world what Sarge was up to. No more rumors of zombies in the night. Now we've got an army marching through the streets in the middle of the day. It should look great in HD."

"Wait a minute," Kyn said. "I thought you turned your back on F."

Veritas looked down. "I considered it. But I gave my word. While you guys slugged it out in the railyard, I snuck into one of the zombie farms."

I chuckled. "Good idea."

"I know. It wasn't mine." He appeared to be looking over my shoulder.

I turned around and saw Gauntlet coming down the stairs. I wanted nothing more than to hug him at that moment, but I knew that would only raise questions.

Gauntlet let out a low whistle and looked around. "I love what you did with the place."

"The HazMats?" I asked.

"Neutralized. Doomstone too."

"Uh, guys," Kyn said. "Pat yourselves on the back later. What do we do about the zombies?"

Veritas looked down, and it sounded as though he was typing on a keyboard. "Well, that's just a matter of firing up Dr. Ayers's failsafe. I already did, sort of, and I tied it into a GPS system. If a zombie tried to cross out of Hogtown, its failsafe activated, and it was taken out. But now I'll just . . ." He smacked a button on his keyboard.

I looked at the larger map. As I watched, all the red dots vanished.

In Hogtown, tens of thousands of zombies had suddenly gone from undead to dead-dead.

Gauntlet squeezed me on the shoulder. "Congrats, Failstate. You did it."

I shook my head. "No, we all did. You held the wall. Veritas activated the failsafe. Kyn swung the battle with Sarge. Everyone else did it too." I walked over to Charlene and helped her get Steve to his feet. "Now let's get up there. I think we've got one more villain to unmask."

CHAPTER 62

BY THE TIME we emerged from the compound, emergency vehicles were flooding into the Hogtown streets. They surrounded Sarge's compound. Soon the entire area was swarming with police, firefighters, and EMTs. The citizens of Hogtown emerged from their buildings, looking frightened but none the worse for wear.

It would probably take a long time for Hogtown to recover from this. The neighborhood looked like a war zone. A lot of the buildings had been trashed, their pristine exteriors ruined. Cars had been overturned and smashed. The streets were a maze of potholes and large cracks. I was willing to bet that Chief Thompson would have kittens when she saw it all.

The other heroes trudged up the street, picking their way through the wreckage of the zombie horde. They looked exhausted. Kid Magnum collapsed against the wall of the compound and heaved a long sigh. Dr. Olympus practically fell out of her exosuit. The only one who didn't appear affected was

Etzal'el. He simply stood on a corner, a pillar of shadow in the midst of the daylight. He nodded to me, and I smiled. Sure, he couldn't see my expression, but I was glad to see he had made it.

T-Ram stumbled to my side and punched me in the arm. "We did it, kid."

"And without getting your head caught in anything this time," I added.

He laughed. "Well, there's a first time for everything."

The VOC vans arrived then. I flexed my fingers into fists. Good.

Agent Sexton burst from the lead vehicle. He strode through the streets and gaped at the destruction. Sexton took it all in and then whirled on me. He shoved his way past Agent Kensington, who continued to survey the ruined streets. "What have you done?" he demanded.

I shook my head. "Drop the act, Sexton. Isn't this what you wanted all along?"

He froze. "What are you talking about?"

Etzal'el's head turned toward me, and he glided across the pavement. Dr. Olympus also strode over, flanked by Kid Magnum and Downtime. Kyn, Gauntlet, and T-Ram followed them. Agent Kensington slipped into the circle between Prairie Fire and Blowhard. Even Veritas arrived in time to join the crowd.

"C'mon," I said, "I know it was you. You're the one who brought Sarge back from the dead. You're the one who funded Dr. Ayers's research. This is all your fault."

Kensington looked between Sexton and me. "What are you talking about?"

"Oh, I almost didn't figure it out," I said. "But then I found out about how the money that should have gone to building me a headquarters is missing. The official line is that the VOC built me a lair at the NCU campus, but funny, no one gave me the keys to it or even told me about it. Sexton took the money and built Ayers's lab instead. According to Meridian, the VOC are experts at building hidden facilities without anyone noticing. Then I learned that Dr. Ayers got access to Mind Master and some of the other supervillains in Valley. But he couldn't have gotten in without VOC authorization. And weren't you in Washington over the summer, around the same time that someone stole a tissue sample from Sarge's grave in Arlington?"

To his credit, Sexton didn't betray anything he was thinking, even though he was surrounded by a group of superheroes who were getting angrier and angrier with each of my accusations.

"So this is what I think you did," I said. "You got the tissue sample. You had them build Ayers's lab in my name. And then you had the professor resurrect Sarge and upgrade his powers. How am I doing so far?"

Kensington glared at Sexton. "Is there any truth to this?"

Sexton's face appeared to have been chiseled from granite. "That's preposterous! I never—"

Veritas made a buzzing sound. "That's a lie."

Etzal'el loomed over Sexton. "Agent Sexton, the truth will set you free. I expect you to see that for yourself. Now."

Sexton snorted. "Back off, Etzal'el. Do you want to lose your license too?"

"Your threats are meaningless." Etzal'el's voice turned to the rumble of an avalanche. "I answer to a higher authority than the Vigilante Oversight Commission. Perhaps you wish to plead your cause with Him?"

Etzal'el burst forward and enveloped Sexton in his cloak. Darkness burst from his form and washed over all of us. Then, just as quickly as it had appeared, the shadows retreated back into Etzal'el. He snapped his cloak open, and Sexton tumbled to the ground. His skin had turned pale, and it appeared as if he had lost thirty pounds. He retched.

"What did you do to him?" I asked.

Etzal'el stepped back from Sexton. "I showed him a brief taste of the ultimate consequences of his sins. Perhaps he needs another?"

Sexton shook his head and held up a hand. "All right. It's true. I did all of that."

"But why?" I asked.

He glared at me. "Because of you."

"Me? What did I ever do to you?"

"You won that license because of that stupid show! We need real heroes, not pathetic wannabes like you. We needed Sarge to protect this country, the way he did before he died. When I learned about Ayers's research, I knew that was the key. So yes, I diverted the funds for your headquarters. I got Ayers access to Valley. But I did it for the greater good, the same as I've always done!"

Kensington signaled for two more VOC agents to come over. "I've heard enough. Come along. I'm sure the director will want to have a long talk with you."

The agents hauled Sexton to his feet, wrenched his arms behind his back, and dragged him back to the vans.

I breathed out a sigh of relief.

"So did you actually know that he did it?" Veritas whispered to me.

I chuckled. "Not entirely."

"Good guess. Sign yourself up as an honorary mindreader."

Etzal'el approached me. "I wish to thank and congratulate you, as well. It has been an honor to battle at your side. Should you ever need my assistance again, all you have to do is call."

"Ditto," Dr. Olympus added.

"But why? I'm not a licensed hero anymore."

Etzal'el turned to Kensington. "That will be remedied soon, correct?"

Kensington's Adam's apple bobbed. He nodded. "I'll start the paperwork as soon as I get back to the office."

Etzal'el's cape swirled around him, and for a heartbeat the entire world went dark. When the sun returned, he had vanished.

"You know what?" Kyn asked. "I think Etz is starting to grow on me."

"Me too. Now let's see what we can do to help out. And then I want to go home. I think I've earned some time off."

I turned to the swarm of little kids that surrounded me. "Are you sure you guys shouldn't go home? It's a school night!"

A chorus of whines filled the evening air. The oldest of the group, a girl around six years old, shook her head. "Didn't you hear? The school got destroyed by those bad men. We get to stay home tomorrow."

Oh. That made sense. "Still, it's getting late, and I'm getting tired."

"Please? Just one more?"

I sighed. "All right. One more. Then you all have to go home."

A cheer went up around me. I smiled underneath my hood and faced an overturned pick-up truck. The truck's rear end had been nearly ripped off, and its windshield had been shattered. More problematic, the engine had been squeezed out of the hood like toothpaste from a tube. I wished I could have been there to see how that had happened.

I glanced at the truck's owner, a middle-aged Hispanic man who stood next to it. "You received the paperwork from the VOC for the insurance company?" I asked.

He nodded.

"And you're okay with this?"

He smiled and gave me a thumb's up.

I shrugged. I rubbed my hands together and then opened my palms at the truck. I probably didn't have to do that, but I had learned that the kids liked the theatrics. I summoned my power and sent a blast of destructive energy into the truck. At first, only the paint peeled away and vaporized, but as I released more of my power, the rest of the truck followed suit. Within a matter of moments, the entire wreck was gone, leaving only a stain on the pavement.

The kids cheered and babbled in excitement. I didn't know how I'd become the babysitter for Hogtown, but as I'd worked to help the VOC teams clear out the rubble from the battle, more and more children had come to watch.

Their self-appointed leader jumped up and down. "One more!"

"Hey!" I said. "You promised. And what do heroes do?"

She stood a little taller. "They keep their word."

"Exactly. Now scoot."

The kids uttered a collective groan but they started back for their homes.

The leader lingered, then she rushed forward and threw her arms around my waist. "Thanks for saving us." She turned and raced down the street, brushing past Agent Kensington and Meridian.

They parted to allow her to pass. Meridian watched her go, then turned to me with a lopsided smile. "Feels pretty good when they hug you, doesn't it?" he asked.

I smiled. "Yeah, it does. So what can I do for you two?"

Meridian and Kensington exchanged a glance.

"Why don't you take a walk with us, Failstate?" Meridian said.

We strolled back along the street. A lot of the debris from the fight had been cleared away already, and most of the ambulances had left the neighborhood. Now it was mostly police officers there to keep things under control as members of the VOC After Works teams assessed the damage and started repairs.

"I've received about half a dozen calls from Mayor Reilly," Kensington said. "She wanted me to thank you on her behalf. Don't tell her that I told you, but she also said she's going to send a petition to the President to see if you can get some sort of commendation."

My eyes widened. If that actually happened, I'd have to be sure to wear my watch and keep my powers muted. A power spike in the White House would likely be a faux pas.

"And I also got a call from Chief Blackthorn. He said to tell you, 'You made us proud.'"

I chuckled.

We strolled past Sarge's former compound. Apparently someone had managed to cut Sarge out of the warehouse's basement. A forklift was loading the large block into the back of an armored semi. Sarge continued to scream abuse at the agents around him. Good thing he didn't see me. He'd probably have a coronary.

"I hear you did that," Meridian said.

I nodded.

"So how about your powers?"

I shrugged. "Not sure. I think I can turn my costume into armor when I want to now, and I seem to be able to do some new tricks." I pointed to Sarge's concrete block. "I'll keep working on it, see what happens. I hear these sorts of things happen to us, right?"

Meridian's eyes narrowed, and his lips drew into a thin line.

"What's going to happen to Sarge?" I asked.

Kensington glanced in Sarge's direction. "Off to the Valley Correctional Facility. Him, Doomstone, and even Raze."

"You're kidding! Raze is going to Valley?"

Kensington nodded. "We have him on tape threatening the director of a local homeless shelter. And there's the fact that he was an accomplice in Dr. Ayers's murder. A vigilante license might give you some latitude, but Raze exceeded it by a lot."

Kensington pulled a purple card out of his pocket and held it out for me. "Speaking of which, I've been talking to Director Bentley back in Washington. Given what's happened, the VOC would like to reinstate you, effective immediately. And, if I may be so bold, you should have never lost it in the first place."

"And his stipend?" Meridian's voice was little more than a growl.

Kensington nodded. "Absolutely. Director Bentley even authorized a bonus for your good work."

Huh. That was unexpected. Maybe I'd take Charlene out to a nice dinner soon.

I glanced at it and then turned to Meridian. "You're still willing to be my mentor?"

Meridian's smile grew larger. "Of course."

I looked back to Kensington. "What about New Chayton's other licensed heroes?"

Kensington grimaced. "Still no word on Shadowfall or Nightsilver. And the Living Quark turned in his resignation two days ago." He brightened. "But I have heard that the Hoplite will be back from her secret mission sometime this week."

I laughed. "Good timing on her part."

"I thought so too." He glanced at the license, then up at me. "Well?"

I stroked my chin through my mask. "Who will my liaison officer be?"

Kensington shifted on his feet. "I thought I would give it a try, if it's okay with you."

I nodded. "That would be great. So . . . do I have to worry about any more jerks like Sexton?"

Kensington shook his head. "The other licensed heroes have been singing your praises. Given the way Etzal'el treated you, I don't think anyone wants to risk crossing you."

That was nice to hear. And scary at the same time.

"Face it, kid: You've become something of a legend now," Meridian said. "How does it feel?"

I grinned. "Not too bad, I guess. Although I don't feel that different."

Meridian clapped me on the shoulder. "Believe me, Failstate, you are different. And it's good to see."

"Well, Failstate? What's it going to be?" Kensington prompted.

I reached out and took the license from Kensington. "I accept . . . on one condition."

EPILOGUE

THE DOORBELL RANG AGAIN.

Mom strode down the hall from the kitchen and poked her head into the living room. "Rob, can you get that? I'm late for Bible study." She adjusted one of her earrings and headed back toward the bathroom, probably for her final primping.

I got up from the couch and slipped to the foyer. I opened the front door and found Mike standing on the front porch.

He smiled sheepishly. "Am I too late?"

I shook my head. "Right on time. Come in."

He nodded and stepped through the door. "So how have you been?"

"Doing better," I said. "They gave me some time to recuperate, and the Hoplite agreed to take up the slack."

"I've never met the Hoplite," Mike said. "What's she like?"

"I'm pretty sure she could break me in half with her pinky. Let's go into the kitchen. Ben's already here."

Sure enough, my brother was hard at work at the stove. He smiled in greetings to Mike and turned toward the center island.

Mom breezed through the kitchen and snared her purse. "You boys have fun, okay? Don't make a mess."

I gave her a hug. "We will and won't. See you later, Mom."

She patted me on the cheek and smiled at Ben. Then she was out the door.

"So do you have any idea why Rob insisted we come here?" he asked.

Mike shook his head. "Not a clue."

"Well, for starters, tonight is a celebration. Not only did we save the city . . . again, but I got my license back." I pulled the purple card out of my pocket and set it on the counter. "That's part of the reason why I wanted to see both of you."

"Wait a minute, I can see where this is going," Mike said, holding up a hand to stop me. "You're going to offer to deputize one of us, right? I've already said no, Rob. I'm done."

"Are you sure?" I asked.

Mike nodded. "Don't get me wrong, I'm going to miss 'the life.' And I'm sure my dad's not going to understand. But I can't do this anymore. I'm out."

"Why?" Ben asked. "You're good at this."

"Not good enough."

I nodded. "I thought you might say that. But you're not backing out of being my friend. And don't think I won't come to you for help—or at least advice—from time to time."

Mike smiled sadly. "Well, okay, I guess."

I turned to Ben. "So if I can't have Veritas as my sidekick, that just leaves—"

"Of course it does." Ben sighed then smiled. "You know what, I'm okay with that. I keep forgetting what a good team we make. If you'll have me as your sidekick, I'd be honored."

"Well, that's too bad," I said. "I have to retract my offer."

Ben's jaw dropped open. "Why?"

"Because of this." I pulled another purple card out of my pocket and slid it across the counter to him.

Ben stared at it for a moment before picking it up with trembling hands. "Is this . . . is it . . ."

I nodded. "Your very own license. Turns out, the Living Quark quit for medical reasons. I had a long talk with Agent Kensington. I told him about what a great hero you are, and I told him that if the VOC wanted to make it up to me, they'd give you a license, as well. He agreed."

Ben mouthed a few words before he launched himself around the counter and scooped me up in a crushing bear hug. "Thank you!"

"You're welcome." My voice was little more than a squeak. "I don't need a sidekick—but I could sure use a partner."

I was worried that Ben wouldn't let me go, but the doorbell rang again, and he put me down.

"That would be the third reason why I wanted us to get together tonight." I grabbed my license and slipped it into my pocket. "I wanted my brother to get to know my girlfriend better."

Ben picked up his license, smiled at it, kissed it, and tucked it away.

I jogged down the hall and opened the front door. Charlene smiled at me and stepped into my arms. She kissed me.

"How are you doing?" I asked.

She shrugged. "I'm okay."

"And your dad?"

Her smile turned a little sad. "He's bouncing back, actually. The doctors were a little worried about him for a while, but they say he's doing better. I think it's because he got to see some superheroes in action. That's all he's talking about now, you know. How great that Failstate guy is."

"Oh, yeah?" I couldn't help myself. "And what about you?"

She smiled. "He's okay. I guess maybe those superheroes serve a good purpose after all."

It wasn't much of an improvement. But at that point, I would take it. "Let's go. Ben cooked. I can't wait until—"

The doorbell rang again. I frowned. All my guests were here. Who could that be?

"Why don't you join the guys in the kitchen, Charlene? I'll be right there."

Charlene nodded and went down the hall.

I opened the door. A beautiful African-American girl stood at the door. She smiled when she saw me. "Hey, there. Nice to meet you for the first time. I just moved to the neighborhood, and I thought I'd stop in and introduce myself. You're Robin Laughlin, right?"

How did she know that? I nodded. "And you are?"

"My name's Kiesha Taylor." Her smile grew, and she leaned in close. "But my friends call me Kyn."

My jaw dropped open. I quickly snapped it shut. "I . . . I . . ."

She chuckled. "How are you doing, F? Holding up okay?" She looked over my shoulder. "I knew back at the compound that she was the reason you wouldn't be with me. I can't say I blame you. She's cute, if you go for that kind of girl."

"How did you . . ."

"It wasn't all that hard. I saw the way you were acting around Charlene there after the battle, and I figured she must be the one. I found out her name from the cops, and then I did some digging. Did you know she recently changed her relationship status on Facebook as being in a relationship with Robin Laughlin? The math practically did itself."

I felt woozy, as if the house were slowly rotating around me.

"Relax, F, I'm not going to make any trouble for you. I just wanted to stop by and say hello. Let you know that I'm not that far away." She stepped in close. "Especially if you ever change your mind about us. Or even just having a sidekick. Ta."

She turned and walked away, a swing in her hips. As she came to the end of our sidewalk, she cast one long look over her shoulder and sashayed down the street.

I shook my head to clear it. Best to just put everything behind me. After all, I had my friend, my brother, and my girlfriend with me. And that was enough reason to celebrate.

ACKNOWLEDGMENTS

Going back to Failstate's world for a second time was a fun adventure, made more so by the people who helped me along the way:

To Jill, my wonderful wife, I'm sorry I keep spoiling the plot for you. Without your encouragement and patience, this story would have only remained a glimmer in the back of my mind. The fact that it's seen the light of day is because of you.

To my boys, who inspire me constantly to be a hero. You've already made my world so much brighter and better. I can't wait to see how you become heroes and save the world in big and little ways.

To my Brain Trust: Joel and Chris. I definitely couldn't have done this for a second time without your help. Your breadth and depth of knowledge was once again invaluable, especially by helping me make sure I wasn't treading on any sacred cows.

To my family, who have been incredibly encouraging as I worked on this, and especially to my Mom, for the proofreading help.

To those who read the early drafts of this story, especially Jill Williamson and Tom Evans. The feedback was invaluable, and the encouragement helped get me through some dry times.

To my agent, Amanda Luedeke, who helped me cobble the plot together and who continues to dare me to dream big dreams, I am so thankful for your advice and encouragement. And don't worry, it'll happen in the next book.

To Jeff Gerke, publisher and editor extraordinaire, your vision continues to astonish me, and I am constantly humbled that you let me tell these stories under your banner. Thank you for your invaluable help in cleaning up how many heroes New Chayton actually needs.

To Carlo Garde and Katja Louhio, the covers are amazing! I am in awe every time I see your work, and I can't see what we come up with for book number three.

To the ACFW, I can honestly say that I wouldn't be published (twice, even!) if it wasn't for you.

To my "extended family" at Marcher Lord Press, thanks for inspiring me with incredible stories and especially for helping me figure out a title for this book.

To the readers, whose excitement for Failstate and his friends is both humbling and terrifying at the same time. I hope you enjoyed the story and will stick with me for the next one.

And last (but never least), to the Only and True God, Father, Son, and Holy Spirit. No matter what I do, big or small, may it all be done for Your glory alone.